the immigrant

by the same author

Difficult Daughters
A Married Woman
Home

the immigrant

MANJU KAPUR

faber and faber

First published in India by Random House in 2008
First published in the UK in 2009
by Faber and Faber Limited
Bloomsbury House
74–77 Great Russell Street
London WC1B 3DA

Printed in England by CPI Mackays, Chatham

A CIP record for this book
is available from the British Library

978–0–571–24406–5

2 4 6 8 10 9 7 5 3 1

For

Amba

Nidhi

Maya, Kranti, Tara

Katyayani

Agastya

&

Miranda House

Part I

Nina was almost thirty. Friend and colleague consoled her by remarking on her radiant complexion and jet black hair but such comfort was cold. Nina's skin knew it was thirty, broadcasting the fact at certain angles in front of the mirror. Her spirit felt sixty as she walked from the bus stop to the single room where she lived with her mother. Her heart felt a hundred as it surveyed the many years of hopeless longing it had known.

And her womb, her ovaries, her uterus, the unfertilised eggs that were expelled every month, what about them? They were busy marking every passing second of her life.

Had she been married, thirty would have been heralded as a time of youthful maturity, her birthday celebrated in the midst of doting husband and children. A body could feel young in these circumstances, look forward to the gifts, the surprises, the love.

Instead this would be the moment that announced her diminishing prospects to a judgemental world.

July 28th, three twenty in the afternoon. Nina's students had, as usual, bunked the seventh period. Their reasons would be: how late they got for coaching classes, how they needed to cook and help and socialise at home, how there were not enough university specials and public buses got so crowded, how eveteasing, anxious parents and girls always vulnerable, demanded the skipping of classes.

Nina stood in the doorway and stared at the three long crooked rows of tables and empty chairs. Though she had known Elective English II would not materialise, part of her job description was waiting for the tardy, lazy, recalcitrant, excuse-making, absconding student.

Her gaze shifted beyond the windows to the tennis court with its ragged, rusted wire fencing, the hostel wing behind it and the distant trees. She felt towards the shabby red-brick building the love of an acolyte. The student-less atmosphere allowed her to feel this love more acutely.

Slowly she climbed upstairs to the department room, put away her register and issued two books on Milton from the library cupboards that lined the walls. In the staff bathroom a hurried pee, her breath held against the strong, foul smell. As she emerged she encountered Kalawati, the all purpose maid.

'Madam, see,' she said, delighted with a spectator, pointing to the reluctant drops oozing from the tap. 'How can I clean without water? Then they complain about my washing.'

The half filled, cracked, discoloured sink was plugged with a black rag, waving bravely from the drain. In it Kalawati was swishing tea mugs, two in each hand, leaving tea rings intact, barely wetting flecks of encrusted powdered milk. These were the mugs the teachers would drink out of tomorrow and Nina wished to see no more. Murmuring indistinguishably she walked away, down empty corridors, passing witness to the sweeper pushing clusters of dirt and paper out of classrooms which were then locked behind him. In a matter of minutes the whole place would be considered clean.

Out the big green double gates embossed with the college emblem, onto the dusty sidewalk, towards the three thirty special. Grit under the strap of her new kolhapuris grated against her sweating feet with every step she took.

Down University Road, left at Patel Chest till the Arts Faculty road, then right towards a line of waiting buses. Students milled around, waiting for the route signs to change. The minute the front of a bus proclaimed its identity, its seats would be attacked and possessed by the lucky few.

Once on her bus, the GK II special, Nina settled down to twenty kilometres of painful thought. Hour by inexorable hour her twenty ninth year was ebbing away. Tomorrow thirty, thirty, thirty. What brightness could any dawn cast on her existence? Colleagues, friends, students, parent—her world was totally female. Would she end up a bitter old spinster like Miss Kapoor of the Economics department, like the Misses Hingorani and Rao of her own, like Miss Lal of History or Miss Krishnamurthy of Sanskrit? Academics was full of spinsters, minatory signposts to depressing, lonely futures.

Yet, education was a gift and she would not exchange the life of the mind for any humdrum marriage. If she was going to settle, she would have settled long ago for one of the men her mother kept dredging up with desperate hope from marriage advertisements.

She wished her mother's happiness was not so dependent on her own. Even now she would be waiting, peering restlessly through the window, readying the tea tray on a little side table, cups turned down, biscuit jar filled, while nearby water killed time in an electric kettle. All in readiness for them to sip tea and exchange the minutiae of their day.

The major topic of conversation in the last eight years had been Nina's marriage—who, when, where, how? The hopes each conversation generated gradually lost their lustre as the years went by and nothing changed. From where could fresh possibilities be unearthed on the eve of her thirtieth birthday? The lack of these, reflected in her mother's dull, mournful eyes, was what she was going home to.

Finally her stop arrived. She turned the corner, and there was the sagging iron gate and scraggly lemon tree of B-26 Jangpura Extension. In front of the house was a tiny concrete space, hogged by the monstrous bulk of the landlord's car shrouded within a grey waterproof cover. A neat row of plants in red pots tried to dispel the ugliness with their glossy green leaves and occasional flowers, but failed miserably.

Nina pushed open the front door and stepped into her home: one small bedroom, attached to a tiny covered verandah which functioned as a drawing-dining room. The front steps provided extra seating. At the back was an angan, in a covered shed to one side was their kitchen, next to it the bathing area, next to

3

that the toilet. B-26 Jangpura Extension had been built as a single unit, but Mr Singh supplemented his income by renting out the front part of the house to tenants who, being female and unprotected, were totally harmless.

'What took you so long? I even waited at the bus stop.'
  'How many times have I told you not to do that?'
  'It was so late, I couldn't help it.'
  'Have you forgotten I come late on Tuesdays?'

Despite the timetable in her possession, yes, the mother has forgotten. Her daughter is going to be thirty, that erodes all reason, all timetables but the one of marriage. Now she has a plan and she is nervous it will not be accepted. While Nina bathes away the sweaty grime of an urban monsoon day, the mother thinks of the astrologer she has to persuade her to visit.

Over tea, Nina listens to the suggestion and considers the desperation it reveals. After what happened to the father they were never again going to believe in astrology. His horoscope had revealed achievement, success and happiness. Like a king's, pronounced his proud mother as he went from brilliant posting to brilliant posting, foregoing the initial years in the backwaters other IFS officers faced. Then, with no history of heart disease, a sudden cardiac arrest killed him at forty five. On and on his mother wailed, was early death too the fate of kings?

Yes, it was. You can't have everything.

This knowledge, so acceptable in the lives of others, was not acceptable in her own. In time honoured tradition she held her son's wife responsible. Instead of looking after her husband, Shanti must have been busy enjoying, enjoying her husband's transfers to all the good European capitals. It took a mother's eye to notice distress, to predict the onset of disaster.

The father had believed in the future, had believed in his retirement, had believed in the beautiful house he would build on a plot he was going to buy in a South Delhi colony. The architect's blueprint would allow Nina to construct a separate

4

unit on the first floor when she grew to need independence. His wife, listening to his dreams, basked in their glow, his daughter, listening, felt lucky to have a future so well taken care of.

The dreamer died leaving his dependents with nothing. The ground cut from beneath their feet, they had no choice but to move to the grandparents' house in Lucknow.

Years of innuendo and resentment followed. The grandmother could not understand Shanti living when Shankar was gone. Shanti herself could not understand it.

Nina hated the atmosphere she found herself in. She hated Lucknow, her grandparents' house and Loreto Convent. The International Academy in Brussels was her real school, Europe her spiritual home.

Anger provided the energy in the house. The grandmother resented her daughter-in-law's existence, Nina resented her mother's meekness, the mother put up with everything because Nina's security depended on her patience. Nina obsessively imagined the day when the two of them would leave this small town hell. Lovingly she embroidered multitudinous themes in the farewell speech to her grandparents, single-mindedly she visualised the job that would enable her to add to the small monthly pension her mother got from the government.

It took seven years. Seven years in which Nina finished school, migrated to Delhi to do English Honours at Miranda House, followed by a postgraduate degree from the university, to end up with a lectureship at her alma mater. Seven years and six months to find this room in Jangpura Extension, and bring her mother to live with her. In Delhi Nina hoped her mother would lead a fuller life; in Delhi the mother imagined a husband could be found who would give her darling the home she deserved.

Neither expectation was fulfilled. The mother refused to indulge in any social life that involved spending Nina's hard earned money, the daughter refused to agree to any groom advertisements or acquaintance threw her way.

She might have been more tractable if she had not fallen in love during her MA.

He was fifteen years older than her, a teacher in the English Department at the Arts Faculty. Rahul liked to love serially. Unfortunately for Nina, he reminded her of her father. She offered him her heart and expected his in return—for surely the combined forces of youth and devotion would persuade him into commitment.

She kept this relationship secret from her mother. She was looking for love on her own terms, untainted by convention and respectability.

Eventually the serial lover moved on. She thought the pain would destroy her. Despite her knowledge of his nature, in her weakened state she succumbed to his blandishments eight months later. Then followed four agonising years dotted with moments of ecstasy as she waited for him to declare that she was the chosen one. But Rahul had always made it clear that he wanted to have his cake and eat it too. Like all cakes this one was chewed, mashed into pulp and swallowed.

Her self-respect finally forced her to choose loneliness over compromise. Silently she grieved, the only men in her life long dead authors.

The mother knew nothing of the anguish, nothing of the joy. In her eyes Nina was a sweet, innocent virgin. Some traditional women would rather not see the things their children go through, those experiences sit so ill with their values. Now she was in the process of trying to convince Nina that astrology was a science too hastily discarded from their lives. Her daughter did not approve of this apostasy. Her turning thirty was no reason to fall for charlatans, even if she was going to suffer a fate worse than death.

'You look so young and beautiful,' pleaded the mother.

This was neither true nor relevant, but in the end the mother's persistence wearied the daughter. Though it was dishonest to provide fuel for irrational expectations, it was still harder to deal with her mother's monumental depression on her birthdays. It even overshadowed her own.

Next morning.
    Birthday girl.
    Nina lay in bed, eyes firmly shut. She wanted nothing of this day.
    Her pillow was disturbed, the sheet pulled, paper rustled. Alas, to share a room with one's mother demanded open eyes. She got up to greet her present joyously.
    'Happy birthday to my darling,' said her mother, holding a parcel carefully wrapped in faintly creased, leftover gift paper. The daughter smiled as she undid the sticky tape to reveal a red and black woven Orissa sari, bought during the Diwali sales of the year before.
    'How pretty Ma.'
    'Your colleagues will like it?'
    Nina nodded. When she came home she would exaggerate each response to replenish her mother's meagre store of pleasure. Her acquaintances peopled her mother's landscape; she was intimate with their personal lives, their vagaries, likes and dislikes. Now at the thought of their admiration she smiled as she carefully folded the wrapping paper, putting it away for the next present.
    The birthday girl noticed the smile and was overcome by self-pity. Both of them were fated to lead lives devoid of men. The mother had fallen through the bad karma of marrying a prince who would die young. The only thing she had to look forward to was her daughter's marriage, after which she would suffer more loneliness. At least the mother had hope. She had nothing.
    As Nina crossed the angan for the toilet, Mr Singh shouted, 'Happy birthday, ji. When are we going to hear some good news?'
    Nina stretched her lips into a grimace.
    'This year, lucky year,' beamed the landlady, pressing her hands to her bosom. 'I feel it here.'

Regrettably these cultured times did not allow Nina to strike the voyeuristic lump in front of her. Instead she vented on her mother. 'How come she keeps such good track of my birthdays?'

'She has your interests at heart,' placated the mother, looking old and slightly guilty. The familiar expression added to the daughter's rage.

'I hate the way she goes on about good news. Every marriage is good news, is it? Stupid cow. What about her marriage? Husband can't even keep the roof over their heads.'

The mother let her rattle on. Poor thing, she had to take out her frustration somehow.

'Don't forget the astrologer's appointment, beta,' she said as Nina left.

As though there was any chance of that. Her treat to all concerned, her husband, her mother, herself.

College. Coffee break, birthday wishes, a few presents. Zenobia, special friend, gave Nina a small bottle of perfume, with *Balmain* written in tiny letters around its rotund middle, suggestive of desire and sex.

Zenobia. Abandoned by marriage after six years, but with parental money and an independent flat. Been there, done that was her attitude to matrimony. Her life was now filled with nephews, nieces, good friends (Nina the chief one), supportive family, occasional sexual encounters and a passion for teaching. She frequently urged Nina to go abroad for higher studies, that being her only chance of finding a decent guy, for Indian men were mother-obsessed, infantile, chauvinist bastards. But all the desperation in the world could not make Nina apply for a PhD.

The friends left college at one thirty in the moist intense heat. As they walked to the bus stand, dampness seeped from their pores, covering both with a sweaty sheen. Nina mopped her face and pulled her sari palla over her head, paltry protection against the solar onslaught. Why did she have to be born in the worst month of the year, she complained. Zenobia agreed. When the monsoon misbehaves, July is a month to hate.

They parted, and Nina pushed her way into a crowded 212. She hung onto the back of a seat, trying to breathe shallowly against the odour freely dispensed from perspiring armpits. Male bodies pushed themselves against her, and she leant firmly into the woman on the seat to her right, hoping she would not have to stand too long.

The bus shook its way through the streets of Delhi. The smells around her were making Nina nauseous. Grimly she put her handkerchief across her nose and glared at the dirty glass windows jammed shut. This same journey was such a pleasure in the mornings, with a seat assured, an hour to go through her lecture notes, suspended between home and college, combining purpose with mindlessness.

She had to change at ITO, struggling unpleasantly against more bodies trying to squeeze into buses. If only she could occasionally treat herself to an auto as Zenobia did, but the habits of frugality ingrained during years of perpetual worry about money, and daily, hourly, weighing of cost and benefit, meant she could never take an auto, not on her birthday, not ever.

So immersed in the world of push, shove, jab and poke, she hung onto another bus strap before being dropped off at the main road next to Jangpura.

The evening found mother and daughter at the same Jangpura bus stop, laden with fruit. 'I hope he likes mangoes,' said Nina's mother, looking uneasily at the three kilos of langra and chausa she had bought from the fruit seller that morning, 'These are practically the last of the season and cost five rupees a kilo, five! I think one or two are slightly overripe, I hope he doesn't mind, I thought of leaving them, but then it would look too little... '

'He will understand that it is the end of the season, and be very grateful,' broke in Nina impatiently, her arms aching with the load. The bus came and twenty minutes later they got off at Shahjahan Road, and walked over to 43 Meena Bagh.

'Please wait, ji,' said the tall grey haired lady ushering them into the glassed in verandah. 'He phoned to say he might be a bit late, he was called for a meeting at the last minute. He had to go, you know what it is like these days.'

Everybody knew what it was like these days. Indira is India, India Indira, we need no one else, certainly not an opposition, D K Barooah, the Congress president, had declared as opposition was jailed, the press censored, demonstrations banned, activists tortured. The most startling objector to be thrown into prison was the venerable freedom fighter Jayaprakash Narayan. Old and frail, incarceration would destroy his health and succeed in killing integrity and conscience.

On the wall opposite the front door was a black and white portrait of Indira Gandhi. Around her was a garland of sandalwood roses. They were in the house of a sycophant, or to interpret it more kindly, a man too scared to be seen as anything but a Believer. Slowly but surely Madam's probing eye delved, knife-like, into every house, every heart.

How feared she was. And how useless. Of her Twenty Point Programme the drive to produce sterile men was the only one that proved responsive to force. Poverty, alas, was resistant. Garibi Hatao. Almost thirty years after Independence that day was further away than ever, though government employees kept long hours in office, too scared to be absent or go home early. This man was obviously an example.

'Papa didn't need this kind of fear to make him work,' burst out Nina. Her tall, vital, handsome father, hair greying at the temples, black framed glasses, clean-shaven face, slightly yellowing teeth, whose laughter was a series of snorts, who could charm with every word he spoke. Were he alive their lives would have been completely different. She tried never to think such thoughts for they led nowhere, but today, on her birthday, circumstances demanded them.

'Your papa was a different breed of man,' sighed the widow. For her every celebration was tinged with sorrow.

'If papa were alive, we would not be here. Nice way to spend my birthday.'

'That is why I say you should settle down. If you married an NRI or someone in the foreign services you could live abroad nicely.'

'I don't see NRIs or foreign service officers lining up to marry me. Get real Ma.'

'Hasn't happened doesn't mean it won't. Everything is possible.'

Even marriage? Even happiness? Even escape?

If a husband could protect her from life in a brutal autocratic state she would marry him tomorrow. All around them countries like Burma, Pakistan, North Korea, Cambodia, China, Vietnam, Afghanistan, Iran, Iraq, Syria, Lebanon, were showing the way to totalitarian regimes, with their repressive measures and violation of human rights. What was so special about this country that would enable them to escape the fate reserved for so many of their neighbours?

Coming, we are coming, wait for us, our millions will soon join you.

Forty five minutes later, as Nina was urging her mother to get up and leave, they heard the sound of a car drawing up next to the house, seconds later its door slamming. 'Namaste, namaste,' twittered a thin, grey-moustached, bespectacled man, deputy secretary, Ministry of Education. 'Sorry to keep you waiting, unexpected meeting. Sit, sit, I have heard so much about your husband.'

The government servant cum astrologer quickly settled down to business. He asked the date of birth, name, added numbers, calculated the planet configuration at the moment Nina was born. He divined enough details of their past to establish even Nina's unwilling confidence.

Now, he claimed, the fifteen year bad period in their lives was coming to an end. The unfortunate arrangement of stars that had governed their destinies was slowly giving over to a more favourable combination. Things were going to change, change quite drastically, he added frowning.

'Marriage?' suggested the mother.

The civil servant peered at the charts. 'Late,' he declared.

It didn't take a genius to predict that, thought Nina. At thirty it was late by anyone's standards.

Marriage would take place this year or the next, went on the astrologer. Journeys were involved, the signs were good for prosperity and happiness. And till where had Nina studied?

'MA,' said the mother.

'Things are not easy if you are educated, the mind needs companionship, the search becomes longer."

Nina scowled. The man should stick to his stars instead of making ridiculous pronouncements.

'And Miranda House you said? Good, very good.'

By now the mother was in a state of deep excitement and Nina in a state of deep suspicion.

Well, at least she has been given enough sustenance to make this birthday less traumatic, thought Nina while the mother clutched her hand on the way back, as though she were already leaving for a new home.

ii

Far away, on the eastern seaboard of Canada, in Halifax, Nova Scotia, a young man stood at the window of his clinic and gazed at the trees lining the sidewalk. It was summer; the air was mild, the sun shining for a change. His long time friend and partner had just walked home to his wife, child and lunch.

Eight years earlier, Ananda had been a practising dentist in small town Dehradun. Unlike many of his friends he had never dreamt of leaving India. His ambitions were simple. He wanted to make enough money to look after his parents and repay them for the time, love and hope they had invested in him.

But these exemplary aspirations were not destined to be realised.

His parents had been middle class professionals, on the lower scale of things. His mother taught at the Convent of Jesus and Mary, his father was a minor functionary at the Forest Institute. They had two children. The daughter studied at her mother's school, and for her BA went to Miranda House, Delhi University. Her lack of academic brilliance was compensated by the genius she exhibited in choosing her partner. The boy had actually been to Doon School with Sanjay Gandhi! Now he was in the IAS, UP cadre. Success was bound to crown your career when you could claim some connection with The Family.

The umbrella of this marriage would cast its shade over the young brother as well. At all times the parents were keenly aware of the potential calamities that could befall their children and a son-in-law added to their sense of security.

Ananda was going to be a doctor. The father spent hours going over the child's lessons with him, making sure there was no question he could not answer, and the son justified this attention by winning scholarships every year. He had to be something responsible, respectable, solvent and being a doctor fit the bill. In class XII he had school in the morning, coaching classes for medical entrance exams in the afternoon and homework at night. But though he was a position holder in the science stream in the boards, he didn't score high enough in those other exams to make it to medical college. It was the first disappointment he had known in anything that had to do with reproducing large amounts of memorised material.

Dentistry was the alternate option. The medical exam entrance forms had demanded he fill in a second choice and now he was forced to see the bright side of things. He would not have to do night shifts. He would get the same—almost the same—respect as doctors did, the same—almost the same—money, but without the insane hours. With more economy and a bank loan, he could set up private practice in Dehradun. The career of a dentist uncle in Canada was painted in glowing colours. Who knew, his future too might convey him across the globe. But for the moment, a stretchable moment, he belonged to his parents.

Dental courses ran on quotas. Ananda was from UP, so for him the obvious choice was the dental wing of King George's Hospital in Lucknow. He passed the interview, and for the five years it would take to qualify he shuttled between Dehradun and Lucknow.

From the moment of his birth Ananda had been surrounded by the rituals of his caste. Before he left home, his parents did their best to reinforce the practices of a lifetime. He was a Brahmin, his body must never be polluted by dead flesh. Low caste boys in the college hostel might try and tempt him towards non-veg, cigarettes and alcohol. Should he deviate from the pure habits they had instilled in him, his mother's heart would break. She assured him of this with her disturbed, devoted gaze.

Ananda was put in a room with three boys who, including the other Brahmin, all smoked. The air was blue with the haze of constant indulgence. He breathed deeply and smelled liberation.

From cigarettes he graduated to alcohol. As he moved from first to second to third year at King George's he found parents allowed their sons a certain autonomy if they were doing well. So, freedom went hand in hand with success. He absorbed this lesson.

Most of his classmates aimed to go abroad. Were they to labour like donkeys for the measly sums Indian doctors commanded? No, never, not while they had wits to fill in applications and patience to endure the year it took to get admission. They would have to qualify again once they were abroad, borrow money for tuition and living expenses and put in even more years if they wished to specialise, but the eventual reward dwarfed these sacrifices.

If the love of his parents meant that Ananda's ultimate destination lay no further than the small town he had lived in all his life, he was son enough to accept this. His parents found him an internship with a reputed dentist in Anstley Hall on Rajpur Road. His future was such a well understood thing between them that discussion was not considered necessary before this was settled.

Ananda worked with Dr Chandra for two years. His hand was deft, but with patients, strangers after all, his conversation was hesitant, his demeanour bashful. Dr Chandra thought he would gain confidence with time, you can't be awkward around people's mouths. Dentists have to be skilled at putting patients at ease, especially since they feel vulnerable as they recline, mouths open, saliva gurgling in tubes stretched across their chins. Each file had to have notes about the client's profession, background, interests and family, so that small talk could be generated, empathy exhibited.

Two years later Ananda felt he had learnt enough to be on his own. His parents broke their fixed deposits to help him set up a dentistry practice further down on Rajpur Road. They applied for a one lakh loan from the State Bank of India with their house as collateral to help finance the office equipment.

This done, they insisted it was time for him to marry, he was already twenty four. Marriage brokers were contacted, the family grapevine alerted, advertisements scanned. Photographs with attached bio-datas began to appear and were judiciously scrutinised before being offered to the son for comment. It would take a few months for her to be found, assessed the parents, but before a year was over they expected to have a daughter-in-law. In anticipation of this, they bought a second-hand car, a Premier Padmini with only thirty thousand miles on it.

Ananda wanted to keep a driver but the parents insisted such expense was unnecessary. They hardly went anywhere; the driver would sit on their heads the whole day and steal petrol. When the bride came and his practice was more established, they could consider it.

'My practice is established,' countered the son, 'and surely you need the car more than my wife, whom nobody has yet seen.'

'May you live forever, may you always be happy,' murmured his mother.

15

The boy felt baffled. It was not a question of his happiness but theirs. 'No arguments, I am keeping a driver. He can get the fruit and vegetables if nothing else.'

The young were so headstrong. What did they know about preserving the life of a car, rationing petrol or saving the salary of a driver? The minute they earned they started to spend. That was not the way, the way was to save, to conserve; how else had they managed all those fixed deposits which had supplemented Ananda's one lakh bank loan? Besides who could trust food bought by hired hands?

The driver was not kept.

Ananda took the car to his clinic, and as always, the parents went for their evening walk to Gandhi Park, stopping on the way back to buy fruits and vegetables, selected only after they had been prodded, smelled and haggled over, piece by piece. One fateful day their rickshaw was hit by a truck speeding through town. They died instantly.

Relatives came. Relatives commented. His parents' karma, his own karma, what could anybody do? If only they could have seen to his marriage, he needed a wife to cushion such a tragedy. His sister kept crying and pointing out that all he had was her.

The son's tears finally came after everybody left. It was his fault, his fault. Why hadn't he forced his parents to keep a driver? Why were they so paranoid about money? Look where it had led them.

He flipped through the Gita his brother-in-law had left him. Do your duty, never think of the consequences; life is full of suffering—that he liked. Every time he read life is full of suffering he felt a mournful resonance deep within him.

Meanwhile his sister took up from where her parents had left off. He was now an even more ideal candidate for marriage: own house, own practice, no parents-in-law to mar this perfect scenario. Offers flowed in, but Ananda had lost the desire to marry. He was marked by fate, happiness was unattainable and he wanted nothing of life.

Destiny though had other plans. His mother's brother, the doctor uncle settled in Halifax for the past twenty years, urged him to come to Canada. In India he would be constantly reminded of his loss, whereas if he wanted to make a fresh start, this was a country filled with opportunities. He sent one through the post: admission forms for the Dalhousie University Dental School.

His sister did not want to lose him to the West. 'I will never see you. You are all that is left of Ma and Baba.'

Her husband scolded her for her foolishness. There was nothing in this country, and how often did they meet anyway? He strongly advocated his brother-in-law's departure. His own luck came through proximity to The Family, and could not be shared. For most of the middle class even the basic things—a phone, a car, a house—took a lifetime. Now this golden chance had landed uninvited on Ananda's doorstep.

Opportunities are very insistent. If you neglect them they promise to retaliate by filling you with regret for the rest of your life. A lost opportunity refuses to hide, it pops out at every low moment, dragging you even lower.

It took six months to settle things. Clothes and household goods were dispersed among people in order of their importance to the Sharma family. First Alka took her pick, then relatives, then friends and neighbours, and lastly the servants. Nothing was thrown away, nothing wasted. The practice was sold, and tenants found for their former home.

His sister came from Agra to see him off. 'Remember if you don't like it, you can always come back,' she repeated many times. Ananda was mostly silent. His situation had changed so much that he already had the mind-set of an immigrant, departing with no desire to return.

Ananda landed in Halifax on the 15th of August, his country's day of independence, as well as his own liberation from it. His uncle, waiting to receive him at the small and dazzlingly empty airport, remarked on this in a distant, nostalgic way.

During the twenty three mile drive from the airport, the uncle expanded at great length on Ananda's goals. The orphaned boy needed to get ahead, brooding was not going to help. He had made a smart move in coming, even though it meant more years of study. Take his own example: hard work and the right profession had made him worth half a million dollars. 'Why do you think there is such a brain drain in India?' he demanded. 'India does not value its minds—unlike here. Otherwise you think we are not patriots? But there even the simple tasks of daily life can bleed you dry.' The uncle shook his head sadly, while his expensive car slid smoothly along the road as though greased with butter. In the undulating landscape, lakes gleamed for a moment, then vanished. Ananda had never seen such empty spaces.

'Where are all the people?' he asked.

'They will come—once we enter the city. But don't expect many, the whole country has barely twenty million—and Halifax only eighty thousand.'

Now eighty thousand and one.

'There, there we are,' said the uncle, pride in his voice as they rose slightly onto a hill which offered a momentary vista of the city sprawled before them. His tone implied that this was the first of many gifts on offer to his nephew. Then came pretty wooden houses, set in green gardens, followed by the high-rises of downtown, all strangely deserted.

'Where are the people?' repeated Ananda.

'Always the first thing to strike our countrymen,' laughed the uncle. 'You'll get used to it.'

Again the spread out generosity of the residential areas, and finally Young Avenue. As they approached, the uncle switched conversational gears; this was one of the poshest areas in town, the Olands, liquour barons, lived right across the street in a huge mansion that made his own place look like an outhouse, but neighbours, nevertheless, neighbours. He could afford to live here because one plot had been divided into three.

The car drew upto its companion outside a garage attached to a yellow house with a black roof. They climbed the steps,

Ananda's eager gaze registering the large picture window, the smaller windows, one strangely set just above a flower bed. The uncle unlocked the front door to reveal four more steps that led up to a carpeted expanse, filled with lamps, deep sofas, silk cushions, shining wooden tables, gilt edged pictures. All this belonged to a doctor like himself.

His first cousins, Lara and Lenny, fifteen and sixteen, were introduced. He was to share the basement with Lenny. The den or the open area between the laundry and Lenny's room had a pull-out sofa which was to be his bed. They had prepared it for him, they thought he might need to rest. Would he like something to eat first? Ananda accepted, and as he ate a dry and tasteless tomato sandwich his uncle told him this was lunch, and everybody made their own.

Too tired to register anything more, he sank into the soft foam of the sofa bed. Against the crispness of the cotton sheet and the fluffiness of the comforter he felt cocooned as though in a fortress.

He slept for hours, through dinner, through half the night. Three o'clock found him rambling in a strange house, too scared to make a noise that might disturb, longing for a cup of tea, unable to even find the bottles of drinking water. He was alone, all alone, with relatives who did not wake with the fall of his feet on the floor, the blood that joined them diluted with the waters of an ocean. The glossy magazine house felt cold and alien. Tears gathered and fell silently as he sat huddled on the soft yellow silk love seat, shivering with grief and cold in his new pyjamas.

The family awoke finally. He was taught how to make tea, he was told of tap water clean enough to drink, he was shown where breakfast materials lay. His helplessness reminded the uncle that boys fresh from India needed to be guided in every step they took.

Breakfast over, Dr Sharma and wife Nancy continued with their explanation of Western domestic arrangements. Everybody had to do everything themselves. They both cooked dinner, but breakfast, lunch, tea, snacks, each one made according to their needs. Washing, ironing, bed making, similarly all on their own. 'You will learn soon, beta,' said the uncle gently. Here Nancy stubbed her cigarette butt into an ashtray and carefully picked a speck of tobacco from her painted mouth, creased by faint wrinkles scratched into her upper lip.

The tightness in Ananda's chest increased. Not even one day had passed and they were giving him rules to live by— presupposing he was an ignorant, good for nothing freeloader. All his life he had been praised for being a good boy. He had assumed responsibility, performed well in exams, done his duty by his parents, met every expectation placed on his shoulders. Carefully he put on a pleasant expression to mask his humiliation.

The uncle and aunt got up. Lenny would show him the ropes downstairs. He must make his bed and get ready. Then, it being such a beautiful day, they would drive out to Peggy's Cove, and follow this with a special Indian lunch in his honour at the Taj Mahal restaurant on Spring Garden Road.

'No, no,' said Ananda politely, trying to convey that he didn't want the familiarity of Indian food so soon after he had left it. He wanted something Western and exciting.

'Oh, don't worry,' said Nancy, 'it will be a treat for all of us. We love Indian food.'

So Ananda went down into the basement to have a shower, carefully moving the curtains outside the tub so they didn't touch him. Water streamed onto the floor. His first lesson on how to bathe in the West and how to clean the bathroom afterwards, followed. As Lenny watched, he mopped the floor, and wrung the dirty water out into a bucket. He felt soiled and desperately in need of another bath, but he grimly ignored these feelings. He could live with an unclean body, he had lived with so much else. Now, said Lenny simply, here is the toilet cleaning stuff, here, you use the brush like this, and he proceeded to attack some brown stains that Ananda, to his mortification, had not registered as his responsibility.

Then the bed had to be remade, yes it had to disappear every day, so people could sit in front of the TV. This was the den (ie not Ananda's room), explained Lenny as they folded the bedding inside the sofa and replaced the cushions.

'In India we had a maid who did all this, I mainly studied,' explained Ananda in turn.

'Lucky man, I could do with a few servants picking after me.'

'It was not quite like that,' said Ananda. He had never felt particularly pampered. Rather they were the struggling ones, always anxious, always trying to make ends meet, clinging dearly to their standard of living through toil and sacrifice. The single servant was an ancient, bucktoothed, grey-haired woman, who had to be supervised into proper labour, who chatted relentlessly the whole time she worked and minded if you didn't listen.

Into the car and out to Peggy's Cove. 'It's down the South Shore,' said Dr Sharma, 'about fifty kilometres or so.' Lovely scenery, spectacular setting. As before the nephew was struck by the lack of people along the way, but this paled next to the beauty of their destination. There, beyond huge sloping boulders lay sparkling waters, glittering grey and silver in the bright sunlight. A white lighthouse marked the edge of land and sea, and as they stood on the rocks the wind tore into their clothes, hair and ears. He knew the place, knew it from Enid Blyton, the place where four children had gone for an adventure along with Kiki the parrot. What would his friends say if they could see him now, he thought, while Nancy took pictures and gulls wheeled and shouted.

Within five minutes the wind had frozen Ananda's bones. And that too in August. What kind of summer was this? His nose began to run, and as he had no hanky he wiped it surreptitiously with his fingers, dragging his hands across his face as if deep in thought. When he could bear it no longer, he excused himself and went into the gift shop. It was warm there. His uncle followed him. 'Want anything?' he asked. The boy shook his head. In his slim wallet he only had the eight US dollars he had been allowed to take when he had left India, dollars he was too afraid to spend. He had been so focused on leaving, it had never occurred to him that money would be an issue once he reached Canada, because of course everything would be taken care of.

When his uncle felt Ananda had drunk his fill of Canadian beauty, they got in the car and headed back to Halifax and the Taj Mahal.

In the red lamplit warmth of the restaurant on Spring Garden Road, Ananda breathed in smells he could no longer take for granted. Bending his head over the menu, he bleakly asked for mutter paneer, while the family bickered gently over what had been good last time and how much of the mutton, chicken, fish, tandoor and gravy items to order: Dad, you swore last time the lassi was too sweet, so why are you ordering it again? And Mum, you cannot eat spicy, though you think you can. Don't forget the pappadums. And Ananda, too bad you are vegetarian, the meat here is really yum.

'You are not eating?' observed the uncle, as he looked at the single naan on Ananda's plate, now cold, and stained red with the oily gravy from his mutter paneer.

In fact his appetite was curbed by memories too recent and too raw to be ignored.

'It's still night for him,' explained Nancy on his behalf.

After the saunf, called mouth freshener, and after the bill, so mammoth for food so familiar, they trooped out. From the car he was shown the Citadel, the graveyard, the pier, the cathedral, Scotia Square, Spring Garden Road, its park. Then on to Dalhousie University, the biggest university in Nova Scotia. Where the uncle studied, where Ananda was provisionally enrolled. And there to the right was the site of the Killam

Library, still under construction, the Student Union Building, the Forrest Building, King's College and the Dome that was part of the Arts and Administration building. He caught a glimpse of department signs on old wooden houses, yes, they said, Dal—Dalhousie—had bought most of the houses around.

The tour of Halifax was over.

To continue bonding with his nephew, Dr Sharma suggested they walk down to Point Pleasant Park, at the end of Young Avenue; they would be back in an hour. It was four in the evening, yet Ananda's eyelids were drooping, his head felt heavy, his body was screaming for a bed. But his uncle had decided he must see this park and it was not in him to be disrespectful.

'It's so beautiful, uncle,' Ananda breathed, as he walked through the wood and saw the sea at its edge, 'so clean and fresh—so few people.' The uncle beamed, admiring for the thousandth time the view and himself for living so close to it.

'Beta, we must talk.'

'Ji uncle.'

They walk on meditatively, the uncle pulls on his pipe, an affectation he has. To help his nephew, now so unfortunate, would be a way for him to pay back the debts a life of fortune had accumulated; a way also of making sure his sister's soul was at peace. As soon as he knew the boy was coming he had spoken to the Dean of Admissions at the Dental School, submitted Ananda's application and explained his circumstances. He was well respected, and they were understanding.

'Thank you, ji,' murmured the tired nephew, soaking in the feeling of being taken care of, by his uncle, the system, the government.

'Meet the Dean, then we will see about your loan.'

The feeling of being taken care of melted away. Of course this was not a world where family sacrificed their all for your success; here blood expected you to stand on your own.

'This is how things are done here,' went on Dr Sharma, his Indianness attuning him to Ananda's discomfort. 'Even Lara

23

and Lenny will take loans. No pocket can stretch to cover higher education, maybe a millionaire's, but not a doctor's.'

'How much loan?'

'Doctors and lawyers are considered good investments, so the whole thing is easily worked out. Right now I will give you a hundred dollars a month, enough to cover some basics.'

He pulled the money carefully from his wallet. The sight of the blue, red, orange and green Canadian notes brought relief to Ananda's soul. He could unclench his fist from around his eight US dollars, could look forward to replenishment every month, could avoid the ignominy of having to ask, so close to begging.

'I will pay you back, uncle,' he murmured. You had to learn fast in the West, it was sink or swim, and Ananda was trying out his strokes.

Dr Sharma looked at the boy, noticed the weariness on his face. Poor child, he had just been orphaned, but what better way to find your feet than student life? If he made things too easy, his nephew, being Indian, might take such avuncular indulgence for granted.

'Let's go back, you must be very jet-lagged—it's going to be light for hours yet. But have something to eat before you sleep.'

The boy looked at him and there never was such an open, unguarded expression on his face again. 'Thank you, uncle, thank you—for everything. I can't—don't want to—go back home, after what has happened—it will be impossible. With your blessings I can make it here.'

'You will make your mother proud if you do well.'

Why did his uncle have to mention her?

After a pause the uncle said, 'One does miss relatives here. I kept inviting your mother—even offered to pay—but she said it was impossible to leave her family and I could not afford four international tickets.'

His mother, his self-sacrificing mother.

'I often discussed it with Nancy,' continued the uncle reflectively, 'but it was not feasible.'

24

Ananda said nothing, he was in too much pain.

Dr Sharma's own sadness increased. He wished he had done more for his sister. Compared to his life, hers had been so mean and small. Though close in age, as children she had mothered him. Well, he would make it up to her son. She would prefer that, and the son himself would eventually realise that good things can come from even the greatest tragedies. Time is a great healer, he told his nephew, who nodded obediently.

They went home, Ananda made himself a tomato, cheese and lettuce sandwich, drank a glass of milk and went to bed.

Getting Ananda's life in order took the better part of two weeks. Dr Sharma went with him to the Dean's office, went with him to the Forrest Building, went with him to the student loan section, showed him the layout of Dalhousie University, this time on foot. With each day Ananda felt more beholden. Because of his uncle he would be in a place where there were no rickshaws, where if truck drivers were rash, they were caught and punished. With so few people an individual life must mean something. 'If God shuts the door, he opens a window,' remarked the uncle periodically.

In India many of his fellow students had yearned after these doors and windows, spent time and money trying to get them open. The brightest of futures anyone could think of was going abroad to study, then staying on somehow.

'Look at me,' Dr Sharma often said, pretending Ananda had a choice of where to place his gaze, 'look at me. I am a citizen of the world.' In other words, every summer they went to Europe. In Rome, Florence, Paris, Venice, London, Amsterdam, Munich, in art galleries, theatres and museums he exposed his family to the finest artefacts of Western civilization. The uncle looked mystical as he pronounced these evocative place names, and Ananda saw his future dotted with similar alluring stars.

Once Ananda, thinking more of his own situation than intending any criticism of this highly successful man, ventured

25

to ask why his uncle did not visit India more often. Were Lara and Lenny not curious about their father's birthplace?

'Arre, beta, last visit, ten days out of three weeks were spent being sick. Such bad diarrhoea—we all had to go on antibiotics. The whole country is crawling with disease, filth, flies and beggars. The children were horrified. How can they be proud of their ancient heritage if they see nothing of it? Very disappointing—and from what I hear the country is practically a dictatorship. One should take the best of one's country and leave.'

'Ji, uncle.'

Ananda had been dyed in a lifetime of study, and such habits were not difficult to return to. The dental course was rigorous, but he welcomed hard work. Long hours in the library stood between him and his memories. In the old wing of the Dental School, he could dawdle, read, feel himself king of the silence, the large windows, the high ceilings. He often returned to work after dinner.

Occasionally he wandered over to the vending machines in the basement. There he drank coffee, ate sandwiches, candy bars and chips. He felt a great fondness for the black, glass-cased monsters. Like his parents, they always gave, never asked. Come ten or eleven he would walk out onto Robie, down the mile to Young Avenue. Meanwhile, this new country was sinking into his heart.

He watched darkness fall earlier and earlier, till night came at four. By February he had joined others in grumbling about the snow and the cold. But in his heart he had not yet had enough, he only complained because everybody else was doing so. And look how efficient the snow cleaning, how manifold the pellets of salt, how pervasive the central heating.

This was the country to live in, despite the cold, the darkness and the never-ending winter.

Diwali and Holi. Every year their dates change, but around the beginning and end of winter come the festivals that make

Indians think with longing of celebrations in the mother country.

Halifax was no exception. Home to four hundred Indian families, home to the India Club whose main aim was to ensure that expatriates did not feel deprived during festive occasions and to expose the next generation to Indian traditions.

Ananda would have preferred not to know when Diwali and Holi fell. With his parents he had eaten special foods on fast days, prayed with them before the gods on Janamashtami, Dussehra, Diwali, Ram Navami, Holi and a hundred other smaller occasions. There was no way he could replicate any ceremony on his own; he preferred complete rejection.

On November 5th of his first year in Canada, Ananda finds himself in the basement of the Equador Hotel. Curtains give the illusion of windows. Tiny coloured winking lights are strung all around. A pundit arranges prayer materials before small images of Ram, Sita, Lakshman, Hanuman on a raised dais. A few diyas are lit around them, more, being a fire hazard, are not allowed. Myriad women are dressed in saris, Nancy and Lara included. Dr Sharma and Lenny are wearing new clothes.

On the other side of the hall is a long table, where the vegetarian feast catered by the Taj Mahal restaurant is laid out. The guests eat, wish each other a Happy Diwali, joyously, festively, wistfully, then emerge into the Nova Scotian night, the wind howling around the women's saris, inflating them like balloons, reaching under their petticoats, chilling their skin before they even reach their cars.

Another hybrid Diwali over.

Later Ananda asked his uncle why he participated. This was a man who couldn't stay three weeks in India.

'To give the children some idea of their background of course, otherwise how will they know our customs?'

Ananda looked unconvinced. His uncle was a fraud. He went on about Canada, and here he was dressing his women up in saris and devouring vegetarian food on Diwali. His own life would be conducted with more integrity—none of this Indian for a day, and Western for the remaining year. The uncle glanced at his nephew. 'Beta, I was once like you. I too wanted to leave my country behind when I left its shores.

'Twenty years ago there was no India club. I am one of the founding members. I realised that if I forgot everything of mine, then who was I? When the children came, it became even more important to keep in touch. Nancy thinks like I do, after all there is something so graceful about our rituals. She loves the opportunity to wear her sari. Then at Christmas we all go to church, that is fair, don't you think?'

'Ji, uncle.'

It was some time after Diwali, when days were shortening so much one barely caught a glimpse of light, that Dr Sharma decided to partition the laundry room to made a cubicle for his nephew. Ananda was bewildered; he was fine on the sofa bed, quietly watching TV during his free evenings and holidays.

He tried to prevent his uncle from spending the money, but his uncle explained—as though to a two year old, that this way he could have privacy. He could use the den of course but his clothes, books and all his personal stuff would have their own place in this little room. He would have a cupboard, his own desk with a tube light above it and a tiny alcove fitted with drawers. Wouldn't that be nice?

By now Ananda knew that privacy was an important issue in this culture and though he felt wounded, he said nothing. His uncle wanted to shut him up in a cage.

Workmen came and in ten days it was finished.

The room had a window near the top of the ceiling that looked onto the skimpy grass of the back lawn. It was this alone that prevented Ananda from dying of claustrophobia. 'You are lucky to live rent free,' remarked Nancy. 'There are many students who pay highly for accommodation in this area, we are so close to Dal.' Ananda hadn't realised he had to show gratitude, his instinct was to feel aggrieved.

'Your uncle always said we don't want strangers in the house, not even a student. He might think differently after you leave.'

Ananda did not respond, he was busy with his own thoughts. He had always considered himself undemanding, never exceeding his hundred dollar allowance, keeping his discomfort over food unobtrusive, with no special requests for meals, despite the woeful sameness of boiled vegetables. Nobly too, he had ignored that those vegetables were sometimes served to him from the side of the meat platter.

Yet his uncle thought fit to settle down on the edge of his bed one day, towards the end of his year at Dal, and say that it was time for him to move to a place of his own. He had been around Halifax long enough to know the ropes.

It then dawned on Ananda that being a relative did not bestow automatic rights, that being an orphan ceased to mean anything after you had eaten hundreds of meals at your aunt's table.

Though proud and sensitive, he was not perceptive. Over the past year he had many times admired his ability to adjust, allowing his TV channel to be changed, doing his own laundry, cleaning the toilet and bathroom. Now as he sought to understand the reasons behind his uncle's suggestion he concluded that the Sharmas must have tired of seeing his face, while he, pushed in his tiny room, felt barely visible. When his uncle had said, 'Family here means different things, beta. We help you be independent. We do not want to cripple you,' he could almost taste the sugar on the pill being used to get rid of him.

With distance the feeling of rejection became less, the understanding more, but the shame remained.

Ananda shone in Dental School. His three years of practice in India gave him confidence amongst his fellow students. He was articulate in the classroom, good with projects and demonstrations, always ready to help others. His particular friend was Gary Geller, who was the same age as him. Thick-set, small bright blue eyes, short blond hair, ready laughter, only child. His father was a dentist too.

Gary had taken a few years off after high school, spending this time working at menial jobs and travelling in Asia. He knew India, he had a broad cultural empathy. High time Ananda stopped clinging to his uncle, he said. He realised that sorrow and the pain of leaving his country made him want to hang on to the familiar. But every young adult in North America left home as soon as possible. Come on, man, it was time to be a bit more Canadian. His parents took boarders (as no doubt the Sharmas would as soon as he left), why didn't he talk to them?

'They hardly know me,' said Ananda, disguising his relieved, tacit acceptance of Gary's proposal—still being taken care of, but a step outside home, and a man has to start somewhere.

'They've met you enough times. Now you speak to them today?' It was not a question, Gary's statements sounded like this, as he was Haligonian born and bred.

The Gellers would be delighted to have him. They looked upon him as their own, and the rent was fifty dollars a week. That very evening Ananda told his uncle who congratulated him on his independence. He was his own blood, he said with great feeling, and the hundred dollars a month were his till he graduated.

Dr Sharma felt he could now stand before his sister on judgement day with his head held high. And the year of listening to the slight barbs Nancy had subjected him to was over. The way Indians did things made no sense to her, though he had repeatedly tried to explain the duty he owed a dead sister's son. Before he had issued the sponsorship, they had both agreed Ananda would spend time with them, but even after years of marriage, Dr Sharma had not realised that for Nancy time meant one month whereas for him it had meant at least a year. He had tried to speed up his nephew's acclimatisation, but grief made the process slow. Now Gary had stepped in, preventing him from feeling too bad about the boy's departure.

'You have known them quite a while, no?'

'Ji.'

'Once you are settled I will visit regularly, alright?'

'Ji.'

Gary helped him shift. One trip in his car was all it took. Lara and Lenny had been ordered by their father to be there to say goodbye. The bonds of an Indian family were strong, he preached, and they said yes Dad, and indulged him—easy since the circumstances involved departure.

'Thank you, Lara, Lenny, Aunty, Uncle, I am sorry for any inconvenience I might have caused you,' said the well brought up boy.

'You couldn't help it,' responded the aunt genially, 'it is difficult when one goes abroad for the first time. But you have adjusted nicely, very nicely.'

Dr Sharma beamed. 'Come and see us often,' he repeated.

'Well, I must say they're going to miss you,' said Gary in the car.

'After making sure I left,' muttered Ananda as they drove away from 807 Young Avenue.

Gary laughed. 'You'll have a much better time on your own, man. One can't have family breathing down one's neck.'

If one was fortunate enough to have a family, thought Ananda. Stoically he stared at the majestic maple trees that lined the roads that led to Gary's house.

'My parents had this room specially designed, and students have been quite happy here, you'll see,' said Gary as he unlatched a little gate at the back. Six narrow steps circled down to a door that opened into the basement. Basements were the students' lot, but this was as different from his old one as night from day. Blinds divided the room into a tiny foyer with a desk and chair, and a larger bedroom. On the wall above were two long, thin windows set close to the ceiling. The view was of grass, but enough light came through to brighten the place. A single step led up to an alcove with a stove and fridge on one side; on the other was a bathroom to wet as he pleased.

It was heaven at fifty dollars a week. Why hadn't he moved sooner? Why hadn't he thought of it?

'Notice the blinds? They are teak. I saw them in India and had them shipped over—you don't get things like this here.'

Ananda had never seen teak blinds at home, but he didn't say anything.

'Better get a phone connection soon,' said Gary, pulling the door shut and handing Ananda a key. 'Come on, Mom must be waiting.'

Dinner was to take place upstairs, in celebration of the new tenant cum friend cum part of the family.

To be served a fish bouillabaisse—we made this for you, because you don't eat meat.

'Mom, Andy doesn't eat meat, fish or chicken, he is *pure* vegetarian.'

The mother looked stricken—here, the salad, the potatoes, the bread, and I can open a can of tomato soup, it will only take two minutes.

As Ananda sipped the thick, red mass produced liquid—for the two hundredth time (conservative estimate)—he thought of his uncle. A Brahmin like himself, but only marginally connected to vegetables. How long could one hang on to caste taboos, for whom and for what? His parents were dead. And he had broken taboos when he drank alcohol in college.

As a first step towards a different future, he now said, 'My uncle eats everything—including beef.'

'Ah yes, Dr Sharma has been here a long time, hasn't he?

'Twenty two years, but he began with meat when he was a student in India.'

'Andy here is a late starter. But soon you will be asking for steak,' Gary rallied.

'Cows are sacred in India, Gary. You must not make fun of a person's beliefs,' said Mr Geller.

'I'm aware of that, Mom—I haven't travelled in India for nothing—but Andy knows what I mean. When in Rome do as Romans do.'

Ananda carried Gary's joke further to show how well he could take the spirit of what they were saying, 'The cows there are sacred, but maybe I will commit no sin if I eat the cows here. Let's see how long it takes me,' he remarked and they laughed, wanting to encourage him in steps he took to be Canadian. His life would be easier if he ate meat.

Ananda had a summer job. He had responded to a notice on the school bulletin board that advertised the position of dental assistant to Dr Cameron in Robie Street.

The interview with Dr Cameron had gone well. The doctor was a tall, stooped man, with thinning hair, a soft voice, tentative manner and blue eyes magnified by glasses. It was a seven hour working day, and if four dollars an hour was acceptable, his assistant (soon to go on maternity leave) would show him the ropes.

The money was acceptable, it had to be, but Ananda took care to inform him that he had been a dentist with his own practice in India. Dr Cameron took equal care to inform him that he was not allowed to even touch a patient till he got his DDS, a fact Ananda was aware of.

From the 1st of June, every morning he made his way to 4098 Quinpool Road. The menial nature of his job galled him. All he did was take impressions, mix silver for fillings, help with flap operations and wisdom teeth removal, prepare injections, develop X-rays, change little paper cups of water, hold and clean the suction, arrange the cloth around the patient's neck and take out files. He had trained a high school pass boy to do this for him in Dehradun. Never mind, he told himself often, in the new world PhDs drove taxis if necessary.

The money he possessed was a jealous mistress; he wished he could stop offering her the attention she demanded, but he was powerless. Each dollar invited his anxious love, each cent demanded his careful protection. Over and over he calculated: twenty eight dollars a day meant hundred and twelve dollars a week. In one month he would earn four hundred and forty eight dollars. Rent was two hundred dollars, the balance two hundred and forty eight would have to cover everything else.

Once the school year started there would be a fresh loan to cover eight thousand dollars of fees, plus living expenses of four thousand five hundred a year. With scrimping and saving, make that four thousand dollars. Total = twelve thousand dollars. The bank would own him, but then the bank owned many students. Starting life deeply in debt was the way things were done here: don't worry, don't worry, you are going to be a qualified dentist.

Dr Sharma approved of his new life. About once a fortnight he dropped in, drank a cup of tea and demanded details of Ananda's finances, job, boss, duties, eating arrangements, friends and landlord. After the written part of the DDS, how much time before he could appear for the second, clinical part? Should he spend more years and specialise? If he joined a practice where there were specialists, he could be the general practitioner. Would he prefer a hospital? And how many more years for citizenship? What about his social life, the boy was always in when he dropped by.

Ananda lied and quickly created some mythical friendships. He couldn't bear that his uncle should find him wanting in any respect.

The truth was that the whole long summer Ananda was very lonely. Weekends were the worst, and he had much time in which to relive his parents' deaths. His isolation pressed upon him and numbed his capacity to break his solitude. In India whether at home or in the hostel he had always been surrounded by people, his life open to inspection, comment and group participation.

Now he realised how much his uncle had done for him. The family cocoon he found himself in had felt uncomfortable and alien, but shreds of Indianness transported across oceans did mean something. Despite all that was said, blood (his uncle) was thicker than water (Gary's parents). They may have said he was like a son, but there was no daily interaction, no constant checking that he was all right. To be fair, they did not check on Gary either, so perhaps this could not be a basis for comparison.

At times it could be a heady feeling, not being accountable to anyone but often towards evening that momentary excitement degenerated into lonesomeness and he grew sick of his see-sawing emotions.

Much thought was spent on food.

As he boiled his vegetables and seasoned them with butter, salt and pepper, Ananda wondered how much his caste meant to him. His uncle pushed him gently towards the eating of flesh. He offered himself as an example. Should one's identity depend on what one ate? If Ananda married a local girl, he would find himself in a difficult situation. When one came to a new country, one had to come wholeheartedly otherwise one could be very miserable. He wasn't telling Ananda what to do, all he was saying was that the boy should think about it.

It was Ananda's own cooking that added fuel to this particular fire. He couldn't bear to eat another boiled vegetable, another sliver of cheese. He wanted to be able to eat fast food: burgers, hot dogs, sandwiches filled with bright pink meats.

Carefully he started with a fish—that almost vegetable—taking his first bite of a fillet soaked in lemon and tartar sauce, asking his mother's forgiveness, but feeling liberated. By the end of the summer he had graduated to processed meats. Culinary convenience entered his life.

His uncle approved.

*

35

At last the long holidays came to an end. Now, with his feet on the ground and the confidence of independent living Ananda could look beyond the seasons, trees, ground, skies, and let his gaze alight on the enticing figures of girls. Not for the young the separation that was mandatory in Dehradun and Lucknow. Here the sexes twinned—arms, legs, lips, anything, anywhere. He stared in fascination until he learned that his innocent looking was considered ill-mannered and obtrusive. Then it was all covert, corner of the eye stuff.

Many twosomes were casual. Sex did not mean commitment. The possibilities this opened were endless, Ananda only wished for the panache to take them. Self-doubt plagued him.

'Why don't you go out on a date?' Gary often urged, concerned about his friend's celibacy. 'Do you have a girlfriend in India?'

Inspired by the question Ananda told Gary about a long ago girl, fellow dental student, weaving a relationship out of something whose strongest feature had been his fantasies.

'Her name was Priyanka,' he started.

'Your girlfriend's?'

'We don't have this girlfriend–boyfriend concept in India,' said Ananda severely.

'Is that why you don't go out? You want to be faithful to her?'

'She was very pretty, lots of boys liked her. In college the ratio of boys to girls was 6:1. Some girls were so shy, they didn't even talk to us,' said Ananda sidestepping the question. 'Lucknow has a small town mentality. Segregation was the norm. Dating was not possible; people would see, talk, the girl's reputation would get spoilt. Of course everything was done, but not out in the open.'

'So, is she still your friend?'

'Some years ago she had an arranged marriage.'

Gary took a moment to contemplate this tragedy of Indian life. 'Is that why you are so sad all the time?' he finally asked.

Had Gary forgotten the death of his parents that even now weighed his heart down with a mountain of stones? Was the absence of some ephemeral girlfriend easier for him to understand?

Yet he desperately wanted to be the kind of person Gary could connect to. His only experience with a girl had concerned not the unavailable Priyanka, but Nandita, bespectacled, plump, dark, with long black hair and a snub nose. Nandita from Kanpur, who had flattered him with her interest, but who had only one thing on her mind, even snuggling up to him in a taxi after suggestively taking her glasses off. He was slow to respond to her demands. Later he heard that she had cast aspersions on his manliness. He had never hated anyone as he hated Nandita.

Three months after Ananda had moved into the Geller home Gary acquired a girlfriend who was training to be a nurse. She had an unattached flatmate, and thus Ananda found himself fixed up with Sue, uninhibited and willing to like him. 'I love the colour of your skin,' was one of her early statements. 'We lie in the sun for hours to get a tan like that.'

This remark grated on Ananda, because he knew that even in liberal Canada an artificial tan was considered superior to natural brown. And if she really did like his colour he didn't want to reveal that all his life he had been considered too dark. Instead he reciprocated by telling her that in India, her skin would be loved.

It was so pale, in places you could trace the green lines of her veins beneath the surface. Her eyes were big and blue, the eyelashes blond fringes, the eyebrows almost invisible arches. Fascinating gold patches glistened in her hair.

Sue smiled and reached for his hand. They had just parked and were walking to a downtown film hall behind Kim and Gary, who were also holding hands. Kim's long white legs ended in wedges. Her skirt was short, her blouse fitting. Both girls were unself-conscious about their bodies, even with so much uncovered. He admired that ease.

Ananda's background, his tragic history, his Lucknow medical college, the stories he told of India, all made him a romantic figure. A few more dates and Sue wanted to carry their intimacy further. Gary continually asked whether they had done it yet. Anxiety and desire grew in similar proportions.

A few weekends later Sue invited him to a Kim-less apartment. She took the initiative, kissing him, unbuttoning his shirt, zipping open his pants, while his hands and tongue followed where they were led. He climaxed before he reached the desired goal, then threw himself face down between her legs, so that hopefully she wouldn't hold it against him.

Later Sue asked, 'Was I your first?'

Yes, she was.

Sue giggled, mused and melted at this. Half an hour later she wanted to do it again. The result was no better.

Next time he took her to his own room. She admired the gay bedspread from Five Seas, the cosy light the papier-mâché lamp threw on the bed, the fluted wine glasses he set out for their drinks, the sitar music he played on his little two-in-one. When he could no longer linger over foreplay, he breathed deeply and desperately, tried for entry, but again to no avail.

Sue, it turned out, felt the need for discussion.

'Maybe you have issues around sex. Here it's no big deal, but in your culture it must be different. Deep down perhaps you are not comfortable?'

'Not at all. I am very broadminded.'

'Well, that's always one possibility. On the other hand you could have a problem. Just temporarily, you know. Some men do, it's nothing to be ashamed of.'

The relationship cooled; a few more encounters and it turned quite cold. The tactful ceasing of Gary's questions led him to believe that knowledge of his failure had spread. He abhorred the experience of Western women, which gave them the ability to compare.

It became worse when Gary started going out with Sue. Sue the voracious. She reminded him of Nandita.

'What about Kim?' he questioned.

'We weren't making it man, Sue is more my type.'

'But still her friend and all?'

'Hey, man, nobody owns anybody.'

'Is that Kim's view?'

'Why don't you ask her if you are so concerned?' snapped Gary. 'Besides she'll find someone else, plenty of fish in the sea.'

The sea could be crawling with fish, but to meet the one his friend was now dating was going to embarrass him terribly.

Gary made no further attempt to fix up dates for Ananda. 'There are always solutions to problems, man,' he said invitingly, but Ananda chose not to get into this discussion. Gary was his dearest friend, but how could he explain a difficulty he barely understood? There was a lack of inhibition in the women he met that excited and alarmed him. He had to match up in some unknown way. After his encounter with Sue he went over his performance in minute detail. Where had he gone wrong? He had so longed to abandon himself in her arms—Sue, who stood for the whole race, who was the book of knowledge.

As he tried to figure out his feelings in the dark watches of the night, he wondered whether his inability to love a white woman meant he had never really left India. Perhaps he was still clinging to his parents, still unable to come to terms with their deaths, still faithful to the notions of purity they had instilled in him. In his more despairing moments he liked to imagine he was indelibly marked by a tragedy that had imperceptibly seeped into his blood, bones and muscle. He who had never failed at anything was now failing in this most fundamental act, an act which even the poorest, meanest, most deprived peasant in India performed with ease.

In his less despondent moments he dismissed these thoughts as trivial rubbish. The fact that his penis seemed to have its own notions made him a little vulnerable, that was all.

The few Indian girls he met in Halifax did not attract him. He was too suspicious of the strings he saw around them. They might be looking for marriage, they might regard any physical contact as commitment, they might get their parents to contact his uncle.

And then too Indian women meant he could never escape his country. His uncle might remember on occasion that he was Indian, Nancy might enjoy playing the native, but for him the basement of the Equador Hotel on Diwali and Holi only evoked the shadows of home without its beauty. He hadn't travelled so far for that.

For a while he was edgy around Gary, wary of Sue's presence and judgement. But Sue met him with her usual friendliness and Ananda was forced to behave as she did. Gary continued to be his natural self, and gradually the trust that had been severely shaken was reaffirmed. Such a friend was worth crossing the seven seas for.

Meanwhile Ananda threw himself into his work. He had done well in the first part of his DDS, he was soon appearing for the clinical evaluation. His skill in passing exams stood him in good stead.

Finally he was a qualified Canadian dentist. Dr Cameron offered him a junior partnership. He was getting old, his back hurt, his eyes were giving him trouble. It was time to semi-retire. Ananda was delighted to prove that he was not the menial he had seemed the previous summer. All those people for whom he had made impressions, mixed silver, filled glasses of water, now all those people were going to see him in his true avatar.

When his uncle posed the big question—did Ananda want to specialise?—the nephew replied that he could not afford to. Gary however was going to become a paediatric dental surgeon. After that the two friends were thinking of a practice together. Yes, professionally things were going smoothly, congratulated Dr Sharma. Now for his personal life. 'Beta, here one is alone. You need a companion. Unfortunately these things are not arranged as they are in India, otherwise—'

The boy blushed, 'Uncle, please, there is no need. First I want to repay my debts.'

Didn't Ananda know that in Canada a wife was willing to support you while you established yourself? Women did demand—some of them—equality, but in turn they also shouldered considerable responsibilities. The boy was good-looking, with sharp features, dimples, smooth skin brownish red in colour, bright intelligent eyes behind black rimmed glasses. Was he gay? Gary?

'Does your friend have a girlfriend?'

'Lots.'

You too could have lots, cried the uncle's heart, you are such a good boy. Any woman would be lucky to have you—steady, faithful, reliable, earning well.

But he had to let him be. His wife was never tired of pointing out that he was obsessed with his nephew. He wasn't, but he had a special empathy for young Indian immigrants, facing his own initial difficulties.

Ananda fixed his eyes on the grass outside the ceiling window, picked his lips with his fingers, tapped his foot against the floor and withdrew into his shell. After a few minutes the uncle left, leaving Ananda free to throw himself face down on the bed. He could smell his uncle's cologne and it made him furious. What he did with his emotional life was his business. They were not in India. In the guise of discussing his future he could not come and say anything he liked.

To himself he could admit how desperately he wanted a girl to love. His experience with Sue had been traumatic, but maybe another? In this country nothing was awarded the faint-hearted.

There was little variation in the next two years of Ananda's life. He worked at Dr Cameron's and saved money. He did not move out of his bedsit, and he did not take a holiday. Gary accused him of penny-pinching—but that was Gary not understanding his ways. Though another loan was unavoidable, he wanted it to be as low as possible. Gary and the nation could go on paying interest on borrowed money, but he saw no necessity to follow suit.

Gradually Ananda lost Gary to Sue. Occasionally he joined them, but he was hesitant about being an awkward third, the bone in the kebab, the fly on the wall of their love. He envied his friend the security of his relationship. Sue was territory he had explored but had not been able to possess. She had been willing but an essential part of him remained hiding in his pants, shy, insecure and frightened. Now she and his friend had found each other and day and night they bloomed.

Gary and he talked of partnership, of loans, rentals, offices, practices, equipment, types of insurance and hiring staff, but when it came to anything intimate, he fell silent. Unlike Gary's, his personal life was confined to the same, monotonous, never varying place.

Many girls were attracted to him, but he could keep nothing going beyond a few dates. Still, he was hopeful. With an understanding partner, sexual prowess could improve. He dropped all those who suggested doctors, they were trying to undermine his confidence. How could there be anything wrong with him when he wanted sex so much? And which doctor did these stupid women think he could go to? He belonged to the medical fraternity, and he knew no sex therapist existed in Halifax.

Two years later Gary emerged a fully fledged specialist. By now Ananda had gained experience and popularity at Dr Cameron's. Being Indian turned out to be his USP. Arranged marriages, elephants, tigers, tree houses, there was no end to his patients' curiosity or misconceptions. There they were, pinned to their chairs by their open mouths, happy to listen to him, willing to be distracted, eager to be enlightened. Dr Cameron was very sorry to see him go.

Gary and Ananda bought a house on the corner of Durant and Leslie Streets. By himself Ananda would not have dared to venture into a future tied up in mortgage payments, but with the security of Gary by his side, he felt bold and Canadian.

Ananda loved the house. It was double storied with brown wooden shingles. Twin hydrangea bushes flowered on either side of the steps, and on the front lawn was a Japanese maple with maroon leaves.

The pair hired an architect to help them convert the ground floor into a dental clinic comprising three offices, a reception with picture windows and a tiny kitchen. A ramp was built for wheelchairs. Upstairs was transformed into a self-contained residential unit that the zoning laws demanded. It had hardwood floors, a fireplace, a tree brushing against the back window and large rooms; a place to die for. Gary fixed the rent, and decided that he would be the one to stay there—if his partner didn't mind. For, he explained, things were getting serious with Sue, and he needed a proper place. Of course, said Ananda, of course Gary must take the apartment.

Nothing further was said. Both saw it fit that Gary should retain the privileges his birth and country gave him. Later Gary would get the slightly larger office with the slightly better view.

Many of the repairs Gary intended they carry out themselves.

'I am not a carpenter,' complained Ananda as they drove towards Canadian Tire.

'You'll learn on the job, that's what we all do. As it is, the plumbing will cost a bomb.'

They sawed, they fixed, they painted. Dr Geller senior helped, as did all their friends. The chumminess reminded Ananda of his friends at King Edward Medical College. How many of them, he wondered, had built their own shelters in a strange land? Truly an immigrant had to be skilled in many things.

Despite Ananda's two years of saving, his debts became oppressive. A friend of Dr Geller senior sold them his practice for twenty five thousand dollars. That was twelve thousand five hundred his share, plus ten thousand on filling materials, five thousand each on new dental chairs, six thousand on new X-ray machines. Then there was malpractice insurance, liability insurance and the insurance for the equipment and office contents. In frightened moments he added his dental school loans that he was paying off at the rate of ten percent interest. Gary laughed at his fears and told him to be a man. In a few years he promised they would be earning so much he wouldn't even notice his payments.

There was much comfort in the fact that he and Gary were a team, consisting of two dentists (themselves), one hygienist and one receptionist cum secretary. If only his parents could see him now. A respected member of society, with a Canadian as partner and best friend. A man of substance in the new world.

In the apartment upstairs, in a place that promised security and contentment, Sue became pregnant. She and Gary decided to do the conventional thing and get married.

Ananda was best man. He stood next to the groom in the church on Spring Garden Road, and drank in the solemnity of the occasion, the vast arrays of flowers, the pews filled with white Anglo Saxon Canadians, quiet, elegant, expectant and well-behaved. The sound of the organ filled the church, deep, moving, sonorous. It had to be the most wonderful instrument in the world.

To marry a white woman would be like marrying the country with your whole body. He wondered whether being Hindu would be a deterrent to a church wedding.

The bride appeared. She was clothed in a sheath-like gown that left her shoulders bare. A single strand of large white pearls ringed her neck, pearl drops dangled from her ears, white gauze flowed over her pulled back hair. Down the aisle she walked, drawing all eyes towards her.

The service began. Ananda's attention wandered through its long recital, till ring, the priest indicated, and Gary turned to him. Soon the couple kissed, tenderly, lengthily, passionately. The audience sighed as the bride and groom trooped off to sign the register in the small side room.

1975. A state of Emergency is declared in India. The nation has had enough of democratic processes declares the Prime Minister, it is time for stronger medicine to cure the body politic.

Uncle and nephew are horrified at what is happening back home. Ananda writes anxious letters to his sister. Won't she think of emigrating? He is not a citizen yet, but he is sure their uncle will sponsor Ramesh.

His sister writes scolding letters back. Ramesh is a trained bureaucrat. Unlike medicine or engineering, that is not a profession with transferable skills. Besides, the new dispensation is making use of his talents in Delhi. Western media with their obsession with democracy tended to blow things out of proportion. India did not need an opposition, India needed economic development, which a strong leadership enabled. The slogans he heard, like India was Indira, Indira was India, were coined to drive this into the heads of the masses. Ananda could come back now—the nation needed its doctors, with his foreign degree he would find that home was the land of opportunity.

What opportunity was his sister talking about? He was still in touch with his old college friends—they were all desperate to leave. Why should he go back?

Meanwhile pictures of Sanjay Gandhi appeared with great regularity in the weekly *Statesman* and *Guardian* that Dr Sharma passed on to the nephew. Dr Sharma was a great believer in news. And the news was all bad. The PM was re-writing the nation's laws. Her party's majority meant that she considered herself free to amend the constitution, to award her office more power and to imprison any dissenter. Parliament was harnessed to her will. States where the Congress did not have enough seats had their assemblies dissolved with President's Rule imposed.

India had become a threatening place. A censored press, forced sterilizations, a factory that never took off, money

45

laundering, kickbacks, torture, with more and more in jail. Each detail became a brick in the edifice of Ananda's love for Canada, the sanctuary. He determined to become a citizen as soon as he qualified.

From time to time Alka brought up her poor lonely brother's need for a wife. Such and such offer had come, what did he think? He always thought negatively. A wife from India meant the India Club, meant socialising with immigrants, pretending they had a bond, when really he found their conversation monotonous and boring. With a superior snigger they compared their own virtues with the shortcomings of their adopted country; look at their domestic life, the way they educated their children, their sexual morality, their marriages, their treatment of the old, etc, etc. Then they talked of Hindi films and songs. Their heads, hearts and purses were permanently and uneasily divided between two countries.

Give him Gary any day.

Alka began to get more insistent.

'Did you think about that last proposal? I can't keep putting off interested people.'

'You should see the way I live—in one room as a paying guest.'

'A wife will help you settle. Ma's spirit will not rest in peace till you are married.'

Ananda thought mournfully of his sexual difficulties, and wondered whether the breakthrough moment would come with an arranged marriage. Certainly he could count on a willing, patient, forgiving, loving partner.

'You have to stop being so fussy. My astrologer told me about this girl, a teacher in my old college, a year younger than you, father used to be in the IFS. She sounds just your type.'

'How do you know what my type is?'

'O-ho. Calm down. I will send her picture, and if you approve I will meet her.'

46

'There is no need for hurry.'

'You are thirty one, you call that hurrying?'

'How can I decide with just a photo? What about compatibility, taste, her ability to live here?'

'Poor boy,' murmured Alka after a pause. 'To think like this makes it more difficult. Marriage is a question of adjustment.'

'You still need a canvas to paint on.'

'So write, phone, get to know her. I am not asking you to marry a stranger. No thinking person can.'

Still, she was pulling him backwards into the arms of an Indian wife. If she could see how respected he was in his community, how immersed in Canada, she would understand his reluctance.

'Why don't you visit me? Get your hotshot husband to wrangle a trip abroad. Must be easy now.'

Alka spent the next five minutes of the precious phone call explaining how Ramesh was not one of those corrupt civil servants used to wrangling trips abroad. He was a loyal and humble servant of the state. He wanted India to progress, and ever since strikes were banned the economy had been improving.

Abruptly Alka rang off. Were things so bad that an ignorant middle class housewife had to sound like a propaganda machine? Was her phone being tapped?

Two weeks later, a photograph. He stared at it, a bland, black and white formal portrait of a girl gazing into the distance. It gave away nothing. Certainly not the state of her teeth.

He first kept the snapshot face down on the table, but after a few days propped it tentatively against the frame containing his parents. Suppose circumstances propelled her from the basement to the clinic?

Picture of wife sitting in the dentist's office on top of the implement cabinet:

Patients ask, who is that lovely lady? She looks so exotic.

With quiet pride he responds, that is my wife, her name is... he opened his sister's letter, ah yes, there it was, Nina. Her name is Nina.

Nina, what a nice name.

Both Indian and Canadian. There are few names like that.

Like Andy? Dr Andy?

Actually Andy is not my real name, my Indian name is Ananda. Means deep happiness.

Really?

My friends call me Andy, and since it is easier to say, I use it myself.

End of conversation, but was it the end of Nina? Her name had been thoughtfully provided, no need for a Westernized version.

By this time Ananda had experienced multitudinous unbearable evenings. It was a little humiliating not to be able to find a companion on his own, but he had to admit there were some things he could not do. This was a very intimate area, and his body showed him who was master every single time.

He came from a traditional background. What was wrong with thinking of a woman from home? His sister would consider the girl's age, education, looks, adaptability and lack of encumbrances. In a way the ground would be cleared. His friends might wonder at his choice, but Westerners, thank god, were not nosy, inquisitive, prying and pushy with their insane curiosity about other people's lives.

His uncle's comments about Diwali now appeared in a more forceful light. If you reject it all, then who are you?

In his anxiety to establish himself he had turned his back on India and Indians. He hadn't been home in seven years. It was time to return.

iv

Nina had not realised that being thirty would be so difficult. Actually she had expected to go on feeling young, alone and strong till she died. Then her body stepped in to make a difference to her mind.

She detected a tiny wrinkle near her eyelid.

'I don't see it,' said her mother.

'You are obsessed with wrinkles,' said Zenobia.

This was not true. The wrinkle was the future and she was afraid. She looked carefully and found its companions around her lips, in the folds of her neck and on her forehead. She grimaced, stretched her mouth to exercise her skin, lathered on rejuvenating cream at night, but the faint lines were faithful to their nature and refused to leave.

Invisible to all except her, these indentations had tentacles that reached into her soul.

She hesitated to discuss this further with Zen. To be so concerned about ageing was weak minded and Zen herself was forty one. But she had lived, her divorce reflected there had been choices in her life. What did Nina have? Socially she was nothing. If she were in her own flat like her friend, if she possessed a little more enabling money, then she too could be brave. Anywhere else but in B-26 Jangpura Extension amidst the heat and damp, ugly walls, the concrete garden, the windows, with the peeling varnish and the grey, splintered wood beneath.

She was only human. Only human, she assured herself, as she witnessed her youth end and her courage ebb.

'What's this all about, Ma?' asked Nina as the weekend approached, and the mother reached for the silver tea set, the one wrapped in an old sari towards the back of the top shelf of the Godrej almirah.

'Somebody is coming for tea.'

'Who?'

'A woman, that's who.'

'Somebody's relative?'

'Might be.'

'Whose?'

'A boy's sister.'

'Sister?'

'Both the parents are dead, so it is left to the older sister to look out for him, poor, poor boy.'

A sister, representing a suitor, followed by another bout of hope with the inevitable disappointment. Why did this have to be her fate? Always hovering on the threshold, never crossing through. She glared at her mother, the most convenient person to glare at. 'Why are you so sorry for a stranger?' she asked sharply.

'One can feel for people, no?'

'You want me to be someone's nursemaid?'

The mother too had her feelings. What had she done to be saddled by a daughter so difficult? Any possibility on the horizon was accompanied by tension and tantrums. 'You are very unreasonable,' she now protested, 'With this attitude what is the use of calling anybody over? You have to *try*, you don't even *try*.'

'Ma, that's not fair. I have seen every man you wanted me to. Can I help it if it never worked out?'

In no meeting had Mr Batra managed to produce anyone she was sure would make her daughter happy. And without that certainty, she could insist on nothing.

'We have to keep on looking. You want to remain single for the rest of your life?'

Nina looked down, and with her finger traced the fortunes of the tiny fish woven into the border of her sari. Her longing for someone to love floated about her in silence.

Mr Batra glanced at her. A one room home in a world obsessed with material goods was not a fit setting for her daughter's sterling qualities. But the astrologer, recognising Nina's worth, had phoned after the birthday visit. He knew a woman whose brother was in Canada; if she wished he could make enquiries, but he would need a photograph. This Mr Batra surreptitiously gave.

'Don't you want to know who he is?' she asked.

'Alright.'

'A dentist. Settled in Canada.'

The daughter digested this information. 'The dentist himself is coming?'

'No, no, his sister. And you know who brought the match?'

'Who?'

'The astrologer. Now say you don't trust astrologers.'

'I don't. I thought his questions had little to do with the stars. He must be paid to do this kind of thing.'

'And why not? Somebody has to. I will pay him myself, one hundred rupees, plus donate another hundred at the Katyayani Mandir the day you get married.'

'You will never be able to afford to marry me to a dentist in Canada, so you can keep your hundred rupees.'

'We will see,' said the mother, hopeful because, regardless of their circumstances, the sister of a boy settled in Canada had expressed an interest in meeting her daughter.

Come Saturday, Mr Batra's anxiety reached hysterical proportions. She cleaned and cleaned, coaxing a dull shine from the old furniture, a dubious transparency from the thick glass in the windows. She soaked dals and imli, she ground the walnuts for her special barfi, she fried namak para. She rearranged the pots in the little cemented area in the front, she plucked a few puny branches and arranged them in two vases. And yet, it all looked sad and dreary, the home of people who had come down in the world.

It was just as well that Nina worked on Saturdays, such preparations made her nervous and angry. 'We have to be taken as we are, surely that is what marriage is all about.'

And the mother retorted silently; as we *were*, people must take us as we *were*. This is not us, this is some dreadful fate that has happened because of our karma.

But she said none of this aloud, Nina despised talk of karma: the opiate of the masses, the bane of Hindu society, the smugness of resignation, the invitation to do nothing.

Sunday. Despite the hot sultry monsoon, the gods have dredged up a cloudy sky, intermittent raindrops and a cool breeze to honour the occasion.

Nina woke to the sound of a mixie; Mr Batra grinding dal for the dahi bhallas.

'Ma, give me a break,' she shouted from her bed, 'do you have to start preparing so early in the morning?'

'It won't take a minute,' called back the mother, not wanting to antagonise her daughter. But the bhalla paste had to be ground, the bhallas fried, then soaked in water, then soaked in dahi. The accompanying tamarind chutney also had to be made, and it was already ten.

Nina emerged, dishevelled and bad tempered. 'Why are you going to so much trouble? Some biscuits will do. It's just tea.'

'You want me to starve her? Will that please you?' Mr Batra's lip quivered. Why did Nina have so little sense of the world? Someone with whom you hoped to establish a connection was coming—you had to make an extra effort.

Nina noticed her old friend, the quiver. Her mother would never understand how degraded she felt by the way she slaved on these occasions.

'If this works out your Daadi will stop blaming me.'

'I keep telling you, don't listen to her.'

It was all right for the young. They were less vulnerable. Nina used stupid words about her mother's endeavours: bought—sold—marriage market. She didn't understand that if a girl was thirty, you had to submit to the process even more.

How the sister ate! Three dahi bhallas, two barfis and fistfuls of namak para. Some perfunctory praise for the homemade but no deep interest in Nina's culinary skills, only questions about the places she had travelled and the things she had done. For a bride hunter she spoke much of herself, her old college, Miranda House, teachers, hostel, English Literature, her passion for reading, but above all it was husband, husband, children, children. The new emphasis on progress was keeping Ramesh very busy. Madam's Twenty Point Programme was left to people like him to implement.

The visit was an hour old before Alka said anything about that simple boy, her brother. After seven years still a paying guest. Orphaned, sensitive, brilliant, doing well, Canadian partner, own clinic.

Then she drove off in an official white Ambassador, leaving them with the suggestion that a letter from the boy might follow.

Mr Batra was jubilant. What culture, such sophistication, no suggestion that if Nina was thirty and unmarried there was something wrong with her, no appraisal of her daughter's monetary worth; instead an appreciation that she was teaching English Literature in an elite college. With such a background, how could her daughter not be happy, how could she not?

Nina was thoughtful. There had indeed been no hint of a demand for dowry or gifts, an issue which had caused some rejections. If anything her eye wandered approvingly over their meagre room, approvingly over Nina's books in the verandah, approvingly over Nina herself, of medium height, of a fairness so exquisite that the natural yellow of an Indian skin was replaced by pinkness.

'See, the astrologer was right,' gloated the mother.

'She made it quite clear that it depended on the brother.'

'If she liked you so will he. What else does he have to go by?'

Abroad. This was the first sign of interest shown by abroad. The grey cool skies of Brussels, the wide streets, the fewer people, the wood panelled library of the International Academy, the hot school lunches, the boy she had exchanged a few glances with, all this came back to Nina vividly, without the barrier of fifteen intervening years. As a first step to a new life, she murmured, 'What will you do without me? Have you thought of that?'

'I can do many things. I can go back to Lucknow.'

'Lucknow? And live with those people?'

'Why not? They are getting old. They need me.'

'You are not their servant.'

'Oh, what does it matter? After you marry, I can die happy.'

'I don't want you to die, nor do I want you living here alone.'

'Once you are settled, I will come and visit you. And I can help look after your children. Help is very expensive there. I have experience of the West.' Her cheeks glowed.

'I don't think we should count our chickens before we have seen the egg.'

'This time everything will work out.'

'So eager to send your daughter ten thousand miles away?'

'For this I have been praying and fasting the last ten years,' sniffed the mother as tears trickled down her withered face and smeared her work worn fingers as she rubbed them away.

'If I get married promise me you will stop this ridiculous Tuesday fasting.'

'We will see when the time comes.'

v

It took three weeks for Ananda to get the letter concerning this visit:

They live in a one room unit in Jangpura. Though clean it is cramped and uncomfortable. The father was in the IFS and she has lived abroad. She studied French in Belgium, where her father was posted for four years. He died when she was fifteen, and life seems to have been a struggle since then. The mother is like Mummy, excellent cook, affectionate, simple. The girl is an only child with grandparents in Lucknow. You will not be bothered by numerous relatives trying to get sponsorship abroad.

54

For the last nine years she has taught English at Miranda House; she spoke very knowledgeably of books, which will appeal to you. A career is important to her, you can decide later whether you want to be a double income family. Her voice is low, her colour fair, she has a straight nose, large eyes and sharp Punjabi type features. Height medium. Her circumstances will make her grateful and loving. They are certainly not well-off.

Here is the girl's address. Should you decide to correspond with her, she will understand there are no obligations. She is thirty years old and sensible.

Give this a try, I beg you. Even though you have taken citizenship at heart you are an Indian, with Indian values. Why else have you not been able to settle down? Thank god you have not chosen to marry a Canadian, like our uncle.

After you set up practice in Dehradun our mother was looking for a wife for you. It is my duty to finish the work she started.

Now it is up to you.

Ananda read this letter several times, increasingly exasperated. How was it his sister managed to aggravate his sensibilities every single time? What did she mean, the girl would be grateful? If gratitude was what he wanted, he would marry a beggar off the streets. And what did she mean at heart he was an Indian? He was no such thing. He was now a Canadian of Indian origin. What did she know of him, they hadn't met in seven years.

His sister reminded him of all that he found objectionable about arranged marriages, with her talk of gratitude, adjustment, double income families and paranoia about future in-laws before he even had a wife. It was disgusting.

He looked at the photograph and wondered exactly how fair she was. Pictures were deceptive. He who appeared so light-skinned in his own knew that.

Thirty—how come still unmarried? The father's death must have something to do with it. People may say that time was a great healer, but such events marked you for life. That was one thing they had in common. No other proposal from his sister had included a French speaking girl. If her knowledge was good she could help him acquire another skill useful in Canada.

He would write to her on the weekend. The post office had some special air mail letter forms printed with the flowers of Canada. She might find them pretty.

A letter to a stranger was a step in the dark; on the other hand he was writing to someone who understood the end goal. That immediately brought her closer.

The flowered aerogramme that was to appeal to Nina's aesthetic sense arrived in Jangpura two weeks later. With a casual air the mother handed it to Nina as she was sipping her first cup of evening tea.

'What does it say?' she murmured involuntarily, staring at her daughter's hand as it slowly sliced the letter open with the back end of a spoon.

Nina instantly held out the still folded page.

'No, no, you read first. It came at eleven o'clock. I knew at once it was from him, such a nice design, don't you think, why can't we do things like this? Your father was always buying paintings by Indian artists to hang in the embassies abroad, maybe he is like him.'

'He's a dentist, Ma, not an artist. Everybody there must be using these things.'

'Come on, read, what are you waiting for?'

This aerogramme held the promise of change, a commodity rare in Nina's world. The anxiety she felt was reflected a thousand fold in her mother's scrutinising face. She pushed her half drunk, now cold, tea away.

Her mother got up and carried the tray into the kitchen. Nina remained on the front steps. From there she could see the arc of the newly completed flyover. Day and night cars zoomed down it, the swish of traffic, the blare of horn accompanied every waking moment of the road facing Jangpura residents.

Slowly she opened the two flaps. The handwriting was legible (his patients must love him), the ink blue (conventional? but then he was a doctor), the style formal, the tone correct (a man well brought up by middle class Indian parents) and the information one could have got from a guide to Halifax. Expectations of romance would have to wait in the wings a little longer. This letter did not invite their presence.

As she mused over the nature of hopes that refused to die Mr Batra came out and sat next to her.

'Well?'

'Read it.'

The mother quickly grabbed the sheet that hung from Nina's hand. The neat, blue, evenly spaced handwriting met with her approval. Respectability and decency shone through every careful statement about his life in Canada. Her instinct after the sister's visit was vindicated.

'It's a nice letter, no?' she asked her daughter, whose standards were not her own.

'I suppose.'

'Then?'

'Why is he looking to India for a wife?'

'He probably wants one of his own kind. That's not hard to understand. Many do it.'

'True.'

'So why criticise him?'

'I am not criticising him. I am just wondering.'

'When do you think you will write back?'

'I'll see.'

'Marriage is a question of luck.'

If luck determined relationships so far she had not been lucky. Not with that creep who could talk of books so well, who was witty, who loved the same songs she did and who had made her pay for every moment of happiness with a bucket of tears. No, she had definitely not been lucky with him.

57

Nina stared at the cars that streamed across the skyline. 'Don't worry,' she said, 'I will reply. My life does not have so many opportunities that I should ignore this one.'

Now it was the mother's turn to stare mournfully at the auto studded horizon.

The letter was taken to college the next day. It lay among the pages of *Paradise Lost* Book I all morning. Nina's intention had been to show it to Zenobia, but when the moment came she hesitated. Nothing might come of the correspondence she temporised uneasily, knowing this was no reason to withhold confidences. Instead, she dismissed her tutorial early, came back to an empty department room, took the letter out and examined it. The flowers, the handwriting, the even lines. Wasn't the fact of the letter more significant than its actual contents? She might have thought this yesterday, if her mother had not darted in with her plucking hands and fearful heart. She who had been so scarred by the death of her father was now looking at the letter of a man who had been doubly traumatised. Her thoughts began to flow and she started a reply in her head. *Dear Ananda, I was so pleased to get your letter. I am sitting in the department room of my college. It is hot and the electricity has gone. Do you remember such times?* etc, etc. Tomorrow she would bring her nice letter pad to college. It was not easy to think at home.

Ananda responded immediately. His answer included details of Gary and Sue, his paying guest arrangement, the money he was engaged in saving. Flatteringly he wanted to know more about her. His sister used to tell them so much about Miranda House—was all of it true?

How should she tell him, thought Nina, what living in India was like? Even in academia the effects of the present regime were felt. A peon of their college had recently been killed. Such murders were no longer isolated. For the past few months the staff had heard rumours, based on accounts by eyewitnesses, of the way in which selected bastis were being razed to make a Delhi Beautiful.

The poor are so stubborn. They do not want to be compensated by land miles away in outlying areas, do not want relocation that would mean hours and hours, rupees and rupees spent in commuting to their sources of livelihood, their pavement shops, their menial transient jobs. They do not want to leave neighbourhoods replete with memories of fathers and grandfathers.

So they have to be taught by force. Police firing and bull-dozers, some deaths, some arrests, some curfews and terror, all this do the job.

The peon's extended family came to college begging for help, they were poor people, they wanted relief, some redress of wrongs, their voices heard, their woes considered; the tears of the poor, never ceasing, always flowing.

Though the staff felt bad, they could do nothing. A year ago they would have organized a march to the prime minister's residence, drawn attention to the atrocity—now it was illegal for more than three people to meet in public.

They took up a collection for the widow. But collections are a one time thing. How long could any amount of money last? They drafted a letter to the editor of *The Statesman* which was never published.

Nina tried to convey some of this to Ananda. Fear was rampant, letters were read and people arrested in the night. She could be imprisoned for the criticism she was implying. Though she told herself that the State could not be interested in an obscure citizen like herself, her pen was not free. At times like these she missed Brussels very much.

Ananda paid more attention to her distress than to the incident itself. In particular he was inspired by her reference to Brussels. Though he had never been there, he could assure her that Canada was equally sane, civilised and secure. On and on he talked of his adopted country.

Nina got to know of Pierre Trudeau, young, dynamic, visionary, charismatic, flamboyant, a leader who he assured her was the envy of the world. She got to know of the lovely city of Halifax, its parks and gardens, its wonderful weather, the coastal climate (the winter was a bit long, the damp and wind were sometimes too persistent, but that was all), its small place charm, its cosmopolitan qualities. She was acquainted with the acceptance he had gained, with the citizenship he had taken because in Rome, he wanted to be a Roman. Then there was dentistry, the ideal profession, a doctor who didn't have to be on call. You could call your soul your own if you were a dentist.

As time passed, Ananda allowed himself to grow more intimate. If she were to ever see his clinic on the corner of Durant and Leslie she would love it. It was a big wooden house and he was half owner of it. Gary lived upstairs, and the rent he gave helped with the mortgage. An architect had redesigned it, but he and Gary had done a lot of the woodwork and all the painting. This was a do-it-yourself culture.

Then there was an India Club, he didn't know if she would like that sort of thing, it was not quite his style. They celebrated Holi and Diwali in the basement of a hotel, and many of the four hundred Indian families in town came. He didn't see why being an immigrant should make him socialise with other immigrants. What did Nina think about such situations, he asked in a roundabout way.

Nina's replies were equally circumspect. They had had a lot of Indian friends at the embassies, but that was the diplomatic life, something she had experienced when young, she couldn't tell how she would feel now. But what Ananda said seemed to make sense.

Nina's mother watched the flow of letters with hope in her heart. She prayed every morning that they would result in a home and happiness for her daughter. To see her well settled was her only remaining wish.

'Canada seems like a nice place,' Nina remarked after two months had passed.

'Many people go abroad for a better life.'

'You had the best of both worlds, Ma. Living abroad, without having to leave home for ever.'

'What is there in this country now? Nothing. You know that as well as I do.'

Nina was silent.

She was walking down a street in Brussels with her mother. The sky was overcast, a few snow flurries had begun to fall. Snow was so magical. She lifted her palm and watched the flakes melt on the red woollen mitten. Her mother laughed, took her hand, and they walked home brimming with the warmth of happiness and material security.

Now Nina longed to put her burden down and escape into a life similar to the one she had known years ago. Daily this longing grew more intense, and each time a letter came it fed into it, until she began to think she was no longer fit for this city.

'I wish Canada were not so far away, Ma,' Nina said after three months.

'How often could we meet if you lived in Bangalore or Assam?'

'It's not the same thing,' said Nina vaguely. The ramifications of psychological distance were yet in the future.

Mr Batra pinched her cheek and laughed. She knew going abroad would suit her daughter: decent, comfortable, easy living, fine food and wine, holidays, access to books, music, theatre, concerts, she would have all the things that had once made their lives privileged.

Came the day when Nina related self-consciously that Ananda was coming to India. It would be a short visit over Christmas, he could only be away two weeks.

vi

In the weeks before Ananda came anxiety reduced Nina to a wreck. She knew they would try their best to like each other, they would not have reached this point if they were not

61

serious. What was it like to experience love within the security of marriage? How did he look? This question at least would soon be answered.

Another small detail. Zenobia did not know that she, Nina, was being courted, that marriage was peeping shyly over the horizon. Though the minutiae of their lives had formed the substance of many thousands of words between them, Nina continued the silence established from the first letter. Nevertheless uneasy lies the head that is used to confiding everything and is now hiding something. A man was coming between them, and that too before she had set eyes upon him. How to justify this?

One afternoon in November.

'You look different these days,' mused Zenobia. 'That Rahul is not back in your life, is he?'

'Does it have to be someone in my life?'

'What else could it be?'

'It's nothing really.'

The friend realised the betrayal and gave her a long stare. They were sitting in the canteen eating Mr Seth's bad chowmein, so full of grease and green chillies that even such devotees as themselves could not finish it. 'What's happening? Why haven't you told me?'

'Nothing was certain.'

'So?'

'Zen, I am sorry.'

Zenobia directed her attention to her slippery noodles while Nina awkwardly explained that there had been no point in making a big deal out of nothing. That nothing comprised the astrologer, the sister, the letters and the forthcoming visit around Christmas.

It was a situation in which Zenobia was bound to feel excluded. At forty one, any chance that her single status would change was remote enough to colour the discussion, though neither of them meant it to.

*

December 23rd. College closes and Nina can focus on his arrival. His plane is landing that night. How soon would he call? Was he careful and cautious, or impetuous like her father, who had been the very centre of gaiety, expeditions, plans and fun. Any resemblance and she would be Ananda's for life.

'What are you thinking?' called the mother, hearing the daughter's restless tossing on the moaning, groaning string bed.

'Nothing, don't worry about me, go to sleep.'

Though this was not possible, the mother said no more.

The next morning Nina was called to the phone by the landlady. The accent was Canadian, which came as a shock. You can get used to it, she tells herself quickly, as she concentrates on sounding attractive, warm and confident. The voice was male, it was aeons since a male voice had spoken to her on the telephone.

'Hi there, how're you doin'?'

'Fine. How was your journey?'

'Oh, not too bad. Long, but not too bad.'

'Aren't you tired?'

'Can't complain.'

'You are obviously a seasoned traveller.'

He laughed. 'Not really. I'm coming for the first time in seven years.'

'That's too long a gap, don't you think?'

So arch, so coy in her nervousness, not knowing how else to be. But he didn't seem to mind. Maybe he was nervous too. 'I got you some perfume,' he confided. 'And some chocolate. I hope you like them.'

'I will I'm sure, but you shouldn't have.'

'Not at all. I know how hard these things are to get in India.'

And how expensive.

Now she wanted their meeting over. It was like waiting for the result of an exam—the day before being the very worst.

She couldn't eat, she couldn't sleep, she couldn't think. Any outcome, pass—fail, disappointment—success, would be preferable to this tension.

Ananda should go back to Canada and leave her to her lonely life. But he had got her presents. The last time she had got presents from abroad was when her father had been alive. He would spoil her with boxes of French perfume. She still treasured them, the tiny empty vials of Dior, Chanel, Paco Rabanne, Givenchy, Yves St Laurent.

Here was another man, with a bottle of perfume for her in his suitcase. Was it cheap or expensive? And the chocolates, her mouth watered at the thought of them. Surely the fact that he had got them revealed much. She would not say anything to her mother, the poor woman would start drawing up lists of wedding guests.

Later in the day the mother is called to the phone.

'You are getting a lot of calls,' insinuated the landlady, venality oozing from every jerk of her flesh laden hips. 'Are we going to get some good news?'

'It is nothing, ji,' whispered Mr Batra. Nina should not hear, Nina should not mind, Nina should not get in a bad mood, Nina should get married.

'Arre, we are family, what are these secrets for?'

By now the phone had been reached, Mr Singh need not be answered right away, and yes, she and Nina could come for tea tomorrow.

December 25th. A beautiful winter's day. Nina was dressed in a pale gold Assam kosa silk sari, with a woven black and red border. The silk blouse was a matching gold, the shawl thrown across her shoulders was her mother's black pashmina. Around her neck was a thin black velvet ribbon on which hung a little ceramic Ganesh medallion, on one wrist was her watch, on the other were thick black and red glass bangles. Mr Batra thought her delicate pearl and ruby set would go down well with the sister, who would influence the brother.

'Sorry, I will not look as though I am dressed for my own wedding—he has come from abroad, he does not expect this—if he doesn't like it, I don't want anything to do with him—will you please calm down—I think it's disgraceful to want to marry me off so much—I really wish this visit was over.'

They took a taxi. The windows were rolled up, Nina didn't want her hair blown about. In the closed atmosphere of the cab the silence seemed more oppressive. No talk was small enough for the occasion.

Ananda was dressed in blue jeans, a grey sweatshirt and Reebok sneakers. Standard casual wear in the parts he hailed from.

'At least put on a proper shirt,' said his sister disapprovingly.

'Why should I? It's just an informal meeting. Don't get so uptight, for heaven's sake.'

'It doesn't look nice. Though they are in such a needy position I suppose it doesn't matter,' said the sister patronisingly.

'Why did you encourage me to write to her if you think they are so pathetic?'

'O-ho, there is no pleasing you. Why don't you arrange your marriage yourself?'

Ananda clenched his teeth. There she was throwing his inadequacies in his face. Who asked her to do anything, anyway? She was the one who kept on and on, and once he agreed, she reduced the whole thing to an economic exchange.

His brother-in-law was wearing a suit, looking smug, pretentious and insufferable. Since Ananda had last met Ramesh, the man had changed. On the way back from the airport in the official chauffeur driven car, Alka had hinted that her husband was at last being rewarded. The present regime was proving beneficial for him. If things went right he might be posted abroad.

'Posted abroad? Where?'

'It's still hush-hush. London. Washington.'

'London? Washington? Good for you, Didi. I had no idea Jijaji was so important.'

Alka smiled mysteriously. 'He has helped with many of the new programmes. You know like removing slums, bringing about some order. All that.'

Nina's letter flashed into Ananda's mind—the collection, the widow, the murder, the anguish. He kept silent. He did not want to be involved. These were the reasons people left this country. Nothing here was clean, all was messy and complicated.

It was when Ananda saw his brother-in-law's house that his full importance struck him. Double storied on Shahjahan Road—how had Ramesh risen in so short a time? Was the school connection so valuable, merit so negligible? He, who had nothing, no advantages of birth or connection, had had to go out into the world to prove himself.

Mentally he kept on proving himself with every fresh interaction. Far from the dazzling older man of his youth, he now found Ramesh pompous, behaving as though only he had the keys to life. But no matter, it was for a few days. He would be dutiful for Alka's sake.

Soon the girl would arrive. He imagined her smiling as he showered her with perfume and chocolate. It was a simple picture, based on some airport shopping; he didn't have nerve enough for more exact visualization.

A taxi drove up. Ananda peered at the two sari clad figures from the window. What should he do about his presents, would giving them at once seem too eager? His sister would probably disapprove. Let her disapprove. He picked up the perfume and chocolate, put them down, picked them up, put them down. First he would see her face, but before he could do that the tension in his stomach drove him to the bathroom.

Meanwhile, outside, seated in a wicker chair under a peach tree, Nina was saying, 'What a nice garden,' and Alka was replying, 'Yes, we were lucky to get this house, it is very central, yet so green. Right next to Lutyens Delhi, you know.'

'Has Ananda got over his jet lag?' asked the mother. 'It used to affect my husband greatly.'

Nina glowered at the grass. Why did her mother have to show that she too was once associated with international travel? Those days were history.

'These things do not affect him much,' said the sister dryly. She wondered what was taking Ananda so long. Really, the boy was behaving like a bashful bride. She hoped he liked Nina, then the whole thing would be settled soon. The girl was looking well enough. In the mild light of the winter afternoon her colour glowed, the black velvet of her necklace set off the pinkness of her skin; it was obvious she managed well with little. Her sari had some perceptible water stains, evidently an old one of her mother's.

'He is still tired, his luggage took one hour to arrive, two hours we were waiting at the airport,' explained the sister when fifteen minutes had passed.

Nina's mother just had time to say it happens with international travel, though we of course had diplomatic passports, when the vision in casual wear stepped out. He settled down in a wicker chair, smiled and said, 'Hi there.'

The girl smiled back, her lips firmly closed over the slightly protruding teeth she was self-conscious about. Ananda's heart turned. She looked so young, as if she were in her early twenties, how come she wasn't taken? She had had a hard life, he would make up for that—she would not know a day's suffering with him.

Small talk flowed as tea was poured, biscuits nibbled, sweets offered and refused. They have not bothered to cook anything, noted the mother, they think that being the boy's side it is not necessary. Thank goodness Nina won't have to deal with many in-laws. But the girl was so stubborn, she would refuse to realise how lucky that was.

Right now she was not saying much. To cover up, her mother asked Ananda at least five times how his flight was.

The last cup drunk, and 'Come inside a minute, I have something I want to show you.'

'Bring whatever it is, out here,' said Alka sharply.

'We'll be out in a second, Didi,' said Ananda holding out his hand to Nina.

Can't wait to touch her, thought the sister. At this rate they will get a very inflated notion of themselves.

He likes my daughter, gem that she is, thought the mother as she watched the two them climb the three steps into the house, and they look so handsome together.

Once in his room Ananda's voice dropped. 'I got you these things, just a small present, picked up at the airport.'

'You mentioned, but I don't know,' her voice trailed off. 'With nothing settled how will it look... '

'I see you as my friend. After all we have been writing to each other.'

She wished now he hadn't got her anything, it made things awkward. He opened his suitcase and grabbed a colourful plastic bag marked Frankfurt Flughafen. 'Here, I hope you like them.'

She peeked inside. A bottle of Miss Dior, and a big box of Lindt pralines. 'How wonderful.'

He put a hand out and touched her cheek. 'You are so pretty,' he said. 'Why, you could pass for a foreigner.'

'Oh?'

'I'm not kidding. And this necklace is nice too.'

'I'm glad you like it. My mother wanted me to wear pearls and rubies.'

'And my sister wanted me to wear something formal.'

They felt a conspiratorial closeness against the older generation, so staid and conservative.

'How about having dinner tonight? Then we can talk in peace,' continued Ananda. 'I'll come and pick you up in a taxi.'

'You know where we live?'

'I'll find it, don't worry.'

Seven was the time agreed upon.

*

They emerged from the house looking conscious. Alka could see her brother liked the girl—lucky thing, a chance to marry at thirty, and live like a queen in Canada. Dangling from her hand was a bright Flughafen bag. Why hadn't he consulted her? She would have told him don't create unnecessary expectations, but her brother had always been foolishly generous. They must have given him a shopping list.

Mr Batra looked misty eyed. Her daughter was carrying a package. Ananda had brought something before he had even seen her. Truly living abroad had not changed the Indian in him. Old world values, respect for people.

She got up to leave. 'Could you please call a taxi for us?'

'Did you like him?' she asked, as a few minutes later as the old Ambassador wheezed its way towards Jangpura. 'He is not bad looking, sharp features, good height. Dark though. And glasses, I hope the number is not too high, these things are inherited.'

'Yes, he looked well enough. I like that he doesn't have a moustache—unlike every other Indian man. And colour doesn't bother me.'

'So?'

'I only met him for an hour.'

'But you don't dislike him?'

'No.'

'What's in the bag?'

The Frankfurt Flughafen package was handed over to the mother, who exclaimed excessively enough over the two items to increase Nina's self-consciousness to uncomfortable levels.

Evening. 'He's coming to take me out in half an hour.'

The mother looked wounded at Nina's day long secrecy, but distracted herself by observing that even the plainest silk sari could not dull the glow on the girl's face. She must like the man whatever she might say.

They went to the Oberoi's, as recommended by his sister, and Nina had to admit there was a certain pleasure in being picked up in a taxi, dining at a fancy place and not worrying about the bill.

Ananda talked mostly about Canada, his friend Gary, his dental practice, his years at Dalhousie. 'Do you think you would like living there?'

'I loved being abroad when my father was alive.'

'You will love it again, I am sure.'

She blushed. He was being very specific.

'And you know French?'

'I did. It's all forgotten now.'

'You'll soon pick it up. Canada is bilingual, you know.'

More specificity. Every word about Canada constituted a proposal. Thankfully it was indirect enough for no immediate answer to be necessary.

He dropped her home. As the taxi turned the bend into the entrance of Jangpura, Ananda leaned towards her and kissed her gently on the mouth. It was a small kiss, but it sealed the proposal and put the ball in Nina's court.

That night Nina couldn't sleep. It was clear he had come determined to marry, barring absolute hideousness on her part. But she hadn't felt the spark of instant attraction. Was that so necessary in marriage? He was decent, considerate, thoughtful, everything his letters had suggested. Perhaps, given time, he would grow on her. Together they would walk the path of slowly growing respect, mutual dependence, create the habits that tied people together like a tree and a vine.

Two days of a suitor and already she was finding the whole thing complicated. Maybe she should just say yes. She wanted a family, she wanted children, she wanted to make her mother happy.

Millions of women married for such reasons. If only they had more than ten days, if only they had not met with the urgency of this decision upon them.

*

Next morning. The mother's probing look, Nina's evasive one.

'Did you have a nice time last night?' asked the mother as she brought the girl her tea.

'Nice enough.'

The mother waited.

'Where did you go,' she asked tentatively.

'The Oberoi.'

The mother's lips trembled, 'At last my girl is being taken to the kind of place she deserves.'

'It *was* nice. First we went to the bar. He had a drink, I had a juice, then we went to the Chinese restaurant, though he said it wasn't real Chinese. He insisted on eating only the things I ate. It was all very expensive.'

'He earns in dollars.'

'It's still a lot of money for just one meal. If I was sure we were getting married it would be different. But I am not.'

The financial inequalities oppressed her, yet in an arranged marriage wasn't improving one's lot a consideration?

At four Ananda came over. 'Sorry to come without warning but I took a chance. I should have fixed up last evening, I guess I wasn't thinking.'

The mother was all smiles. 'Come, come beta, we are not so formal here. It's so nice to see you, we had such a lovely time at your sister's yesterday. I must call and thank her properly.'

'She was mentioning how wonderful it was to have you over,' said the young man politely.

The formality of the sister out of the way, Ananda looked around the small place, and, turning to Nina, asked to be shown the colony.

They needed to be alone, though she had no idea what she would say; she was still in a hundred minds. Meeting him had not made decisions about her life easier.

'Look,' said Ananda, as they walked, attracting the curious eyes of neighbours sitting out to catch the last bits of winter sun, 'My sister is pressing for a decision and I like you.'

She was silent. Thinking she wanted a romantic proposal he cleared his throat, 'Will you marry me?'

'I'm not sure,' she faltered, alarmed.

'How long do you think you will need? I'm going back in ten days. I am a dentist, I have patients, I can't keep coming here.'

She detected the irritation in his tone, and fought her inclination to feel guilty.

'For years she had been harassing me about marriage, and when she does get it right, the girl is not certain. Just my luck,' said Ananda gloomily.

Nina's heart softened. Poor guy, so dominated by his sister, she seemed quite horrible.

'Well, my mother is pretty paranoid about my marriage too, but we must resist them.'

'I have no desire to resist,' said Ananda handsomely.

Nina smiled at him. He took her hand, and they continued their walk through the colony.

Another sleepless night for Nina.

Another morning with mother and daughter not talking about the issue at hand.

'I'm going out for the day,' announced Nina.

'Oh? Where are you going?'

'Zenobia is taking me to Dasaprakash for lunch. I need to have something else in my head besides marriage.'

'Alright, beti,' said the mother meekly.

So Mr Batra was alone when Ananda dropped by. He stayed for an hour, she gave him tea, they talked. There was none of Nina's indecision about the mother, she was all suppliant and appealing. To her Ananda presented himself as an eligible, well-off professional, settled in a first world country, an honest, upright citizen, a man who understood about caring and sharing, someone Nina would never regret choosing.

Nina's mother was so moved that she decided that Ananda was a replica of her late husband. There was that same dynamism,

72

that same forward looking quality that had led him to emigrate, that same traditional streak that induced him to come home for a bride. A rare and unusual mix of Indian and Western. Who could ask for more?

Zenobia and Nina sat in the darkness of Dasaprakash lingering over dosas. 'It's just too rushed, Zen, I don't even know him—though he seems quite keen. And that too after living in the West for seven years. How can I be sure there is nothing wrong with him?'

'You can't,' said the friend sapiently.

'Though he doesn't seem a murderer or a rapist, nor could he have a wife tucked away somewhere. No parents putting pressure.'

'Why has he been single so long?'

'His parents' deaths, then immigration, then dental school, then settling down?'

Were those enough reasons? Neither of them was sure. He was too unknown and giving up, they focused on the known. Nina—she wanted to settle down, she wanted children, she could continue in the same rut for years, longing and hoping. He had got her presents, showed a generous nature, was willing to like—to love. This could be her last chance. What were the odds of marrying after thirty? Did they know *anybody* who had managed to cross this Rubicon? And she did *like* him—as for romance, she had to live in the real world. It had come her way once and brought a few highs paid for by many lows. She had to remember that where God shut the door, he always opened a window. Ananda was the window, if later he morphed into a closed door she could divorce him. Risks were inevitable if one wanted change.

The friends decided Nina would ask for six months in which to give her answer. She couldn't rush into marriage with someone she didn't know. Ananda lived in the West, he was sure to understand that.

When Nina came home she was met by her mother's freshly composed paean to Ananda. He had dropped by unexpectedly, had stayed to talk to her, so considerate, so thoughtful, so friendly. Smart, intelligent and sensitive, not like his sister. He spoke so sensibly of his life there, of what it would mean to a girl like Nina, how it would probably be easier for her than for most.

At last, at last, her daughter had a decent offer, thank God there was somebody to take her out of this little room and give her the life she deserved.

Nina looked at her mother. The thin face was sallow, the glasses on it were pale pink plastic, square and nondescript. The eyes behind them were large, brown and anxious.

'I'm not sure, Ma, it is such a big step. And so far away. It means leaving everything, job, friends, you. If anything happens, I'll be left with *nothing*.'

The mother ignored this nonsense. Of course, Nina would find new friends, a new job. One couldn't stay in one place forever. 'You like him?' she asked.

'Well, yes.'

'Then beta, what is the problem?'

'It's not enough.'

'Marriage is a question of adjustment.'

'I feel nervous. So far away with a person I hardly know.'

Why did her daughter refuse to recognise that it was necessary to have a man to protect one from the vicissitudes of life? Somehow she had not managed to teach Nina the concepts of safety. She didn't know of Nina's struggle to resist her mother's fears, didn't know how afraid she was of their becoming her own.

Age and fear divided them. The mother was certain she saw the path to the daughter's happiness as clearly as the road into Jangpura from the bus stop.

'You can always divorce him,' she said at last. Once the girl was married, experience and maturity would demand she make wise decisions.

'Why marry then?'

74

'Because the boy is good. As for your other objections, nothing will become clearer no matter how much you think.'

Zenobia's very sentiments.

The evening of Ananda's departure. They had just had tea, and were sitting on the front steps of B-26 Jangpura Extension, hidden from the road by the bulk of Mr Singh's car. The door behind them was closed, Nina knew her mother would never open it; privacy was essential for the realisation of love and the mother's ambitions for her daughter. The sun had set, and the last light of the day was fading. The streetlights flickered on. As it grew darker Nina and Ananda shifted closer to each other.

'I will miss you,' said Ananda.

He heard a faint sigh. Her head was on his shoulder, his arm around her, he could not see her face. Every time a car entered the lane, huge shadows were cast on the walls of the house. Then relative darkness for five seconds before another car appeared.

'Does this go on all night? Don't you get disturbed?'

'We are used to it. Besides you may have noticed how dark and thick our curtains are.'

He said nothing. Seven years away and the country assaulted his senses like it might have done any foreigner's.

He shifted down one step, pulling her with him, so that they were more completely hidden by the car. 'I love you,' he whispered. He was leaving the next day and already he felt desolate.

'So soon?' she murmured back.

'I have always known my own mind.'

Again the sigh.

She was clothed in a thick sweater and a shawl, plus six yards of sari. His arm around her waist felt nothing but padding, and he slipped his hand under her sweater so he could feel her skin. She became very still, and he grew more conscious of her weight against him. There was some knit material loosely tucked into her petticoat.

'What's this?' he asked, pulling gently at it.

'In winter when it is very cold I often wear a vest instead of a blouse,' she replied, not moving, waiting to see what he would do.

His yanking increased. 'Just a second,' she whispered, 'you will pull my pleats out this way.' She sucked in her stomach, freed the vest.

It was an invitation and he responded. His hand caressed her stomach, brushed against her breasts. More delight, she was not wearing a bra; beneath the outer volume of clothing she was very accessible.

'I love you,' he repeated, his heart beating, his body warm in the cold night.

She pressed herself closer. Gone was the awkwardness of words. With his free hand he turned her face towards him and nuzzled her lips. Her mouth opened, his tongue slipped in, to be met in eagerness by her own. His hand played fast and furious with her breasts, now no barriers between him and them. Involuntarily she opened her legs slightly; with alacrity he followed that invitation as well.

Nina's body spoke its own language, coming to the fore in those insistent moments, treating as secondary her fears about distance and marriage. Her breathing told him this and he was satisfied. In his bones he felt this was the girl for him, and there by the wheels of Mr Singh's Ambassador he did his best to make her feel the same.

'Well, has she made up her mind yet?' asked Alka sarcastically as he entered the house. 'Or is she going to wait till the plane takes off.'

'At least she is not looking for a meal ticket.'

This was ignored. 'She is being mighty fussy. Where else will she get a man like you?'

'Let it be. The girl has a right to ask for time.'

'Already defending her,' taunted the older sister. 'You didn't need time. Why does she?'

'She is giving up more than I am, it's not surprising that she should be cautious. I would feel the same in her place.'

Alka stared at him. So he was already under the girl's spell. He looked happy, and she didn't have the heart to puncture his joy. She just hoped this Nina would be worth that warms flushed look.

Six hours later when Ananda boarded the British Airways flight for London it was with a sense of loss. He was reminded unpleasantly of seven years ago when he had left, putting his youth and the deaths of his parents behind him. When would his life be sorted out, when would he have someone of his own? He was glad he had not told anybody in Halifax, should his hopes be dashed, the distress would only be his.

vii

No sooner did Ananda depart than Nina found her life empty. Two weeks and she had grown used to the pleasures of a romantic involvement. Away from him her own doubts seemed less substantial.

Now when his letters came, Mr Batra did not ask what was in them, Nina reacted so badly. It was useless explaining that she just wanted to know how he *was*, what was wrong with *that*?

Instead she frequently inquired, 'What does Zenobia think?'

'Nothing much.'

Mr Batra had spent many years fearing Zenobia's influence over her daughter. Despite her parents' efforts to ensure a respectable second marriage, she remained alone in her barsati, thinking independence worth the pain of loneliness.

'You don't know the kind of people they want her to marry,' said Nina angrily, but was it possible there was no one suitable for the high and mighty Zenobia?

Nina usually did not take kindly to Mr Batra's comments about Zenobia. Now she thought if only her mother knew how much Zen's views and her own coincided, her dislike would vanish. But she would not give her that pleasure.

The months passed.

Each day brought Nina face to face with her problem, should she or shouldn't she? She grew sick of her indecision. If she didn't say yes, she might regret it all her life. Twenty years down the road she could see herself alone in B-26 Jangpura Extension, growing old with the landlord's children, the spinster of the English Department, her body dry with longing for a child. Then Ananda promised her such a future, laced with choices, edged with beautiful snowflakes that glittered through the distance, promising at the very minimum change, novelty, excitement. To push her over the fence Zenobia and Mr Batra held out the tantalising option of divorce. She should not resign straightaway, she should just take leave. All doors open, escape routes planned. Now jump off the fence. Go, Nina, go.

She did jump, as they had hoped, known, predicted she would, jumped to join legions of women who crossed the seas to marry men living in unseen lands.

In the nineteenth century they departed from their northern homes in boatloads, voyaging to Australia, Asia and the Americas. They left behind countries that had offered neither men nor security, left behind hopeless futures and lonely presents. In the women of the homeland, the waiting men saw helpers, family makers and standard bearers.

In the twentieth century it was the Asian woman's turn. The immigrant man needed a bride who would surround him with familiar traditions, habits and attitudes, whose reward was the prosperity of the West and a freedom often not available to her at home.

For his part the dentist had turned to his own kind after seven long years. His wife would share his money, body and success. She would know and appreciate the distance he had travelled, and he in turn would guide her on her journey. For what did immigrants want but a better life, not only for themselves, but for others whom they could assist and patronise. These thoughts fell into place only after he met Nina.

After Nina said yes, Ananda experienced a sense of achievement. He had courted, at the same time he had completed what his mother had set out to do. He recognised his sister's role in this and felt closer to her.

Once she had made the decision, Nina became calmer. Her torture was over. She was moving towards a new life, and she allowed herself to feel the excitement of this.

As for Mr Batra, she looked positively bridal as the weight of Nina's thirty years lifted from her heart.

Letters between the engaged pair doubled. She who dealt in words all day came home from work to pen hundreds to him, a running commentary on her thoughts and feelings, shyly revealing her expectations of happiness. Now between his neatly spaced blue lines she was free to read every meaning she wanted—desire for her, impatience for marriage, an eagerness to build a future together

A few times Ananda asked whether she would like to work once she came. He would be away all day, she might get lonely.

Nina would investigate all that once she got there. She knew it wasn't easy to get a teaching job, but she had no experience of anything else. When she considered all her years of study and preparation, doing nothing for a while seemed no bad thing.

Once a week Nina went to the university post office to get her sheaf of onion skin papers weighed. She bought stamps for the precise amount, gummed them onto a thin airmail envelope, which she then had franked before her wary eyes. She numbered her letters so Ananda would know when one was missing and be appropriately desolate.

Almost every weekend Nina visited Alka. Ishan and Ila called her Maami; she was already their aunt. For Nina it was novel to feel part of a larger family, her interest assumed and gladly given in every matter under discussion. She could wander around the kitchen, open the fridge, ask about Ananda's favourite dishes. (Later she realised that Alka had got it all wrong.) Ila hero-worshipped her—it was the age—and wanted to come to Canada as soon as possible. On the evenings of these visits, Nina gratified her mother by recounting every tiny detail. Mr Batra was always greedy for more.

Alka presented Nina with an engagement ring, a rectangular cut ruby surrounded by Basra pearls. 'My mother got it from Burma. How she was looking forward to this day.' The ring had an old-fashioned prettiness, and Nina slowly put it on her finger, abandoning fantasies of Ananda and diamonds. She was too old for that sort of thing, she had better watch herself.

The wedding was fixed for December. Ananda, the uncle and his family, friend Gary and Gary's parents were all coming. The uncle wanted to stay at the Oberoi Hotel; its central heating and running hot water would soften the harsh realities of Indian living. Gary and his parents were booked at the Gymkhana Club. A colonial relic, it had an atmosphere no money could buy.

Ananda and Nina wanted a court marriage—less trouble, less expense—but Alka insisted that ritual alone could satisfy the spirit of her parents. They compromised on a simple ceremony at the Arya Samaj Mandir. Canadian dollars were to be spent on a reception held in the Rose Garden of the Gymkhana.

Though the groom was adamant that the girl's side be put to no expense, Nina did not want to start married life as a charity case. She took a loan against her college provident fund, determined to pay for the wedding and the subsequent breakfast. Every day Nina and her mother counted their rupees, now free to flow into the future with all their might.

Meanwhile the mother worried about the daughter's trousseau collected during her husband's postings abroad: sheets, towels, linen, cutlery, kitchenware. Were these items to be shipped to Halifax or stored in Alka's house?

Ananda objected to both possibilities. The transport money to Canada would buy such household articles twice over, and Alka would not want to be burdened by them. As for memorabilia, the practical eye looked coldly on books, letters, old diaries, cotton saris, lecture notes and decided they could not go.

Ananda had made sure that none of the traditional demands involving gifts and money be made on the bride's side. All the immigration paperwork and the price of the air ticket were his. A bed of roses was waiting for Nina. Mr Batra hoped the girl would not make a special effort to seek out the thorns.

The summer holidays began, mother and daughter trapped in the heat of Delhi. At night they slept in the small outer space, squeezed to one side of the car, on two string beds which were propped against the wall in the day. They wet their sheets, so they could fall asleep with some coolness against their bodies. By five in the morning the summer sun drove them inside, Nina to bed, the mother to the kitchen.

For the first time in years, the never-ending summer with its dusty, searing winds was bearable. Every day was numbered, the last one of its kind. The last May, the last June. Nina would soon break out of this prison of heat. As she sweated, and fanned herself during electricity breakdowns, she could scarcely believe that for the rest of her life she need never be this hot again.

Valiantly the duo dealt with the flies that came with this particular ointment.

Homesick? Home was just a flight away.

Especially if you had money, and money was what the West was all about.

The world was getting smaller. Distances were all in the mind.

College started. At a meeting during the first term Zenobia announced that their Lit Soc secretary was engaged. Family, sex and marriage would soon be hers.

The colleagues looked at Nina's blushing face. How did it all start? How long had it been going on? And the boy, the boy, the boy?

Nina was careful to describe her courtship in a way that prevented the department from denigrating her as an arranged marriage type whom age had made desperate. Though the wedding was fixed for December, her own departure was not so certain. Her fiancé was doing all he could to expedite the immigration process, but much of that could only start after the ceremony.

viii

Ananda was affianced. It was time to let his uncle and friend know. He looked forward to neither conversation. Both of them had hoped he would find a wife in Canada.

An engagement is a big thing to hide. When his secret grew so large he could look at neither person without feeling guilty, he decided to start with his uncle. As it so happened Lara and Lenny were home from their respective universities for Easter weekend. Dr Sharma had invited him over for dinner and Ananda planned to break the news then. A wedding trip to India needed ample notice.

He sat with them at their dining table. The food was at its Sharma best: glazed ham, duchess potatoes, fiddlesticks with lemon butter sauce, an elaborate salad with fresh mustard–honey dressing, crisp brown rolls. All this was accompanied by a French red wine.

Mellowed by the feast, the drink and family feeling, Ananda allowed himself to imagine Nina sitting at this very table next year. He looked at Nancy and thought his fiancée was a hundred times more beautiful and elegant. And once she wore Western clothes she could pass for Italian or Spanish.

By now the family was on dessert. Fruit compote with rum flavoured whipped cream. During a pause in the conversation, Ananda took a photograph from his wallet. 'This,' he said, 'is the girl I am going to marry in December. You are all invited.'

It was a bombshell, yes, it was. They were flabbergasted, they exclaimed, they examined him with more interest than they had in seven years.

Was it an arranged marriage?

How long had he known her?

How had they met?

Was that why he had gone to India?

What was he going to do about the immigration papers?

How much family did she have?

What did this girl do?

How old was she?

She looked pretty in the picture, what was she like in real life?

Ananda answered patiently. Dr Sharma grew quite emotional. They would come for the wedding. His children were half Indian; it was time they discovered their roots. Lara declared her father always sounded so soppy about India, if he cared that much, how come they didn't go there more often? And could she please bring her boyfriend? Lenny said he wanted to go to Goa. He had heard the beaches there were fantastic.

And so the evening passed.

Now for the friend. Gary might wonder about the secrecy, might question the explanations, but he knew friendship recognised the clear divide between public and private and beyond a certain point there would be no probing.

It was Friday—come and have a beer with me, I have something to tell you, was how he put it. Gary immediately looked concerned. No, nothing was wrong, he had good news and he wanted to relate it properly.

'So, I gather this is not your average arranged marriage,' remarked Gary at the end of the story, thoughtfully nibbling his chips and sipping his beer.

That Indian marriages were barbarically arranged, that strangers were forced to cohabit, was a universal perception, and there was nothing Ananda could do to change it. Useless to assert the influence of modernity, to suggest variations, to indicate that in the cities it was just arranged introductions, and where in the world did that not happen? The Western eye, viewing things from a ten thousand mile distance, had no use for trifling nuances.

'No,' said Ananda, aiming for truth of intention rather than cold fact.

'All these years and you never said anything.'

'What was the point of talking when nothing was sure? She lives with her widowed mother whom she did not want to leave.'

So the mother died?'

'Noooo.'

'You managed to prevail upon her? I thought—or at least Sue thought—there might be a girl involved the way you suddenly went to India.'

Gary continued to marvel and speculate; all these years and the faithful lovers were going to be united, that was a tale in itself. Sue would be thrilled. Ananda was a little confused as to who Gary thought he was marrying, but he was not about to venture into explanatory quagmires. Instead he tried to persuade his friend to come for the wedding. He had been Gary's best man, now Gary owed him one. It was about time he made a second trip to India.

By the third beer Ananda's face grew flushed and he willingly supplied details. Their courtship, the long wait, and yes, that was the reason he could not be serious about any other girl, though he had tried. When he left India, it was with no strings attached, but seven years later, Gary, those very strings, still existed. Her feelings were unchanged, and her mother was now all for it. In India mothers were very hung up about their children's marriages and it was clear the girl could not find an Indian that suited her. In different ways they had both considered other options.

As he talked he felt he was describing a person who could easily have been him. That the story differed in a few minor

84

details was immaterial. This was a narrative that knit his life together and made sense of his Canadian experiences.

Later Gary insisted on coming home with him and announcing the good news to his parents, who in turn insisted on opening a bottle of champagne. Sue was called over, and again the whole story of the courtship was related, the long relationship, then the long engagement. In the Geller eyes, the existence of Nina explained many things. They only wished Ananda had mentioned her earlier; it would have saved many hours of useless speculation.

Ananda insisted they attend his marriage. They were like his family, and families came for weddings. If he didn't take his baraat from Halifax, then where on earth would it come from?

That night Ananda went to bed with a light heart. His marriage now felt more real to him. The baraat was getting ready, the guests were excited. He would ask his sister to book the Gellers rooms in the Gymkhana. They could walk from their room to the reception. He imagined his uncle, with his fear of germs and disease, would want to stay in a five star hotel. Tomorrow morning he would phone his sister. He must move out of the basement, perhaps by November. No point spending money before he had to.

He knew the Gellers would like Nina. She was the perfect mix of East and West. Her devotion to her mother and her willingness to consider an arranged introduction proved her Indian values, while her tastes, reading, thoughts, manner of speech and lack of sexual inhibition all revealed Western influences. As a wife she would show the same qualities, bringing patience and understanding to any little problem that might crop up between them. He saw now that many of his difficulties with women in Canada had come from his anxiety to prove himself. Nina and he had the luxury of their whole lives in which to sort things out. He put his hand protectively around his organ and caressed it gently. Poor thing, it had had

85

a hard time. At this sympathy the organ stiffened eagerly. Yes, a hard time, but now that trauma was going to end. A loving mistress was about to enter the picture.

Months passed, and finally it was Nina's last day in college. A year ago she had walked these same corridors expecting Ananda's imminent arrival; now she was going to marry him. On the 27th of December they had an appointment at the Canadian High Commission.

The groom and the foreign guests had arrived. The Sharma family came in stages; first the Goa bound children, ten days later the parents. Sue had been too nervous about exposing her kids to Indian germs to come, but the rest of the Gellers, along with Ananda, had flown in the night before. The Gellers were being put up at the Gymkhana courtesy Alka's connections and Ananda's money. Ananda assured them they were not allowed to pay; Indian tradition dictated that the utmost hospitality be shown to baraatis, if he could have afforded it, he would have bought their plane tickets. They respected tradition too much to argue.

Nina found this odd. Another tradition she had been brought up in said you did not take anything from anybody. Besides, traditionally it was the bride's side that paid for baraatis, and that was just the sort of custom no enlightened woman had patience with.

Tonight they were all going to congregate at the club. Nina would be seeing Ananda for the first time in a year. Along with the Gellers, the Sharmas and the Alkas. Clearly it was an introduction to the bride dinner, and she felt nervous. She didn't like being on display.

It turned out there was no cause for worry as everybody was determined to like everybody. There were enough new people meeting for the first time to keep questions and answers flowing. Ananda and Nina greeted one another shyly. During the past year their most intimate moments

86

had centred around visions of their future which they had shared in letters.

Two days later, December 26th, the Arya Samaj Mandir in Mount Kailash Colony. It is eight in the morning and still misty. Guests clutch their shawls around them. Birds twitter in trees next to the temple compound. In the covered verandah a bridal couple are seated before a fire, flanked by their parents, opposite a pundit. The onlookers sit on white sheeted mattresses that surround the bride and groom. Nancy and Lara are wearing saris that Nina's mother had long ago purchased for her daughter's in-laws, Lenny and his father are wearing the silk kurta pyjamas she had bought during the Diwali discount sales from Khadi Gramodyog. This family, half Indian, half foreign, stand out and are explained again and again. As are the Gellers, also wearing Indian clothes. Friendship that comes from so far away is deeply admired.

The bride wears a deep rose Kanjeevaram sari woven with gold flowers. The bridegroom looks self-conscious in his silk dhoti-kurta. The pundit intones Sanskrit slokas, while the astrologer gives elaborate explanations in English. From time to time the family murmur among themselves that these explanations increase the beauty of the ceremony; obviously Ananda is keen to understand everything.

Mr Batra's eyes are moist, her smile brave. Such a sincere boy, listening so intently, and such a beautiful girl, cheeks flushed, eyes luminous, face framed by the sari that covers her black glossy hair. Even Zenobia, sitting behind them, doesn't look too bad. Now that Nina can no longer be her companion, maybe one day the poor woman will find someone.

One hour and the pheras are over. Nina and Ananda are married. Family and friends smile, nod and congratulate each other. Presents for the couple are piled onto their relatives. The breakfast that has been paid for by Nina's provident fund will now be consumed. Idli, dosa, vada, puri-aaloo, chola-bhatura, chilla-chutney, dahi-parantha, fruit chaat, lassi, Assam tea, south Indian coffee; all the possible variations of a pan-Indian breakfast are theirs to feast on.

The registry of the marriage will take place at Alka's home in the afternoon. Through the influence of Ramesh's IAS contacts, the registrar with his register will come over to save them the trouble of going to Tees Hazari. Mr Batra is tearfully reminded of the days when she too had benefitted from the connections all important bureaucrats enjoyed.

Alka whispered to her that soon they were going to get a posting abroad, but it was taking time to finalise. A lot of people were envious of Ramesh and sought to obstruct his rise.

'In what capacity?' asked Mr Batra, jealous of IFS prerogatives. What was the use of the foreign service if postings were distributed so widely? Might as well scrap the whole thing.

'As a consultant.'

'For what?'

'National security.'

'National security?'

'Yes. But please keep this to yourself. I am only telling you because now you are family.'

'Where?'

'London, maybe Washington. It's all in the hands of the above.'

'Nina will be very happy to have you near her. God willing Ramesh's posting will take place soon.'

The reception took place that evening in the Rose Garden at the Gymkhana. Nina's red silk temple sari had once belonged to Ananda's mother. The motifs were exquisite, its embroidery of genuine gold thread. True, forty one years of lying folded in a trunk had given it minute cracks along the folds, but all heirlooms show a certain amount of wear and tear. Besides, declared Alka, there was no point in buying saris when you were going to live abroad.

So Nina stood stiffly next to Ananda, moving her hands carefully so that her jewellery did not catch the thread work, lifting her feet gently, so her heels did not rip the delicate, ancient fabric. Family and friends greeted, congratulations and gifts accepted, drinks drunk, food eaten, and at last the day was over. The bridal couple could leave for their honeymoon destination, the Oberoi Hotel.

In a car festooned with marigolds, they moved from the place money couldn't buy, to a place screaming for every rupee you made. 'Now he is yours to look after,' said Alka as she left them in their hotel room. 'He has given me enough trouble all these years, God knows.'

Her powerful presence lingered in the room. 'Thank goodness we are free of Didi,' murmured Ananda. Nina smiled and put her hand in his. He was her husband, of course she would look after him.

She started by worrying about expenses. She knew NRIs did stay in such hotels, but anxiety about money had been her companion since infancy, and it asserted itself on every possible occasion.

Ananda on the other hand was flush with dollar confidence. His ability to spend in India (unmatched by any such extravagance in Canada) had to be savoured fully.

'When you work abroad, things look different.'

'My friends and I have come here a few times for coffee, but that was all.'

'Call them over now for a meal,' said Ananda expansively.

'I don't want to share you,' murmured the wife.

'You can invite whomever you like,' he persisted, 'A few patients, and it's all taken care of.'

The bridal night. Now that the moment was close, Nina felt shy. Ananda closed the door and grabbed her. His hands leapt all over, under her blouse, her petticoats; they forced her on the bed to enable an even speedier exploration of her body. Startled, she tried to slow him down, but in five minutes he had come, five minutes and he had not even entered her. The rest was done with his hands, but that was stuff she could have done on her own.

Ananda disappeared into the bathroom. Nina had imagined a very different consummation. As she lay in bed she tried to transform reality into a scenario that would not confuse or upset her. Togetherness was the important thing. To be critical of how it was achieved was against the spirit of marriage.

Involuntarily comparisons arose. Rahul, with his obsessive talk of sex, endlessly curious about what she felt in what position, this technique versus that. So much so that at times she felt objectified. At his desire to penetrate from behind she had been outraged, what did he think she was? His little virgin, he replied, who needed to be educated so they could feel as much pleasure as possible. That was what love was all about.

Later she giggled, and you call me a virgin.

You still have vestiges, I have to be very careful to remove them all.

Virginal or not, what she had felt with Rahul was alive.

Back in bed, Ananda gathered her in his arms. 'I'm sorry,' he whispered, 'sorry it was over so fast. It's been a long time.'

'That's alright,' she said lightly.

He stroked her hair. 'You are worth waiting my whole life for.'

Her own grip around his body tightened. Thus clinging to each other, exhausted by the day and by each other they fell asleep.

She woke to his caress.

'Darling,' he whispered.

They were going to try again.

As he whipped off his pyjamas, she caught a faint hospital-like smell. 'What's that?' she asked, momentarily distracted from anticipation of what was to come.

'What?'

'That smell.'

'I don't smell anything.'

'Are you sure?'

'Yup.'

'Maybe it's the hotel cleaning stuff.'

He closed her mouth with a kiss.

She kissed him back and slid her arms around his long slender waist. If he didn't smell anything, it must be her imagination.

This time he did make it inside her.

For less than a minute, but the marriage had been consummated. They both felt the importance of this.

'I love you,' he said.

'Me too,' she replied.

With this established he jumped out of bed, looking handsome and boyish, thought his wife. 'Come, let's go to the pool. It's such a beautiful day.'

'It's *December*.'

'So?'

'Too cold.'

'Look at all those people next to it.'

'Foreigners. Crazy.'

'Not at all. Besides I am a foreigner too, and I want to go swimming.'

'I don't have a swimsuit.'

'Can't you swim?'

'I can, but there was never any place to go.'

'Well, now there is.'

'But no swimsuit.'

'Let's buy one. I noticed a women's wear shop in the lobby.'

'It will be frightfully expensive.'

'In dollars?'

'I don't think in dollars.'

'One patient will take care of this swimsuit, now come.'

So Nina ended up spending thirty dollars on an item she was sure she could have gotten for a hundred rupees in one of the Connaught Place shops. Daringly she fell in with Ananda's notions of money spending. She was on her honeymoon, this was not the time or place to indulge a lifetime's practice of market research.

A few hours later in the cool bright sun, she darted about in the pool, long hair streaming behind her, free and easy, swimming around her husband, touching him as he was touching her. She held the marble ledge, leaned back into the sun warmed water and closed her eyes. It was hard to imagine she was in the same Delhi she had lived in all these years. Ananda stroked her between her thighs, she in turn brushed repeatedly against the front of his swimsuit; he twisted his legs around her, she escaped, he chased. And so it went on, easier than the night.

He disappeared to order drinks and snacks. She floated on her back and took in the many stories of the hotel towering over her, indulging in the fantasy of being mistress of her future, her life, her happiness.

The entire family was coming for dinner. 'Let's get this over with,' said Ananda as, following Alka's suggestion, he booked a table at the plush French restaurant on the ground floor.

Mr Batra came early. She sat in the lobby, looking around her, glorying in the fact that her daughter was a resident in this great five star hotel. This was where NRIs stayed, where the Sharmas had stayed till yesterday. Now they were in the Lake Palace in Udaipur, spending more dollars on local colour and luxury. The Gellers were trekking in Nepal. So strange that the foreigners should be doing things more cheaply.

Patiently she watched the lobby clocks tick past the appointed time. Her daughter would be in the arms of her husband and she didn't want to disturb them. When she was just married how many hours they had spent in bed! Nina should make the most of every minute with Ananda. He was such a nice boy.

The Alka unit arrived. 'Arre Aunty, what are you doing, sitting here all alone?'

'Waiting for you,' smiled Mr Batra.

'Where are Nina and Ananda?'

'They should be coming.'

Really, Nina's mother was impossible, she couldn't do anything on her own. The bride and groom were summoned downstairs. Together they walked into the plush Cote D'Azur, to be seated by a great wall of glass that overlooked a garden artfully highlighted by hidden lamps.

Mr Batra nervously scanned the menu, unable to order at these prices, even at someone else's expense. Her spending impulse had withered through years of very mild usage.

Ananda scrutinized the wine list, seemingly unfazed by the astronomical charges, while Nina reminded herself of the patients who would take care of everything.

Conversation darted towards Halifax, and the value of relatives there. Not to mention friends, friends who had proved that water can be as thick as blood when it came to journeying to India for a wedding.

Alka observed that if they got their posting abroad, it would be nice for Nina to have family nearby. The children would miss their new aunt.

Ananda said things were pretty grim in India, it would be good if they got their posting, but why was it taking so long? Hadn't it been imminent last time?

Ramesh said Alka was too innocent to understand the workings of the government. Postings abroad could take years. Besides, Ananda might or might not know, but the leaders were doing their best to put India on the fast track to success. The people who maligned them, especially the foreign presses, did not understand how the Indian system worked. Democracy had proved a waste of time. India needed icons, they needed a strong hand. Look at what China had managed to do with a firm power base.

Nina fell silent as she took cold butter curls from the chilled silver dish and carefully put them on her bread roll. Ramesh was so pompous and stupid, just because he and The Son had been in school together did this mean he could misrepresent every fact? She hoped they never got their posting.

93

'Don't look sad,' said Alka, noticing her downcast expression.

'I'm worried about my mother,' said Nina quickly. 'I am all she has.'

'You'll be in touch.'

'It's difficult without a phone.'

'Ah yes, it does take long to get a phone. Have you applied?'

'Three years ago.'

Ramesh was listening. 'Don't worry. I'll look into it.'

Her irritation could not continue under this show of concern. A phone would make her mother less isolated. What could she do but accept the offer, and smile—though the smile stuck in her throat? And later on when Ananda said appreciatively, 'That was nice of Ramesh. You didn't even ask,' what could she do but agree?

The second night.

She spent a long time in the bathroom. Was she looking alluring enough? The nightdress she was contemplating so earnestly was a white thin-strapped affair, with little eyelets worked into the diaphanous fabric and a narrow pink satin ribbon at the neckline. She had bought it with Zenobia at Connaught Place. At the thought of her friend an unsought tear explored her cheek before being mopped up with a piece of hotel tissue.

When she came out of the bathroom she saw Ananda was asleep. She clattered around noisily, drinking water, putting off the lamp: no result. She snuggled next to him, shook him a little: still no result, only the faint sound of his snoring.

Should she wake him up? No, her poor husband must still be jet-lagged, and hadn't he mentioned working hard and sleeping little before his departure? He had only been in India five days. Besides her own needs, she had to think of another person's as well.

She wished she had packed books for her honeymoon. Reading was her usual soporific. She tossed and turned, tossed and turned, getting more and more agitated, the white eyelet nightie mocking her all the while. Eventually she fell asleep, sighing into her pillow, marvelling at the man whom no amount of tossing and turning could wake.

The next morning Ananda redeemed his husband status by jumping on her before she was fully awake. True, the penetration was over even more quickly than the day before, but Ananda tried to make up for it in other ways. Afterwards he looked at her adoringly.

'All these years I've been so lonely.'

She pushed her hands though his thick soft hair, 'No longer.'

'No longer,' he murmured back.

She loved her husband, she did. And she didn't feel the slight itchiness in her vagina that she did yesterday. Maybe her body cavities had to get used to his emissions, she thought as she made her way to the bathroom.

Alone, in the plush bathroom of the Oberoi, she absorbed the soft white towels, the little soaps, shampoo and lotions, the running hot water, oceans of it, so different from the mingy bathwater she heated in tin containers at home.

Her husband was giving her the best of everything. Was she going to be so unreasonable as to demand penetrative orgasms as well? Thus her thoughts as she jumped into the shower. Her husband followed her and drew the curtain back to tenderly stare at her as she soaped herself, then he watched her some more as she tied the pleats of her sari. As she gave a final tug to the hem he put his arms around her and crushed the careful folds of her palla.

Her own arms bent around him, she gazed into his face, her heart creeping towards her eyes. 'Love me,' she said.

He laughed and pinched her cheek, 'I already do.'

That night dinner with Zenobia. Nina felt nervous about the occasion. Would they get along? The glue of blood would not work here, just the glue of friendship, where different pressures worked upon the joints.

Zenobia was taken to the Chinese restaurant on the rooftop. 'You can't take her to a very expensive place—she won't like it—it will seem like showing off, and don't order imported wine—it's too expensive,' cautioned Nina beforehand.

Husband and friend were both civil to each other. Zenobia plied him with questions about dentistry, but he withheld a similar enthusiasm about her life. Nina felt embarrassed. Why couldn't he at least return the compliment of interest? But it did not occur to him, instead he looked complacent. Dinner over, and I have to go, said Zenobia, bye, phone me when you can to the wife, nice meeting you to the husband. It had been the shortest dinner Nina had ever had with her friend.

Meanwhile, their interview at the Canadian embassy. They went with the wedding invitation, wedding photographs, evidence of the year long correspondence, and the marriage certificate that the registrar had given them.

They waited in the lobby. Nina was nervous. Suppose they denied her a visa?

'Of course you will get a visa. I am a citizen, they cannot deny my wife entry,' said Ananda, flipping through her old passport. 'You can speak to them in French if you like.'

'Heavens! My French is not good enough. Is it necessary?' Nina had noticed the two languages all over the embassy compound.

'Not necessary. But sure to help.'

They waited silently along with others. Through the glass they could see a big white courtyard with fountains playing in small blue-painted pools. One woman was reading on a bench, under a small tree. No other people. Nina wondered what the rest of the building was like. It was so massive.

A man descended. 'Sharma?' he asked.

Ananda stood up.

The man joined them. He had their papers in his hand. Letters, certificates, pictures, everything that established them as bona fide.

'So, you are applying for an immigrant visa?'

Nina nodded.

'How long have you been married?'

'Two days.'

The man looked up briefly, his gaze arrested by the bangles on Nina's hands. Ananda rustled his papers. 'I am a Canadian citizen. I have known my wife for a while. As you can see from my visa entries, this is my second visit in a year.'

The passports were examined closely. Nina thought she had never seen a man with so little colour in his face. His hair was a kind of grey-brown-blond, his eyebrows and eyelashes similarly lifeless.

'There seems no problem,' he finally said.

Husband and wife breathed a sigh of relief.

'Shouldn't take more than three months.'

'Three months!' exclaimed Nina.

'We were actually hoping that my wife would be able to accompany me,' said Ananda.

'We have to proceed strictly in order of application. There are plenty of others before you.'

'Is there no way?'

'I'm sorry. Those are the rules.' He got up to leave. They watched his retreating back, solid, unapproachable, impermeable to pleas or bribes. The door buzzed; it was for them, they had to go.

They were silent as they walked out onto the spacious driveway. Past the round of green lawn with a fountain playing in the middle. The chowkidar came out of his little cabin and lifted the bar that lay across the gate.

'Never mind,' said Ananda holding her hand, 'three months will pass quickly. I'll phone you often.'

'Yes, it's not so bad. Didi had said it might take two–three years.'

Ananda snorted. 'That's in the US.'

Back in the hotel. Didi phoned. Nina sat on the bed and listened. Ananda was getting angry. This was not your India, where bribes and connections worked. He didn't want to take her into the country under false pretences, otherwise of course she could have got a tourist visa.

A silence in which Nina could hear Alka's voice, faint, quick, excited.

He put the phone down. She sidled up to him, put her arm through his and laid her head on his shoulder. 'What was Didi saying?'

'She thinks one can't move two steps without her husband's help. If he interferes, a perfectly straightforward case will take ten times longer. Things don't work on pull in Canada, why can't she understand that?'

The bride rubbed her cheek against her husband's shoulder. They were not going to leave together. She would return to Jangpura after the Oberoi Hotel, to Miranda House after the winter break.

'Are you disappointed?' she asked.

'I thought this might happen.'

'I didn't.'

'You thought everything would fall into your lap?'

The sharpness surprised her. She drew back. 'You did say that as a citizen you were entitled to marry whom you liked.'

'Of course I am. But that doesn't mean papers are granted in one day. Three months is nothing.' Hadn't she already agreed to that? Nina had not realised the adjustment process her mother had spoken of so long and so lovingly would begin the moment she married. She put her arms around her husband. 'The main thing is that we enjoy our honeymoon. I can certainly wait as long as required.'

'I shall count every minute till you come,' said Ananda gallantly.

He recovered his old tone, and she recovered hers by laughing.

That evening the family dropped by. They congregated in the coffee shop to discuss this new development. Arguments flew thick and fast. Ramesh wanted to use his contacts. Ananda was positive this would backfire, Alka implied they didn't know the extent of Ramesh's contacts.

The married couple thought secretly, what was the rush? In an unseemly fashion both were immediately aware of the advantages of staying apart. In their thirties, the single life was what they were used to, and now for a while longer they could contemplate in solitude the adjustments that accompany any marriage.

'We'll come to take you to the airport tomorrow night,' said Ramesh in the lobby. 'Then Nina will stay with us?'

Fortunately Nina had a mother, whom she pleaded as an excuse. Alka looked arch and said they would not accept her absence for long.

The third night. Ananda's flight was at three in the morning, he had to get to the airport by twelve. Nina's mother was coming to the hotel, and so were Alka and Ramesh, coming to escort Ananda to the airport, to escort the new wife back to B-26 Jangpura Extension.

ix

Nina returned to Miranda House a married woman. On the surface everything was the same: address, students, classes, bus routine, masses of corrections, department meetings, third term anxiety about exams. She never anticipated though the respect that came with marriage, a tiny shift in focus, and there it was; Nina Sharma, an accepted member of society, married, bound for the Western big time. The clerical staff demanded sweets, Kalawati accused her of forgetting her in her happiness and the Principal congratulated her.

As far as Zenobia was concerned the intensity of the friendship ebbed and flowed in a pattern initiated by that first announcement of Ananda's arrival in Mr Seth's canteen. Nina was married, she was waiting for an immigrant visa, she was going away. These were the lines that divided them, their friendship could not stand the weight of so many new beginnings.

Ananda phoned two or three times a week. Nina had to force herself to be nice to Mr Singh for their conversations were long. They already had a past to share, the wedding, the stay at the Oberoi, Gary, the uncle, who asked about her all the time. Nina in turn related news of Alka's family, of her mother, of college. Truly marriage was a fine thing. No detail was too small to be conveyed.

They also had their future, one that would take place in her flat, as Ananda insisted on calling it. It was a nice modern flat. Gary had suggested he buy a house, but a house was too much work, constant attention to repairs, messing about in the garden, dealing with the snow, plus all the equipment needed for coping with these things. An apartment was more practical.

Nina could connect to none of this. The important thing was that they should be together, even a mud hut would do. As she talked Ananda felt more in love than ever.

Meanwhile election fever was in the air. Many interests coalesced to create the Janata party and to provide a coherent opposition to fight the PM. For a moment their individual differences mattered less than a united protest against the Emergency that had been declared two years ago.

The forces of dictatorship seemed so firmly entrenched that Nina voted Janata in despair rather than hope.

It was a day of miracles when the results declared that Indira Gandhi had lost. The Emergency was over. Firecrackers went off all night, cars hooted, people shouted in the streets, Janata has won, Janata has won. Morarji Desai was sworn in as prime minister. Nobody had thought it possible. Nina described all this to Ananda, detail after detail. Across the seas he echoed her joy in more reserved, let's wait and see tones.

Three months later and the call from the Canadian embassy came.

This time she could look around the glass and concrete, the lawns, the fountain, the French and the English brochures with a sense of ownership. She had been accepted. They knew. They smiled at her, greeted her warmly. She was in the process of crossing oceans to be one of them.

She gave notice in college; she would finish the term and leave on the 1st of May. Ananda sent her ticket. Delhi—London—Toronto—Halifax. She collected it from British Airways and stared at the three red and white pages that comprised her departure from India.

At home she could not escape the sorrow of leaving her mother. Every glance at the sad pathetic face, pinched cheeks, badly dyed hair, eyes blinking behind spectacles marred her happiness. She had been her mother's life since her father died, now that life was going ten thousand miles away.

'Don't worry about me, beta,' said Mr Batra, constantly endeavouring to reassure. 'Don't worry about me. I will be all right. If need be I can go back to Lucknow.'

'And be their unpaid servant? Promise me you won't do that. You know you can always come to Canada.'

'Yes, yes, I know. But you can hardly arrive there with your mother.'

Yes, first Nina had to go.

It was as difficult parting from Zenobia, and a great deal less simple.

'Promise me you will come and visit,' said Nina again and again.

Zenobia refused to allow this cheap comfort. 'It's expensive, you know that. I don't have a husband earning in dollars.'

Departure time was definitely ebb time in their relationship.

The tears Nina hadn't shed before, during or after her wedding, all came pouring out days before she was to leave. They came unsought, at all hours, trickling down her cheeks, hidden from her mother, mopped furtively only to come again. This was her true vida—to her home, her friend, her job, her mother, everything.

Alka made soothing noises as the office car drove them to the airport. 'Don't worry, we will look after her, you will feel better once you reach, this is the lot of women, what is one to do.'

They parted at the airport door. Alka put her arm around Mr Batra's heaving shoulders and led her back to the car. And that was it. Mother and daughter were separated, as is the fit order of things.

In the plane Nina sat hunched in her tiny seat. It was the middle of the night. As the flight took off she had to fight her nausea. Panic-stricken she tried not to vomit, breathing deeply, closing her eyes, repeatedly swallowing the saliva that flowed into her mouth. Her head felt too heavy for her neck, her jaws were clenched, her temples throbbing.

In Delhi she had been soothed by animated discussions of how small the world had become. Stupid, she had been stupid. She looked at her watch that marked distance in the changing time zones of the earth. Half an hour. Hours and hours, minutes and minutes, thousands and thousands of seconds more. And during every one of those seconds the links between her and home stretched tighter and tighter.

The last time she had travelled internationally had been sixteen years ago, when she had flown back from Brussels, her father's coffin in the hold of the plane. In these intervening years she had never thought of that nightmare journey, blanking it out as completely as she could.

Now she was married and in a place that allowed her to throw a cautious glance backwards. She could see that child returning unwillingly back to India, homeless, fatherless and dislocated, her destiny changed forever. It had taken all this time, and much doubt and anguish, but as she travelled westwards, she felt her life shifting onto the track it had been forced to leave. This despite the pain of leaving her mother, and the uncertainties in her future.

She began to shiver with the assault of the air conditioning and wrapped her thick silk palla around her arms. Trolleys of food and drink came and went. She took a tray then returned it untouched. 'Ask the air hostess for a pill,' said the matron next to her, 'that's what I had to do the first time I went to visit my son.' (By now the woman had gleaned all there was to know about Nina.) Grateful to be reminded that states of mind can have pill-like solutions, Nina asked for one, and on a tray came a little paper cup of water with two white tablets—they will work in half an hour, promised the air hostess.

Gradually, the pills she had ingested kindly closed her eyes. Her head fell against the seat, her mouth dropped open. For the next six hours Nina slept, scrunched up and oblivious. The stewardess woke her as the plane started to descend, 'Fasten your seat belt, please.'

She sat up, hair dishevelled, limbs cramped. She couldn't believe it. Heathrow. London. England.

Nearer the earth they came and there it was: a white city, tall buildings, large, sprawling, a grey-silvery river. 'Sweet Thames run softly till I end my song… Sweet Thames run softly for I sing not loud or long', 'The river sweats/ Oil and tar/ The barges drift/ With the turning tide', the mighty river of the opening of *Heart of Darkness*; O Thames, I come from far away shores to greet you, receive me your foster daughter, who loves your literature and language better than her own.

The plane lurches slightly as it hits the tarmac. The foster daughter looks out at the great silver wings dotted with tiny raindrops. The passengers heave, rise, pull open the overhead luggage bins, haul out their bags and unable to sit a moment longer, jostle in the aisles till the doors open.

The long windowed tube connecting the plane to the airport is new to her. Purposefully she follows the arrows pointing to transit.

She crosses a sweeping woman, long handled mop describing damp concentric circles on the floor. She is salwar kameezed, with gold hoop earrings, a face brown, worn, lined and shut. Punjabi, fellow country woman, we are sisters, you and I.

Just then the woman does look up, but so blankly, it is obvious that the sari clad lady in front of her strikes no chord, her kindly gaze, her twitching, ready to smile lips mean nothing.

Heathrow: miles and miles of duty free glitter, seduction encased in lights, each dazzling item rivalled by adjacent companions. Nina glutted herself with looking; she had no money to buy as was obvious from her demeanour and shop assistants kindly ignored her. She rifled through postcards: the Tower of London, Westminster Abbey, St Paul's Cathedral, Buckingham Palace, the Thames River, the Lord Nelson Column, Trafalgar Square overrun by pigeons, names and places that found a faithful echo in a heart taught to beat to English Literature for so many years. So near, yet so far. Wistfully she drank from a water fountain, then made her way to the gate that would take her to Toronto. Her feet hurt in new closed shoes.

In the waiting lounge Nina gazed at the raindrops still sliding off the big glass windows. Everything outside was grey: the sky a pale grey, the planes a silvery grey, the tarmac a blackish grey. The colour was soothing; there was no need to respond to it, all her responses had been absorbed by the shop lights, vortexes which reached out to people and sucked them in.

Two hours passed. The departure lounge filled with confident, well-dressed people, looking as though they owned the world. For the first time in her life Nina felt out of place. Wrong clothes, shoes, handbag, bag. Maybe in their eyes she was like the woman sweeping. If Ananda were here, would both of them seem the same? Outwardly they might, though he was West and she was home.

She looked down at her book to block out these useless thoughts.

Half an hour later they were requested to proceed for boarding.

*

104

The flight to Toronto was much easier than the flight to London. Nina could concentrate on the film, it was bright outside, the food was better and she could eat.

Looking at the British Airways magazine, it occurred to Nina to figure out where she was going to live. What and where were Canadian cities anyway? Toronto, ah, there it was, why it was practically in America. And Halifax? Where was that? Good heavens, almost half a page before Toronto. Right by the edge of the sea. Why was she going to Toronto if Halifax came first? She wished she had been more alert when she had been told about these travel arrangements instead of bored and switched off.

The plane started to descend. Saliva filled her mouth, nausea overcame her and as the wheels touched the ground, she retched into the brown paper air sickness bag. She wondered if this was an omen.

As they go through immigration Nina clutches her passport apprehensively. She notices the many glances cast at her bangles, the bridal ones that enabled every Indian in the nooks and crannies of the globe to identify her as newlywed. She covers them with her shawl.

When Nina reaches the counter, the immigration man demands to see her husband. He is in Halifax, says Nina nervously. She is told to step aside. She waits. The white people queuing for entry into the country look away, the coloured ones have pity in their eyes. Will she be deported?

She is ushered into a small empty cubicle with neon lights, and no windows. It looks like a jail, which is where Nina feels she is heading. She sits down and stares straight in front of her. After a while a woman appears. She smiles briefly, takes out a form and begins to fire questions.

When had Ananda first come to Canada, who were his relatives here, who were his relatives in India, what did all of them do, where did they live? What did her husband do, what was the name of the partner he worked with? Where all had she travelled, who were her parents, what was her education, what were her professional qualifications?

Nina has no idea why this is happening to her. She has a valid visa which had taken three months to acquire. She is decent, respectable, god fearing and worthy. If deported, she doesn't think she can make the plane journey back again.

The immigration woman examines each page of her passport suspiciously. Nina's claim that she has married a citizen needs to be scrutinised despite the paperwork. The colour of her skin shouts volumes in that small room. She feels edgy; she is alone with a woman who makes no eye contact, for whom she is less than human. Suppose they found a way to kill her? That would be one less unwanted immigrant.

Now she is being asked for proof of marriage.

'How did you meet your husband?'

An astrologer is clearly not the right answer. 'Our families are old friends.'

'How often had you met your husband before you married?'

Nina cannot think of a reply, the question is repeated; Nina says with distances so great, they wrote more than met, as can be seen from the number of these letters.

This is a weak answer, but thankfully the woman has had her fill of torturing her. She examines the photographs, the wedding invitation, the marriage certificate, all that Ananda had asked her to carry—just in case you get someone unpleasant. Well, she had got someone unpleasant.

Rage fills her. Why were people so silent about the humiliations they faced in the West? She was a teacher at a university, yet this woman, probably high school pass, can imprison her in a cell-like room, scare her and condemn her. Though she was addressed as ma'am, no respect is conveyed.

Nina has been used to respect. It came with her class, her education, her accent, her clothes.

Here a different yardstick is used to judge her.

A short note to her husband:

Dear Ananda

This is not your country. You are deceived, and you have deceived me. You made it out to be a liberal haven where everybody loved you. This woman is looking for a reason to get rid of me. I am the wrong colour, I come from the wrong place. See me in this airport, of all the passengers the only one not allowed to sail through immigration, made to feel like an illegal alien. See, see, see.

Love Nina.

Finally she is allowed to go. The woman thanks her for her time and urges her to have a good day. Nina leaves, by now three inches tall.

Numbly she walks down the corridor. She feels soiled, accused of trying to take something not rightfully hers. In her heart she holds Ananda responsible for her humiliation, while her mind accuses her of unreason. He is not to blame for attitudes found in this country. If he is responsible for her coming here, she is responsible for having chosen to marry an NRI. There exist some rotten eggs everywhere.

These things happened. It was bhind her. Forget, forget. Forget the injustice of her treatment, the slurs on her marriage, her helplessness, forget all in the glitter of shops and the lights of the Toronto airport. Have some tea, hot, with a touch of sugar, redolent with the fragrance of the Darjeeling hills.

Ananda had given her some Canadian money. She goes to a restaurant. The tea comes in a bag. She swishes it around in the cup, takes a sip and finds it devoid of flavour.

She does not like her introduction to the new world.

Part II

Nina sits inside another pane, numb and weary. She drinks, eats, breaks the roll, spreads the butter, bites into the cheese, sips coffee, occupies her hands and mouth, and hopes her mind will follow suit.

The plane begins its descent. She cranes her head towards the window, to be greeted by masses of trees, and a few white buildings. Somewhere there is a husband waiting with her new life. Her immigrant status, no matter how closely examined, no matter how unpleasantly conceded, could not now be taken away. She supposed she had won, she was on a plane, looking at buildings as they came nearer, one of them her home.

The plane did its runway thing and stopped. Nina could see stairs being wheeled. With no immediate connection between plane and building, Halifax was obviously old fashioned. Already she was in the position of comparing the West with the West.

She had so much to tell the apprehensive, waiting Ananda. She had almost been deported. What would he say to that? He would share the knowledge and the shame. Just a few more minutes before they met, no barriers now between her and him.

Inside. Her first taste of the sparseness of people scattered through space. Could this really be the airport of a city? In front of the carousel, she waits, her hand on the luggage cart. That hand stands out, covered in bangles, gold, red and white with painted black circles. In this northern light the bridal turns into meaningless plastic. She pulls her shawl forward, a burkha for her wrists. Arms invisible, she waits for her luggage.

Across the barrier Ananda was getting impatient. He jiggled the car keys in his pocket, inspected the passengers as they came out—why was his wife taking so long? Was she in trouble, had she made the journey safely? He had not been in contact with her since she'd left India. Three flights, plus immigration and customs might be confusing for someone who had never travelled alone. He looked out of the glassed wall onto the huge car park. Soon he would introduce his wife to his car—a silver-blueish dream also known as a Saab. He thought of her transportation means in Delhi and grimaced. Anxiously, he turned back to the passengers—ah there she was. Swathed in metres of silk and wool, only her face visible above the trolley she was having difficulty pushing.

He moved forward to grasp it.

'Hi.'

She looked troubled. 'They stopped me at Toronto.'

'What? Why?'

'It took ages and ages.' The mortification, resolutely kept down during the flight, coalesced into a brief sob. 'They kept asking me questions.'

'Questions?'

'How long had I known you? When were we married? Where were we married? How had we met? What did you do? It was like the bloody inquisition.'

'Calm down, Nina, calm down. This is standard.'

'They were treating me like a criminal.'

'Some people get into false marriages in order to gain entry, or to stay on; they were just making sure this was not the case,' he said lightly. 'If it never happened, there would be no need for such questioning.'

'They wouldn't treat a European or American like that. Why me? Every paper was in order.'

'Sometimes you get a bad guy, you can't help it.'

'They did it because we are third world.'

'Don't be silly. These things happen.'

He was coaxing her into accepting and then forgetting what had happened. If they lacked the ability to do this, they would never be able to enjoy their new country. The situation made them vulnerable, one could hardly start fighting in an immigration cell, deportation would be the certain result. Ananda's way of handling it was expedient. Nina now turned to him and smiled. He took her hand from underneath the shawl.

Outside she caught her breath. The light was slanting and lay gently on the cars in the vast parking lot, touching the trees in the distance so that they shone green. The sky was blue, so blue, and there were puffy white clouds floating in it. The air was kind and temperate.

Pride of ownership gleamed in Ananda's eyes. 'See, how clean, how spacious,' he said performing the introduction. 'Even the air sparkles. Ah!' He closed his eyes in rapture.

She squeezed his hand. 'Yes, it is truly wonderful. Just like the mountains of home.'

Nina did not respond to the Saab. She was still too upset, supposed the husband as they started to drive through the countryside with its many trees, lakes and the odd car or two. Nina remarked on the slim evidence of a Canadian population to be told there were only twenty million people in the whole country.

Then Halifax spread before them, gleaming in the sun, small and sweet. 'Like it?' asked Ananda, turning to her and laughing. He knew he was presenting something of value, civilized, ordered and therefore beautiful.

'It looks wonderful,' she breathed. 'Reminds me of Brussels.'

'Brussels is *European*. This is *North America*.'

'It's the *West*.'

'Well,' said Ananda, who had never been to Europe, 'wait till you drive through. It's like a garden.'

It went on, tidy, neat and pretty. She exclaimed, he was encouraged to point out more Haligonian wonders. Finally they entered a complex of apartment buildings, halting in front of the highest and ugliest.

'This is the only block with a lift. From the flat you can observe the whole city, even the Arm—the North West Arm—the bit of sea water that comes into Halifax.'

'My, an ocean view,' marvelled Nina, the hitherto landlocked one, as they rode the elevator.

'Your new home,' announced Ananda as he turned the key in 612, Hollin Court, and ceremoniously ushered Nina in.

She faced a tiny corridor with a little kitchen at the end of it. To the right were two rooms, a drawing-dining with a picture window, behind that a bedroom, and opposite a bathroom, a blinding vision in pink.

Nina would not have thought there was so much to show in one tiny apartment, but there was: the drawer for her clothes, her cupboard space, the peculiarity of the bathroom taps, how the stove operated, where the switches were, where the spices were, where the bathroom cleaners were, how to put on the TV when Ananda wasn't there. 'And the rest you will learn by and by.'

Eagerly Nina followed her husband from knob to switch. Her new place looked comfortable, compact and cosy, unlike those terrible rooms in Jangpura that her mother would inhabit alone.

To get rid of her sad feeling, she said, 'Show me the sea, you said there's a view from the house.'

'Arm, I said we could see the North West Arm from the—and it is not a house, it's an apartment.'

'Whatever it is, just show me.'

He parted the net curtains in the bedroom, 'There.'

'Where? I can't see.'

'*There.*' He jabbed at a thin black line in the distance.

'Oh.'

'I told you it was not the sea, it is more like an outstretched arm.' He drew her close to him. 'One weekend I will take you out of the city so you can see the ocean properly. We can drive down the coast, go to Lunenburg.'

She would have to wait before she saw her image of the ocean: vast quantities of yellow sandy beach, grand foamy waves, white gulls circling in the brilliant blue sky and their own wobbly line of footprints as they walked hand in hand next to the water. She threw her arms around his neck, and nuzzled his lips. 'That's so sweet of you, I have never seen the sea—and the house is perfect, I shall be very happy here.'

'Of course you will,' he said pecking her mouth before disengaging himself. 'Now I thought we could order pizza for lunch. How about a special combo with pepperoni, anchovies, olives, green peppers and onions. Nothing in India quite compares.'

'I thought you were vegetarian.'

'At home they think I am. But here I eat what everybody else does, it is simpler and convenient. You too will get used to it.'

'I won't.'

Meat had never crossed Nina's lips in thirty years, how could she change now? She thought of the recipes her mother had anxiously written down for her, the special pickle she had given her so lovingly, that she had secretly carried these ten thousand miles. Five years old, a delicacy of blackish, salt encrusted pieces of lemon, their pale seeds glowing against dark skins.

'Well, I can get you a green pepper, mushroom and olive pizza. That should do,' decided Ananda, reaching for the phone.

In the bedroom, Nina sank to the carpet in front of her suitcases. Though she needed her toilet things, she hesitated before opening them, for all of home lay within, and she was scared of pain. Her mother and she had packed together, trying to cram within the trousseau that had been collected over a lifetime.

Slowly she fit the tiny keys in the locks. She took out her saris and stroked the intricate woven surfaces. Benarasi, Kanjeevaram, Orissa patola, Gujarati patola, Bandhani; she had fancied carrying all parts of India to Canada in her clothes. She spread the brightest one on the bed, and gazed at the magic of the green, yellow and red Gujarati weave.

'Look, Ananda, look.'

He came, looked, remarked that it would get dirty if used as a bedcover, and would she hurry up, the pizza was coming.

112

Men didn't know about saris.

She hung their radiance on hangers, shut them in the cupboard and drew comfort from knowing they were there.

ii

Next morning. Her shoulder was being shaken. 'I'm going now, I'll call you,' said a voice.

An enormous effort and she managed to unglue her eyelashes a fraction. Who was this man? Into her blankness he repeated, 'I'll call you.'

Her husband. 'But—but what about breakfast?' she asked, heaving under the bedclothes.

'I've already had it. If you need anything, here is my work number, here, see, under the clock.'

The front door banged, and she was left in silence. Alone, she was alone. Luxuriously she welcomed the exhaustion that forced her eyes shut.

When she next opened them it was noon. She lay in bed a long time, looking at the grey sky hovering over her through the large window, gazing at the blue and white stripes of the quilt, noticing the jumping green digital numbers of the clock radio. She snuggled deeper into the bedding, it was so cosy and she was so comfortable. There was no one to shout, get up, get up, it's getting late, no task that would suffer by her staying in bed, no person whose loneliness she had to assuage. Only Ananda, who was at this very moment filling the teeth of Canadian children. (She brought to mind he had a family practice.)

Eventually lying in bed became boring. She must explore, she must examine her territory in private. Boldly she strode about in her nightie, the shape of her breasts visible, as was the shadow of her pubic hair. No servant, landlord, landlady, neighbour or mother was there to see. After years of night and day protection against the eyes of the world, it felt strange to abandon the shield that had defended her modesty.

Eat, she must eat. She stares at the pink meat slices, milk, eggs, bread, butter in the fridge. She holds the cold bottle of grape juice in her hands, 1.99 dollars—just 1.99. Welcome to the land of plenty, Nina. Remember how impossible it was to drink grape juice in Delhi? The last time you had it was courtesy Zenobia's birthday at Dasaprakash, and it cost sixty rupees. Now it seems practically free.

She found a long stemmed glass, and poured the juice. It wasn't quite the fresh, thick, pulpy taste she remembered from the south Indian restaurant at the Ambassador Hotel, but it was grape juice, and caused a similar puckering in her mouth. She poured herself another glass and continued to drink slowly. If nostalgia came she would fight it.

The phone rang. It was her husband.

'Hi.'

'Hi.'

'How are you doing? Everything all right?'

'I have just gotten up.'

'Jet lag, sleep it off.'

Sleep some more? Oh all right.

'Have you had lunch?'

'No.'

'Make yourself a sandwich.'

'There is only meat.'

'Eggs? Boil some eggs. Or try the peanut butter in the cupboard. We'll go shopping in the evening. I would have come home, but I have to catch up on patients here. Sorry about your lunch.'

'That's all right.'

'See you, bye. Have to run.' He put the phone down, and silence caught up from where it had left off.

Eggs. He had told her to boil eggs.

She attempted to light the stove but it resisted stubbornly. She rummaged some more in the cupboard and came up with milk and cereal, easier than putting peanut butter down her throat, which seemed a very viscous, unsubtle, peculiar smelling mass.

114

It was strange to have no sign of any living thing around her. When was Ananda coming home?

She resumed her roaming, opening every drawer, peering into every cupboard. On close scrutiny there did seem to be a thin film of dust in the apartment. She found a damp blue and white cloth lying bunched up next to the sink and started.

For an hour she cleaned, with much examining of each object her duster wiped. There was nothing to disturb her. No landlord, no sound of traffic, no vendors, no part-time help to clean and swab, no mother who chatted while she worked. Chores finished, nightie clad, she stretched on the sofa and flung her legs over the cushions.

She closed her eyes, she was tired, so tired. She would get up just before Ananda came home she told herself as she drifted off.

Five o'clock. There he was, bending over her, shaking her. 'Are you all right?'

She looked at him. Again the slight shock.

'Did you eat?'

'Cereal.'

'You must be starving. Come on, we better rush, the grocery store closes at six.'

'I haven't had a bath.'

'Doesn't matter. Just put on your clothes.'

'Aren't you going to have tea first?'

'Tea? I don't have tea in the evenings. Do you want some?'

'No, it's all right.'

'Hurry then, the supermarket will close.'

After some hesitation Nina put on her plainest salwar kameez. It was silk with embroidery at the neck, sleeves, and borders. She wished she had some ordinary clothes, but what with getting married and travelling to the West, ordinary was out of the question

'Don't you have anything else?' asked Ananda, eyeing her splendour dubiously.

'I have my saris,' offered his wife.

'Oh, never mind, let's go. We'll have to see about some clothes for you this weekend.'

In the hallway Ananda took her hand. 'Are you tired?' he asked tenderly.

She laughed, 'After sleeping the whole day? It's you who must be tired.'

'Naah. I'm used to coming home and shopping.'

'Do you have a lot of patients?'

He gave a modest smile, 'Oh, I've been here a long time,' He hummed and swung her hand down the long corridor to the elevator.

'What name did you say the car was?' said Nina, making up for yesterday's neglect in this area.

'It's a Saab.'

'What's that?'

'A Swedish car. Gary thinks European cars are a waste of money, but man, Swedish design makes this one classy car.'

Her husband had a car so exclusive she had never heard of it. In a single stroke she had outpaced the status symbols of home.

Down, down the building, down into the dank, dark, neon-lit basement.

Rows of cars. She should get acquainted with them, they were more plentiful than people.

'One of the reasons I chose this building was that it has underground parking,' explained Ananda. 'Otherwise in winter it's a real hassle plugging in the car to keep it warm, scraping off the snow, takes much longer to warm the engine too. The people in older apartments are not so lucky.'

Ananda had the air of Santa Claus as he took out the keys and the central locking system clicked open. 'I thought this was a sophisticated colour. Indians come here and buy such showy things. Red, blue, black. No taste.'

Nina could see before her a car, pale grey, long, sleek,

handsome, capable of gliding, smooth and slick over bump-free spacious roads. Her admiration was warm.

They drove around the apartment blocks of Hollin Court, across the road into a shopping complex. The trip had taken thirty seconds. 'It's so close!' Nina exclaimed.

'Yes, we only drive when we need to stock up—otherwise you can walk to the market.'

Nina stepped out of the car. The morning clouds had abated to reveal patches of clear sky. The slanting mellow light seemed to prolong evening into the hours that belonged to night. Even in a parking lot there was something wondrous about it.

'Is it always so beautiful?' she asked.

'When it's not raining. This is one of the wettest places in Canada.'

'Rain? Oh how lovely.' Rain, always welcome, always a respite from heat, heavy, pounding, lovely, beautiful, grey and white rain.

'Wait till it rains. It's not like India.'

'I know,' said Nina, neatly jumping over the last sixteen years and landing under the leaden, drizzly skies of Brussels.

They walked into the Dominion Supermarket. The slight chill outside was replaced by warmth. The silk salwar kameez was doing nicely, thank you very much, thought Nina as she folded her pashmina shawl and tucked it inside her handbag.

The couple wheeled a cart down the aisles, past such colour and promise that Nina felt she would go mad with the bounties of infinite choice. Like the airport, only a thousand times better, because here she was not a deprived onlooker but a consumer ready to be consumed. It would take her days to digest the delights of one supermarket, a lifetime before she could be indifferent to its charms.

The adult pleasure of wallowing in a sea of material goods was entirely new to her. Eventually she would experience exhaustion at the claims made on her senses, but for now she was all ardent response and eager reaction.

Ananda was indulgent of Nina's indiscriminate urges. No, no, not so much grape juice, or so many chips or biscuits, that's a dip, we don't want so much dip, only sugarless candy and gum, I am a dentist, no, put them back. Amused he led her firmly to the meat, fruit and vegetable section. Where there was no dirt on anything, and a certain quality guaranteed in the purchase.

Gratified by the success of their first grocery shopping, Ananda wheeled the laden grocery cart towards the car. On the way home he elaborated on his sagacity, 'You run out of something, you just whip down and out—of course in winter you have to wear warm clothes, the wind is a little strong sometimes, but living so nearby, what does it matter?'

Back in the apartment building basement, Ananda took out a small trolley from the trunk. For taking groceries up, no servants.

'We never had full time servants at home either, and I wish we had trolleys,' said Nina.

They unpacked together. 'I've never bought so much junk in my life,' joked Ananda as he flipped open a can of beer. Nina felt the delectation of a pampered child.

Then they cooked in the small kitchen, rice, dal and raita for Nina, with an additional grilled fish for Ananda.

'Is this how you eat every day?' asked Nina.

'Hell, no. I just fry some hamburger patties, whole wheat bun, salad on the side, or I grill some fish with a bit of lemon and butter. On the weekends I may make a steak, sirloin or T bone, with some mashed potatoes and peas.'

'So you never eat Indian?'

'Too much trouble, too much time. I only cook Indian when I have guests, they seem to expect it,' he added gloomily.

'So, you are doing this for me?'

'Until you get used to something different. I've made enough dal for a week.'

Could his care and consideration be equalled, could she have married a better man—no, thought Nina, no. The institution of the arranged marriage was alive and well so far as she was concerned. Mentally, she sent a message to Zenobia and her mother, *I am all right, don't worry, he cooks most of the food and freezes tons of dal for me, stay well, love Nina.*

That night, in bed, Nina was more prepared for the brevity of their sexual encounter. It was easier to not compare Ananda with his predecessor in a different country. 'Welcome home, darling,' said Ananda, putting his arm around his wife afterwards. And that was the main point, wasn't it? Not her orgasms, but the fact that she was home.

'Thank you,' she murmured to a husband who was already asleep.

She put in some tossing and turning before drifting restlessly to the other room, over to the unit on which rested the TV, and quickly unearthed its single literary treasure. *The Mountain and the Valley* by Ernest Buckler, inscribed with love from Sue, was evidently unread from the stiffness of its pages. Well, might as well get to know this country. As she read on, the book gripped her. She had not realised rural Nova Scotia was so interesting. She would like to meet Sue, perhaps borrow other books.

And now she remembered, Ananda had said no point shipping, with the same money you could buy a new library. This remark drew the days ahead into some shape. To read as much as she liked with no disturbance! 612 Hollin Court began to seem like paradise.

Or so she thought at night. In the day it was sleep, sleep, sleep. 'It's just jet lag,' said her husband, as he woke her up for dinner the next day. 'Some people get it very badly.'

'You didn't?'

'I can't afford to. Not with my patients waiting. It's all right for you, take your time.'

Did he not suffer, crossing nine different time zones? Or was Canada so deeply embedded in his body that waking, sleeping, he moved to its rhythms? One day her system too would move to a different beat.

For now, after a restless, wakeful night, sleep came upon her like the most artful lover in the day, and despite her determined efforts to resist, claimed her for his own. The tiredness of her life, the hardships, the journeys in buses, the baking summer sleeplessness on a calefacient bed, the nagging discomfort of two miniscule rooms, all melted into soft pillows, sweet smelling sheets and a springy mattress.

Two nights later she finished *The Mountain and the Valley*. She had a greater sense of Canada with this one book, than after all her husband's conversation. At dinner she demanded more reading material.

'I'll ask Gary.'

'What'll I do in the meantime?'

'Watch TV.'

'TV?'

'There is the remote. And there, the guide.'

Nina had never watched TV in her life. She required the printed word to fill the spaces in her mind, the leisured turning of pages, the slow absorption of words, the occasional re-reading. She wondered whether this suggested some rigidity of outlook.

iii

Certain Indians become immigrants slowly. They are not among those who have fled persecution, destitution, famine, slavery and death threats, nor among those for whom the doors of their country slam shut the minute they leave its borders.

These immigrants are always in two minds. Outwardly they adjust well. Educated and English speaking, they allow misleading assumptions about a heart that is divided.

In the new country they work lengthy hours to gain entrance into the system, into society, into establishing a healthy bank account. Years pass like this, ungrudged years because they can see their all sustaining dream of a better life coming true.

As far as citizenship is concerned, a divided heart means that the immigrant clings to his status, feeling that to give up his passport is the final break in the weakened chain that binds him to his motherland. That day does come however.

The steps towards it are varied and not necessarily slow. Sometimes trips to the home country bring a disillusion and bitterness that the immigrant has forgotten how to cope with. Is this how it is here? So corrupt, merit stifled, such malfunctioning of every civic amenity, where your last ounce of energy is spent in merely keeping the wheels of daily life oiled and running. For men this logic works particularly well. Ok, let's be loyal to the country that has done so much for us.

In fact the years it takes to qualify for citizenship are needed to adapt, bit by bit, day by day. To stop finding little things strange and confusing, laughable and inappropriate. Wear the shoe on the other foot, sister, brother. They think the same of you. Get rid of the schism, become enough like them to be comfortable, merge and mingle. From East to West, over and over.

Forget the smells, sights, sounds you were used to, forget them or you will not survive. There is new stuff around, make it your own, you have to.

When it comes to buying, yes in North America clothes are mass produced and wonderful, food is plentiful, pre-packaged and cheap. For a long time the immigrant looks upon these things with joy. This is what he has come for. The price he pays for leaving the uneven artistry of home is not very high.

Work is an easy way to integrate. Work engages the mind and prevents it from brooding over the respective merits of what has been lost and gained. Colleagues are potential friends.

The immigrant who comes as a wife has a more difficult time. If work exists for her, it is in the future and after much finding of feet. At present all she is, is a wife, and a wife is alone for many, many hours. There will come a day when

121

even books are powerless to distract. When the house and its conveniences can no longer completely charm or compensate. Then she realises she is an immigrant for life.

Nina cries, feels homesick, sometimes adventurous, often forlorn. The minute she gets up she is at a loose end. Languidly she approaches her housework: dishwashing, bed making, cleaning, stretching every task out, slow, slow. She keeps the radio on, listening to music, advertisements, the CBC and its take on Quebec separatism and Pierre Elliott Trudeau. It seems a big issue here.

This done, she puts on her silk salwar kameez, fast becoming her uniform, goes out to wander around. She admires the Nova Scotian summer, so cool. She buys junk and nibbles it on the way: chips, chocolate, candy. She ruins her appetite, but she doesn't need much of an appetite to do justice to the canned soup and toasted sandwich that will be her lunch.

Once home she takes off her shoes, which had been deceptively comfortable in the store, but now pinch like her old ones did.

Books bought from the grocery store fill her time. They are as cheap and trashy as the food she indulges in. Basically she waits for Ananda to come home, then she will talk, often the first words of the day. She writes frequently to her mother and Zenobia. Her letters are very cheerful.

Ananda knows she is lonely, but hopes she will settle down quickly. A teaching career would be ideal, but in the West the road to a teaching job is long and arduous. She has to have a PhD, she has to have published.

Nina insists that not doing anything for a while will be pleasant, however the statement lacks its earlier buoyancy. Ananda tries to come home early so they can do things together.

Women in Love is her first film in Halifax.

How strange the halls in the West are, thought Nina, holding on to a bag of buttered popcorn and surveying the miniscule number of people that made up the audience. Did they even make a profit? At home crowds milled around film halls, the black market in tickets was brisk. Here, come here, plenty of room for all.

The film credits started, Ananda took her hand and they became a regular couple, for all to see. Nina directed these visuals towards her mother and colleagues. Ananda directed them towards his uncle, aunt, Alka, Ramesh, Gary, Sue and the students at the school of dentistry. Look, look at the clasped hands, at her head resting against my shoulder.

Nina soon became distracted from the drama on the screen by the couple sitting directly in front of them. The man had his arm around the girl's shoulders. Every so often their faces merged, their lips locked in kisses. Why couldn't they wait till they got home? How long had they known each other, was this a new love or an old one, clandestine or legitimate? She marvelled at such passion in a public place, while her hand lay in Ananda's, so coy and shy compared to the fecund model in front.

Those two lived on in her imagination long after she had forgotten the details of *Women in Love*.

Later as they were driving home, 'Did you like the movie?'

'It was lovely,' though actually *Women in Love* had too much sex for Nina's taste. She did not like direct evidence of how different her own experience was.

Ananda looked pleased.

'But it was very different from the book. In fact,' she said, warming to her theme, 'I much prefer *The Rainbow*.'

'Do you?'

'Oh yes. I read everything Lawrence wrote, but his blood thing is overrated. What do you think?'

'As a medical student, I did not get much time to read.'

Perhaps that was just as well. Only a fool would be influenced by the whole Lawrentian sexual mystique. If one applied books to life one had to distinguish between the prescriptive, descriptive, metaphoric and realistic.

She grabbed her husband's hand. He pressed it momentarily before releasing it. He did not encourage affection on the road; too unsafe, too reckless, one should focus on what one was doing.

'Did you know insurance rates are the highest for young unmarried men below twenty five?'

'Really?' How much the man knew!

'They are considered very reckless.'

Nina twiddled with the knobs of the car radio, and was rewarded by a Beatles song: *Here comes the sun, here comes the sun, it's all right*. She hummed and tapped her feet while her husband drove in silence.

That night Ananda couldn't wait to get inside her. No foreplay, no kissing, just jam it in. Nina tried to take his head in her hands to suggest some preparation, but he was too impatient. The green glow of the digital clock cum radio sitting on the bedside table illuminated the seconds for one minute, and it was over. She didn't even have time to speculate on the whiff of hospital odour, similar to the one she had smelt at the Oberoi. As she reached for his hand, he sighed,

'That was better, wasn't it?'

She murmured an assent. What this said about his standards, she did not care to consider. Besides, her body had decided to object to his emissions again. She rose to pee in the pink bathroom. Washing herself liberally, she wondered how long it would take her to conceive.

She woke up late next morning. From the stillness in the apartment she could tell Ananda had gone. He insisted she not get up for him, insisted beyond politeness, and she wondered whether he saw her as an intrusion. On his own for almost ten years, he must value his space. It couldn't be easy to share everything with a still unfamiliar wife.

Rubbing her feet together, she lay in bed, eyes shut, enjoying the pleasure of perfect idleness. It was beautiful outside and the mild sun, clear blue sky and stringy white clouds called to her. She decided to surprise Ananda by planning and cooking dinner on her own. That meant she would have to touch meat, but such a moment was inevitable; it was not really fair that, because of her sensibilities, her husband had to cook his carnivore dish after the stress of work.

Tea in hand, she settled down with *Canadian Cooking at its Finest,* a book her husband loved. When I called so and so, I cooked such and such out of this, and boy, they couldn't believe it had been made by me. Sue even said she was reminded of her mother's cooking.

A glossy picture of a pork chop caught her eye. The recipe sounded easy with paprika, sour cream, peppercorns and bay leaves. Hopefully it wouldn't be too bland. She got up, had a bath, put on her uniform and wended her way to the nest of shops across Hollin Court, that semi-circle of magic and desire. There was the Dominion Food Store, her old friend, the Shoppers Drug Mart, Canadian Tire, Scotia Bank, Nell's Green Thumb, Flo's Bakery, Canadian Post.

Each shop felt like a treasure trove. These very things Indians yearned for at home, here hers to possess. Alone she could exhibit her third world immigrant self, no witness to the depths to which a former academic had fallen.

Today she started with the Shoppers Drug Mart, really a shopper's wonder mart. The drugs were confined to a small counter at the back, scarcely noticeable. The real drug was to her senses.

Starting down the corner aisle she passed sunglasses, mittens, gloves, in various sizes, colours, prices, textures.

Turn a corner stacked with special discount shampoos, then down another aisle to meet shaving creams, hair dyes, shampoos for every conceivable hair type, fragrance, different brands, marked down ones, bargain ones, store brand ones.

Turn the corner stacked with discounted bags of sweets. Colours of the rainbow glowed from bags of gums, jellies, boiled candy, chocolates, peppermints, caramels, toffees, mouth fresheners: the deep reds of cinnamon and cherry, the greens of mint, the blacks of liquorice.

Slowly around another corner, skirting the pyramid of two for one toothpastes.

To move on, down the aisle to body lotions, to meditate on her skin type, to compare prices and brands, to wonder how long it would take for one bottle to finish before another could be bought.

Around the corner to bath salts, bubble baths, bath creams, bottles and cubes all promising beautiful, glowing skin in a miasma of perfume, if one could bring oneself to lie in a tub and be surrounded by one's dirt.

And then the counters where the agents of beauty were displayed: nail polish, lipsticks, mascara, eye shadow, foundations, with brushes to put these things on. And creams, thousands of creams to defeat age, blemishes, wrinkles, sun, water, dryness, oiliness—a cream for every second of the day and night.

A girl advances towards her. Would she like a free demonstration?

She is startled. It is more important to look than do. She rushes on to the savouries: potato chips in myriad flavours, barbeque, sour cream and onion, plain salted, garlic, cheese, then past the corn chips, the onion rings, the Cheetos, the tins of Pringle.

Turn the corner, past the stationery, the greeting cards, pencils, pens, office and kitchen equipment.

Down another aisle, past toilet paper, tissues, sanitary towels.

Endlessly picking up and putting down, staring, staring. So much variety takes away her power to choose because everything beckons.

She comes away with full eyes and empty hands. This was not about need, it was about plenty, and she feels sick from gorging.

Dissatisfied, and out of tune with herself, she angrily walked to Dominion's. Why had she wasted so much time gazing at things? Firmly she walked past the aisles in a straight line; pork chop, sour cream, paprika, bay leaf, tinned peaches, cake mix, bought purposefully, without looking right or left. To do this was a test of character.

Her character tested, she lapsed into dreaminess before the window of Nell's Green Thumb, visualising a home full of flowers, imagining suspended pots flowing over with myriad shaped leaves.

And then to reward herself for her steadfast behaviour in Dominion's she visited the bakery to buy a cupcake, eat and feel sick. It was too rich for her, too full of white flour, which settled like a stone in her stomach, making her feel dull and full for hours afterwards. Still the sticky sweet taste soothed her.

One day she would have looked her fill, satisfied enough longing to feel replete. On that day she would float through the semi-circle of shops, going straight towards the things she needed, above the blandishments of the material West. That day she would have clarity of mind and heart. She thought these things as she trudged up the little hill to 612 Hollin Court, bearing her produce in a backpack.

Ananda was going to be offered peaches in cream. Both of them liked tinned peaches, so big, yellow and syrupy. And he was going to get a crisp fresh salad with blue cheese dressing, the one he loved, that was evidence of his sophisticated preferences. And chocolate cake with cherry burgundy icecream.

She ate this same ice cream for lunch, rested, then put on an old shirt of Ananda's over her salwar kameez to start the cooking.

Rub garlic on the pan, braise (explained by the glossary) the chop, stab it gingerly with fork, mix sour cream, paprika, five peppercorns, salt, throw in pork chop, shove in oven, reflect on how lonely it looks, hope the husband will like it. Now cut up the salad, boil peas, mash potatoes, make cake from the stuff in the box, open peaches, lay table. Set wine glasses, unearth candle stand, insert three red candles. Use Indian table mats, part of trousseau. Rest aching legs, ignore counter covered with peel and packages.

A key turned in the lock.

'Surprise!'

'My goodness. What is this, a party?'

'A party for *you*.'

'My,' he repeated, coming to kiss her. She lifted her face eagerly.

He poured himself a drink while she briefly described her expedition to the Hollin Court shops. I went, I bought. Then they sat down to eat.

'Do you like it?' she asked, surveying him from behind the egg shaped glow of the non-dripping candles. 'I couldn't taste the meat, but I know you are fond of pork chops. I hope it is all right?'

Ananda looked up, mouth full. 'Very good,' he said appreciatively. 'How did you manage to cook like this?'

'*Canadian Cooking at its Finest*.'

'Wonderful book. Sue said her mother couldn't prepare better spareribs.'

'You mentioned.'

'These people are very particular about home food.'

'I know.'

'And you are fitting in nicely.'

'Thank you.'

'Hey,' he said, 'you haven't finished your wine.'

Nina gingerly sipped the sour tasting liquid.

Ananda beamed, 'Californian. Three dollars a bottle. Tastes the same as French, so why pay good money for a name? Now—what's for dessert?'

The wine made Nina feel high and melancholy, like looking at the sky from the apartment window and feeling her solitude. She shook herself. 'Cherry burgundy ice cream, chocolate cake which I baked, peaches with cream.'

'*Three* deserts. Wow. '

'Well, I couldn't decide—so I thought why not allow you the choice.'

'At the clinic today I never thought I'd be getting such a spread. A real change from bachelor days, I can tell you.'

Nina bustled about with many dishes, while Ananda cleared the plates.

Much was eaten.

Then Ananda said, 'You sit, and let me do the washing up.'

'I will do it. You have had a hard day at the clinic.'

'But you bought the stuff. If you had waited we could have done this together.'

'I have nothing much to do.'

'Well, relax.' He solicitously poured some more wine into her glass.

'I don't think I can drink so much,' offered Nina.

'Nonsense. Just a light Zinfandel.'

Nina sat and sipped. Ananda washed; she could hear the splash and clatter of dish against water. He came out of the kitchen, rolling down his sleeves.

'There, that's done.'

'Yes. Thank you.'

'Hey, no need to thank me. Here we share everything. You cooked, I wash, it's perfectly fair.'

'Yes, well.'

In the silence that followed this, sadness flowed over Nina. She had fed on his appreciation all evening and still it wasn't enough. What can one do with a hungry heart?

'What's the matter?' he asked, looking at the face that mirrored these thoughts.

She shook her head.

'Has anyone said anything to you? Today at the store?'

'No, no—the store was fine.'

'Everybody is very nice here.'

'I'm sure.'

He pulled her onto his lap and caressed her. His shirt smelt of Tide and fabric softener, of cigarettes and the faint odour of sweat. Maybe the wine was making her feel like this.

Her mother: things take time. In the end patience and love achieve their own rewards. A woman's duty is to understand this.

She wondered if this had been the philosophy that lay behind her parents' perfect marriage. There was no way she would ever know.

That Sunday they were going to the uncle's for lunch. About time, thought Nina. It had already been a month, and she was keen to set down roots that would make her feel more at home. In India these relatives had seemed peripheral, more tourist than family. Now her perception had changed. She wanted to be close to them.

'Which sari should I wear?'

'Sari? Won't that be too formal?'

'Of course not. They've been to India, they understand the way we dress.'

'Well, people are casual, keep that in mind.'

'I wish I had got to know Aunty better at the wedding. And Lara and Lenny.'

'She's not really an aunty like that. It's pointless to think of them as we do of relatives back home.'

'Why? He's your uncle. Lara and Lenny are like Ishan and Ila for me.'

Ananda snorted.

'Is there nobody here you are close to?'

'There's Gary. And if Sue weren't so awfully busy with her two children, she would be the one to help you.'

Nina had noticed the absence of Gary and Sue. Was it always going to be like this, just her and Ananda?

All set for social contact they drive to Young Avenue, the wife in a gorgeous patola sari, the husband informal in blue jeans and a sweatshirt. With his wife by his side, he feels he can venture briefly into his past.

'I lived in that house for a year when I came.'

'Why did you leave? Much better to stay with relatives than be a paying guest.'

'Naw. It was time to move on. Be independent.'

'I suppose it's easier here. They would be so hurt at home if one ever tried to do such a thing. Imagine if I had left Mama. All the extra money, all the pain, then the safety, the difficulty of renting, no, it would have been inconceivable,' she ruminated. With only Ananda to talk to, she talked considerably.

'Parents are different.'

'True.'

'He helped me a lot in the beginning, but that didn't mean I had to go on being dependent. He is very family minded; he came all the way for the wedding though four tickets cost him two thousand dollars.'

'That's not cheap.'

'Well, he is a doctor.'

They turned into Young Avenue, 'the best street in Halifax', promised Ananda as he manoeuvred the car into a parallel parking situation against the curb. Despite Ananda's caveat, Nina fantasised a Nancy who would take to her, invite her for tea, make efforts to alleviate her homesickness because she was a new addition to the family.

The door opened, and there was their pant-suited, welcoming aunt. How marvellous you look, great to see you again, welcome to Canada. At the head of the stairs was Dr Sharma, beaming, welcome to Canada, what a pleasure to see a woman in a sari, so that Nina for a moment could stop feeling overdressed.

They sat on fat stuffed chairs, and drank dewy glasses of white wine smelling of fruit and flowers. 'How happy I am to be here,' thought Nina as she answered the questions they were asking about how had she settled down, what did she do all day and was her mother well?

That done, the uncle and Ananda began to discuss Indira Gandhi's trial by the Janata government.

They will never have the guts to find anything against her, claimed the uncle. Ananda disagreed; if Jagmohanlal Sinha of the Allahabad High Court could find her guilty in '75 she could be found guilty again. The uncle said that the Nehru name would protect Indira no matter what she had done. Out of office she would play the sympathy card. It was one thing for the Janata to defeat her in the elections, but as prime minister, Desai would find keeping conflicting interests together more difficult. Not even a year and a power struggle had begun within the coalition.

That was irrelevant, said Ananda impatiently, infighting was a political reality in India, but getting rid of a dictatorship demonstrated the people's ability to stand up for their rights. No matter how much charisma Indira possessed, there was no reason why she would not be convicted.

Nina listened with the familiar sense of depression that the state of India always caused. After the Janata had won there had been so much hope. Democracy had triumphed and in that euphoria she had left. But here were Ananda and Dr Sharma using the same old rhetoric of hopelessness and corruption reflected in letters from home. What did it take? A revolution like in China?

In the end, those who could leave did, because there was nothing to keep them. A good example was this room, in which three of India's drained brains were discussing their abandoned country.

Nina turned to the aunt, 'I would love to see where Ananda lived for a year. I have heard so much about your house.'

'Of course, my dear,' said Nancy. 'These men can talk about politics for ages. Come.'

She was shown everything. The three bedrooms, study, the semi-basement, the rec room, the laundry room, the miniscule cubby hole that had been specially built for Ananda. The sight of the tiny wood panelled space appalled Nina; how had he managed to survive certain claustrophobia? 'Poor boy,' went on the aunt, 'it took him so long to be independent, but then I guess he was used to a different way of doing things. Why, he couldn't even wash his own clothes! Lenny at fifteen was far more self-reliant.'

'Really.'

'Oh, yes. Lenny—or Lara for that matter—would never have stayed with an aunt or uncle for as long as Andy did.'

'Andy?'

'Lara and Lenny prefer to call him Andy. Now I do too.'

So this was the scenario that lay behind Ananda's reticence. Her heart filled with tender hurt on her husband's behalf. It was quite clear that Nancy was not going to be another Alka. Longing for India gripped her, then slowly dissipated as they climbed back upstairs and settled down to a beautifully laid table.

Whatever Nina might have thought of Nancy, she had to admire the plates, the crystal and the silverware, so solid and elegant.

'We normally don't eat like this,' said Nancy, 'but this is your first time here.'

'Yes,' beamed her husband. 'I hope the food is to your liking.'

'I am a vegetarian,' confessed Nina, looking at the rounded hump of glistening brown bird, a long sharp knife and a big shiny fork resting on flowered ceramic holders on either side.

'I thought you might be, so though the turkey is in Ananda's honour, the extra veggies are in yours,' said the uncle gesturing to the rolls, salad, potatoes, beans and a small plate of cut tomatoes.

'Even Andy here was a vegetarian, but he changed fast enough when he had to cook for himself,' remarked the aunt.

Ananda said, 'When in Rome do what Romans do.'

'That's what I always say,' said the uncle, sawing away at the turkey.

'Brij started eating meat in India. It made it so much easier once he came here,' commented Nancy, handing over the plates one by one.

'My best friend in college was non-veg,' confided Brij. 'I used to go with him to dhabas, and watch him eat tikka and kebabs. Try it, try it, he kept saying. Once I did, I never looked back. Of course no one in the family ever knew.'

The aunt laughed while the children focused on their requests of light, dark, breast, leg. Nina smiled politely.

Her fingers rested on the thick padding of the table. The cloth stretched over it was lacy white. Each place had silver napkin rings, the milk and water were in green glass jugs. To the left of her plate was a little wooden bowl full of salad.

In front of her was a cupboard filled with crystal, china and porcelain. Next to it, at a slight angle, facing the stairs was a grandfather clock, with Roman numerals, the pendulum swinging in a glass fronted door with a design etched onto it. The rich dark wood resonated with age and money.

All around her were sparkling clean windows, filled with the green from trees that were lit up by the sun, playing out patterns of light and shadow.

So this was fine living, thought Nina, as meat servings over, she helped herself to beans with almonds, duchess potatoes, a roll and butter from the silver butter dish.

'You must be used to curries,' remarked Nancy as the family dug into their piles of food.

By now she knew the reference was not to the North Indian curry she knew, made of yoghurt, chick pea flour and dumplings—no, this was a reference to every Indian dish, wet, runny, dry, spicy, veg, non-veg.

'She's lived abroad a lot,' put in Ananda.

They did ask where, they were not entirely disinterested, but her father's posting had been so long ago, she had been so young and so much had happened since, that she did not like talking about Brussels. She fingered the knife and picked it up to look at the flowered design along its handle.

'Part of my wedding silver,' offered the aunt.

'Very beautiful.'

'Don't get silver like this nowadays.'

'I see.'

As the evening progressed, Nina felt let down by the family's self-absorption. There was no offer of I will lend you books, I will take you to shops and libraries, I will help you settle down. She was there as Ananda's wife, as his responsibility, a vegetarian, who needed to acquire the food habits of the West in order to adapt comfortably.

By the time they left Young Avenue visions of intimacy had been firmly put to rest. She had only just come to Halifax, but already she felt the emptiness of a single pea rattling around in Ananda's tin can.

'Well, what did you think?' he asked.

'They have a beautiful house,' she said carefully, 'with really fine silver.'

'We can also get fine silver, what's the problem?'

'Nothing, nothing.'

'It's nice talking about India with Uncle. He's pretty well informed. And it's a link with home.'

It was not her place to voice that if that was all, it was not much. He looked at her out of the corner of his eye. She would find her feet soon, then there would not be this useless hankering after relatives. She hadn't had many in India from what he could tell, so why was she expecting those kinds of ties in Canada, of all places.

The next day, 'See, I got you a surprise,' he said as soon as he walked in.

'What?'

He opened his briefcase.

'Books!'

'Yup. I asked Linda to get some.'

'Linda?'

'Our hygienist.'

'Oh, thank you.' She turned them around in her hands. *Under the Volcano* by Malcolm Lowry and *Who Has Seen the Wind* by WO Mitchell. With a book how could she be lonely? She looked at him gratefully. He held his arms out, she willingly pressed her body into his, then pushed his mouth open with her lips and played with his tongue. He responded by carrying her to bed.

A few minutes later Ananda was washing up in the bathroom. He gazed fondly at his limp damp organ; at last it was doing its job. There was penetration, there was satisfaction, there was the pleasure and security of marriage. There was no need to be so tense, he told it, no need at all. Things were going fine.

Sexuality was beginning to be studied scientifically, he had heard Masters and Johnson claimed a high rate of cure for premature ejaculation, but thank god, he would not have to go through the humiliation of medical investigation that his desperation had forced him to consider. He recognised this attitude as inimical to perfect health, but he would feel great shame if he had to submit his orgasms to the scrutiny of a doctor. And with the help of his dental anaesthetic spray, he had consummated his marriage.

iv

The phone rang.

'Caall from India,' said the heavily accented English of an Indian operator.

'Yes, yes,' said Nina.

Her mother's voice, clear and loud as though next to her, her mother talking, carrying her back to Jangpura, linking her to something beyond marriage and husband.

'Ma. How come you are phoning? From where?'

A small giggle. 'From home. Just imagine, I only booked the call five hours ago.'

'That's pretty fast, Ma. You sound as though you were in the next room! How did you get a phone?'

'Ramesh dug out my application and claimed special priority on the grounds that I was a widow, living alone and in poor health. The instrument came yesterday, the number today. A thorough gentleman. Like Ananda.'

'That was nice of him.'

'I never expected such promptness. After our conversation in the hotel he kept chasing it up. On his own!'

She expanded on this until the operator interrupted, 'Three minutes up.'

136

'Wait wait, one minute please.'

'Madam, you waant, you extend another three minutes.'

'No, no, too expensive.'

'Ma, give me your number—so I can phone you. I'll phone you right now.'

'Time is over, Madam, you waant to continue?'

'No, no,' said Mr Batra, even while Nina was shouting, 'Yes, yes,' into a phone that suddenly went dead.

She sat there, flushed, her mother's voice still in her ears, made possible by a phone delivered two months after her departure, something that normally took years. She could only be grateful, very grateful. Happiness spread through her.

That night it was Ananda who dialled two international calls through the operator, first Alka to get Mr Batra's phone number, then Mr Batra. From the Canadian side there were no time constraints, and Nina and Ananda spoke for fifteen minutes. Ananda assured his mother-in-law they were both very happy and when was she going to come and visit? Let the baby come, she would be there. The call ended, Nina sidled up to him affectionately, oh, thank you, thank you, this makes such a difference. Ananda smiled modestly. It was really because of him that her mother had got a phone.

The connection with her mother took Nina back to her pre-Canada self. After this conversation she felt as though she had woken up, ready to feel more grounded in Halifax.

'When am I going to see where you work?' Nina asked her husband the next evening.

'Well, it's half day tomorrow. I can pick you up, take you to the clinic. From there we can go to the Taj Mahal on Spring Garden Road. An Indian couple runs it and they serve pretty decent food.'

Indian food. Oh, all right. Let's see what they make of Indian food in Halifax.

*

The next day at twelve thirty Ananda picked her up, and five minutes later they were there, before a sweet red wooden house, set on a road with large old trees, gardened on three sides, hedged on two, with a ramp and four steps leading to a porch with an engraved glass door. Nina was base enough to wildly desire such a place as a home, but her desires would have to wait, Ananda told her.

This was among the best locations in town, immigrants cannot start with sixty-seventy thousand dollar properties.

The clinic was closing for the week, and the place was empty of patients. Nina was introduced to Mrs Hill, the receptionist, and young, wholesome looking Linda, who laughed brightly when she thanked her for the books. Gary was not there, but his office was, large, garden facing, with toys, a musical mobile and a sofa, homier than her own home. Ananda had a more business-like view, porch, hedge, sidewalk, cars.

No wonder, with an establishment like this, her husband was in love with Canada. Her memories dredged up the government hospital where she and her mother went for their teeth, crowded, with queues involving many hours, resignedly put up with because the government paid.

'So lovely to meet you,' said Mrs Hill, maternal, middle aged, smiling, grey hair done in curls around her face, red lipstick, glasses dangling on a gold bead chain down her white clad chest. 'We are so pleased Andy has married. And my, what a catch. He looks just like Omar Sharif.'

'Come on, Mrs H.'

'Oh, but everybody says so,' added Linda.

After a bit more teasing, Ananda left, followed by demands that now at least he had to throw a party.

In the car, 'Why do they assume you look like Omar Sharif?'

'Oh, for them, any Asian is the same.'

'But he is Egyptian! At home nobody thinks you resemble Omar Sharif.'

'I'm telling you Canada is truly international. They don't believe in narrow boundaries.'

'Maybe it's like us in college thinking all Chinese look the same. I swear I often couldn't distinguish between my northeastern students. And I could never say their names.'

'I don't think it is the same. We are shamefully ignorant of the northeast though it is part of our country. Omar Sharif is not Canadian, but still they know, still they relate.'

If that was so, who would they associate with her? Sophia Loren? In Brussels she had frequently been mistaken for an Italian.

'Gary could have asked anybody to share the practice, but he asked me.'

An Asian, an Omar Sharif.

They sped downtown towards the Taj Mahal. Eight tables with red shaded lamps in a darkened room. A pleated sari hung on the wall, a miniature Taj Mahal glowed in red lights under a glass case on the counter, photographs of exotic, touristy places in India decorated the dingy walls, as unfamiliar to Nina as to any other client.

She was going to tell Ananda she wasn't the kind of Indian to respond to camels or colourful dancing girls, when the smells caught her mind and shut her mouth. Turmeric, yellow turning into brown as it bubbled in hot oil, red chillies that crackled as they roasted, onions and garlic that turned pink then brown, releasing sweet sharp smells, tomatoes that became soupy as they were swished around, cumin and coriander that gave out pungent flavours, these smells and imagined sights travelled across the world from north India to eastern Canada to kick her sharply in the stomach.

'Do you come here often?' she managed to ask.

'Only to bring friends who think that with me they should be eating Indian food. I prefer places like Mike's Ribs.'

They sat at a table for two, glanced at the menu decorated with friezes from Mughal architecture and ordered chicken do piyaza, palak paneer, dal, raita and naan.

139

Naan. Nina hadn't had a roti item since she left home. She traced the pattern on the plastic table mat impatiently with a toothpick.

The food came. Not bad, not bad at all. Not exactly like home, but distance blurred the distinction.

'We can go to Mike's Ribs next time,' she offered bravely.

'That's my girl,' said Ananda, looking at her tenderly. He chomped on his chicken 'Quite good, no?'

Nina nodded.

'I find the chicken here far tastier than at home,' continued the husband, 'at least these birds have some meat on them.'

'I'll take your word for it.'

A pause before Nina started asking questions. 'How come the previous dentist wanted to sell such a beautiful house?' She heard the cheerfulness in her voice and flinched. She distrusted cheerfulness, and always looked for the darker feeling beneath it.

'It's a long story.'

'Oh, do tell.'

'Gary's father's friend wanted to retire.'

'Why, was he old?'

'Not by the standards here. Late sixties. But dentistry is hard on the back and eyes. It's minute work and you have to bend all the time. Besides, the sound of the drill can get on your nerves after forty years. Once we graduated, he sold us his practice.'

'I could work forever in a place like that.'

'His practice was on Quinpool. But we were two, we needed more space, so we bought this house. I thought we could manage in a cheaper location, but Gary insisted the two of us could afford the down payment. The Gellers maintained that a nice clinic would give our practice added value. As it has. A lot of the neighbourhood children come to us.'

'If it's such a fancy place, where did you get the money?'

'The bank. Where else?'

'Isn't the interest high?'

'That's the way things are done here.'

140

'So how much is the loan?'

'Forty thousand. All these years, saving, saving, no trips home, living like a student, so I could hold my head high. At the time I put ten thousand down from my own pocket. Of course getting married, those two trips to India, the wedding, then your ticket, all this meant four thousand more.'

Nina thought of the expenditure at the Oberoi, the uneasiness he had brushed aside, the patients that were supposed to make up for everything, 'I didn't know the wedding would pinch you financially.'

'One needs a nest egg. Gary has both his and his wife's parents to rely on, should any difficulty come up. People who are new to this country have no such cushion.'

'Didn't you mention Gary lived upstairs?'

'He did till the second kid. Then his father helped him with the down payment on a home nearby.'

'Maybe I should look for a job?'

'Don't be silly. We are starting a family—what is the point?' He put his hand over her own. In the silence that fell between them he finished his chicken, she her palak paneer. Finger bowls with a sliver of lemon in hot water were put before them, and the last touch of home was presented in the saunf and mishri that came with the bill.

They got up. Ananda looked around as they emerged from the cave-like atmosphere that was the Taj Mahal. 'This place needs more people, otherwise it'll shut down. The Bengal Tiger on Quinpool has already closed. It's not easy making it in a new country.'

Outside, the day was summer time Nova Scotian: breezy, cloudy, sunny, cool and kind. This was the day on which Ananda led Nina to the Halifax Regional Library, a lovely old grey stone building, at the bottom of Spring Garden Road, set slightly apart at an angle. There was a small lawn in front, benches, trees and a statue of Churchill. Engraved across the top was Halifax Memorial Library.

The mourning that the smells of India had engendered in Nina vanished as she was made a member. Feverishly she scanned the titles. European, English classics, American, Canadian fiction—authors she had never heard of. She confined her selection to Stephen Leacock and Madame Bovary; she intended to come back very soon. With a steady supply assured, she could live secure and happy between the pages she read. Smelling the paper, touching the covers, devouring the words—in book heaven.

Each day now had its purpose enshrined in the Halifax Memorial Library. It was amazing how direction appeared in her life with just one compelling destination. She almost always finished one book during the night, but even if she didn't need to borrow, there were magazines to read and newspapers to flick through. As she walked she swung her tote bag in a simulacrum of carefree gaiety. Passing the speciality stores on Spring Garden Road she felt superior to her star struck material self, who had stared so longingly at things in the Shopper's Drug Mart. Here there were the fresh baked breads, cakes, biscuits at The Baker Man, the imported sweets at the Candy Bowl, the French perfume, socks and soft cashmere sweaters at Mills, the jewellery at Birks; there were all these things, but their allure was restricted because she was on her way to the library, and the fact that she had no time to waste was mapped in her hurried, severe, abstracted gaze.

v

'Gary has invited us over this Sunday, isn't that nice?' Ananda beamed, 'I knew he would.'

Nina had also known he would. If Ananda's best friend and colleague didn't invite them, who would? The wonder was that this invitation had taken some months to come.

Continued Ananda, thoughtfully examining his bottles of wine, 'I've helped him a lot around his house. His is an old construction and this is a society in which people do things for others.'

'So is ours,' said Nina, defending her society, its virtues radiant through the mists of distance. 'After all Ramesh got my mother that phone.'

'That is not the same thing. Family and pull don't count.'

'Why not? How does it matter in what way you help people so long as you help them.'

'Can you really not see the difference? Here, it's clean, above board, not dependent on birth or connections. It's your own skills that are important, what you can do with your *hands*.'

What was so great about that? Any carpenter/ plumber/ electrician would do. Pull was so much more potent, it made the difference between having and not having. But she didn't want to agitate her husband.

'I didn't know you were a handyman,' she said soothingly.

'One has to know a bit of everything: plumbing, electricity, woodwork. In the West it's more economical to be self-reliant. Just see if there's some wrapping paper in the last drawer of the desk.'

Nina found wrapping paper, neatly folded. He spent so much time helping them, still he had to take something. Was that how things were done here, give, give and give? She resented every fold of the thick coloured paper around the bottle.

'I don't see you socialising much with Gary.'

'Just before you came, I was over every weekend helping him with the rec room for his kids in the basement.'

'You can still help him, you know.'

'He won't hear of it. Couples do things together in this country.'

Another definition of marriage.

'It turns out they are expecting a baby. Sue was very sick, that's why he hadn't called us. I knew there was a reason,' ended Ananda triumphantly, all Nina's unspoken accusations answered by this one fact of nature.

'You said they already have two children.'

'They want a large family. Maybe because he himself was just one.'

'You mean they practise no birth control?'

'How should I know? I don't ask him these things.'

'But at this rate they will end up having ten children,' tittered Nina. It was strange to think of an educated man as much at the mercy of his body as any villager in India.

'People are not so different,' said Ananda stiffly.

'Of course there are universals, but still, many factors do determine differences. One reads about it often.'

'Life is not all books.'

She kept quiet. There might be those who thought life was not all books, but she was not one of them. Her husband was the outer world of telegrams and anger that EM Forster described in *Howard's End,* she represented a dark inner world of feeling, instinct and intuitive wisdom. She was Margaret Schlegel, he was Mr Wilcox; she Constance Chatterley, he Clifford.

He took her acquiescence in his world view for granted; it was so obvious and sane. She turned her attention to the sari she was going to wear, a brocade purple and turquoise tanchoi. It was slightly creased, she would have to iron it before Saturday.

'My God, they'll think I've married a Christmas tree.'

'Isn't it a party?'

'It's a barbecue. People will be wearing jeans and T-shirts.'

'I didn't bring ordinary saris.'

'Here, all saris are extraordinary. Wear your salwar kameez.'

Nina put the brocade away and wore one of the five salwar kameezes she had been living in since she came.

It was a nice day, that is, the sun was shining. They walked across the complex to Quinpool Road, and the breeze played, chilly, about Nina's ears. Her tropical blood yearned for a shawl, in the height of summer. 'Wait till it's winter,' said Ananda, his standard response to every statement that reflected cold. She now accepted his pride in winter and its horrors.

Down Maple Street, across Elm Street, twenty minutes later, 1902 Peach Street. A child's tricycle lay confidently on the grass. A swing on the porch exuded certainty that its cushions would not be stolen, nor its surface marred with pigeon shit.

Ananda walked up the steps, swinging his wrapped bottle of wine. He pushed the door open and the house drew him in, down the back steps into the yard, followed by his wife.

'Andy, Andy,' cried a little girl with red hair, rushing towards his leg and hugging it.

'Hey, how's my baby?'

A tall woman, blue eyes, long curly blond hair, clear pink skin, came smiling up to them. 'Hi,' she said, holding out a hand which Nina took limply. 'I'm Sue. Welcome to Canada. We've been meaning to have you over for so long, but I just haven't been feeling well.'

'Please, it's no problem,' murmured Nina.

'Wow, don't you look stunning! Look at that, what do you call it?'

'Salwar kameez.'

'Gosh, it's so pretty.'

If this was pretty, what attention would the sari have elicited? She was glad she hadn't worn it.

Introductions followed. Gary's parents, Sue's parents, Melissa the daughter, John the toddler, some more dentists. Nina smiled, received compliments for her costume. No she had never been to Canada before, she loved it, the trees, the coolness, the library facilities, the few people, everything so different and interesting.

Yes, Nina gratified her audience with her appreciation. They thought she was a nice girl, she looked exotic in her silk, gold jewellery and bindi, but she spoke English so well, they could understand everything she said.

'Hey, Sue, my wife needs some clothes. Something practical.'

'Sure. We could go to the mall and try something out.'

Nina hesitated, 'I don't know if they would suit my figure. Indian women are either pears or apples.'

'I wish I could wear clothes like yours, graceful and feminine. But,' she gestured to her jeans and T-shirt, 'old fuddy-duddy, that's me.'

'Oh no,' protested the couple anxiously.

Sue laughed.

'Ananda has talked of nothing but you and Gary since we first met,' said Nina.

'We've been wanting him to settle down for a long time, we are really, really glad to meet you,' confided Sue in turn.

Nina blushed.

I'll help her in any way I can, thought Sue. Since our blind date, I've wondered who he was going to end up with, and here he is with a girl straight from India. They say arranged marriages are quite successful, perhaps the women expect less. Maybe that's why he had to go there for a wife; I wonder how his problem is. She *seems* quite happy, but it's still early. Are they trying to get pregnant? Andy would make a wonderful father.

'Andy is so much part of our family. Did he tell you he is Melissa's godfather?' she said.

'No, no, he didn't tell me. But he keeps mentioning how the two of you are like family to him.'

'He is just darling. We both thought Andy would be ideal—he is so patient, look at him,' and Sue waved her orange juice at the four year old who at this moment was clutching Ananda's long, jean clad leg, and shrieking, 'Andy, Andy, gimme a ride.'

The smell of barbecued meat rose into the warm blue air. Gary advanced towards them bearing a paper plate with barbecued pork chops, 'Is potato salad all you are eating, Nina? Is there anything else I can get you?'

They discovered she was vegetarian. Her husband was called to account, why hadn't he told them? Cheese sandwiches appeared. With a plate respectably full, Nina sank into a garden chair, watching Ananda and his goddaughter. He *was* good with children, how little he minded the length of time

146

Melissa dangled from his leg, how exemplary his patience with her demands.

On the way home.

'Did you like Sue?'

'Yes, of course.'

'And Gary?'

'Him too.'

'His parents? Did you talk to them?'

'Not much.'

'You must next time. After all I lived with them for many years.'

So this was more about their reactions than her own liking-disliking. Had she passed the test?

They were walking fast. Clouds had suddenly darkened the sky. 'Unpredictable weather,' said Ananda with relish, 'But I think we'll make it home before it rains'.

They neared Hollin Court and the wind briskly froze Nina's ears. She shivered as goosebumps appeared on her skin. 'Tunnel effect,' said Ananda pointing to two big buildings, a school and an apartment block on either side of the road.

Nina was not interested. Her thoughts centred around her warm home and a cup of hot tea, while her husband's darted obsessively back to the party, worrying, assessing.

'Here I'm thought of as a cultured man, as Canadian as everybody else. So I don't want folks to get the wrong impression.'

'What impression?'

'That you are a traditional, backward Indian girl, like some of these women you see at the India Club. Can't even speak English properly.'

'How can you live here and not speak English properly?'

'Some immigrant types straight from the village—they speak English, sure, but would rather not.'

'They couldn't possibly have thought I am like that.'

147

'I know, I know. I'm just warning you. Especially, you know, since we married the way we did.'

Nina now understood the cause of his anxiety. People here probably had very archaic notions about arranged marriages. As Ananda strode along, shoulders straight against the cold Canadian breeze, Nina glanced at his smooth brown skin, his jet black hair, the emphatically Indian eyes, the unmistakeable Indian features, the Indian accent that lurked behind the Western.

'Since we aren't from here, your friends must make allowances. Besides, beyond a point, how does it matter what they think?'

The husband was silent, and the wife realised, of course it mattered what people thought. They were the ones among whom he, and now she, intended to pass their lives, and it was important they be understood for what they were, rather than be judged by stereotypical ideas.

She took her husband's hand, and swung it in her own. He had had such a hard time after his parents died, she was certainly not going to question the edifice he had built.

He looked at her and smiled. Several people at the party had told him how good looking his wife was, her dark complexion was so striking. He mentioned this.

She grunted. It still felt strange hearing the word dark applied to her, in India she was among the ones with a prized fair complexion.

'They liked you, I could tell,' said Ananda, squeezing her hand. 'You'll have no problem making friends here.'

'I miss Zenobia.'

'Well, it's easy enough to find others to take her place.'

'It takes time, I suppose.'

'These people are initially reserved, not like Americans, who start washing their dirty linen the moment they say hello.'

'Really? They seemed very friendly.'

'You are my wife, that's why they accepted you immediately.' Yes, they had, now that she thought about it. It hadn't been like that strange awkward lunch at Uncle Sharma's, with Nancy showing no special interest in her and saying all those things about Ananda. No, this afternoon had certainly not been like that evening.

Once home, Ananda gratified his wife by insisting they make love immediately. Maybe this time you'll get pregnant, he whispered, though he did not last long enough for such hopes to persist.

Still, thought Ananda, sexually he was doing better than before, even without the anaesthetic he sprayed on his penis to delay his climax. He felt uneasy about using it too frequently; it was meant for teeth after all, not for tender female depths. And although Nina had not complained, except to remark on the smell, his own sensations were unpleasantly affected.

He knew he still had miles to go before he reached his goal of pounding some woman to sexual pulp, but with marriage, he had gained confidence. One day he might try again with a white woman. He loved his wife, but he didn't want to feel that she was the only one in the world he could have sex with. What kind of man would that make him, with his masculinity so limited? His lack of control rendered him very vulnerable, the anxiety of it grew cancerously inside him. Every female patient lying in his chair with her mouth open, giving herself trustingly to him, made him imagine an alternate sexual scenario. Her attractiveness, her responses, were immaterial; his sole concern was, could he do it? At these moments his touch became tender, his voice lower as he assured her she would feel no pain, the injection would only take a second.

He was a doctor, bound by professional codes, and his fantasies sometimes disturbed him.

At least he was lucky in his wife, a good woman, never saying anything to make him feel bad. As he came out of the bathroom, full of ungratified needs and sexual resolve, she smiled at him and asked whether he would like some tea. He could hear her hum in the kitchen as he put on Beethoven's Fifth Symphony, one of his favourites.

As immigrants fly across oceans they shed their old clothing, because clothes maketh the man and new ones help ease the transition. Men's clothing has less international variation; the change is not so drastic. But those women who are not used to wearing Western clothes find themselves in a dilemma. If they focus on integration, convenience and conformity they have to sacrifice habit, style and self-perception. The choice is hard, and in Nina's case it took months to wear down her resistance.

Looking after her Indian clothes was time consuming and exhausting. Everything had to be washed by hand, then hung on hangers from the shower curtain rod to dry, then the ironing board had to be hauled from the closet so the clothes could be ironed meticulously. And ironed again whenever she wore them, for this fabric crumpled easily.

In Brussels her mother had worn saris everywhere, thick Kanjeevarams even in the snow, underneath her winter overcoat. Lovely, lovely, had been the unanimous response. But to go with all this, she had imported Indian domestic help

Nina's clothes demanded the local dhobi, the corner presswallah, not washing machines. So when Ananda declared enough was enough, she had to graduate to Western, she acquiesced.

He hadn't thought his wife would need so much prodding. Once dressed in a certain way, it would be easy for her to blend in; she was lighter in colour than he was, her origins not so obvious. In her silks (praised at the party as exotic and dazzling) she was too much of an exhibit.

The weather helped him win his argument. Although in the summer she was quite comfortable in her salwar kameez, as it grew colder, the wind dug sharply into her silk clad legs, the damp ground made the hems of her salwar dirty, while constant scrubbing left the edges ragged. She couldn't live in such clothes for the rest of her life, she knew that.

To the Halifax Shopping Centre then, to those giants in standard clothing, Eaton's and Simpsons, that flanked either end of the mall. Ananda's patriotism meant that he preferred Eaton's, the all-Canadian store, to the offshoot of Simpson-Sears, USA.

Once there he hunted out a salesgirl while Nina surveyed the racks in the woman's section. Blue, black, grey, brown, white, these were the dominant colours.

The salesgirl's X-ray vision looked through the kindly, concealing salwar kameez to the awkward body beneath and asked, 'What would you like? A skirt? A dress? Tops? Slacks? Jeans?'

Nina disguised her apprehension with a look of deep thoughtfulness that she hoped could be interpreted as Eastern mysticism. 'Pants?' she said, her voice disengaged and distant.

'Jeans,' clarified the husband.

'Try these for size.'

The stiff blue material pinched her waist and hurt her crotch. She tried squatting in them; the discomfort grew. Looser, I want looser. In a larger size, she could slip a hand in the waistband, but still the material felt hard and stiff against her skin. Her bra stuck out in points under the knit material of the accompanying shirt, her belly bulged visibly against the material. She looked so awful she could not bear it. Averting her head from the mirror, she stepped outside the trial room.

'That looks nice,' said Ananda enthusiastically.

'I feel uncomfortable.'

'They'll feel better after a couple of washes,' said the salesgirl.

The jeans were agreed upon. So were two dark baggy shirts. For the first time in her adult life Nina was wearing assembly line clothing.

It was a beginning, thought the husband. She did look ungainly, he had to admit. Despite her foreign service background, his wife was quite traditional. He smiled at her.

'You'll get used to it,' he said, and she said that if she looked nice to him that was all that mattered. He put his arm around her and thought again what a good woman his wife was.

Nina has new clothes. She is going to the library and on the way she will check the number of covert glances she is able to dis-attract. As she walks the familiar roads her gaze flickers here and there, but her surroundings respond with indifference. She could be any jean clad woman with a colour co-ordinated blue shirt. There is comfort in this anonymity. She strolls through the public gardens, stops and stares at the ducks. They swim in the waters with an air of belonging, regally swallowing the bread people throw at them. They are there to be admired, and they do their job well.

As she hangs over the railing, a young man sidles towards her. 'Nice, aren't they?'

She nods uncertainly.

'Where are you from?'

It is broad daylight in a public place. 'Guess,' she says, in her accentless English.

'Italy?'

She nods.

'Wanna have a coffee?'

Alarmed, she ceases to be an adventuress from Italy and subsides into a housewife from India. Quickly she leaves the park.

In all the time of wearing salwar kameez no one had accosted her. Now in jeans, she is accessible to the whole city. She looks down at her clothes with some friendliness. Maybe in time she will get used to her belly jutting out (it hadn't stopped a man from addressing her), get used to thick stiff material between her legs.

The Candy Bowl arrives. She nips in and spends 14.95. It is just as well men do not accost her every day.

The library, and our newly clad Nina disappears inside it. Assimilation brings approval, and the checkout counter woman assures her she looks wonderful.

*

Autumn came. Sue phoned. 'Nina? Would you like to go to the Halifax Shopping Centre to look for your coat and boots? I promised Andy I would do this, and I'm sorry, I just haven't had the time.'

Nina hastened to convince Sue that she had not felt neglected.

'Afterwards I thought we could visit the Atlantic Winter Fair?' Sue went on with her upward lilt. 'The children love it. We could go directly from there. The fall colours on that road are really nice.'

'Won't the children get bored buying a coat?'

'It shouldn't take too long—and you'll get to see a bit of our Nova Scotian culture as well.'

'I'd love that.'

'Fine. I'll pick you up in half an hour.'

Nina used that time to experiment with her clothes. The jeans and shirt of course, but she tried her shawls in various draping combinations so that she seemed more herself in the mirror. Finally she decided that a red shawl in folds till her waist and Ananda's grey all purpose coat made her look quite attractive. Would Sue think so too?

Sue did. 'My, you look nice. What a lovely stole, it complements your skin, we sit for hours to get a tan like that.' But Nina is not interested in fairness or darkness; they have their standards, she has hers and never the twain shall meet. She wants information.

Last night, perhaps in consonance with her new look, Ananda had asked Nina to call him Andy. She had refused. It was foreign, Christian, Western, and to use the word Andy in her own home would be to carry alienation into the bedroom. Ananda had not persisted, but the very fact that he had asked suggested desires she found disturbing.

'Sue. Can you say Ananda?'

'What's that?'

'Andy. His name is Ananda.'

153

'I did realise you were calling him something different at the party, but I thought that was a pet name.'

'No, no, it's his actual name. Andy is not a Hindu name.'

'Well, fancy that. He always said call me Andy.'

There was a subtle distinction between *call me Andy* and *my name is Andy,* which Sue was perhaps not in a position to appreciate. To sensitise her, Nina briefly described Ananda's efforts to assimilate.

The granddaughter of immigrants, Sue was completely understanding. 'My grandfather changed his name from Dmitri to Jimmy. His last name from Philippoussis to Phillip.'

'Jimmy doesn't even sound like Dmitri,' objected Nina.

'He wanted a total change. My grandfather didn't do things by halves.'

'Didn't your grandmother mind? She must have been used to Greek names.'

'I think she felt the same way. They were very poor. They met on the boat they came out on, and married soon after they landed. They were grateful to this country, they thought of it as their home before they had even seen it.'

'What about their identity?'

'Oh, they had the one they wanted. Canadian. They made every effort to mingle as fast as possible. Even though their English was limited, they didn't insist their children learn Greek. Then my mother married a Scottish Canadian, and I married someone of Polish origin. End of Greece.'

Dmitri—Jimmy, Ananda—Andy. If you looked at it from this end it made sense. New beginnings, new names. Didn't Hindu families change the bride's name if they felt like it? Hello Canada, we are married. Now change my name.

What about colour? Dmitri could call himself Jimmy and get away with it, his skin was a shade of white. What assimilation when your body stamped you an outsider?

Never, for a moment, in all her years at home, had she to think about who or what she was. She had belonged. Only now was she beginning to realise how much that meant.

154

In the back seat John kept up a steady chant: horsy, horsy, horsy, horsy ride horsy.

'Yes dear, you'll ride a pony once we get there.'

'Ride horsy, ride horsy,' repeated John insistently.

Sue spent five minutes nosing around for a space in the parking lot, then John was put in the stroller, Melissa's hand taken and now Simpson's or Eatons?

'Let me see,' she murmured, heading towards Simpson's. 'They did advertise a pre-winter sale of camel hair coats—maybe with a lining...'

'Gimme candy, I want candy,' started Melissa, her attention caught by a lollipop a little boy was sucking.

'No dear, you only get candy on Sundays. It's not Sunday yet.'

'Candy, I want candy.'

'No dear.'

'CANDY—I WANT CANDY.'

Nina felt responsible for Melissa's behaviour. It was her coat that was causing it. 'We can come another time,' she offered.

Sue ignored this, turning her attention to her daughter. 'Now Melly—if you don't say another word about candy, I'll give you some caramel corn at the fair. But otherwise not even that.'

Melly shut up. Nina was impressed by the effective discipline.

Sue explained, 'I don't like bribing them, but when they see other children eating candy, they can't help but want. Well, other children will end up in the dentist's chair, but they are too young to understand that.'

They walked to the Simpson's end of the mall and into the ladies' section. By now Nina had developed ambitions as to how she wanted to look in Western clothes. Tall, slim, elegant, at ease in a good quality coat that she could swish about in. She liked what she saw of the camel hair, the same colour as her tussar saris—golden beige, sophisticated, understated, attractive. 'Here's a nice one,' said Sue, 'it has a cape, very in this season, with a belt and a detachable lining.'

155

Nina looked doubtful. A belt would showcase her stomach, her shoulders would be widened by the extra material of the cape. She tried it on, and the tall, elegant image of herself faded before the reality of the mirror.

In the end she bought a coat in which she would not be noticed, an ordinary camel coat with a detachable lining, two ugly raised plastic beehive buttons, a small unobtrusive collar; a coat with no character. This cost her ninety five dollars.

Boots followed, plain brown low-heeled boots to match the coat.

'Well, that's done,' said Sue brightly, as they headed towards the car less than an hour later.

'Yes,' agreed Nina, her heart heavy at the thought of what lay in the parcels she was carrying. She reminded herself that clothes were for comfort and protection, looks came afterwards and were not essential to the more enduring values of life.

They hit St Margaret's Bay Road, crossing a lake that reflected the sun in a silver rippling sheet. Trees glittered with incandescent reds and yellows. Above them the sky was a deep blue and in the distance a bank of rolling dark clouds shaded into peach at the edges.

Nina gazed at this spectacle. The sky reflected such a variety of moods, gentle, melancholic, tender, romantic, fierce; she could look at it forever. Finally she said, 'I hope those clouds don't mean it is going to rain. The Fair will be quite ruined.'

Sue looked puzzled. 'I do have a couple of umbrellas in the back.'

Now Nina looked bewildered. 'Won't the children get wet?'

'It's not far.'

This was even less clear, and Nina took refuge in silence.

The Atlantic Winter Fair. Oh, it is *inside a building* realised the immigrant, for whom fairs were associated with Diwali, with stalls around a maidan, rising dust, a friendly winter sun, crowds, rides on elephants, bangle sellers, paper lanterns, firecrackers, earthen diyas and all kinds of delicious food.

They queued up for entrance tickets and once inside, John started his chant again, 'Ride horsy, ride horsy, ride horsy,' while Melissa cried, 'I want candy, you promised.'

Caramel corn bought, they headed towards the petting farm. Ponies, sheep, goats, calves, pigs, all there to be petted. John and Melissa rode ponies. Then they saw a hog race, then they circulated among the many animals, all so fat that not a bone could be seen.

And then to the barn, row after row of horses' rumps, beautiful gleaming rumps: black, dark brown, brown, roan, red, gold, a few greys. Their tails were being plaited, their coats brushed, their manes clipped.

Announcements were being made. The competition of jumpers in the speed class was about to begin.

'Ride horsy, I wanna ride horsy,' said John, toddling towards a huge chestnut, eighteen hands high. A young girl with Anna written on her sleeve was holding its reins. 'I don't think so,' she said. 'Look how big he is.'

'Wanna ride horsy,' repeated John, who barely reached the horse's knee.

'John, come here,' called Sue.

John didn't budge. Sue grabbed him irritably. Having children in the West is no joke, pondered Nina. Complete absence of help along with constant demands. And Sue would soon have a third. What life would she have left?

'Ride horsy,' repeated John as his mother dragged him towards the rink, saying, 'You rode that nice pony, remember? Now we'll see the big horsy jump.'

They settled into seats high above the rink. The dirt was raked, ten jumps set up. One by one, the horses came, cantered around to warm up before starting their rounds of seventy seconds. The spectators groaned at every railing knocked over, clapped loudly at the successful few.

It was soothing, watching these horses, noting their strange names: Holly Go Lightly, Bluestreak, Thunderbolt, Winner, Ascot, It's No Trouble. The hall was warm, the fresh dung had an earthy, moist smell. The horses were big, healthy and glossy, their movements fluid. Nina too groaned, held her breath and applauded with everyone else. She felt part of the crowd, the fair, the city, the province, the country.

One day she would be sitting here with her children. All this would seem very natural to them; their minds would be imprinted with Canadian images from the day they were born. It made her a little sad that they should be so different from their mother. On the other hand, they wouldn't have inherited the template in the mother's mind where every experience contained a hidden double. If she saw a horse, it stood against the emaciated beast back home, if horse droppings were cleared she was reminded of the way cow dung patties dried in the sun, if she wandered around a fair it was against the vast backdrop of Diwali melas. Compound images shuttled to and fro in her mind, faster than the speed of lightning, covering thousands of miles, there and back, there and back, there and back.

She broke her silence by saying, 'I am so glad you brought me here. Our fairs at home are very different.'

Sue smiled indulgently. It was axiomatic that for the immigrant everything was new; she took it for granted that Nina would want to imbibe this culture as fast as possible. Like Dmitri Philippoussis. Sue could not imagine differences that hurt the senses and pained the mind. No, she couldn't imagine such a thing, and because she lived in Canada, it was probable she would never have to.

Ananda was very pleased when he heard about Nina's day.

'Nice of Sue.'

'Do you want to see the coat?'

'Sure.'

The middle aged, frumpish, bulky, inelegant creation was modelled. 'I think it makes me look old.'

'Nah. You look fine.'

'Should I take it back?'

'You bought it, Sue helped you, she would not have let you buy something unsuitable. Why are you being fussy? '

Because in winter enough bulges could be hidden for even her to appear glamorous, and this coat meant she had failed before the first snowflake fell.

vii

Till Nina came to Canada she hadn't known what lonely meant. At home one was never really alone. The presence of her mother, the vendors who came to the door, the half hour gardener who watered their plants, the part time maid who washed and cleaned, the encounters with the landlady, all these had been woven into her day. When she mourned her loneliness to Zenobia, it was a romantic companionate loneliness she was referring to, not the soul destroying absence of human beings from her life. She had worried about her mother's lack of companionship after her marriage; it would have been wise to have spared a thought for herself as well.

Day after day passed without her speaking to anyone but Ananda.

'Why is it that we hardly see uncle? It's just us two, alone in the whole city with no one to care if we live or die.'

'People are busy here. We meet them for family functions.'

'Like birthdays?'

'Birthdays! That's not a family function. No, like Thanksgiving and Christmas, occasions like that.'

'Thanksgiving and Christmas! That's all?'

'It's a big thing. Nancy does them very well. For Thanksgiving, pumpkin pie, turkey and stuffing, fresh cranberry sauce. For Christmas, presents under the tree, stockings with our names on them and a traditional dinner. It is nice to have somewhere to go on holidays.'

Her husband was talking another language. Canadian perhaps.

Her most intense social gesture was a nod. One could go to a shop and buy something without a word, the prices were all written, no need to ask, suspect, haggle or accuse.

If she had a baby, the next twenty years would be taken care of. Her interest in Canada would grow, her child's home after all. Would s/he have an accent? Read at an early age like her mother? Shine in school like his father?

Ananda's thoughts of their child's future were on a grander scale. He should aim to be prime minister of Canada. If no NRI had so far reached high office, there was a first time for everything. The country had been made by immigrants, and that included people like themselves.

This when incidents of racial hatred were frequently reported in the newspapers. In Toronto the other day, students had beaten an Asian travelling on the subway. The *subway*—a public place.

Ananda feels it is useless being frightened by such incidents. Intimidation should not be allowed to succeed.

Meanwhile Nina's biological clock ticks on and the sounds echo loudly in the Canadian vastness. Every time she has sex she imagines her egg fertilised, and every time she has her period she wonders whether this is a miscarriage; the bleeding is so plentiful, the pain so intense. Her childlessness is reinforced daily.

Morning time in the city was mother and child time, no single young adult woman could be seen on any of her walks. Her visits to the HRL coincided with reading hour for pre-schoolers. Among them she saw the shadowy figure of her own child, listening intently, intelligence gleaming from large dark eyes.

Her mother too is concerned. The word patience, ricocheting across the planet, assumes a tinny quality, and the mother eventually stops using it, suggesting a doctor instead. Ananda doesn't want to hear the implications of this. They have not been married that long, what is the hurry?

Nina decides to phone Sue. A woman with a third child on the way would be qualified to guide her.

'Oh, hi,' exclaimed Sue with obvious pleasure. Nina felt gratified. 'How are you? I've been meaning to call, but Melly came down with a cold. I didn't want to invite you over, in case of infection, you know?'

'Infection? With a cold?' repeated Nina. At home people coughed and sneezed in your face and thought nothing of it.

'Yes—isn't it terrible?' repeated Sue. 'But now everything is fine, just fine. She's gone to play school.'

'Sue, if you are not too busy, could I come over? I need some advice.'

The forlorn tone in her voice was obvious. Sue chastised herself; she should be paying more attention to the girl. Andy had a heart of gold, but sometimes that wasn't enough.

Sue welcomed her cordially. Over coffee, to avoid a single awkward pause Nina nervously asked about Melly, her cold, her symptoms, enough questions to persuade an onlooker into thinking the child had a terminal illness.

'And now,' said Sue, when she had had enough, 'about that advice?'

Nina started by wanting to know where she could look for a job; she had ten years experience in Delhi University, but Ananda was quite categorical that she was not qualified to teach here.

'He must know,' said Sue, but she did believe it was quite difficult. People spent years trying to get tenure after their PhDs.

The very thought of a PhD made Nina tired. She didn't want to study, her brain had grown weak with fiction and idleness. Besides, what was the point; even after years of labour there was no job guarantee.

The topic she had been nerving herself to mention came naturally from the pregnant mother's lips. What about children, did they plan on having any?

161

Nina blushed, guilty of barrenness. Some involuntary tears as she told her story. Sue leapt up and pushed a box of Kleenex at her.

'Oh, don't cry, don't cry,' she murmured. Encouraged, Nina sobbed, 'It's so awful,' into the soft clutch of flowered tissue in her hand.

Abruptly she felt ashamed of herself, using her situation to gain sympathy and comfort. See what being in this country had reduced her to.

She left the house having agreed to come over for the next meeting of the La Leche League. This was an association of nursing mothers and Sue knew that two or three of them had had trouble conceiving, it might help for Nina to talk to them.

On the appointed day Nina is introduced to ten mothers with matching babies and toddlers.

White faces stare at her, interested, curious, friendly. Sue drew the League's attention to the fact that Nina was new to this country and needed advice. They had plenty of experience, at the very least they could point her in the right direction. Now, Nina, take the floor.

Nina describes her monthly waiting, along with her monthly despair. 'If only I were home I would have somebody I could talk to, ask is there anything wrong, am I worrying too much, should I see a doctor, is it too early, am I being as alarmist as my husband insists, how much time should I give it? I am thirty two. Is it already too late?'

The women looked concerned and sympathetic. Their collective wisdom touched on many things. The stress of being in a strange country could be a reason for not conceiving. Or the husband might be producing sperm that was insufficient, immobile or misshapen, or it could be some hidden infection or alcohol or nicotine, or age, or too long on the pill, blocked tubes, fibroids, irregular periods, faulty ovulation; it could be any one of a hundred things, known or unknown. Sometimes after every test and treatment in the world, the couple still did not conceive. The anxiety and strain often took the desire out of sex, and then the marriage often broke up.

Though medically speaking, infertility was not specifically a woman's problem, it was she who bore the brunt of this particular deficiency. Her feminine self in question, she could end up hating her body. Its female functions, the period, the blood, the cramps, the inconvenience, the dry breasts useless and without purpose, were all reminders of the child that was not to be. It could get so bad that even the sight of a baby or a pregnant woman caused pain. Therapy worked at times, but nothing could really take the sense of loss away.

There was always adoption, an option for those not wedded to biological maternity.

Nina listened with alarm. She had not realised her vague dissatisfaction was the precursor to such drastic things.

Alone, in all the room, her fertility was in question. Her menstrual blood, even as they spoke, was soaking into a sanitary napkin, her stomach cramping with an unfruitful cramp. She looked down at her lap and fiddled with the strings of her purse. Now her back began to hurt. How soon before she could go home and lie down?

But these women were into action, not lying down. If initially her husband was unwilling, she could make a preliminary visit to the doctor. Her husband would soon come around when he realised medical attention was necessary. These procedures could take a long, long time, she was absolutely right in wanting to start.

Sue said Andy was the sweetest man; he must be in some kind of denial to not be supportive.

Another said she was free three hours every morning when David went to playschool. She could accompany Nina.

Hearing his name, David stuck his head out from under his mother's T-shirt. His mother laughed and said though almost weaned, he always nursed at meetings—it was seeing all the babies that made him want to suckle.

'How old is he?' asked Nina curiously.

163

'Three.'

'We believe in the bond between mother and child,' explained Sue, 'and in nursing as long as both are comfortable.'

How strange, thought Nina, that the La Leche League should have this affinity with villagers back home. It was the second time she was led to question assumptions about the so-called backward and developed worlds. Here it was developed to nurse for years, to stay at home with your children, to decide to fulfil your motherhood. Development allowed you to have the luxury of choosing a way of life from the practices of any part of the world. That was developed, not the age of the child dangling from your breast.

Finally the meeting settled down to the business of the day.

La Leche League pamphlets were circulated, containing descriptions of various items: backpacks and frontpacks for babies, carry cots, books on nutrition, baby welfare, family welfare.

Nina studied the pamphlets, again aware of her cramps. Her failure to produce seemed all the more poignant in this room profluent with life.

But apparently there were other problems with the female body besides an inability to conceive. Breastfeeding was not the simple, natural exercise she had thought it was. You had to be careful about your diet, your mood, the way you sat, the angle of the baby's head, the position of the breast. And then that devastating common thing was discussed: the disappearance of milk.

There were instances when the milk turns recalcitrant. The baby cries, the worried mother gets tense, the milk retreats further, in frustration the bottle is wielded. The milk objects violently, and really plays hide and seek. What the mother had thought was a temporary measure becomes a feeding pattern in earnest. The mother is in despair—what's the use, with breastfeeding her nipples hurt, her uterus hurts, everything hurts. She wants to give up. Which is where the La Leche

League steps in and says, there are other women like you, with troubled breasts, minds and hearts; courage, meet, compare notes, receive support and all will be well.

Not for nothing was the association's name derived from the Spanish leche, meaning milk. Yes, thought Nina, when she became a mother, she too would come to every meeting. She looked around at the bobbing babies heads, and the bits of white—very white—breasts she could see. Oh, if only that day would come when she too cradled a nursing baby in her arms. Just look at these women, grounded, rooted, connected to the earth by those pulling, plucking mouths, by those searching little hands, by the soft skin and round staring eyes, the tender skull with blood throbbing visibly beneath the sparse hair. How could these women nurse their wrongs when they were so busy nursing children, drawing out the process into years? There obviously was no place in their lives for solitary brooding.

Though Ananda was predictably pleased with her morning at Sue's house, he asked for no details and she provided none. There was a storm inside her, created by raising the possibility of infertility in front of a group of women and finding her fears were real.

Helplessness, loss of control and a lack of confidence in her femininity. That was a sterile woman's profile.

If Nina felt more in charge of her circumstances she wouldn't have blamed Ananda so much. From his point of view, waiting was understandable. He didn't have a clock marking time inside his body. Other distractions occupied him daily.

She told herself this was not about finding fault; this was about being united and doing what was necessary to have a child. They each had to understand how the other felt.

It was Friday evening. 'Let's go out,' said Ananda.

She preferred to stay home. They ordered pizza.

The Papa Pepito's guy came and delivered. Ananda opened a beer, poured Nina some juice and started on his pepperoni-olive-mushroom affair with relish.

'My, you cannot beat Papa Pepito. So much better than Pizza Pizza, Pizza Express or Domino's.'

Nina just ate. She couldn't tell the difference between one pizza and another.

Did Ananda remember, she asked, when sated with food he sat back, sipped his beer, remarked, this was the life, and smiled at her fondly, did Ananda remember her visit to Sue's?

Of course.

Well, Sue was a member of the La Leche League, an association of nursing mothers and she had gone to attend a meeting.

Ananda's look of satisfaction turned to bewilderment.

Sue had suggested she come to talk to some of the mothers who had had trouble conceiving.

And?

There was so much information about infertility! So many reasons, to do with either the man or the woman. And, incidentally, not conceiving after six months if you were under thirty five qualified as infertility.

'What rubbish.'

If he liked, he could check with Sue, she would corroborate all this.

Ananda pointed out coldly that he was a doctor, he had the medical fraternity to consult if need be.

'Then please, please, Ananda consult *someone*. Am I the only one here who wants a baby?'

At this he lost his temper. It was the weekend and there was time for lengthy confrontations. Of course he wanted children, but there was no need to get het up before even a year was out. To get pregnant as soon as you married was a very stupid, backward thing to do, it was more important to settle down first.

That was exactly why she wanted a child, to settle down, to give her days focus in this new country. What was she to do with her time, it wasn't as though she had a life.

'You were the one who didn't want a job just yet.'

'But that was when I thought a child would follow. Even my mother keeps asking... '

When she thought about it later she could not understand why mention of her mother should make him so angry. He said all kinds of unreasonable things such as: if there was anyone she had left out of her discussions, please to let him know, he would fill that person in also, he hadn't realised getting married was such a violation of privacy, and maybe if children were so important to her, she should have suggested a fertility test before the engagement.

Though startled, she held her own; there were others who cared even if he didn't, she said.

Back and forth, back and forth, the anger mounting, the words meaningless, except to wound.

Ananda retreated to the next room to remove the obdurate Nina from his sight. He went over his position in his mind, and found it impeccable. He wasn't being stubborn, he was being sensible. His body told him to relax in marriage, but how could he with this kind of performance anxiety on his head? He knew the way infertility tests worked—the woman keeps a record of her basal body temperature, there were ovulation times when you had to have sex, there was a test of post coital fluids, a detailed test of semen, a medical searchlight trained on premature ejaculations; hunt, hunt for the problems in him, in her, sexually, physically. Was his penis going to feel inspired by such relentless scrutiny? It was still in a delicate stage, managing penetration but not long or deep enough to satisfy him. Marriage had done much, but there was more to be conquered. They should get to know each other in comfort and peace. Was their personal happiness more important or some baby?

What was left of the weekend passed in silence. They had never had a major fight before. Each felt violated and refused to make conciliatory gestures. Nina brooded over her situation for a few more days before picking up the Yellow Pages to look for gynaecologists. She chose the first one, Dr Abbot.

The appointment made, she wondered whether to tell Ananda. No, what did he care? At least she was doing something about her problems, she was venturing into the unknown, she was expanding into Halifax in ways that made her less dependent on her husband.

She took a taxi to the doctor's office on Quinpool. A nurse at the reception took down details, and then she waited in the small room with no windows or warming lamps, a stack of well-thumbed magazines—*MacLean's, Time, Redbook*—on the centre table. She flipped through one, looking at words, her friends, at present unequal to the task of comfort and oblivion.

There were three other women, all looking at magazines, as alone as she was.

What would it be like to see a male gynaecologist? Most of the doctors in the Yellow Pages had been men, perhaps she should have done a little more research?

Well, it was too late now. She stared at the terracotta pot of ferns in the corner, its feathery plastic leaves artfully spilling over. At home her mother would have come with her, or Zenobia. She would never have been allowed to do something like this on her own.

Her turn came after forty minutes.

The doctor sat across a big desk and smiled at her firmly. The card the nurse had made was in his hand.

More smiling, now from her side, placating, pleading.

'What exactly is the problem?'

It was easy enough to talk, to describe the length of the marriage, the fear of age vis-à-vis pregnancy, the feeling of isolation, the not knowing what to do.

The questions began. Menstruation, contraception, abortion, pap smear history, sexual activity, sexual disease history, general health, pelvic surgery history, maternal gynaecological history, parental disease history, alcohol, nicotine and weight history.

168

Then followed a discussion of insurance coverage, diagnosis and treatment costs, drug costs, procedures concerning correction of possible defects and the time they took. Of course, the full plan of action could only be decided upon once the husband had his tests done. One third of all infertility cases stemmed from male causes, of which the majority centred around abnormalities in the sperm.

Here, here was a pamphlet answering some commonly asked questions, with details of various support groups. This was a trying time for couples, and it helped to meet other people who were going through similar problems.

Thank you doctor.

Now for the examination. The pap smear, the checking of fibroids, the general health. Immediately she felt tense.

The nurse came. 'Come along, dear.'

She was shown into a tiny cubicle.

'Just slip off your pants and lie down.'

'Why?'

'So the doctor can look at you'.

'In my country we don't do this.'

'Really? Then how do they examine you?'

'I don't know.'

'It'll be over in a minute. Lie down.'

It was a horrid little windowless room, fluorescent lights set in the ceiling, tiny, with just one high bed covered with a white sheet and a large lamp near it. She stood irresolutely by the bed.

'You'll have to do this many times, dear,' said the nurse. 'Might as well get used to it.'

It was with a sense of shame that she slid off her pants and panties and lay down on the table. 'Put your feet here,' said the nurse. Now her legs were spread wide open, facing the door, the world coming through. And there the doctor, squirting gel on his glove clad fingers, inserting a metal contraption into her vagina, aiming the light between her legs, peering inside, scraping some tissue off, pressing on her stomach, feeling around and around.

'You can get dressed now,' he said, and left.

There were two other closed doors, she had noticed, two other women lying on tables, waiting for the doctor.

Dr Abbot was a pervert, decided Nina, as she stood in the outer waiting room; why else would he, a male, want to specialise in this branch of medicine?

'When would you like your next appointment?' asked the receptionist.

Could she phone and let her know?

She didn't care so much about having a child now. These walls, this room, was inimical to it. She wanted to be outside, she had had enough of inside. Slowly she left the apartment block and started walking. The sky was grey, a few brown leaves still clung to trees otherwise bare.

Would she ever have a child? She had not thought beyond a visit to a doctor, that had seemed a big enough issue. Now she realised there was a world stretching beyond; a preliminary check up didn't even begin to scratch the surface. And after all that time, trouble and expense, it wasn't even guaranteed that a baby would be the result.

'What's up,' said Ananda that evening, 'why are you acting so strange?'

They had still not resumed friendly relations, but this was an olive branch of sorts. Nina mashed her dal in her rice, scooped yoghurt from the carton and jabbed viciously at a Five Seas imported slice of mango pickle.

It was easy to blame him for all she was feeling, so easy, she was frightened at how quickly she fell into that trap. She tried to control herself. Babies did not come through accusations.

'You didn't feel it necessary to see a doctor,' she said as neutrally as she could, 'about why we weren't getting pregnant, so I went myself.'

Now his turn to be silent. What had driven her to take this step, he would have gone, he wasn't saying no, he just wanted time. But that, it seemed, was impossible.

He hid his feelings. 'Well, did anything come of it?'

'A lot.'

'What?'

'He didn't think I was being alarmist.'

Of course he wouldn't. This was a culture that visited the doctor after one cough, after one degree of temperature, after one twinge in a tooth. He knew the next step in this process would be that he too go to the doctor. Then would follow his own testing, then reports, specialists, sex at specified times. Nina would become more demanding. As she recounted details of the visit, he could just see the shape of the future and he didn't like it. He was not ready for so much invasion of his privacy, not ready for all this effort to try for a child when he barely felt married.

'What about the costs?' he asked cunningly. 'Insurance doesn't cover it.'

Her face fell. 'I believe they cover the diagnosis.'

'But the tests? Some of them are quite expensive—believe me, there is no end to testing. First tests, then treatment, then more tests, then treatment, and as I said only the basic ones are insured. Are we ready for all that? I still haven't recovered from the expense of the wedding.'

She could think of nothing to say to this. Dr Abbot had said very clearly, they both had to be equally committed, otherwise it was not going to work. If Ananda was not as desperate about children, there was little she could do. Already she could see her dreams falling into fragments around the dining table. Tears gathered in her eyes.

Ananda looked at her. He had not found it so difficult to adjust when he had come, but perhaps he was made of sterner stuff. He drew her onto his lap.

viii

Early mornings were the hardest. Often Nina stayed in bed, not happy, not unhappy, scenes from home floating in her mind, jostling next to images of Spring Garden Road, the Halifax Shopping Centre and the Public Library. Sometimes she read, sometimes she put the clock radio on to introduce the sound of human voices.

One morning as she was twiddling the radio knobs she heard voices in Hindi, background to the commentator's British accent. Her hand trembled.

He was reporting the Kumbh Mela, held in Allahabad every twelve years, for the devout Hindu an extremely auspicious event.

'Today is the day of the Maha Kumbh, the day the spiritual blends with the ordinary, when the muted murmur of millions of pilgrims, marching to the Ganga, are matched by the early morning war cries of the Naga sadhus. Two crore faithful will bathe in this river today. The confluence of the Ganga, Yamuna and the mythological Saraswati has turned into an ocean of human beings immersing themselves in the holy waters to the chanting of Vedic hymns, blowing of conch shells and beating of drums.

'Now, it is the naked sadhus who are waiting for their dip. It is four thirty in the morning, the auspicious hour started at three. The atmosphere here is simply incredible; as far as the eye can see, there are pilgrims from all four corners of India gathered on the banks of the Sangam, waiting their turn to immerse themselves. There is the Maharajah of Kapurthala, mounted on a horse. Previously he mounted an elephant, but after last time's stampede elephants have been discouraged. Over there are the akharas, bearing their standard in front of them; on the right has just passed a very colourful procession of village women, balancing sacks on their heads. The naked sadhus are getting restless, they want their turn—oh, now it is their turn, they are descending into the water. It is a bitterly cold morning, there is a mist and the sun has yet to rise, but nothing deters these pilgrims from the icy river.'

The words reverberated through Nina, though she was as much a stranger to the Kumbh Mela as anyone in Canada.

Educated, secular and Westernised, she had never had anything to do with ritual Hinduism. From so far however, the crowds, the pilgrims, the piety, the cold river, the morning mist, the sadhus, all called to her. Somewhere they beat in her blood and now, in a foreign land, she was as guilty of exoticising India as the tourist posters in the Taj Mahal restaurant.

Over dinner Nina told Ananda about the Kumbh Mela.

He grunted.

'Do you know it?'

'Of course.'

'Oh. Well, hearing about it over the BBC made me realise how special it was.'

Unlike Nina, Ananda knew firsthand how special it was, because he had gone there as a pilgrim when small. 'Once my mother insisted on going,' he offered, willing to share a memory, something he rarely did if it was set in India.

'And?'

'My father didn't want to brave all those crowds, but my mother was very insistent. She hardly ever asked for anything, but who knew what would happen in twelve years she said, and so we all went. There was certainly not another opportunity in her life, so it turned out she was right.'

Nina was astonished. She knew no one who went on pilgrimages, not even her pious mother. 'How was it?'

'I don't remember. I was only five or six.'

But he remembered something. Getting up when it was still dark, shivering on the river bank, the sound of conch shells, his father carrying him as he waded into the freezing water, his mother holding his sister's hand, people, people all around in the growing pale of morning. Then later on the train ride home, the family feeling they had all accomplished something, being light hearted and gay. And still later, the discovery that his sister had lice in her hair.

He remembered the sharp smelling kerosene oil his mother repeatedly massaged into Alka's scalp, the long, wooden, fine-toothed comb used to drag the dead lice out of her hair, the tick of his mother's finger nail as she squashed the eggs on an old newspaper. The tears of humiliation in his sister's eyes—she would rather die than go to the Kumbh Mela again.

'Did your mother feel something special?' asked Nina wondering, as she always did, whether to break into memories that might be painful.

'Huh?'

'Your mother. It must have been a big thing for her.'

'Must have. She was quite religious. Maybe she got what she wished for. Certainly she didn't have to live without my father.'

Nina's heart ached for her husband. After her father died, she and her mother had spent long bitter years reconciling themselves to the full scale emptiness in their lives. In addition to the man they adored, they had lost status, housing, security and their future. In a moment, Ananda too had plunged from everything to nothing. She reached for his hand.

'Maybe one day we can go,' she said, trying to make up for the losses in his life.

'Naw—once is enough. Bathing in a river full of other people's germs can't cleanse you. Now I know better.'

'The Ganga is supposed to be naturally pure. My mother even drinks the water. Nothing happens to her.'

'But not the river that has two crore people splashing about. How hygienic do you think that is?' snorted Ananda and thus concluded the conversation about their mothers.

During her long sojourn in bed, next morning, Nina thought about the Kumbh Mela. Something that had barely crossed her consciousness for thirty two years had become the subject of two days' reflection.

Yearning for home did strange things to the mind. Even though she despised cheap nostalgia, the way she had reacted to the Kumbh Mela was proof that living in a different country you became a different person. Here she drew comfort from caressing her breasts, imagining them in a wet sari in the waters of the Sangam. From there her mind wandered to all the soaked heroines she had seen in Hindi cinema and how very buxom they had looked.

There she was, doing it again. At home, wet sari clad heroines were ignored as part of the blatant devices of commercial cinema, certainly never identified with.

Misery such as hers could have no immediate end, she decided, as she stroked herself into another morning in Canada.

Her interest in going to the library waned. It was hard to sustain the same passion for books when they served as appetizer, main course and dessert as well. It seemed another lifetime when, as a teacher, she had read for her profession, when she had thought for a living.

The children, among whom she had once seen her daughter's bright eyes, became noxious to her, their thin high voices pierced her skin. Already the prediction at the LLL was coming true; the very sight of them made her sad. When would the hatred of her body start, she wondered gloomily, the next item on the agenda.

She changed the direction of her walks, turning to the book of nature, perusing it in Point Pleasant Park. If it was windy or drizzly, she walked in a long waterproof coat of Ananda's, the material flapping around her knees, a silk scarf tied around her ears, her nose, running slightly from the cold, wiped frequently by a tissue clutched in her hand.

I am in a place, five hundred or was it six hundred–seven hundred million of my countrymen would give their eye teeth to be in. I have a Saab, a General Electric fridge, a washing machine, a dishwasher, running hot water, I can eat and drink whatever I like. Don't look at the bad side, her mother used to say. Look at the good.

But just having to tell herself this seemed so pathetic. Did the people who lived in these houses with the blank windows ever count their washing machines? She could see two, three cars parked in the driveways of the houses on Young Avenue; did the inmates look at them every morning and think how lucky they were? Then why should she?

Because she was brown? Third world?

And the answer echoed through the quiet, tree covered atmosphere of Point Pleasant Park—yes, yes, yes. Now be grateful for the rest of your life.

She was trying. If she started telling Ananda how miserable she sometimes felt, cause unknown, he told her to be positive. Who can argue with positive thinking? No one. She was the culprit.

Her mind wandered back to the astrologer. Was it only two years ago that he had predicted her life would be transformed? His words had been seen as words of promise. They didn't convey how much stress she would undergo while assaulted by changes, changes so thorough that she felt rootless, branchless, just a body floating upon the cold surface of this particular piece of earth.

Part of that birthday treat had been the scooter ride back home with her mother, which allowed them to be exposed at street level to all the pollutions of the road. Now she longed to breathe the foul air, longed to sit in a scooter rickshaw and have every bone in her body jolted.

Home. That was what she wanted. The park, the trees, the harbour, the view, everything was so pretty, but it failed to satisfy her heart. Maybe if her mother could share it with her, it would have made a difference. She could imagine her thin worn face, her gnarled hands, happy in her happiness. Happy. The whole planet would be better off not searching for something so ephemeral.

On the way back she passed a deserted children's playground. Swings, sand pit, jungle gym, benches, all unused. At home no space, large or small, was ever free of people. She remembered the rows of jhuggis in the nalla near her house, without sanitation, water or toilet facilities. The children there spilled onto the pavement, playing, shitting, begging.

In her disorientation she could think wistfully of children shitting, when in all her years of living in Delhi, her strongest feelings about jhuggis had been that they were a filthy, ugly nuisance and why didn't the government do something about them. Every morning on the way to the bus stop, her sari fastidiously lifted, she had stepped around multiple turds and continued on her way, only peripherally registering them and their implications. Now, even those faeces were transported to the playground with their owners, along with other starving children, beggars, the homeless, the brutalised, the charred, the raped. These wide open spaces could provide them with a place of rest too.

At the corner store she stopped for a long time. The woman who ran it was an Indian, and though she avoided Nina's gaze, her presence made the store comfortable. There was one of her own kind running the shop, even if she did have a Canadian accent. Up and down the small aisles, looking at products crying out for the money she was dying to part with. Slowly she chose. Corn chips. Salt and vinegar chips. Onion and garlic dip. Mint and coconut chocolate. Cinnamon sweets. Buttery shortbread biscuits. Then sugarless gum, because her teeth were going to feel yucky. Oh, and they were out of milk and yoghurt, these were needed to weigh the shopping down in the scales of sanity.

Lugging these things home, Nina couldn't wait to open those packets and sink her teeth into the soothing stuff. Thank God this stuff was so cheap, or Ananda would notice the amount she spent on rubbish.

ix

'When should I make the next appointment with the doctor?'

'Which doctor?'

177

'The gynaecologist said we should go as a couple.'

'What reason did he give?'

'Well, his initial findings were normal so far as I was concerned.'

'That's good.'

'Not good enough. We need to investigate some more.'

'Will you shut up about doctors?'

'Why are you being so rude?'

'I'm sorry, but please don't go on talking about this. We'll go when the time is right.'

Temporarily she gave up on doctors to start nagging him about sex. 'If we had it frequently, maybe a sperm would make it to an egg.'

'Are you implying it's my fault we don't have sex more often? Don't you know how much I want it? But while you just sit around and relax at home, I am at the clinic working hard to make a living. Unless I get a full night's rest, I can't concentrate the next day. Dentistry is very fine work, you know.'

Dispassionately Nina observed that Ananda got offensive when he felt attacked. This was not a nice trait, but she ignored it for the moment, wondering whether she was wrong in thinking that her appetite for sex was greater than her husband's. It was true though, he did need to be rested, his hands needed to be absolutely steady and he often complained of pain in his lower back. She wondered whether she needed to be more empathetic, but the state of permanent sexual frustration she was in made it difficult. It grieved her that Ananda had no notion of how she felt. Her idea of matrimony was a husband who was a little more alert to the discreet clues she let drop. Long moments were spent gazing at herself in the mirror, in her underwear or sexy nightie. In the soft glow of the pink tiled bathroom, she looked dazzling. Her bare skin, the curves of her body, her black hair falling over her shoulders, all were delectable. Desire rose in her as she communed with her reflection. She pushed her breasts up, and gazed at the seductive cleavage that would surely drive any man to fondle. Having a husband should not have meant such lonely desperation.

For years and years Nina had masturbated, hoping the day would come when a loving partner would circumvent the furtive, dissatisfied feeling this left her with. Thrice a day on average, and this restraint only due to the fact that she was working. Guilt ridden, she would promise herself, this is the last time, but her restlessness made this impossible.

Though married, the last time was nowhere in sight. After dinner, when she tried to get cosy with Ananda he would often say later, I'm tired. And Nina would feel humiliated at what seemed a reversal of gender roles; she the monstrous cornucopia of appetite. He never noticed, never asked what she had been doing for so long, when she marched determinedly towards the bathroom, sat on the toilet, opened her legs, jammed her fingers in, leaned back and closed her eyes.

In the beginning she had construed their problems to lie in their unfamiliarity to each other; even her body told her this in an itching which subsequently disappeared. His needs were obviously different, and she didn't want to impose, hesitant about putting him off. If only she were in India, with more difficulties in her daily life, with more heat to sap her energy, with more obligations.

At night when her discontent reached epic proportions, weary of books, she would creep from her bed to turn on the TV with the volume low. She flicked the remote and was greeted with variety, the spice of life. Occasionally she got up to fetch something to keep her company: grape juice, taco chips, salsa, chocolate, cherry burgundy ice cream.

Hours later, when she had watched enough TV to put her in a calmer, more insensible state of mind, she could brave Ananda's recumbent, sleeping, snoring form again. But often, once in bed, she became wide awake. Maybe if she did it one more time, sleep would come. With a strong sense of duty her hand slid between her legs.

In the library, in the supermarket, every magazine Nina picked up showcased sexual fulfilment. Articles leapt to the eye, demandingly, accusingly, tauntingly: how to please your man, how to get your man to please you; quizzes about performance, seduction, techniques, adventure, libido, fantasy, daring, communication skills, verbal and physical etc, etc. She read them with fascination, hating every word. She wished to live a quiet contemplative life, she didn't take kindly to this invasion into her private domain, these ratings on scales from A to D. That D = F was clear and where she ranked was also clear.

Above all, the magazines emphasised mutuality. Desires, fantasies, feelings, all were to be shared. Togetherness was the essence of a successful relationship, and in sex it was particularly important. Women, do not feel shy, your man needs to know how you feel, he is not a mind reader, come on, tell him.

It was all very well to tell Western men. Judging from her reading they were more aware of communicative lacunae than their Indian counterparts. Though Ananda was always making out he wasn't quite Indian. This would be the acid test, surely.

That evening after dinner, with a bad feeling in the pit of her stomach, Nina broached the topic she hoped would be taken in the spirit it was intended.

'Ananda, are you satisfied with our sex life?'

'Why?'

'Because I feel—I just feel—there is room for improvement.'

'There always is.'

Now she had taken the plunge, she had to swim. 'It's too short, not even five–ten seconds. Surely that can't be normal. I love you, but when it is over so quickly I get frustrated. Maybe this is why I have not conceived. Dr Abbot did ask whether we enjoyed a normal sex life and I didn't know what to say. When we go together, we can discuss it in greater detail.'

'What good will that do?'

'Knowing where one stands is important, surely.'

'I do my best,' he said coldly. She was like the others, judging him all along. Even this Indian girl, his wife whom he had travelled so far to get.

Nina sensed his withdrawal and was horrified. 'Ananda, that's not fair. Don't condemn me for what I feel.'

No response.

She put her head on her arms in hopelessness.

He looked at the locks of black hair spread on the table. Left to herself she tended to exaggerate things. He pushed his chair back and held out his arms. Nina responded; who else was there for her in this whole country?

'I feel so lonely,' she confessed, playing with his tie, stroking the faint bristle on his chin and cheeks, caressing his little rotund belly.

'You have me,' he replied, husband-like, hauling her securely onto his lap. This was a subject he was more comfortable with. 'And maybe it was a bad idea not looking for work immediately.'

'But there is nothing I can do.'

'There are always things if you don't mind a basic wage. That's how I started.'

Whenever there was a problem he suggested work, distracted her by its possibilities, then nothing came of it. Ignoring the issue of basic wages, she slid onto the floor between his legs, unbuttoned his shirt and pressed her cheek against the soft hair of his stomach. 'I want us to be happy,' she whispered. 'That is what I want to work at. We should tell each other all our feelings. I don't want any shadows in our married life.'

Ananda gripped Nina's hair so hard, she had to suggest they move to the bedroom. They had sex, and Ananda did his best to compensate by lingering long over her body. As Nina washed up she felt much lighter. Fluctuating emotions were part of the adjustment process, it was important to recognise that. For now, they were going across the street to buy groceries. In marriage, the power of shopping together cannot be underestimated. Planning the week's menu suggests a stronger future than sex ever can.

181

A damp wind started up as they emerged from Dominion's, and Nina gratefully got into the car. She could cope with the light drizzle that passed for rain, but it was the wind that drove her mad. It reddened her ears, made her nose drip, her eyes water, turned her hands into frozen blocks.

That night it was Ananda who lay awake instead of Nina. Why was he like this? If his wife felt there was something wrong, despite fooling him initially, what hope was there? In the porn he read, men could go on forever, ejaculate, then go back to it for a few more hours. Was this pleasure never to be his?

He tossed and turned. The green numbers on the clock changed steadily. The arranged marriage had not, after all, been the perfect solution. The canker of failure had entered the house and forced his back to the wall. He thought of the Masters and Johnson he had read, when seeking some clarity into his condition.

They had been very clear that the older definition of premature ejaculation, defined by less than two minutes inside the woman, was now passé. Sexual experience was too complex to be judged by such crude criteria. A diagnosis of sexual dysfunction depended on the partner, the situation, the length of arousal, the mutual satisfaction. Above all, it was a behavioural problem rather than a psychological one, and there were simple technical solutions to it.

Maybe he should get in touch with them. There were others like him, he was not alone. The tragedy was that he was only exploring the possibility of sexual therapy now, when marriage restricted his choices. For a brief moment he looked at Nina's sleeping form with hatred.

x

Distance grew between them. Nina felt imprisoned by the stress and assured him there were other things besides sex in marriage.

Relationships had to develop, feelings had to be shared, surely he understood that? It was only her tension about a child and her age that drove her to find solutions, otherwise she knew things took time, of course she did.

Everything she said made it worse. The single assurance that would have made it better was not forthcoming; that whatever he did, however he was, she was happy with him.

The silence continued. To break it she suggested going in for couple therapy. Had he heard of Masters and Johnson? In the library there were magazines—*respectable* magazines like *MacLeans* and *Redbook*—that mentioned their work. The Halifax Memorial Library did not carry their books, but she could order them through inter-library loan. She was sure there was a lot they could learn from them.

So now her academic eye was trained on premature ejaculation. First his wife was the expert in infertility, then in sexuality.

'I don't need you to tell me about Masters and Johnson. They have been around for a decade, you know.'

'Then you are aware they treat couples in their clinic in St Louis. And claim an eighty percent success rate. Why can't we go?'

'For how long have you been researching this?'

'I have not been researching this. I just read about it in some magazine.'

Nina looked worried. She didn't understand why he had suddenly turned hostile—surely he was aware he had a problem. Sex was a form of communication, and if they couldn't communicate on this most basic level, what about everything else?

If it was a behavioural problem, there was a behavioural remedy. In the West people relentlessly scrutinised the quality of their lives; they demanded solutions for everything. Why had he never explored those options? Suddenly the unpleasant thought came that this might be why he had come home to look for a bride. Was this the kind of man he was? Passing off shoddy goods to the innocent East? She did want to know this answer.

'Are you telling me you *want* to go to Masters and Johnson?' he demanded.

'If it will help us, why not? They are doctors, they specialise in couple therapy.'

'How is it that you know so much about this?'

'From reading. That's how I know anything.'

Just as he thought. She had studied the subject.

She put her arms around him, slid her hands inside his pants and caressed his faulty, furtive organ. 'Please, darling, it will make such a difference to our marriage. Don't you want to have better sex?'

He shuddered. The one word yes would mean acknowledging his inadequacy. And that hurt too much.

The penis she was cradling got smaller as it tried to escape her searching hands. She got the message. She had never heard that penises did very well on their own, but if this one wanted to try, it was welcome.

She wished she were home. Home was the place to be if something was wrong. Private issues were not public knowledge, suffering and deprivation were taken for granted, and you learned to accept your lot. No doubt the fatalism of the East had much to do with this attitude, but when you looked at the bottom line it read, yes, you can live.

A few weeks later Ananda emerged from his absorption in an affable mood. This mood demanded that he take Nina to the Taj Mahal, drink red wine and tell her that he was going away for two weeks. One week would be spent at a dental conference in San Francisco, the other at San Diego with an old school friend.

Nina was glad Ananda was taking a holiday. Honesty had led to a platonic relationship in bed. Neither of them wanted this, but it was what they had gotten over the past few weeks.

'I wish I could come,' she said wistfully. 'I believe California is beautiful, with the sea and the mountains. A college friend of mine is doing her PhD at Berkeley. Maybe I could stay with her while you are at your conference, then we could visit San Diego together?'

'I'll take you another time.'

'Why not now? We can take a holiday, distract ourselves from all this. Come on, Ananda.'

He got irritated. Why was she always wanting him to do things differently? 'The conference is paying for my ticket, which is really expensive. I don't think we can afford it.'

The temperature had dropped to zero. The trees waved stark black branches against an unremitting pallid sky. The wind was icy. Occasionally the sun shone, but that meant nothing. It would have been nice to be able to step out without tons of clothing, to see blue skies, to experience a warm sun rather than a cold one, thought Nina self-pityingly as Ananda prepared to leave for San Francisco.

She had wanted to spend a special evening with him before he left. A candlelit dinner in a nice restaurant; home had been the scene of too many quarrels lately.

But Ananda said they were going to eat at uncle's, uncle had been complaining of neglect. And so another evening of politics, of here versus there. Talk of rival parties trying to unseat Morarji Desai, who was eighty two years old, who drank his own urine, whose son was corrupt. Madam was bound to come back to power as soon as this government fell, she was just waiting in the wings. Meanwhile Trudeau would not be able to delay elections beyond next year.

Eventually the uncle turned to Nina—how was she getting on? Didn't she get bored staying at home all day?

'Yes,' said Ananda, Nina did get bored. She went to the library of course, but she needed employment of some kind.

In a recession finding jobs was difficult, remarked the uncle. Trudeau had created a deficit and unemployment was growing.

'Any job,' said Nina, she was not particular.

But, said the uncle, it should be in keeping with her education. There was no point in doing menial labour and being paid the minimum wage.

No, they agreed, no point.

If they planned to have a family, said Nancy, it was better to start soon.

Nephew and niece-in-law smiled politely. Ananda remarked that Nina was still getting used to the country, after all they had just gotten married.

Uncle grunted. That was not an occupation. Maybe she should study further, Dalhousie had an excellent reputation. Get a B Ed, then she could teach in the school system. Sooner or later the recession would recede.

They would think about it, said Nina, when Ananda didn't respond.

On the way home Ananda was strangely abstracted. All Nina's attempts at conversation failed. Perhaps it was just as well they had been at uncle's house instead of their own; at least he had shown animation when they discussed Morarji Desai.

This abstraction continued till Ananda's departure. Nina could see he was making an effort to appear normal, which increased her dismay. He was hiding something and she had no idea what it was.

With Ananda gone Nina had even less to do. Alone, her thoughts grew darker. The hollowness of the landscape reverberated inside her, with no people, no conversation to even glaze the surfaces. Hour after hour, day after day could pass without a single word uttered.

How much did Ananda earn anyway? He never told her so she couldn't judge whether they could afford an extra ticket or whether he was trying to avoid taking her for some other reason.

On the plane to California Ananda had six hours to think about his situation and the lies he had told. He didn't even know why he had lied. Nina would have been enthusiastic about any move to overhaul himself sexually, participated in the process wholeheartedly, but, he argued with himself, as a husband did he want his wife to expose her most private moments to a sex therapist? Especially when she didn't have to, the problem was after all his. Of course the therapist would only show sympathy—but he was a doctor and he knew how prurient the curiosity behind the professional facade could be. Then she too would be encouraged to reveal her feelings. Call it inhibition, but he didn't want to start out with Nina complaining about his sexual shortcomings, though he had to admit she was the one most affected.

This was a journey he preferred to make on his own. If he improved, he could tell her. If he didn't, this would be one failure about which she need never know.

That was the big comfort. No one need ever know. As he flew through the vast skies of North America he felt liberated. Such an adventure would never have been possible at home. And if he came back with his manhood improved, perhaps he might really turn into an Omar Sharif.

When he had finally taken the step it had been easy, but it had taken marriage to push him. He owed Nina that.

It had been shortly after their last fight that he had phoned Masters and Johnson and described his problem.

Did he have a partner, they asked.

The single word no escaped his mouth, impelled by forces he did not examine.

They were sorry, but they only did couple therapy. If he so wished, they would be happy to give him names of therapists who took on single clients.

Yes, he so wished.

Dr Hansen in San Francisco had had excellent results in this area. Here was the number.

Over the phone, Ananda truthfully answered the many questions Dr Hansen asked him except the crucial one about whether he had ever been in a relationship.

'Not really,' he said.

It was simpler that way. It might also be true. All his adult life he had been alone with this problem; it was the background to everything. For years he had felt abnormal, with a hidden disfigurement. There was a lacuna where an erect, virile, nicely performing penis should be, which was reflected in the depths of his eyes when he looked at both men and women.

Two weeks of therapy, Dr Hansen had promised, and he would be a changed man. A changed man. He tried to imagine life without this particular torture and failed. Still he was travelling towards hope, and hope is a very potent thing. He would have two doctors (Dr Hansen worked with his wife) bringing all their expertise and knowledge to bear on him.

It was going to cost him heavily. Each day of treatment was a hundred dollars. With hotel and plane fare the whole thing came to almost three thousand, American. He had told Dr Hansen he needed a cheap hotel; the expenses were already crippling him.

He understood his concerns, said Dr Hansen. Usually they recommended a hotel on Telegraph Avenue to their clients. It was near the clinic, they saved on commuting time and money and they got a specially discounted rate for their two week stay.

It was afternoon when the plane taxied into the San Francisco airport. Ananda took a cab, marvelling all the while at the sun, the tropical vegetation, the palm trees. So this was California. He hadn't felt such warmth outside India.

The drive was long. They crossed a bridge to enter Berkeley on the other side of the Bay. He felt the smallness of Halifax; the road system here was enough to dazzle. Finally he arrived at the Carlton Hotel. His room was pleasant, with huge windows overlooking the street, a small balcony with an awning, a double bed, muted lilac and blue bedspread. He could see a clock tower in the distance.

He phoned Nina—yes, he had reached all right, the weather was nice and warm, he was looking forward to bringing

188

her here one day. The hotel the conference had booked him into was very nice, centrally located in downtown Berkeley. There were other doctors booked into the Carlton, he looked forward to spending time with them over lunches and dinners. He would probably walk to the conference venue, just a few blocks away. Tomorrow was a long day, he was particularly interested in the sessions on root canals, he might not be able to phone her, but she was not to worry. Here was the number of the hotel, but she was only to use it in emergencies, he was going to be pretty tied up.

Phone call over, he lay down, exhausted. Everything was now in place, he must sleep, his appointment with Dr Hansen was for ten the next morning.

He leaves early, the address of the doctor's office in his hand. On Shattuck Avenue he finds a narrow white building, no 1214. Up the stairs to the second floor, to an office and receptionist, she probably knows why he is here, but never mind, never mind, there must be streams of people in and out all the time. The floors are wooden, the sofas pale stripes, the cushions silvery green. The door opens: 'Ananda Sharma?' 'Yes.' 'Max Hansen,' dressed in jeans and a white shirt, about fifty years old.

Ananda is led into the inner room with big windows, a tree waving its benign branches outside. Here, Max and Carla begin the journey that will explore Ananda's psyche and root out all offending matter.

First some reassuring facts. This was a condition that was eminently reversible. (They did not use words like cure because that suggested disease.) They gave him statistics about premature ejaculation, percentage of men affected, how often, what ages, rate of improvement. Though sex was ultimately dominated by the mind, the success rate of talk therapy was low; you could spend years, thousands of dollars and still not get anywhere. When frustration built up, performance suffered. Tension led to unsatisfactory sex, which furthered anxiety. Sexual therapy disrupted that cause and effect. Once it was proven to the client

189

that he had staying power, then confidence built, leading to better performance, etc, etc. Their job was to provide methods to enable this process.

Ananda asked apprehensively whether not having a partner would affect treatment. They laughed genially. Some doctors insisted on partners because they felt that emotional commitment made the therapy more effective. While that was true, such an attitude condemned the unattached male to perpetual misery. They themselves had had great success with surrogates.

Now the procedure was this. The surrogate—her name was Marty—would meet him at his hotel. In consultation with them she would set limits on how much and what kind of contact was permissible. There was to be no penetration the first week. It was essential to learn how to relax, and they placed great emphasis on breathing techniques. Marty would also teach him how to exercise the pubococcygeus muscle, pull it back, hold it, let go (same as for urine); you can do it anywhere, and as with all exercise, the more often he did it, the stronger it would be.

In sex there was no goal to be reached, no performance on which one was judged (Nina, are you listening?). They would teach him to take pleasure in his body, to focus on the sensations. He would just feel, that was all he had to do.

After every session Marty would meet the doctors and give them her feedback. Based on this, there would be a counselling session with Ananda. The counselling session would be taped, and Ananda would have to listen to it in the evenings, as often as he could. He would be surprised at how many insights emerged during this exercise.

They sent him back with some books: *Male Sexuality, Male Sexual Response, Together in Bed, Sexual Myths*. Marty would meet him at his hotel at three o'clock. In the meantime he was to read, read, read.

Ananda left 1214 Shattuck Avenue with a light heart. Professionals, the professionals were taking care of him. He was bound to improve. He had no time to waste in restaurant dining; there was a McDonald's around the block, a burger would be his lunch.

Once done, the good student hurried back to his hotel, only stopping briefly at the drugstore to buy breath fresheners. A surrogate was coming; maybe the books would reveal techniques that would enable him to perform better. He settled down to *Myths about Sexuality* first, flipping the pages quickly to see what information it would yield. Initial arousal, excitement phase, full arousal, plateau phase (this is what he yearned to prolong), orgasm, then resolution after orgasm and the time it took to reach the plateau phase again.

PE was reversible; ten percent of men had it, many more experienced it in varying degrees. Ananda decided he could be included in varying degrees. Hadn't he known some success with Nina? He looked at his watch. It was already two thirty. He took a shower, shaved, brushed his teeth, used mouthwash, used aftershave, deodorant, and walked around the room chewing breath fresheners. He felt intensely nervous.

The hotel phone rang. Marty here. Come on up, Marty, Room 201. She was dead on time; he liked that in a woman, though of course she was not a woman, she was a person of the medical profession.

The door bell rang. His sexual helper was young, blond, with freckled skin, tight clothes, somewhat plain. 'Hi. I'm Marty.'

'Hi, Marty. Come in. Dr Hansen told me about you.'

She smiled warmly. 'I am so pleased to meet you. I have always wanted to visit India.'

'Yes. Well.'

'So here is what we are going to do. I'll be with you for two hours. We'll spend at least an hour of that time in bed, maybe more if necessary. Meanwhile you must let me know what goes through your head. Whatever it is, no matter how small. Max says that things that don't seem relevant are often the most revealing.'

He just stood there, nerve-wracked.

191

'Let's get into bed,' she said.

Should he draw the curtains?

If it put him at ease.

It definitely did.

A dim and gloomy light filled the room.

'You prefer it like this?'

'Should I not?'

'Hey, there are no shoulds and shouldn'ts. You must go with what you feel.'

'Alright,' he said uncertainly.

'We can take our clothes off now.'

'Do you want to use the bathroom first?'

'For what?'

'To take off your clothes.'

'Would that make you more comfortable?'

'I don't really know how this works.'

'Would it disturb you if we undressed in front of each other?'

'Not at all.'

But he couldn't help turn his back a little. He knew it was irrational; she was going to see him anyway, touch him anyway. Alone with her though, it seemed the most unnatural situation in the world. How had he gotten into it? He heard rustling, the screech of a zipper, the fall of clothes on the floor.

'What are you thinking?'

He turned. She was standing there naked and he was unable to look at her directly. A covert glance informed him that she had large, high breasts, sturdy muscled legs, narrow shoulders, square feet. Her body made her face more appealing.

'The whole thing is a bit cold blooded, no?'

'We are here by mutual agreement. So, no, I don't feel cold blooded.'

'But I am a stranger to you. Don't you feel awkward?'

'I would hardly be in this profession if I did. I like helping people, makes me feel I am doing some good in the world. Come lie down. Let me know why you are so uneasy.'

192

He got into bed with her. She started stroking him, running light fingers over his skin, commenting admiringly on its colour. 'How does that feel?'

'Nice,' he said politely.

She laughed, 'You have such good manners. Now relax, tell me what you are thinking.'

'Dr Hansen also stressed relaxing. But it is hard in these circumstances.'

'Yes, in the beginning it's a bit strange, but you get used to it. Talking helps.'

Encouraged he confided, 'They keep saying relax, relax—Dr Hansen, the books. Feel your sensations, empty your mind, concentrate on the moment, and if I could, I would, but I *can't*.'

'You are right, it's difficult. But together we can do it.'

She was clearly a nice girl. A tiny bit of him unknotted.

'Let your mind follow my fingers. Close your eyes.'

He closed his eyes. There was that light touch on his shoulders, travelling down to his stomach, venturing to his thighs, parting them, stroking the insides, coming back to his chest.

It felt so wonderful, another knot in him untied.

'What are you thinking?'

'I love what you are doing to me.'

She smiled at him and continued. After a few minutes he grew tense, he couldn't help it. It made him nervous to just lie there, not reciprocating. He cleared his throat.

'Yes?'

'You're doing all the work.'

This time she laughed, 'Honey, it's not work. I've just been touching you for seven minutes. It's fine to enjoy your body, there are no responsibilities attached to this.'

Her fingers moved gently over him. In the dim light he could see her white body against his brown skin. Usually he lay under covers when he was naked, even with Nina, but there was too much activity going on here to allow that. She jumped down to take a bottle of lotion from her bag; she was going to give him a massage. Obediently he straightened himself.

Not like that. Lie on your stomach.

He found she meant to sit on him.

Firmly, on his buttocks she positioned her own fair bottom, shifting every two minutes to continue the sure, steady movements of her hands. No place was too private for her. Eyes shut, he followed her touch with every nerve.

Two hours later the session was up. As she dressed she told him he had been wonderful, did he know that? It took courage to expose oneself, but he had managed to overcome his uneasiness. Most men took a long time to loosen up. He was doing great, just great.

He doubted that, but Marty insisted that it was so. He should trust her, she had the experience.

In the evening he walked down Telegraph Avenue, looking for dinner. The place was dotted with cheap student places. All around he could see people in every kind of ethnic variation. In Halifax you had to look hard to see an Indian, here the place was crawling with them. He spent a long time just walking up and down the sidewalks, enjoying the warmth, the sight of so many young people, the shops open much later than in Canada, the streets buzzing with life. It had been a full and momentous day.

When he was tired, he went into an Italian joint and ordered a spaghetti bolognaise. Dutifully he tried to finish—he hated waste—but found it impossible. He returned to the hotel, phoned Nina, assured her that the conference was very interesting and then succumbed to jet lag.

Next morning at Carla and Max's, the tape recorder was put on—and the session began. Marty had given them her inputs, now they wanted to know what his experience was: how had he felt when she stroked him, massaged him, was he tense, what were his thoughts.

His thoughts throughout the whole thing had been of two kinds. He had managed to derive pleasure from what she was doing, but there had also been embarrassment and discomfort.

Yes, they said, that was the reason traditional sex therapists preferred to do couple therapy. They felt you could get straight to the point.

Ananda studied his shoes.

So discomfort was entirely understandable, continued Max, and many clients had to work to overcome it. As a medical man, Ananda knew that there were some things you couldn't do yourself, like fixing your teeth or testing your eyes. Even dentistry could be awkward; after all it was an intimate experience, leaning close to a person and putting your hands in their open mouths. We are used to it, that's all. Ananda just had to think of sex therapy in those terms. Embarrassment was also a matter of conditioning and habit.

Ananda agreed. He was spending too much money to do anything else. Of course they were right, it was a matter of conditioning.

They applauded his attitude; it would definitely make things easier.

Tomorrow Marty would continue with her stroking. By now the process would be more familiar and his sole concern should be his own pleasure. It was up to him to get as much as possible out of these two weeks. These methods worked, their success rate was very high. Marty would also teach him breathing exercises that would help reduce tension. And for two weeks he was not to think, to worry, to get anxious or to speculate. All that was their domain, he was only to enjoy himself and (they laughed) do all his homework. His input would decide the ultimate result.

Slowly Ananda walked back to Telegraph Avenue, armed with the tape he had to listen to, along with the little machine that would play it to him.

He ducked into a pizza joint for lunch. Thoughtfully he chewed the slices, barely tasting the pepperoni. What had Max said? He should not be so concerned about what other people thought, this was not an exam. There are no shoulds or shouldn'ts, there is no judgement; whatever he did was him, uniquely him. Every person was different. Towards Max Hansen, Ananda was rapidly feeling all the love a boy feels for his father.

Afternoon, and there was Marty.

This time she stroked his penis, his scrotum, his thighs, murmuring from time to time, 'What are you thinking?'

'What did Max tell you about me?'

'He told me you are more concerned about others than yourself.'

This did not sound too bad. In India one was praised for this.

'Just let go. Take a deep breath, slow and regular. Focus on the air going in and out of your body. You're making very good progress.'

His mind cleared a bit. These people liked him.

In response his penis stiffened.

'I am going to go on doing this, if any thought comes to mind, tell me. Any thought, any fantasy—anything. We're here to help you.'

Her body was warm next to his, her hand persuasive. As instructed he lay back and did nothing, but with more confidence. Maybe this wasn't going to be so difficult after all. Her stroking went on; involuntarily he raised his hand and found her breasts. His eyes flickered shut, and he shifted closer. His wandering fingers touched a slight seam of ridged flesh, and his medical senses awoke. She had had breast augmentation.

'Why did you get this done?'

'To feel good about myself.'

'Were your breasts small?'

'B cup. I wanted a C.'

'Oh.'

'Do you find that strange?'

'So feeling good is important enough for you to undergo surgery?' He had heard that sometimes the silicone leaked, or that the tissue around it grew hard. As a procedure it was definitely non-essential. And how much had she paid for it? There was no insurance that covered cosmetic surgery. She would have had to save for ages.

She giggled, 'Oh I managed, but let's concentrate on you instead. Does the scar disgust you?'

'Oh no, no. I was just wondering.'

'If it does, you can tell me.'

There is only so far one can go to change one's nature. Telling girls who are cradling your penis that their breast augmentation scars are disgusting was beyond him.

'I'm a doctor, I have seen all kinds of things.'

And so the session ended.

That night as he listened to the tapes, he heard himself: hesitant, tentative, unsure, even afraid. He heard Max repeating he should relax in a hundred different ways. It was all very well to tell his little friend down there to relax, but who was listening?

Gloomily he rewound the tape, though it was no fun listening to himself. He heard Carla telling him that he seemed a responsible, caring person, worried about the needs of others. It was about time he worried about his own desires and feelings. He sighed and picked up the phone.

'Hey Neen.'

'You sound in a good mood. Did you have a productive day?'

'Yeah.'

'How is the conference going?'

'These Americans really do thorough research. Some of the papers are very interesting.'

'How come you are not giving a paper?'

'Maybe next time I will. And then you come with me.'

He could hear her chewing something, and the flavour of her peppermint sweets filled his mouth. She would love that, she said. She was feeling lonely, she missed him.

Yes, he missed her too. She would never know how much.

He was sounding quite romantic, teased the wife. Maybe he should go to more conferences in California.

He laughed and so did she, each feeling pleased with the other as they put their respective phones down.

Next day, Max informed him that his session with Marty had seen an important shift in his attitude; her impression was that he had been able to relax and enjoy himself more. What was his own assessment? Had he felt less pressured?

Ananda said he hadn't felt so tense, though he didn't know whether this situation could be replicated in normal life. Perhaps you could lie back and do nothing with a surrogate, but a partner expected more.

There were no rules in sex. In a relationship, he and his partner could work things out in such a way that both received pleasure. It was not all up to him, the things he was learning here were his, to be used in a relationship.

Ananda looked doubtful.

And masturbation, continued Max. What about that?

What about it?

Did he do it? How long did he last?

Ananda was horrified. Of course he didn't do it. He had stopped once he reached college.

Many people suffered guilt over masturbation, observed Carla sorrowfully.

No, Ananda said, he did not suffer guilt. It was something he had outgrown, that was all.

Sexuality was not something one outgrew.

Perhaps, but masturbation was.

That was the traditional view. But it was just another form of sexuality. Besides it was good practice, when he was giving himself pleasure, he had to please no one.

That evening when Ananda heard this tape, he felt he was on the verge of an important breakthrough. Another form of sexuality, giving himself pleasure, it was not all up to him. The words floated through his head inducing a strange state of languor. Sexual feeling flowed through him, he felt young, untrammelled, free.

Two hours later, numbed by the time difference between the Atlantic and Pacific coasts, Ananda drifted off to sleep.

One week was over, and he still hadn't had what he considered sex. When he raised this point, both Carla and Max laughed. Of course he was having sex, it was all sex, every bit of it. The stroking, the touching, the myriad physical sensations. Had he enjoyed himself? Yes, he had. Then he was having a successful sexual experience. There were no goals in sex, they repeated, no point to be reached, nothing to be achieved; the journey was the destination, from the first step on.

Suppose, he queried, he had a partner who did not understand this? Who only focused on the duration of penetration?

If necessary, they could do a one week session together. It would be very detrimental to the treatment if she persisted in this attitude. They could not answer for the consequences.

On the seventh day Marty sat on him, assuring him all the while that all he had to do was enjoy himself, feel the sensations. She interspersed her thrusting with holding his penis in a tight grip, a technique developed by Masters and Johnson and very effective. She taught it to him, so he could practise it during masturbation. During sex he could teach it to his partner as well; she knew of PE cases where the client managed to last the whole night just doing this.

What would Nina think, where had he learned all this from? He would have to tell her. Openness was the key to a good relationship, he knew, but he didn't want to face questions or recrimination. It was his life. Besides, she had told him he needed help.

Marty sensed his attention was wandering, and the inevitable tell me what you are thinking followed.

'I am thinking,' he said, 'that it might be a bit difficult to explain all this to a partner. She may not agree to—you know—do it quite your way.'

Marty smiled. 'Trust me, if she truly loves you she will. It will do wonders to your relationship. My boyfriend also had a little bit of this problem. I didn't mind, but it really bothered him. He worried about it so much that we went in for couple treatment—and he has never looked back. So I speak from experience.'

'Your boyfriend?'

'Yeah. Never looked back.'

'No, but doesn't he mind?'

'Mind what?'

'This. What you do?' How to put it without insulting her? 'Isn't he jealous of your contact with other men?'

Marty was made of sterner stuff. She was in a therapeutic situation and paid to not mind anything.

'It does bother him. But he also understands I'm in a caring profession. I want to help other people.'

There must be other ways, was his intuitive Indian thought, but hey Andy, she's helping you, is she not? Somebody has to do these things, otherwise how would men get over PE, how would the world function?

'Still, I can understand his objections. I don't think I would like my wife—when I have one—to be a sex therapist.'

Marty smiled and said no more.

Next day, Max asked him whether he associated sex with shame? In certain cultures this was normal, but he needed to be aware of what he felt.

Ananda denied everything.

Then Carla asked him whether he had a problem with female sexuality; did he consider it on par with men's?

As a doctor, of course he knew it was on par with men's.

Did he have any problems with Marty's role in his treatment, did he consider her a cheap woman, like a whore?

Of course she would have told them, that was part of the structure, so though Ananda felt betrayed, he was not surprised. 'What did Marty tell you?'

'Only that you thought her boyfriend might have issues with her work. Were you putting yourself in his place? Transference is quite common.'

How he wished he had never opened his mouth. They would think he was not progressive, just another backward, conservative Indian.

There is no emotional right or wrong, but it is essential that we recognise our feelings. For example he might feel uncomfortable with a woman's expressing herself sexually, many traditions equated this with looseness. Being aware would help him deal with it, and he had to deal with it because it interfered with pleasure.

Ananda said he was not sure he agreed with them.

They replied that he didn't have to agree with anything. But he should give these matters serious consideration.

While listening to this tape Ananda wondered whether he was old-fashioned. He didn't feel old-fashioned. The fact that he was doing this therapy meant he was an open, enlightened man. There were some things that Carla and Max could not understand, understanding and sympathetic though they were.

Two weeks later Ananda's therapy ended. He has lasted almost twenty minutes inside Marty. Dr Hansen assured him that his present condition would be permanent as long as he continued to follow the techniques they had taught him. His three thousand dollars had been well spent. Flushed with achievement, he set off for the long journey home. He felt there was a sexual world waiting to be conquered; the prowess he had not had as a bachelor was now his. Nevertheless, the timing of the whole thing was a bit unfortunate. He wanted to test himself in a wider arena, but he had to make sure his wife never got to know. He loved her, but his grief over his sexual ineptness had a much longer history.

*

Nina hadn't realised how much she was going to miss Ananda. In this country he was her anchor. Along with the missing, however, came uneasiness. On the phone he was simultaneously loving and evasive, especially once the conference week was over. He refused to give her the friend's telephone number; she might disturb the household, he would call instead. Was he really in California? She just had his word for it.

She brooded over his behaviour during daily walks that grew progressively longer as her mind grew more disturbed. The short chilly days lent themselves well to her moody shuffling down the sidewalk and into Point Pleasant Park. In the Park she looked at all the dead leaves on the ground, brown, damp, shrivelled, waiting to decompose into the earth and give up their leafy natures. If Ananda was having an affair somewhere with an ex-patient during an assignation that lasted two whole weeks, what would happen to her? Should she return home, announcing her failure to her former world? No, anything was better than that. He would have to give her alimony, she would move out. The cement of children was lacking in this marriage.

The wind whistled past her ears and tore at her bent head. Her hair whipped across her eyes. How much colder would it get, she wondered. When would it snow?

The whole country is air conditioned Ananda had said. What would he say in winter? The whole country is a refrigerator? Let's sell ours and put the food in the snow; we can save so much money.

On the last day of Ananda's absence, Nina got a job. It was perhaps inevitable that her trips to the library would coincide, sooner or later, with a notice announcing the need for part-time help. She gazed at this notice lovingly—an answer to a prayer, another gift from the library—knowing in her heart that this job was meant for her. She was directed downstairs to the head librarian.

Here she put on her charm, 'I come almost every day, this is my home away from home. I used to teach literature in India, now I am getting to know Canadian authors. I am working my way through the stacks, and I would love to unite my knowledge of books with more practical experience.'

This kind of job usually went to graduate students, was Nina sure she would be happy with something so temporary?

Nina was absolutely sure, couldn't be surer.

A few more questions, and the job was hers. It would eat into her time with Ananda at home, but maybe in the new dispensation that would not matter so much. She wondered how he would take the news.

In the meantime Ananda was flying back. It was Saturday, his head was full of his treatment. In the past two weeks, he had experienced more sexual fulfilment than in his whole lifetime. His suitcase was crammed with books Max and Carla had recommended. Perhaps Nina would be interested in reading them. She was a reader after all, and it would allay her fears. In the last week she had been suspicious, demanding to know his phone number, asking him whether he was having an affair, what was the matter, why was he sounding strange?

Nina was waiting for him impatiently. As soon as he entered, she threw her arms around him—where were you really? Why did you sound so peculiar, now tell me the truth.

His own grip tightened, he murmured, I love you, don't get hassled, and carried her to bed. They pulled each other's clothes off. He introduced his penis to her, her old friend and betrayer. Look, this is how you have to hold it.

Why, she demanded.

He told her in the briefest possible manner. I went for sex therapy, I didn't tell you, I felt embarrassed, also I wasn't sure how humiliating it might be for you, but see, see, it's working, it's working. Already I've been three minutes inside.

The sudden information, the realisation that her suspicions were partially justified, the penetration that lasted longer than it ever had, the squeezing of the penis that she now had to do; all this was too much for Nina to absorb.

I am not going to touch it. Why didn't you tell me? You were lying.

Though she tried to break away from him, he held her tightly. She was naked, and he caressed her over and over—sorry, sorry, I had to do it by myself, don't you see, I was so scared I wouldn't succeed. It's been like this for so long.

He put her hand back where it belonged. Tell me, he said, if the end does not justify the means.

She gave a reluctant giggle.

They had sex all weekend.

Ananda kept an eye on the clock next to the bed informing her each time of the minutes he had lasted. Nina was so relieved, pleased and startled by his performance that she was initially quite enthusiastic about his sense of achievement.

Monday morning came. Ananda departed for his clinic, leaving Nina with the whole day to go over what had happened to him, to her, to their marriage. He had staying power, demonstrated twice on Saturday, then twice more on Sunday.

How often had she longed for this? Her body felt sated, its agitation calmed. She moved around the apartment, tidying, putting things away, thinking of dinner, of how she had even forgotten to tell Ananda about her job.

She opened his suitcase to make sure it was empty before putting it away, and there, lying in it, were several books. Slowly she picked up the fattest, *Male Sexuality,* by one of America's leading sex therapists said the blurb.

There were many sections. Male arousal, female arousal, myths about the rock hard penis, better communication = better sex, what to keep away from the bedroom, doing what she wants, doing what you want, breathing exercises, relaxation techniques, masturbation, assertive sex, premature ejaculation, getting what you want out of sex. Scattered through the book were examples of men with problems, and how the sex therapist had helped them.

Nina closed the book and stared at the cloud serrated sky for a long time. Like fertility, sex was another country.

The book certainly gave her more insight into Ananda's problem than Ananda himself had been able to do. Curiously she picked up the next one, *Together Always*. This one, concerned with dysfunctional sexuality, exuded firm and resolute hope. Dr Epstein maintained it was possible to have a good sex life even with premature ejaculation, even with infertility, even if one was non-orgasmic, even through vaginal dryness and pain, even if arousal stages were vastly different. Human beings were not like animals, they came with their own histories and traumas. And the first place any trauma exhibited itself, in its full glory, was sex.

The first place.

The last book, a thinner, more lightweight volume, *Couples in Bed,* had a cover illustration of a beaming man and woman lying under a sheet, bodies entwined, emanating satisfaction and happiness. She opened it. Anal sex, erogenous zones, oral sex, communicating about sex, stroking, massaging, this is ok, that is ok, everything is ok if both of you want it.

As with the other book there was an emphasis on communication along with a great many examples. Good sex meant a good life. She couldn't bear it.

He had gone about the whole thing in such a secretive manner, with his talk of conferences and root canals. That did not seem like very good communication to her.

The books talked about sex and sex therapy with partners. What had it been like with a surrogate, she wondered. He had been gone for two weeks, had he had sex every day with someone else? That was more than they had ever managed to do.

So it was more unusual alone. What did this say about him that he had preferred it this way? The depth of his insecurity, or the depth of his desire to shield her from the prying eyes of doctors? He must have known she was willing to do whatever it took to have satisfying sex. After all, she had suggested couple therapy, but instead of seeing Masters and Johnson together in St Louis, he had preferred to go alone to Max and Carla in California. Ananda's rationalization, that he did not want to expose her to humiliation, made no sense. That decision should have been hers. On the other hand, he did have more staying power, so why was she looking a gift horse in the mouth? Surely it was wise to quietly accept this improved situation, rather than spoil it with questions.

Ananda came home beaming. He threw off his coat and came to embrace her. He had missed her all day, he said nuzzling her neck. Her smell lingered on him, he hadn't showered that morning because of its fragrance.

Nina was not capable of holding onto grievances in these circumstances. He was so much more open and genial, it was amazing. Seeing the change in him made her realise how heavy his burden must have been. They cooked together, they laughed. She told him about her job, he was delighted. He wanted to hear all about the interview, he was sure she had made a good impression. It was gratifying to know that all her reading had come in useful.

After dinner they made love. She felt close to him, lying in his arms, marvelling once more at the change in his performance.

Again her thoughts went to the surrogate. What had she done? Maybe if she knew, she would be able to do the same for him, so that he would not have to lie so much. It was her wifely duty, and now was the time to bring up this issue, before time had dulled its lustre and forgetfulness set in.

His face was pressed against her shoulder, his hand was slack over her breast.

'What was the surrogate like?'

The hand tightened a bit. 'What do you mean?'

'Was she good in bed?'

'Sexual acrobatics was not the point.'

'Did you feel attracted to her?'

'No.'

'Then?'

'It was a professional relationship. Attraction did not enter the picture.'

'But surely it's necessary.'

'You don't have to like the face of your doctor.'

'Still you were able to have sex with her? What exactly did you do?'

'Why do you want to know?'

'So we can do the same things here and you never have this problem again.'

'She wanted to know how I felt.'

'Well, so do I,' said Nina, sounding a little offended.

'It was different.'

'How? You're not telling me how.'

He lost his temper. 'It's obvious how. Sex with your wife can't be the same as sex with a total stranger in a medical situation.'

Vague terms. She withdrew a little from him, his hands on her body heavy blocks of stone.

'You read so much, why don't you read about the role of surrogates in sexual therapy?'

'Right. All the books you have brought home talk of the importance of couples in this kind of therapy, the importance of trust and understanding.'

Ananda crossed his arms on his chest and stared at the ceiling. Nina felt annoyed. Here she was, trying to be understanding, and he refused to reciprocate. 'Isn't a prostitute also a sexual professional?' she asked.

He had not expected his wife to be so narrow-minded, she was the one who had nagged him to seek help, and now she quarrelled with the form it had taken. It looked to him as though she had some kind of ego problem.

Sadly, it seemed to her that even good sex did not ensure a happiness beyond the act. She should not have said anything, confining communication to the non-verbal was perhaps the best thing at this stage. Maybe he hadn't had time to read his books yet.

They did go to sleep, with a rift between them they felt uncomfortable about, but did not know how to remove.

After that night husband and wife observed a truce. Nina did employ the techniques that Ananda had demonstrated on the day of his arrival, he did show her the books he had brought back. Read them if you like.

Meanwhile he timed himself. As a confidence building measure it was essential, he told her.

When it came to counting his thrusts inside her, she rebelled. Ananda, it is about love, it's not only about performance. Even those books say so. She quoted chapter and verse. 'See?' she said, flipping the pages and finding the section, 'see what it says.'

'And see,' he said pointing to another section, 'where it says how to put your partner off. Criticise his needs. Undermine his self-esteem.'

'I don't do that.'

'You do. Don't you see, it's one thing getting over the problem, it's another keeping up with the improvement. I don't want to backslide to the pre-therapy stage. That's a lot of money wasted for one thing.'

He realised his mistake as soon as she asked, 'How much?'

'Oh, with this and that it came to quite a bit.'

'How much?'

'I kept paying in stages, I haven't yet calculated the whole.'

She didn't believe him. He who knew where every cent went.

Quickly he said, 'If it bothers you I won't do it.'

'What?'

'You know, the counting bit.'

A bit warily she smiled at him. 'Thanks darling.

He kissed her. 'Anything for you.'

She leaned against his arm. 'Above all I want us to have a solid relationship, with us sharing everything. You are all I have in this country, you are the reason I am here.'

He tried to reassure her. 'Things are much better now, aren't they?'

'Yes, they are.'

'It's because of you I went for therapy.' He hugged her again.

Left to himself, Ananda whipped out his little notebook, and noted the date, the thrusts, the length of time inside. Nina need not know about these notations, but they really were necessary for his confidence. The longer he could stay in her, the more triumphant he felt, the better pleased with life, the more loving towards his wife. As yet, she was unable to properly appreciate this.

He hid the notebook in his toilet case and zipped it up. Just looking at the figures made him glow with pride. They could go to the gynaecologist now. There would be no awkward questions, no embarrassment. He was ready for anything. The first thing that needed to be done was a sperm test. Maybe he would start with that.

It was good, thought Nina, that in the middle of all these changes she had a new job, a place with purpose, co-workers, timings and salary attached to it. True those timings were in the evenings and weekends, when Ananda was free, but it was only ten hours and he didn't seem to mind. 'Once you have this experience, maybe you can apply for something full time,' he remarked.

The important thing was to get an entry into the system. From small things big things come, but from nothing comes only nothing.

Outside it was very cold, and Ananda sometimes urged her to take the bus to work, but she preferred to walk. It was fun for her to imagine herself an Arctic explorer, braving the elements. By now she had all the clothes required, and the attitude too, as she walked head down, in pants and closed shoes, woollen socks, thick scarf around her nose and ears, camel hair coat with the lining attached.

All around Nina were signs of Christmas. Up went a tree in the foyer of the library, up went imitation snow and Christmas decorations in shop windows. Santas sat enthroned in malls, against huge ceiling-high trees and scenes of the nativity outlined in winking lights. When she and Ananda went shopping she could see boxes of Christmas decorations on sale everywhere. She stared at these shiny things in Lawton's Drugs and Dominion. She wanted them, her fingers itched to beautify a tree, it hardly mattered if such was not their custom. She asked Ananda whether he had ever had one, but no, his uncle's was enough for him.

Still he came home one evening with a small tree in a tiny pot, bought from a woman on Jubilee Road for fifteen dollars, bought specially for her. Even with nothing on, it was perfect.

'I hope nobody will think we are Christian.'

'Who's to see us?'

Her first 20th of December in Canada. Nina was racing against the wind on her way to the library. She was going in early today. It was still light though overcast, the trees were all bare, the branches outlined blackly against a pale sky. Nina's nose was running, a shawl was wrapped around her head, the ends tucked into her coat collar. She was thinking of the letter she had written Zenobia, in which she had joked about her Christmas tree, given details about the part-time job.

This letter contained many lies, mostly of omission. It was so hard to convey the whole truth, everything seemed but partially correct. If only she could talk to her, if only she had a single solitary friend here. As she was thinking this, flakes began to fall. She stopped in wonder. There was much she had forgotten about snow. That it could be so quiet coming down, that it could spiral about so madly as it floated to the ground, that it could be so different from the straighter path of rain. Next to the silence of snow, rain was brash.

She held out her hand, but the flakes melted as soon as they hit her glove. They were also melting on the sidewalk. She stuck her tongue out, but she felt nothing except the cold. Quickly she broke into a trot; she had to share her excitement with somebody.

Once inside the library, she darted to the information desk. 'It's snowing,' she burst out.

The lady looked over the long room to the end where the windows were. 'The weather forecast did predict flurries,' she said calmly. 'Is this your first snow?'

'Not quite,' said the radiant Nina, 'but I haven't seen it for a long, long time.'

'Well, you'll see plenty of it here,' said the lady and went about her business.

Part III

Nina met Beth in the library.

Beth had long brown hair that hung limply down her back, large brown eyes and a face that looked earnestly at the world through a pair of glasses. She was doing her Masters in Library Science.

'What do you do?' she asked Nina in turn.

'Nothing.'

'What's that then?' She pointed at the trolley that Nina had loaded with returned books, and was now arranging spine up, according to code.

'A part-time job, paid by the hour.'

'As is mine. If we don't consider our work important, who will?'

Next Saturday morning, Beth bounded up to her. 'Listen,' she said, taking some books from the cart and flopping onto the carpet next to her, peering at the bottom shelf, 'I'm starting a group—it was one of my New Year resolutions. Interested?'

'Depends on what kind it is.'

'I had in mind a support group designed to strengthen ourselves. We would function on feminist principles but also use co-counselling.'

'Sorry, but I've never heard of co-counselling.'

'Oh, that's all right. Not many people have. In California I was part of such a group for two years. We create therapeutic situations for each other, it's just great. Cuts out dependence on a professional, besides being free and effective.'

'I see.'

'The first meeting is Thursday afternoon. Would you like to join?'

'Sure.'

'Great. Now, I gotta run. I have my story telling session in five minutes. See you?'

Ananda was suspicious. Why was Nina going to meet a bunch of women she didn't even know? He didn't hold with bra burning feminists; why couldn't she continue with that nice group of Sue's? As for sharing her thoughts and feelings, she had him.

'Why shouldn't I join a group? When in Rome, do as the Romans do.'

Ananda was not amused. She had to choose the best from the West, not blindly follow any and everybody. As he detailed his objections, anger submerged Nina. Sharing, when he could go to California without telling her? The La Leche League when she was not even pregnant? Bra burning feminists? If there were any around she hadn't met them, and surely he was too intelligent to stereotype. She was lonely. And she was going to the meeting.

'I need to find my feet in this country. I can't walk on yours.'

The following Thursday at three in the afternoon, Beth drove Nina to Quinpool Road, and stopped outside a large, ramshackle, double storied wooden house, home to ten. They shared rent and household chores and saw themselves as a brave new alternative to the nuclear family.

Inside was light, colour and mismatched furniture that harmonised through the ideological power of the co-op. There were armchairs with colourful throws, a faded brown velvet sofa and a black beanbag. A dark red carpet was spread on the pinewood floor. A huge overflowing ashtray rested on a coffee table which, once a small door, was now stained with many water rings. The bay window had thin white net curtains drawn across, through which could be seen trees and an occasional passerby.

The group comprised of eight women. One Asian, Nina noticed with pleasure. Later she was introduced as Go-Go; her real name, Gayatri Gulati, had been abandoned as too difficult for foreign tongues.

'We all have problems,' Beth started, 'and we all need help, right? Now, how are we going to get it? So far, the only way has been through professional counsellors, therapists, psychoanalysts, usually men, usually with biased attitudes that are considered normal. As a result, male–female power equations are further replicated, with the difference that the woman is now paying for this shit.

'For those who are new to co-counselling it is the theory that in order to avoid dependence, we provide mutual help to each other. In a clinical setup the anxieties and problems women have tend to be treated as neuroses, rather than the result of stress that comes from coping in a male dominated world. Often women feel inadequate, powerless, even sexually vulnerable because of professional therapists.

'The raison d'être of this group is to provide us with a safe place in which to express ourselves, to grow without fear of criticism, where our individualities will be nurtured and strengthened.

'When we feel comfortable with each other, we will chose partners and interact on a one-to-one basis. Twice a month, we will meet as a group to discuss general issues. Questions?'

Suppose they said the wrong thing?

Gave the wrong advice?

Ended up harming instead of helping?

Created dependency without knowing it?

Beth waved a slim blue book. 'Here are the guidelines. Please try and get hold of a copy, if you can't, borrow mine. Obviously I'm not talking of clinical situations, I'm talking of empowering ourselves. We are not, not, I repeat, here to solve each other's difficulties, but to help our partner work through her issues on her own. When you only listen and give no advice, there is no question of saying the wrong thing.

'For starters we could discuss some of the problems we face as women. No one has to get personal, or give details they are uncomfortable with. Above all, we practise absolute confidentiality.'

Maybe some of the details were disguised, but getting personal didn't seem to bother anyone. Nina heard of sexual harassment in the work place, of women having to struggle with housework, child care and a job, while the husband watched TV, of a mother who suspected her estranged husband of molesting their daughter, of a jobless husband who resented every cent his wife made, of infidelities that came in all guises and with all justifications.

As they spoke, Nina grew tense. Her turn was coming. What was bothering her most at the moment? Her inability to conceive or Ananda's going to California without telling her? Among these women, she became conscious of how hostile his secrecy had been; why had she accepted his explanations so easily? She was now less enthusiastic about a baby, but this only made her feel empty. All her expectations of marriage and her future had been bound up in motherhood.

She looked at the faces around her. Eight white, one brown, sympathetic, caring and concerned. As she started to talk, she realized what a burden she was carrying. She yearned to put it down.

So came the story she never imagined telling in these circumstances.

Her husband needed a certain kind of therapy, she would not go into details—they nodded understandingly—and though it was preferable to treat couples, he had lied to her and gone alone. Now she felt used, excluded and angry. He claimed the end justified the means. He accused her of being unsupportive.

She wasn't even sure whether she had any business to object, because indeed the eventual result was good. If she continued to feel resentful, wasn't that spoiling what she had, as well as undermining her husband's confidence? God knew she didn't want to do that. It had come at too great a cost. Alone in this country, she was emotionally, financially and socially, heavily dependent on him.

Nina's words found a tender home in this room. They had all experienced such negation. Blame was a power game, a way of making the woman uncertain and confused. Eventually it could silence her. Whatever his reasons, she had to give legitimacy to her own feelings. It took courage to discuss something so personal, they appreciated that.

Nina felt more alive than she had in days. Talking, sharing, it was amazing what it could do. She looked at her audience with gratitude. Blame, yes, it was a way of silencing. How she was going to fight was uncertain, but she hadn't been wrong to mind, not wrong at all.

Beth now pointed to a little pile of books on the table; some of these are quite good, write down your name and the book you borrow in that notebook.

Nina picked up *The Second Sex*, heard of, but never read.

Lore, graduate student, said, 'That's a good one.'

'I don't know it.'

'"One is not born, but rather, becomes, a woman." The book is still an eye opener for us.'

'Does she say that?'

'Beginning of part ii.'

'You know the book well.'

'I should. I've taught it.'

And the meeting was over.

'How was it?' asked Ananda, standing in the kitchen, frying a steak. There was rice boiling for Nina, yesterday's dal heated, a little side dish of yoghurt with onions and tomatoes cut up, some salad and packaged mashed potatoes. Looking at him she felt guilty. Hopefully, he would never know how she had betrayed him.

'We are going to counsel each other, but that's not all. It's also a feminist group. We borrow books and discuss issues. Look, I got this.' And she laid *The Second Sex* on the kitchen counter, moving to the cupboard to take out plates and glasses.

'Simone de Beauvoir? Is she one of those bra burning woman's lib types?'

'"One is not born, but rather, becomes, a woman,"' she repeated for his information.

'What?'

'That's what she says in this book. She wrote it in 1949, not quite the bra burning era.'

'Why are you reading it?'

'Because what she says is really relevant.'

He looked at her uneasily. 'But why do you want to read such stuff? You are not deprived in any way.'

She stood next to the table, the open book in her hands, turning the pages slowly, apparently unreceptive to his words.

'Well?'

'I read a novel of hers in college, *The Mandarins*. And this book is really well known.'

'Is she famous?' Ananda asked, as they sat down to dinner.

'Uh-huh.'

'Well, eat up,' he ordered, as he grasped his steak knife and lovingly eyed the chunk of meat oozing reddish brown juices. 'Want some?' he asked as he made the first delicate cut.

Nina shook her head and began mashing the dal and rice together with her fingers. From time to time she dabbed frugally at some chilli pickle. She wanted to finish quickly and get on with her book.

But Ananda had other plans. 'Ooh, your lips are so hot,' he said, nuzzling them with his own. 'I can taste the chillies.'

'Really?'

'Um yes,' and he drew her to the bed.

As the act proceeded, she caught his eye on the clock. She pushed it away. It fell with a cracking sound.

'What are you doing?'

'I don't want to be timed.'

'But baby, each time I improve I feel better. Don't you want me to feel better?'

'Of course. But like this it becomes mechanical. I don't like that.'

'This is a real turn-off.' By now he was out of her.

'Your looking at the clock is a turn-off for me.'

Angrily he retrieved his precious clock. 'Is it because you have gone to some meeting and become a women's libber that you are saying all this?'

She said nothing as she understood that one way or another, he was determined to time himself and she had no choice but to agree. The many pages of *The Second Sex* that historicised her sense of powerlessness were still unread.

Though Ananda found sleep, Nina was cursed with wakefulness. Carefully she slid out of bed and walked to the living room sofa, where she could put on the light and start reading her Beauvoir.

She leafed through the first part—she would read all that biological and historical stuff later. Right now she was looking for an answer as to why she was the way she was.

A woman, an Indian, an immigrant.

Which came first?

Her female self, according to Beauvoir. From her first breath, the processes that formed that being were set in motion.

'One is not born, but rather, becomes, a woman.'

Reading, she found much of the text alien, yet she could not deny the centrality of Beauvoir's thesis, that women are defined in relation to men. In the end hadn't she given up everything familiar because of man and marriage?

Tired of her thoughts, she put the book down and turned to the soporific of TV. It was almost one in the morning—when, oh when, would she feel sleepy. The screen flashed to a clip of a couple heaving and panting. As Nina watched, the camera lingered lovingly on shut eyes, moving backs, interlocked hands, hair spread on pillow, again backs humping up and down to the tune of heavy breathing. One, two, three minutes and still not over. Ananda should be watching this, not she. He could count the minutes, assess the similarities, analyse the techniques. Irritated, she switched off the TV.

Next morning she woke with a headache. Ananda, with his usual consideration, quietly made his own breakfast and left, pecking her on the cheek.

'How are you doing with *The Second Sex*?' asked Beth.

'Good.'

'What are things like in your country? You have arranged marriages, don't you?'

'Yes.'

'Jeez, fancy marrying somebody you don't even know.'

'Many people prefer it actually. It has the advantage of social and family sanction, you are not alone to deal with your problems, it is more convenient to fall in love after you marry than before. And certainly it frees you of some of the sexual burden Beauvoir mentions.'

Nina could defend arranged marriages in her sleep, she had been asked about them so often. To her horror, she had even begun to sound like her mother.

'But to decide to spend your whole life with someone you don't even know,' Beth protested. 'It's so weird.'

'If you are used to the idea, it is not strange,' continued Mr Batra. 'The parents, the main arrangers, look at the whole thing dispassionately, taking into account family background, likes, dislikes, income, everything. Often these marriages are greater successes than ones made on the basis of emotion.'

'Yes, but what about chemistry?'

Chemistry was a powerful but impermanent thing. Suppose you were attracted to someone besides your husband, then? A broken marriage and sorrowful children was the result.

But, argued Beth, at least the marriage was built on a strong foundation. Of course everybody had to work at their relationships, but that didn't negate her argument.

219

That was just her point, said Nina. In the East, there was a basis for marriage that went beyond chemistry. Couldn't she see that?

Beth looked doubtful.

'In traditional societies things work differently. And if you are pretty sure you are going to get married, no matter what, the compulsion to attract male attention is not there. For example, at home nobody talks of being too fat, or thin. And then because it is arranged, the whole extended family has an interest in keeping the marriage going. India doesn't have a large divorce rate, for example.'

This was irrefutable, and Nina retired to the stacks feeling vindicated.

Two weeks later, at the co-op house on Quinpool Road.

They sat around and the sharing began.

Nina said she loved *The Second Sex*, but couldn't identify with much of it. It was too—too—*Western*. All that stuff about being objectified, the emphasis on the body, grooming, beauty, sexual attractiveness, she couldn't connect to this kind of consumerism. It's not that women back home were not subjugated, but class and privilege overrode gender issues. Indian society was in some ways, quite feudal. Look at the power vested in the Nehru family. And she herself. Her education and background had privileged her. Even though she was poor, she had the status bequeathed to her by her dead father.

But that was the point, said Go-Go. That status was male derived.

'Underneath the emancipation,' said Lore, 'the Western woman may not be better off than her sisters elsewhere. We have privileges that make it harder to uncover our inner servitude. Without awareness, we can be both manipulated, and manipulative, exploited as well as exploitative.'

They broke for refreshment, congregating in the large colourful kitchen, placing tea bags and instant coffee into mugs, helping themselves to milk and sugar, dipping hands into a packet of cookies that Beth had brought.

As Nina and Beth drove back, Beth said ruminatively, 'I like what you said about Indian women. We do tend to think of women as a universal category, but there are many differences. For example, all that stuff you mentioned about arranged marriages in the library the other day. Made me think.'

'I'm glad,' said Nina gloomily. In fact she wished she hadn't done such a good job defending arranged marriages. It put her in a false position—she hadn't wanted an arranged marriage, had only entered into one when she had no other choice, and after a long courtship. Her marriage—arranged by herself? Fate? Circumstances? Alka? Her mother? Her age? She looked at *The Female Eunuch*, lying on her lap.

'This book was just the greatest,' said Beth, 'My husband loved it too.'

'Your husband reads these books?' Nina asked, as she ignored the rope of envy that pulled against her heart.

'Yes, he does. I said to him, "Honey, you have to keep up with me, I don't want to be going through this stuff on my own." We both lived with step-parents, and know how easy it is to drift apart. What about your husband? What is he by the way?'

'A dentist.'

'Some of these med school guys can be pretty reactionary. Of course not your husband, I don't mean him.'

They were nearing the apartment building. 'I wonder what Ananda has cooked for me,' said Nina. 'Last time he had made steak for himself and rice and spicy yoghurt for me.'

'Wow! Don't you eat the same food?'

'I'm vegetarian.'

'Gosh I don't know where we'd be without our burgers. We can't afford steak, lucky you. See you next week,' said Beth, letting go of the clutch and driving off to her hamburger dinner.

Nina nodded, and walked slowly up the six flights to her waiting meal.

'Hi,' said the husband, bustling about the table now that she was here.

There was her rice and dal, there was her husband, who was interested in where she had been, who was pleased when he saw her, who she knew was committed to her.

She just had to separate her reading from the life she led. What could she do with those ideas churning in her head; could she refuse to be her mother's daughter, refuse to make the best of what she had?

After dinner Ananda put an envelope in her hands.

'What's this?'

'A surprise.'

'Oh really? What?'

'Open it and see.'

```
Quantity: 2.0 ml
Reaction: Alkaline
Liquifaction: Liquified in 20 minutes
Total count: 70 million
Motility:
Active: 85%
Sluggish: 5%
Dead: 10%
Grade of Motility: ++++
Morphology: 90% normal
10% abnormal
Occasional pus cells seen
No parasites seen.
```

'What is it?'

'My sperm test.'

'Sperm?'

'That's right.'

Needing to absorb this, she sat down. 'How come you did this?'

'It was on the cards, wasn't it?'

'Yes, I suppose. But you know, you never said anything.'

'I wanted it to be a surprise.'

Him and his surprises. A little fewer in her life would do very well.

He read her thoughts. 'Now you aren't going to object, are you? I knew it was the next step, and you must admit it was something I had to do alone, anyway.'

'By yourself, yes. Alone, no.'

'You are always finding fault. I thought you would be pleased.'

She scrutinized the swimsuit shaped breasts and pelvis hanging from a rod, which illustrated the cover of *The Female Eunuch*. What would Germaine Greer have done in her situation?

'It was not easy to do, in case you're interested.'

With an effort she said, 'Really? Why not?'

'If you noticed, we didn't have sex for two days. Then I had to masturbate at the testing centre. They had porn there.'

'Porn?'

'*Playboy. Penthouse.*'

His enjoyment seeped into his voice. She glanced at him. 'I guess it's hard to feel erotic in a doctor's office,' she said to keep the words going.

He felt erotic enough in his own, but this the innocent need not know.

'I had to be careful not to spill a single drop. They wanted the whole thing.'

'So, when did you go?'

'Oh, last week.'

And he had just told her.

He looked at her face. He still wasn't getting the reaction he had expected. 'Don't you want a baby anymore?'

'Of course I do. You know that.'

'Well, this is the first step. Or the second, if we count your trip to the gynaecologist.'

'Why shouldn't we count it?'

'We should count it, that's what I said.'

'No, you said *if* we count it.'

He looked at her and saw a mad woman.

She said no more. It was clear the nuance she was pointing to had escaped him. This was going to be another sleepless night. Well, her reading matter was ready.

'So, everything normal with the sperm.'

'Yes, everything normal with the sperm.'

Late that night, Nina shifted to the living room sofa and started perusing *The Female Eunuch*. As with *The Second Sex* much of it didn't sound as though it reflected her situation or those of the women she had known in India. And yet, and yet, it talked of freedom, rebellion, courage and integrity, it talked of joy in the struggle. It suggested that security was not happiness, and that neither depended on fertility or a husband's sexuality.

Late, late, she retired to bed, alone with herself, her future still as unclear as on the day she had wed.

Ananda's sperm was normal. But was it wise to lose yourself in a child, just because you had nothing to do, and these were the expectations with which you had been brought up?

How gently the group would make her examine her feelings, how much less harsh they would be towards her as she decided she was a fool.

The elation Ananda felt at the result of his sperm test lasted many days. All he wanted was to be normal, and at this late age his ambition was being realised. His body was behaving the way it should, his bodily fluids had the required composition, his erections the required duration. If now they didn't conceive he could hold his head high and say it was not because of him. Maybe not because of Nina either, but somehow that didn't seem so crucial.

'My, you look happy these days, Dr Sharma,' said Mrs Hill.

'Indeed Mrs H, life is good.'

Marriage obviously suits him, thought Mrs Hill, he should have gotten hitched long ago. His wife is adapting well from what I saw.

ii

After a month, the group decided they were ready for individual counselling sessions. Each had to chose a partner. When Gayatri chose Nina, Nina found her good manners did not allow her to say, I want Beth. That would hurt Gayatri's feelings and to console herself she reasoned, perhaps it is just as well, Gayatri is Indian, Gayatri will understand. Maybe Beth will always see me in terms of my arranged marriage.

Gayatri's part of town was at a height, curving above the Northwest Arm, gardens with fences, low slung houses, with clumps of now bare bushes softening their corners. Every brick indicated gracious contented living. The struggles of life over, one arrived at the view of the Northwest Arm, and with the spectacle of the sun gilding the water, spent one's happy days.

So Gayatri was rich. Living in a white painted house, green shuttered, with a green front door and a brass letter slat glinting neat and gold in the middle. Behind the fence she could see a black Labrador wearing a red coat. Gayatri had a dog. Gayatri lived in a house on a winding road. Gayatri from India was really from Mars because she had all this.

She climbed the three steps and rang the bell.

Inside everything was plush. A big TV, wall to wall carpeting, with a few richly hued oriental rugs scattered here and there, brass figurines, Indian paintings.

'What a lovely house, such a lovely neighbourhood,' breathed Nina. 'You should see my little apartment, it's so bare.'

Gayatri beamed. 'It is rather nice,' she said. 'But then we have been living here for many years. It's all because of Mummy-Daddy. Don't worry, your time will come. Indians generally do well.'

Still living with her parents, a girl who studied in order to lay claim to a separate identity, who traded in carpets as a pleasant variation. Whose father went to Kashmir several times a year, a girl who spoke in terms of our dealers, our shops, our retail business, our export rejects, whose speech reflected no dissatisfaction with her family or herself. What did she want out of co-counselling?

Then she felt ashamed of her small-mindedness. What did material plenitude have to do with inner freedom? Gayatri was a sister in more ways than one, she needed her support as sisters did in a male world. Thus ennobled, she accepted tea, loose Darjeeling tea, along with mathri and pickle. The flavour of home imbibed, they held hands and looked into each other's eyes, because that was part of co-counselling. Only Nina remained silent.

'Say anything. Anything that comes to mind,' encouraged the co-counsellor.

The loneliness, Ananda's therapy, her sense of betrayal, her mother and Zenobia, the thought of her whole life ahead of her—how, how could she bear it? Obediently she started to describe all this when the tears came, thousands for each of the above. She cried, till her eyes burned, her nose was raw from wiping, the tissue box next to her empty and her lap full of soggy balls.

Co-counsellors are not supposed to advise or probe, they are only supposed to encourage, facilitate and understand, but half an hour later, Gayatri asked gently whether she would like to say anything.

No, nothing.

One hour later, a shaken and limp Nina made her way to the bus stop. Crying was therapeutic, but so long that poor Gayatri could not even have her half hour session? The scale of her tears had been contrary to co-counselling ethics. She thought of Germaine Greer. Did male eunuchs also cry?

'Well, how was it?' asked Ananda in the evening.

A second passed before she answered, 'Do you know where they live? On Myrtle Avenue. Overlooking the Arm. Such beautiful houses.'

'Myrtle Avenue, huh? Hundred thousand dollar properties there.'

'Really?'

'What does she do, this woman?'

'Lives with her parents. They import carpets from India.'

'Why is she in a group like yours? I thought you said it was mostly university people?'

'She's doing her PhD, along with business on the side. Strange combination.'

Ananda said nothing more about Gayatri as they sat down to eat. Instead he held forth on Canada as a land of opportunity. These people she had gone to meet hadn't started from scratch like students. If you came here with money, making money was so much simpler. Then to do business where there was no corruption, no bribes, no bureaucratic inefficiency, no hurdles deliberately put in your way, why, the sky was the limit.

If their house is anything to go by, they have soared, agreed his wife, caught in the coils of jealousy once it was made clear that such a house was available to her as well.

'One day we too will have as nice a place,' said her husband competitively.

'Really?'

'Really. You saw uncle's house. He is a dentist, an immigrant like me.'

'Will our house have hardwood floors?'

'Sure.'

'And a fireplace, with a fire?'

'Of course.'

'A patio where we can cook in summer?'

227

'Why not?'

'How lovely that will be.'

'We live cheaply, it shouldn't take very long. You can also have the kind of silver you saw in Uncle's house.'

'But I thought you didn't like to shovel snow and mow the lawn?'

'With a snow blower removing snow will be easy, and if the grass isn't too long you can mow it.'

'I have never cut grass.'

'I'll help you if it's difficult, but everything here is electric, so you don't have to worry.'

'Ok. But how come you have changed your mind about apartment living?'

What could he tell her? That now he was certified normal, he was ready to enjoy life? That finally his focus could move outside his body, to the city around him? That he knew status was associated with houses and not with apartments?

'We could try and find a house near Gary. Would you like that?' he went on.

Near Gary, near whomever, what did it matter? It was not as though neighbours were interfering in this country. 'Any place is fine, it depends on the price.'

'Naturally.'

Next week it was Gayatri's turn to visit Hollin Court. They drank tea bag tea and held hands as Nina listened to Gayatri. Parental pressure to marry an Indian, and while she wanted to please her parents, she had come to Canada when she was so young, it was hard for her to adjust to the idea of an arranged marriage. Yet it was not as though she had found someone on her own. She loved studying, but she was lonely, very lonely. Kipling was the man in her life, she thought of him day and night. Being in the group gave her clarity. Like Nina she thought a lot of this stuff didn't quite fit the Indian paradigm, yet how could one throw the baby out with the bath water? As a woman, she felt caught between her Indianness, her parent's expectations and her own desires, which she had to admit were confused.

Here a few tears emerged, but they were mere dew drops compared to the flood unleashed by Nina, when her turn came.

A month later, the group met at Quinpool Road for a review session.

'She doesn't say anything, she just cries,' reported Gayatri. Everybody looked at Nina with great interest. Nina blushed, but reminded herself that such reporting is in the interests of awareness. You can't be embarrassed by awareness.

'Why is that, Nina?' asked Lore gently. Waves of compassion and curiosity came from the group.

'I don't want to talk about myself. What can anybody do? They can do nothing, I can do nothing.'

Listening to her, the group thought, this was the woman who had been bold enough to talk about the most personal details in their very first session. Why is she so stuck now? What can we do to help?

Beth said, 'The purpose of the group is to explore yourself, not to offer explanations. It is not important that we know why you are crying, but Nina, it is very important that *you* know.'

'Everything is very strange,' she said in a rush. 'I used to be a teacher, in fact I taught for ten years before I came here. And now I do nothing. I have not even been able to conceive. Am I locked into stereotypical expectations? I don't know.'

'If you really want a baby, that's fine.'

'I don't know what I want. At home it was much clearer. I feel so lost here.'

'Feeling lost is inevitable in a new place—and if you are a woman without a job, far away from your own friends and family, it must be doubly hard. I thought of you when I read this.' Here Lore flipped open her copy of Shulamith Firestone's *The Dialectic of Sex*, page 101. 'Every person in his first trip to a foreign country, where he knows neither the people nor the language, experiences childhood.'

The group nodded, agreeing with Lore. Nina agreed too, though whatever her difficulties, she hadn't considered language one of them. But as a metaphor, yes, she was a child, learning to walk on a different piece of earth.

In the coffee break, she disappeared into the bathroom to stare at her woebegone face in the mirror. Get a grip, she told the reflection. Nothing is going to change, not here, with this group, not with Ananda, not anywhere.

The co-counselling sessions continued.

'You need to do something,' pronounced Gayatri, breaking the rules by offering advice, while brandishing her fine porcelain tea cup.

'I know, but what? I am qualified for nothing.'

Gayatri frowned. 'This group is to enable you, not to encourage helplessness.'

'Didn't I get a job at the library? How am I helpless?'

'Is a part-time job enough? How much do you earn a month?'

'Two hundred dollars.'

'Why are you satisfied with so little?'

Nina had come to Canada in the throes of hope and love, that was why it was taking her so long to adjust to the necessity of a career. She pointed this out.

Gayatri collected herself.

'Listen, you've been here less than a year, eventually you'll find your way. But Indians do succeed abroad; you find them flourishing everywhere.'

The hands on Nina's own felt heavy, while the moisture on her palms grew. The heat was turned on too high. 'If I could get pregnant, it would be so easy,' she said.

'Suppose you never do?'

'I'm not sure.'

'We are conditioned to think a woman's fulfilment lies in birth and motherhood, just as we are conditioned to feel failures if we don't marry.'

'It's one thing to read this stuff, it's another to suddenly start thinking differently. I'm not sure I can do it.'

'In time, perhaps?'

'Time won't do a thing if I can't alter my expectations.'

'By being in this group you have taken the first step towards change. If you didn't feel the need, you wouldn't be here, would you now?'

'True.'

The session ended.

'Should I call a taxi?'

'No thanks, I'll walk.'

Outside it was cold and still. She could see the icy underside of the trees lining the sidewalk. Here and there, the yellow piss of dogs streaked the snow, especially near lampposts. The piles of snow pushed against the side of the road were coated with black. She had not realised how dirty winter could look in the city. Nor how quickly she would tire of being an Arctic explorer.

Once inside her apartment, she sank into the red vinyl bean-bag she had persuaded Ananda to buy in order to (vainly as it turned out) enliven their place. She looked out of the window. Though not yet four, it was almost dark. She could hear the wind howling around the apartment. Whatever life she hoped to have in this place, she could no longer go on walking to her destinations and count the journey part of the experience. It was too cold, the wind too biting.

It was true, she might never get pregnant, never have the meaning of her life automatically granted to her. She and her mind were going to be on their own, with crying jags at co-counselling sessions, that revealed ghastly inner depths into which she would rather not venture.

When Ananda had come, it had been easy for him. He had enrolled in the Dal Dental School and now he was a respected member of society.

She thought of Miranda House. To replace such a job, she would have to enrol for a PhD, repeat MA courses, then bolster her cv with academic publications. Those years and those tasks were like huge boulders pressing the life out of her—though every year people left her country in droves for just such futures. Maybe she could be like Beth, study to be a librarian. She could continue what she was doing, but with respect and a future. As a part-timer she only got minimum wages, it was essentially a student's job; under thirty five hours a week.

She heard the key in the lock. Ananda was home.

Ananda had also given some thought to her problem. 'You should do a B Ed, then you can teach in a school.'

'I don't want to. I used to work in a *college*.'

'So what? The schools here are not like those at home.'

'No schoolchildren—no matter where they come from.'

'So you tell me, what is it that you have in mind?'

'How about a library degree?'

'A library degree?'

'It's worth trying.'

In reality neither of them knew much beyond doctor, lawyer, teacher, engineer, bureaucrat—these species that came out of the Indian middle classes.

'Well, why not?' said Ananda slowly, considering the idea of his wife as a librarian. He would make a brief phone call in his uncle's direction tomorrow.

'If I don't like it, I can always switch.'

This gay assumption struck him as frivolous. Thoughtlessly she would spend time, money and effort, as well as take up valuable space in a professional course. Though the West was about choice, those choices claimed responsible appraisal. 'Life is not a game. If you are so unsure, why go through all the trouble?'

'Because I have to do something that ensures me a job I am suited for, where I won't take forever to qualify.'

And that would give her independence, she thought but didn't say.

232

At the very least it would give her focus and take care of her moods, he thought but didn't say, and then admired himself for his positive thinking. If only his wife could learn from his example.

Ananda was disappointed with Nina's response to his sperm test. He had expected her to be more appreciative that there was nothing wrong with him. Now he was left with the disagreeable feeling that it was up to him to push the fertility tests through. Granted he had said they would be expensive, and that insurance did not pay for them. But he had never meant they should not investigate. Irritated he accosted her—what happened, first you were very enthusiastic, you found a doctor and had a checkup, now when it is time for the next step, you suddenly lose interest?

She looked up blankly from the book she was reading. 'Lose interest?'she repeated.

'In our child.'

He was maligning her maternal instincts. 'I could never lose interest in our child,' she retorted.

'Then?'

'You were right—it's too soon. I have to find my feet... '

'I know, I know. You can't walk on mine.'

'Exactly.'

He didn't understand what was so special about her feet. Immigrants had to find their way, of course, but instead of following his advice, she preferred to go to some women for help. He hoped their child would make the family more whole, give them all a greater sense of belonging. 'We can still go ahead with the tests. They may take a long time, and we aren't getting any younger.'

She smiled at him wanly. It was nice that he said we when he meant you. If only this heavy feeling would lift from her heart. 'I don't know,' she began and stopped.

He controlled his exasperation. She was going to ramble, and at the end of it all his head would spin. Studying literature for over ten years took you away from the real world.

233

'I miss home—I miss a job—I miss doing things. I feel like a shadow. What am I but your wife?'

'That's a good place to start,' he tried to joke. She didn't answer, merely sat there looking at the closed book in her lap, her finger inserted between the pages, some dreadful looking book with a female torso slung from a rod.

'I'll let you go on with your reading,' he said sarcastically.

She bent her head, annoyingly taking his advice.

Later Ananda thought that Library School was a good way to explain to the world why there weren't any children. Not that anybody was asking. But in the two years it would take for her to finish, anything could happen. The pressure to become pregnant would be reduced, and the whole thing would happen naturally.

Meanwhile he too should take advantage of this time to do a little exploring of his own. He had a secret that gave him a frisson of pleasure whenever he thought of it.

It doesn't rain but it pours.

A life that three years ago was a desert so far as women were concerned, now had a wife and a mistress. The first had lead to the second. And the second had made all the moves.

Poor Mr Hill had broken her leg and needed to rest for two months before she returned to work.

Mandy was the result.

She was young, ten years younger than him, it later turned out. This was her first receptionist's job. The third Friday she had said she would stay back and sort out some records. Ananda, it so happened, needed to stay back too. Their first fuck happened there on the hallway carpet. She was so uninhibited, all over him, kissing, licking, sucking.

'Please,' he protested modestly, his voice faint, 'what are you doing?'

'You are my first Indian,' she said, 'When I saw you I wondered what it would be like.'

'Do you always think things like this about the men you meet?'

'Sure, don't you?'

'I'm a man.'

'Oh, come off it. Hasn't anyone told you that men and women are not that different?'

Ananda was nothing if not a professional. He couldn't carry on an affair with the office receptionist, and he waited impatiently for Mrs Hill to come back. 'No more, my darling, not until she returns.'

Mandy was not however the slave of circumstance. 'What about my place?'

'Where is that?'

'Clayton Park.'

'That's pretty far.'

'It's all I can afford.'

He knew no one there. Yes, Clayton Park suited him.

'So how about this Saturday?'

'You are free on Saturday?'

'My wife works at the library, it's a part-time job she has.'

'Holy shit, I wouldn't work on Saturday, not if you paid me double.'

'Well, sweetheart, she's not like you.'

'I can see that.'

So Saturday afternoon saw Ananda driving to Mandy's apartment in Clayton Park. She lived on the seventh floor: two rooms, a TV, wall to wall carpeting, mattress on the floor, beanbags.

'Can't afford much,' said Mandy as she followed Ananda's eye.

'Hey, you should have seen me as a student. I had nothing for years and years.'

'But you've been a doctor for a while, surely?'

'I had debts to pay, and I'm perhaps not as old as you think.'

She giggled. 'Come here.'

He may have been the doctor, older and definitely more educated, but in ways that surpassed his imagination, she soon demonstrated who was the expert in the field of love.

He went home that first afternoon in a slight daze. A—he had committed adultery. His wife must never know. B—there was no way he could give this up. It was too splendid a thing. C—life was full of surprises and new experiences. He owed it to himself to do them justice.

'Hi,' shouted Nina, as he walked into the apartment.

'Hi, darling,' he replied.

She waited expectantly for his kiss, but he scurried into the shower instead. Mandy had given him a shower, but the smell of sex still lingered in his nostrils.

Nina heard the water running, and her heart sank. That meant sex, meant the clock, meant postponing the shopping till they had finished, and dinner would be late. Still, it was the weekend, they didn't have to be on such a tight schedule.

Fifteen minutes later, a freshly shaved, damp, fragrant husband put his arms around his wife. 'How're you doing, baby?'

Baby. She cringed, then ignored her feminist reaction. 'Fine. And you?'

'Never better. Shall we?'

'Sure. But what about the shopping?'

'Later. This is more important.'

He lifted her, she put her arms around his neck. Ananda was being so romantic, it was rather wonderful she had to admit, even if he did call her baby. And the best part was that he didn't look at the clock even once.

Ananda found everything about Amanda exciting. He loved her hair, a fine pale gold, darkening slightly towards the roots. Even after he realised that some of its more dazzling effects came from a bottle, he continued to be dazzled. And her skin—unless you made love to a white woman, you did not realise what fair really meant.

He was mesmerized by its slightly mottled hue, its blue veins, the pinkness of her nipples, her delicate eyelids, the thinness of her skin. He bought a small travelling clock and placed it next to the mattress.

'What's this for?' demanded the mistress.

'I need to time myself.'

'But baby, you're doing great.'

'It's not that. It's part of the doctor's orders.'

'Which doctor? Gary?' she giggled.

'No, the ones in California.'

The story came out. 'But baby, you should have come to me,' said Mandy.

'I would have, if I had known you.'

'Well, now you do, and if you paid them, you have to pay me.' She looked so knowing, so young, so after his money in such an obvious way, so willing to be his, that he could barely bring the next words out. 'How do you mean?'

'A dollar for every minute you are inside me. Any part, baby,' she whispered, slithering between his legs, and drawing his penis deep within her mouth.

He agreed.

It became a game with them—how much money he owed her. Mandy kept the notebook, writing down the figures while Ananda held her on his lap. Every time it reached fifty dollars they would spend it on furniture or clothes for Mandy, charged to his credit card, chosen from a catalogue. Ananda had never thought an Eaton's holiday special could be such an erotic object.

She was so inventive, he was amazed.

'How do you do it,' he murmured, 'my new found land. My Newfoundland.'

'Hey, I'm not a Newfie,' said the ignorant Mandy.

'It's from a poem by Donne. When my sister came home from college for the holidays she used to read out poetry to me. She said she didn't want me to become a one dimensional science type.'

But Mandy was not interested. Her curiosity was directed towards his wife.

'Didn't you say your wife used to teach English?'

'Yes. In the same college where my sister studied in fact.'

'Is that how you met her?'

'Through my sister, yes."

'Your sister arranged it?'

'In a manner of speaking.'

'Couldn't you find someone here?'

'Oh, her father died, she wanted to emigrate, so I married her. It was to help her really.'

'That was nice of you.'

'I'm a nice guy.'

'So it was just a marriage of convenience, right?'

Even a blind man could see where the innocent Mandy's questions were leading, but a married man can always play for time.

'Well yes, but I'm responsible for her. She has to get settled first, poor thing, she feels quite lost here.'

'Mandy—Andy, our names match.'

'They do indeed.'

Afternoons such as these fixed Ananda's thoughts quite firmly on Nina's future education. His wife was so trusting, so easy to deceive that his love for her increased exponentially. 'Any time you want my help just let me know,' he frequently said, as he watched her painstakingly go through the Library School prospectus, tick possible courses and double-check her choices with Beth on the phone.

'Thank you, darling.'

'You know how much I want you to settle down. Then you'll be happier.'

'It's better now that I have this to do. Otherwise all one thinks about is how infertile we are.'

'I'm not. Don't you remember that report?'

'Yes. But the doctor said I was ok too, remember?'

'I'm always willing to go for further checkups, that's why I even went and got my sperm tested.'

This conversation was supposed to be about her happiness, not their shortcomings. With an effort she put it back on course.

'Now I have got this to look forward to, I feel more settled, don't fret about me.' She smiled at him. 'You really are a worrywart, you know.'

So, he had her permission, albeit inadvertent, to go back to his secret life, to linger over scenes of sex and passion with Mandy, to compare the two in bed.

Mandy encouraged him to be wild, free, uninhibited, playful. With Nina he was his mother's son, his sister's brother, the good husband, playing out a role he had been trained for since childhood. Nine years in Canada had not dimmed the need to be this person.

No wonder he had not been able to succeed with white women before. He needed to stabilise this part of his life. There were too many unseen pressures that had spoken through his body. He smiled lovingly at his spouse.

'What are you grinning at?'

He shook his head—nothing, it's nothing.

Over Christmas and into the New Year, Nina worked at her application processes. In grave oversight she had left her degrees at home. Now her mother dug them out of the cupboard, went to the market to make photocopies, went to Miranda House to collect references from her daughter's former teachers, as well as certificates testifying to the length of her teaching experience. She sent the whole thing to Nina by air mail registered post. Nina counted the rupees stuck on the packet and mailed back a hundred dollars that would cover every incidental expense. This lessened fractionally the guilt she felt about the trouble to which she had put her mother. Locally, her only task had been to get a testimonial from the HRL.

Nina spent weeks over the essay that would accompany her application.

Why did she want to become a librarian, how did she think she could contribute, what were her goals?

Difficult. She didn't know what her goals were, but that was not something anybody need know.

Glibly she wrote about her proficiency in English, her long study of literature, her love of books, her eagerness to combine the skills she had been taught in India with newer ones acquired in this country, her wish to contribute to society.

She didn't believe all she was writing, because she was nervous about a profession that wasn't completely academic. I can always change track if I don't like it, she told herself, this is a place that allows change.

Ananda repeated her assurances right back to her. 'The important thing is to start somewhere. You don't want to teach in a school, you can't teach in a university, what options do you have? I've talked to people, it's a good career,' that is, Mandy had a cousin who was a librarian.

'Really? Who?'

'Some patient. I mentioned my wife was joining Library School and you should have heard her go on. Wonderful occupation, much better than working in an office, you meet a lot of people, jobs are comparatively easier to get.'

'Yeah, Beth says the same.'

'In life you have to have courage.'

'It's a professional course.'

'That's what you need, don't you?'

He was being so supportive she decided it was churlish to hold on to her grouse about the California trip. Maybe there were some things a man had to do alone. And maybe it would have been unpleasant and embarrassing, revealing such private details before unknown American doctors. Hours had been spent over this issue with Gayatri and the group, now she was bored by it. It had stopped bothering her; she let it go.

He was becoming a better lover too; she hardly had to resort to herself. In deference to her, he had even stopped looking at the clock. She owed it to him to stop complaining about his transgressions.

On the last day of January, Nina dropped off the first part of her admission form at the Registrar's office, and the remaining part at the office of the Assistant Administrator, Admissions, Library School. For all her doubts about this as a career, she hoped she would be accepted. In four weeks she would be coming this way again to submit her application for a scholarship.

The pavement was flecked with pellets of salt, there were huge banks of snow on either side of the path. Her boots had a little leak in them, she had not applied enough water repellent, and the salt had traced wavy lines along the surface of the leather, making them look hideous. Her toes felt like tubes of ice. The sky was a pale blue with strips of cloud. With the wind chill factor, it was definitely below zero. In Delhi at this time, flowers were beginning to bloom, the gentle sun would be caressing all its denizens, and everybody would be out in gardens, parks, roundabouts, relishing the few weeks before the heat came.

She took a slight detour, reached the warm red façade of Fader's, entered the drugstore, sat on a high stool at the small sandwich bar near the window and ordered a strawberry milkshake. The course description lay in her bag and she took it out to read again. It sounded technical and different from anything she was used to. Perhaps her love of books had made her a maverick.

The next time she walked to the Killam Library, it was for an interview with the head of the Library Science Department, Dr Claude Cunningham. The weather had changed. No need to wrap a shawl around her head, wear her heavy, ugly coat or walk against an icy wind. The sky was overcast, but the air had a warm undercurrent to it. The huge piles of dirty sidewalk snow were melting, here and there some blades of grass could be seen.

Dr Claude Cunningham was a lovely man with an English accent, interested in her qualifications, her experience in libraries, how she saw her future, why had she switched from teaching, why not go in for a B Ed, or a PhD, might her bent not be more academic?

At this Nina paused, but the thought of the stiff competition for thirty five seats decided her against complete honesty. Her year at the HRL had shown her how much there was to libraries, she wanted to deepen that knowledge.

The Head was receptive. Her hours there could qualify as the work experience that was compulsory. She did realise that graduate school was full time, any job that took more than ten hours a week was discouraged? Yes, she had read the brochures, yes, thank you Dr Cunningham, thank you very much.

When Nina told Ananda about the interview, and that Dr Cunningham had talked as though she were already part of the school, Ananda's confidence soon overshadowed her own more tentative hopes. 'There is no doubt you will get in. You read so much, you have work experience, you have been a teacher of literature, you are serious and steady. In fact I am hoping for both admission and financial assistance.'

Nina looked at him gratefully. Things were getting better between them, the early despair and uneasiness had slowly abated.

A few months later Nina got the letter they had all been hoping for.

She stared at it, this promise of a degree recognised by the Association of Commonwealth Universities, and with it the possibility of a job anywhere in North America.

Ananda was triumphant. The fee waiver especially moved him; this is a generous system, the worthy are always helped. Of course its renewal was dependent on an A average, but Indians always excelled, nothing to worry about.

Her admission warranted a phone call home. Her mother's response was predictable, first the warmness of approval, then the anxiety that sounded like accusation. As a student, would she be able to give Ananda enough attention? Might she not be a drain on his resources? And did this mean she was postponing having a child, she would soon be thirty three.

Nina gritted her teeth. Her mother was such a vehicle of patriarchy, why was her concern for her daughter always expressed through worry about Ananda's well-being? As for a child, both of them thought they could still wait a bit, she wasn't that old after all. Besides, if it didn't happen, it wasn't the end of the world.

'Don't worry, Ma,' shouted Ananda into the phone, 'this is wonderful news. With a fee waiver it'll hardly cost anything, and she'll have a Canadian qualification.'

The mother was forced to be content with things not having turned out the way she had imagined. Pictures of children and a loving grandmother grew dimmer.

From the uncle there was wholehearted approval. Respectable integration always to be welcomed, and beti, don't worry if this doesn't pay very highly, you have a doctor for a husband. Gainful occupation is more important than money in your case.

The group was pleased. From being controlled by circum-stances, Nina was taking the first steps towards autonomy.

Sitting across from her Gayatri felt all the pride of a parent. Of course Nina would perform brilliantly, and keep her scholarship.

Beth told her she would never regret her decision; she had loved every minute of her two years at Dal. Now that she had gotten a job for fourteen thousand five hundred dollars at Acadia University, she and Jerry were moving to Wolfville.

Her colleagues at the HRL greeted the news with enthusiasm. Nina had taken a bag of small chocolate bars to work—trying to replicate the distribution of sweets such news would engender at home.

The ones Nina felt least close to were the most elaborately rewarded. Gary and Sue were treated to dinner at La Gondola, down by the train station. The atmosphere was warm; the wall-paper red velvet, the place crowded, the candles on each table romantic. The paper napkins bore the legend of Papa Gino, poor boy from Italy, now enterprising immigrant. She hoped she would be as successful as Papa Gino.

The two couples talked and laughed and everything seemed right.

The rest of the summer passed in anticipation of fall. Nina noticed her status had risen, both in her group and in her place of work. She was following the path her husband had trodden when he came here all those years ago, getting a degree that would affect the makeover of her Canadian identity. Two years was a small price to pay for such a metamorphosis, said Ananda.

iii

When Nina's life as a student began, she was afraid she would not only be the sole foreigner, but also the oldest among thirty four young Canadians, sticking out like a sore thumb.

But she had underestimated the wide reach of North American education. The thumb had companionable fingers—there was a student each from Malaysia, Lesotho, England and the USA. Others from Saskatchewan, Alberta, Quebec and Ontario also claimed foreigner status, while fifteen came from the Maritimes. As for age, one woman mentioned a grandchild, several mentioned children, many mentioned spouses.

For the next two years, hers was the comfort of being part of a student body, no longer the outsider, one of many bound together by a huge, squat, grey institutional building, five floors high, crammed with books, learning and administration.

Ananda was fond of constantly reminding her how lucky she was. Unlimited facilities were at her disposal. She thought of the torn, vandalised books she had had to do with in Delhi

244

University, of all the texts it was impossible to get, even in a library, and she agreed wholeheartedly.

The technical aspect of the course was apparent from the start. If she had doubts about learning to do rather than think, she reminded herself that for an immigrant changed situations meant changed priorities. Her group assured her she had to move in ways that enabled rather than disabled her.

In accessing books for others, she had to learn how to wield the keys to what lay within, rather than open the locks herself. In the first semester, there was a whole course on how to catalogue, pin, fix and locate the quantities of print that had been spewed into the world since Gutenberg's invention in the mid fifteenth century. From reports to books, skittish behaviour was common, as texts refused to confine themselves to one category.

The Killam collection was catalogued according to the Library of Congress system, while the lab in the Library School had books catalogued under the Dewey Decimal system. Students were expected to know how to use both, to be able to decide where a book's rightful place was in all the miles of library shelf. They had to know how to look up reference material and track down articles. Nina's respect for professional librarians grew. This was the grind they passed through before earning themselves places behind reference desks in the libraries of North America.

Now Nina was the one to get up first, before Ananda. Her day started at eight thirty, whereas he only had to be at the clinic by nine. It took fifteen minutes to walk to the Killam. On the mornings she was too tired to get up early, Ananda would drop her.

She worried that he might mind the hours spent away from home. 'I know how hard a student has to work,' Ananda assured her. 'Since we don't have children, it's not such a sacrifice.'

Damning words. She searched his face for signs of grief, but there was none.

'Do you mind?'

'You didn't seem much interested in my sperm report.'

'Healthy sperm doesn't necessarily lead to a baby, otherwise we would have had one by now.'

'We'll examine our options when your course gets over.'

'Yes, we are in the land of technology.'

'Exactly.'

As Nina walked to and from the university, brilliant leaves showered their benefits on her and turned her preoccupied mind to beauty. Her second fall here, her sense of wonder was still as keen as she watched autumn colours shade into the austerities of winter. She often emerged from school when it was dark, and wanting to shake off the sense of closed spaces, she chose to walk home, instead of calling Ananda or taking the bus. All through the long winter she walked, through the snow, the wind and the drifts. For the second time, she marvelled at the intricate designs made by bare branches outlined against the sky. Initially so dark, branches and twigs whitened under puffy snow covers, then in times of slight warmth and subsequent freezing, became encased in slick and shiny ice, lengthening into points here and there. She wrapped the warmest of her shawls around her head, trying to protect her ears against the burning cold, trapping the moisture of her breath against her skin.

One of the drawbacks of the Killam was that classrooms were completely sealed off. Most of the library sessions took place in room 406, on the fourth floor, around the corner from the Department. It was a room of three stone walls, with curtains on the fourth side shielding them from the corridor. Push those aside, and you could see an identical wall on the opposite end of the concrete quadrangle.

Gradually Nina got used to being cocooned in white fluorescent light. The claustrophobia receded along with memories of how open everything was in India. Her old self was, day by day, overlaid by the new things she was experiencing.

At Library School, they considered themselves a self-contained family unit within the larger university framework. They had their own lab, reference sections, classrooms, lockers, notice boards, coffee and tea centre with oven-toaster and fridge, an informal seating area where they had what they called fireside chats with the head once a week to discuss department news. As a scholarship student, Nina had to look after the lab on the other side of the staff rooms, re-shelve books, make sure the room was clean and tidy before their get-togethers.

Friday noon was usually reserved for guest speakers. The second time Nina saw the librarian of the HRL was when she came to talk about issues of censorship at the local public library and how to handle them.

By Friday evening, a party feeling pervaded as staff, students and spouses gathered over drinks. When Ananda came, he let it be known that he was a graduate of the Dental School, a place where his uncle and his partner sometimes gave lectures to dentistry students on Friday afternoons. Maybe when Nina became a librarian and brought home the bacon, he could become a student again and specialise.

The nascent librarians looked at him, smiled, nodded and appeared interested. For the first time he was socialising with people Nina knew, instead of the other way around. She found she was afraid he would say something to demonstrate how Canadian he was. All said and done, she preferred the smaller gatherings.

iv

Among the students of the Library School was one who looked upon Nina and found her attractive. Anton liked Asian women; he found them warm, intelligent, gentle and empathetic. Settled in America, he himself was two generations away from the Russian peasant. His hair was blonde, short and curly, his skin somewhat weather-beaten, his small eyes a bright blue, his hands and body square, his height medium.

During coffee breaks he often headed towards her, 'My wife is Indian,' he said.

'Indian?'

'Like you. Though she speaks differently.'

'What part of India?'

'It's the West Indies. Trinidad.'

Foreigners understood nothing. 'We don't consider that India.'

'Her grandparents came from your country.'

A pause.

'What does your wife do?'

'She's a nurse in a children's hospital.'

'How come you are in separate places?'

'It's cheaper to study here, and the American Library Association recognises it.'

The break over, they drifted back to class.

Before one of the get-togethers: 'Introduce me to your husband.'

Nina couldn't think of one thing they had in common, but replied, 'Sure—if he comes. He can't always attend. I used to work part-time on Friday evenings, so he started fixing to do other things then.'

'What is he?'

'Dentist.'

His face crinkled. 'I don't think I know any dentists. This will be a first.'

'Yet your teeth are perfect.'

'I mean socially. I was too scared of my dentist to ever want to know her.'

'Ananda is not at all frightening.'

'Or what would you be doing with him?'

*

When Ananda did come, Anton sought him out, but found him full of Canada, his dental setup and his achievements. His wife's brother, a little less genuine than his Lakshmi, also tended to talk like this; maybe some male immigrants caught the competitive bug easily.

'I see you have met my husband,' remarked Nina, the Monday after.

Anton smiled his brilliant, white, even-toothed American smile.

'Yeah.'

'Well, what did you think?'

The smile went as he looked at her. 'Not good enough for you,' he said, and turned deliberately into class. She was left confused—which meant that Anton had succeeded in his intentions. Their first field trip in December was his target. By then he hoped to persuade her into something more intimate.

Library School assumed an excitement for Nina that she hadn't anticipated. Everybody was so nice and friendly. By now she and Anton had fallen into a bantering relationship. They were both married, and to keep things clear, she made frequent references to his wife and her husband. He in turn would grin and turn the conversation back to some personal aspect. Were all women from her country as intriguing? Why, Nina countered, did he want her to generalise about millions of women? And so on—inconsequential, but for the undercurrents that made each word significant.

Soon it was accepted that they had lunch or coffee together. He was easy to talk to, but her tendency to linger over what he said bothered her. Here in Canada, men and women often connected on platonic levels, it was such an immigrant-like thing to be disturbed by some man who paid her attention. Perhaps she should go back to India. No question of platonic levels there. Every male–female interaction was suspect.

In December Ananda paid three hundred and fifty dollars so that his wife could go to Ottawa to tour the National

Library, the National Science Library and the National Archives.

Mandy entirely approved of the field trip. 'Who knows, maybe she'll take a lover there,' she teased, watching Ananda's face.

The husband regretted the impulse that had made him tell Mandy about Nina's trip. He normally preferred to keep the two parts of his life separate, but the prospect of all that lovely free time had dented his usual caution. 'My wife is not like that,' he said briefly, and it was the words 'my wife' that led to their first fight.

He supposed she was *like that*, hissed Mandy, well, he could take his fucking clock, get out of her life and stay out. She was tired of being second. He should get his priorities right.

It took an hour and many promises to calm her down. For the four days that Nina was going to be away he would spend every night with her. He would show her his apartment. He would take her out for dinner. Now he had to go.

Mandy knew he was referring to the function at the Library School, something she always made it very difficult for him to attend. All summer, Friday evenings had been hers, the wife had her part-time job, she had the husband. She saw no reason for this arrangement to change.

How on earth did people manage affairs, wondered Ananda. They were not as he had imagined, smaller versions of a relationship; they functioned on another plane. The many lies and exhausting time juggling that went into meeting, heightened the intensity of each encounter. He and Mandy made love in its rarefied atmosphere, and he frequently told her he would die without her, she was his saviour.

Filled with the guilt of this, he couldn't fight with Nina even when she was irritating him. This artifice lessened their relationship and made it seem superficial. Love for Nina began to wear the face of responsibility, and when he was with Mandy he naturally felt less burdened.

Sometimes his life seemed unreal to him; all his desires were being fulfilled after his marriage. He wished he felt a little happier, but now the only place he was fully himself was when he was peering into people's mouths. Then everything fell away; he was doing something he was good at and which brought him recognition.

As he drove home from his assignation, he thought of the empty spaces marriage had filled, the comfort of routine, the daily companionship, the substance that his parents had been trying to provide him with when they died, now at last his. It was marriage too that had given him Mandy; in his mind his wife and his mistress were inextricably linked. He neared Hollin Court and automatically began to think about the evening menu. Nina was going away, he wished he had time to make her something special, but Indian food was so labour intensive, he often ended up unfreezing the batches of dal he made on the weekends. That, along with rice, cumin peas and raita, would be her monotonous dinner.

Ananda parked his beloved Saab, quickly had a shower to get Mandy's smell off him, put the rice on to cook, took out a portion of dal from the freezer, cut up onions and tomatoes that he would fry to spice it up. Thankfully they always ate late on Fridays.

The doorknob turned. There was his wife, somewhat paler than usual, but then, she did insist on walking in all weather.

'Dr Cunningham asked about you. I was hoping you would come.'

'I told you I couldn't.'

'Still, I was hoping.'

'Well, we are together now. Come, I've made you your dal. And the rice is about to be done.'

'I'm sick of rice and dal.'

He looked at her in surprise. 'I thought you enjoy what I make.'

She did, and was very thankful that he took care of all the meals. 'I don't know what's the matter with me.'

'Well, you can always try meat.'

It was a meaningless statement. She wished they could connect more. 'Why don't you come to Ottawa next weekend?' she now asked—what a brilliant idea, she would kill many birds with this one stone.

His back was turned. 'I'm not sure that's such a good plan. You'll be working, what will I do?'

'Only from Monday to Thursday. Some spouses are going up on Friday for a holiday. We could also have one. Have you even been to Ottawa?'

No, he hadn't.

'Then it's an opportunity. Come on, Ananda, we hardly spend any time together.'

'That's because you are so busy.'

'I know. It is getting a bit much.'

'Who wants to go to Ottawa in the winter? They say spring is the best time. It's sister city to some Dutch place and thousands of tulips bloom then.'

His entanglements meant he could never spontaneously agree to anything.

Nina put her arms around him. 'Tulips may bloom in spring, but in all these years you have never seen them. Why start now? Please come. Library Science is taking up my whole life.'

'Well, you seem the happier for it.'

She stared at him doubtfully. Was there sarcasm behind those words? 'What do you mean?'

'Nothing. What should I mean?'

'I don't know. Never mind. What about us?' And what about the fragments of her scattered self lying about the place? They needed to be collected by her husband's hands and kept close to his chest.

'I'll definitely try to make it. Ok?'

Gary was delighted when Ananda told him he might join Nina in Ottawa. Ananda began to feel he had little choice in the matter; in some ways he desired Gary's approval more than Nina's.

Two months earlier he had told Gary about Mandy, a revelation that turned out to be a terrible mistake. His motives had been simple—by sharing his secret with his best friend he had sought to extend his pleasure more fully.

He had invited Gary for a drink; it had been so long since they had gone out together. A pub was needed in order to fully savour his friend's reaction, to perhaps even indulge in confidences regarding Max and Carla, so long withheld, to share with him the triumph of his sexual progress.

But Gary proved unreceptive, despite the close, smoky atmosphere of the pub, despite the beer they were drinking, despite the chips and peanuts they were munching. The Dental School Gary, the one who slept around and urged him to do the same, had disappeared into a strait-laced father of three. 'Everybody feels like straying, man, doesn't mean you do it. You got her all the way from India, like just yesterday. Now you have telescoped the seven year itch into less than two. No fair, man, try and give it up, it just gets worse. Otherwise divorce will be the result. I've seen it happen every time.'

After this judgemental attitude, never before seen in his friend, any mention of the trip to California was unthinkable. Instead Ananda was reduced to making lame excuses for his behaviour: arranged marriages—not like here—same expectations don't apply—which even he could tell made him sound like a callous bastard.

Gary looked sceptical. They finished their drinks quickly in an atmosphere that had become strained.

Now here was an opportunity to show his friend that his heart was firmly in place with wife and home.

'I've decided to come,' he said, holding his wife in his arms the evening before her departure.

'I'm so glad. What made you decide?'

'You're right, we should spend more time together.'

She hadn't really thought he would agree and she was

pleased. To see a part of the country that was new to both of them would be fun, even though it was winter.

'Uncle has recommended the Ambassador Hotel. I've booked a room for us there.'

Nina wiggled with pleasure. 'It'll be so nice, Ananda. Just the two of us.'

'Hey, what is it here?'

The two of them among many shadows. 'We've never really had a holiday together. Now we'll be doing what I wanted to do when you went to California.'

'Baby, why are you bringing that up? I went on work.'

She said nothing, not wanting to enter into an argument. She wished she wasn't so distracted all the time. Even sex had become perfunctory. The weekend was bound to bring them closer.

Next day, the Library School contingent reached Ottawa. Snow fell lightly and steadily, masses of it lay everywhere, making Halifax look positively tropical by comparison. Nina hoped the bus ride from the airport to the city centre would be long, so she could absorb the wonders of the nation's capital.

Anton was sitting next to her. Had she ever been to Ottawa before? No, had he? No.

They gazed out the window at a city so clearly less provincial than Halifax, that for a moment she could understand people's disdain for the Maritime capital. Dr Evans, their accompanying teacher, pointed out a few landmarks. There, the Rideau canal frozen over; tulips bloomed along its banks in spring. There, the Ottawa River, and there, beyond that they could see Parliament Hill with the Houses of Parliament, the Supreme Court of Canada, Wellington Street coming up next, with the National Library and National Archives.

'Impressive,' remarked Nina, staring at the distant, gothic green spire rising from Parliament House. Anton agreed.

'But you couldn't really think so, not after New York.'

If she could think so after New Delhi, why couldn't he think so after New York, he countered.

She laughed. Fancy comparing New York with New Delhi. It showed how little he knew.

Fleetingly he dropped his hand on her arm. Later, she thought of that instant many times. Was that when she should have been on guard? But how could she have known? In a plane full of people, Anton drops his hand on her arm, she looks at it startled, he removes it, smiles boyishly, she reads charm, friendliness and contrition in that look, and smiles back to show no hard feelings.

What could she have done differently, knowing as little as she did at that moment? She was the person she was, and compared to her later self, that person was a reckless babe in an unfamiliar wood.

The hotel that had been booked for them was a small one off Laurier, in the centre of town and walking distance to Wellington Street. The bigger rooms were shared by two students, the small ones on the sixth floor were single occupancy. Nina's was so tiny she could stand in the middle with both palms pressed against either wall, but she felt fortunate to be alone. The package deal included breakfast, other meals they paid for themselves.

Over the next three days they toured the National Library, the National Science Library, the National Archives. A librarian was a keeper of records, to which there will never be any end, Nina realised, stunned by the plethora that lay in these buildings.

Collection management they called it. Management of newspapers, periodicals, any bit of text to do with ethnic, aboriginal, immigrant or student communities. Diaries, letters, films, documentaries, textual records, architectural drawings, maps, watercolours, sound recordings, music, theses both post-graduate and doctoral, microfilms, manuscripts, medals, seals, posters: all were collected.

They had portraits of Canadians, thousands and thousands; and when it came to photographs, books and drawings, the figures were in millions.

The oldest film in the Archives was dated 1897, the oldest portrait of a Canadian 1710, before the country was even a nation. Since 1957, every publisher in Canada had had to send two copies of each book they published to the National Library. All the publications of the federal and provincial governments, every bit of data ever commissioned, was filed away for the benefit of Canadians in particular and the world in general.

The Archives were the nation's memory. No detail was too small, no record too unimportant for it to store. This was the information Nina had to learn how to access.

She felt a little disloyal to her own country, at the idea of servicing Canada in such a thorough manner. If she was to be a successful librarian, she would have to change her way of thinking, in more ways than she had anticipated.

Thursday night. To celebrate the last day, the graduate students went to a pub cum restaurant downtown. The air was blue with cigarette smoke. In the spirit of adventure Nina held a tentative cigarette between her fingers. Before her was a second glass of beer.

She was sitting next to Anton, as indeed she had for practically all their guided tours. His hand had touched her many times, on the neck, shoulders, arm, small of the back. It was so casual that it seemed stupid to make anything of it. Besides she liked the way he listened to her, liked his intelligent comments, his jokes about meagre Canadian history. 'They have a complex about America,' he opined, 'that makes them want to document everything. This is Canada they think,' said Anton, gesturing towards the Archives, 'this here, folks, step right up, step right up, and see the pictures of every Canadian that ever lived in this huge and wonderful country—wunnerfuul,' he went on, imitating some unrecognisable native Canadian, 'and right here, folks, is every book these people ever wrote—right here, folks.'

All this delivered in sibilant whispers, enclosing them in a light-hearted space of their own. She tried to shake off the attraction of this by looking at him severely and saying, 'In our country, people consider Americans self-obsessed and insular. At least Canadians are not like that.'

He put his hand on his heart and sketched a mock bow. 'Guilty as charged, Ma'am. Where do we stand next to a country like yours?'

She had to laugh. He was so different from Ananda, who could never talk about nations without a deadly earnestness.

Now the trip was over, things would go back to usual. She felt a little sad, allowing herself a brief moment in which to visualise a different scenario for her life. A happier one with less adjustment, less struggle.

'And so,' said Anton, examining her as she silently contemplated her glass of yellow liquid, a red Hudson Lager logo stamped on the side, 'we have finished our crash course in Canadiana.'

She smiled but said nothing. Ananda was coming the next day, and Ottawa was the place for aspiring immigrants to soak in the country's sense of itself.

He tried again, 'The archives of India must be huge—such an ancient country.'

But not so intent on documenting itself, replied Nina. In fact, warming to her theme, it would be nice if India had a similar sense of urgency so far as their records were concerned. There were certainly more people who would benefit, the Indian population being what it was, and the Indian migration scene being what *it* was.

'What is the immigration scene so far as you are concerned?'

'Permanent settlers.'

'Ah! So the Canadiana is up your street?'

'Certainly up my husband's.'

'He likes it here?'

'Loves it.'

'Really? Doesn't miss home?'

'Both his parents were killed in a road accident, which traumatised him considerably, as you can imagine. He was already working as a dentist when his uncle persuaded him to come here, said it would help him recover. In addition he helped him get into Dental School. Now he practises privately with one of his classmates. You can see why he would feel loyal to this country.'

'Where do you fit in?'

'An arranged marriage two years ago.'

Was that right?

Yes, Anton, that was right.

It was almost nine. One by one their classmates left them, pleading fatigue and the pressures of the next day.

Nina and Anton lingered.

She felt daring. It was easy here, drinking, smoking, asserting something, probably her sexuality. Looking at Anton she said, 'So, you like Asian women.'

'I do,' he replied. 'And you?'

'What about me?'

'How do you feel about white men?'

'I know nothing about them.'

'And been here so long.'

'Been married and here so long.'

'I'm married too. But it's stupid to confine yourself to one person for your whole life. What about adventure, what about experiencing differences? Nobody owns anybody, you know.'

'Does your wife agree?'

'Sure. Besides, what she doesn't know can't hurt her,' said Anton as he put his hand over hers. Nina looked down. His hand was dry and hard, it felt odd.

Anton was patient. The vibes between them were delicate, probing vibes, emanating from her as well as him. They got up to leave. The hotel was six blocks away but Nina rejected a taxi, guided by the thing that hung in the air between them, that needed time to develop.

He took her arm and put it around his waist, doing the same with his own, fitting her against the contours of his body. He did it naturally, they looked like the zillions of couples she had seen walking around the university campus. Through months of Library Science, she had gazed covertly at those couples, and now, in appearance at least, she was one of them.

They entered their hotel, he suggested the inevitable. He too was on the sixth floor in a single room, his Halifax hope realised.

His Halifax hope?

Yes. He had been wanting to make love to her from the first day of the first term. She had such a remote, princess-like air. He liked everything about her, she was pretty, intelligent, perceptive.

In that order?

Yup—he was a man after all, an admirer of beauty. And he really loved her skin, the way she looked, the way she walked, so different from Western women.

They were in the elevator, they were in the corridor, they were at his door, they walked in.

He sat down on the narrow bed and pulled her close. His hands were big and square, the nails broad, she marked the contrast between them and the gentleness of his touch.

Her loneliness welled up and overcame her. You might as well do this, and see what it is like. He started kissing her, drawing her legs up around his body. His hands were under her clothes, pulling, tugging, while her own hands, for the sake of politeness and reciprocity, were making less definite gestures around his shirt buttons.

But he didn't need her. He reared up, whipped off his shirt, slid off his pants and then back he was on her, caressing, probing, and then—are you on the pill?

No.

Ok.

He pulled a condom from his wallet—*his wallet*, he must have been prepared—but this was to be digested later. For now he was in her, sliding into the wetness that had been increasing all through their walk back.

Little moans began to escape her—were the walls of the hotel thin? Could anyone hear? Anton seemed not to care, then neither did she. The moans grew into soft screams. On he kept—she found herself arching, she found herself offering her breasts to him, she found herself whimpering, she felt wet and hot, she felt driven beyond the point of herself, her legs thrown across his back, eyes glazed, arms around his neck, and then down, down his back, her fingernails digging into the skin.

She came and came, begging him to stop, she could take no more, before he came too.

They collapsed into sleep, his arm around her stomach; she snuggled into him until she woke up to pee.

This was not a good moment. She saw the unfamiliar white body, her large handbag on the floor, her notebook and the pamphlet containing National Library facts beneath the scattered clothes.

What had she done? She hurried to the bathroom and quietly shut the door. If Anton woke up what would they say to each other? Now that we are lovers—were lovers—have been lovers—the most accurate tense escaped her.

As she peed, she felt the soreness of her vagina. That she liked. She had lived. Who can feel guilty about living? Judging from the evidence and the sexual therapy centres, every citizen in North America regarded good sex as their inalienable right. It was her right too.

But she wanted to get out of the room. She did not like being so starkly confronted by the sight of naked Anton expanse. Quietly she put on her clothes, picked up her things. Should she wake him, but then what was the point? This episode was not something that could lead anywhere. Its effects were in her mind, and there they would stay.

In her room she wrapped herself in a shawl, stood next to the window and glanced out. It was not yet dawn, though she fancied the darkness to be lightening. The streetlights were still on. She craned her neck to see little flurries dancing around the lights. Their small frantic movements told her it was windy.

Briefly she relived the night, then thought of her husband's arrival. They would be staying in a better hotel, they would see more of Ottawa, perhaps try skating on the canal, look at snow sculptures.

For the first time she had a sense of her own self, entirely separate from other people, autonomous, independent. So strange that the sex did not make her feel guilty, not beyond the initial shock. Easy, she was amazed it was that easy. Her first lover had taken her virginity and her hopes, her second lover had been her husband, her third had made her international.

Day arrived. At twelve, Nina took a taxi to the Ambassador Hotel, to wait for Ananda arriving by the evening flight. She left without seeing anyone.

She checked in. Yes, said the receptionist, her husband had said she would be coming in earlier. The room was on the ground floor to the side. It was still snowing, bigger flakes now, covering the branches of the one tree outside with a layer of fluff. She sat at the bay window and watched the snowflakes swirl through the lace curtains. Inside the room was a double bed, a TV, a fridge, a writing desk, a cupboard with an ironing board and iron, and pink satin-covered hangers. Ananda had obviously intended for them to stay in style. It was romantic of him; he was really very sweet.

She enveloped the room in a distant gaze—a woman of the world, a lover of men. There was a strange smell coming from her body. Thick, sweetish, strong, a dimly recalled sex smell. Even her vest smelt of it; she blushed at the odour. At home she and Ananda never had baths, considering it a dirty Western custom. Now she filled the tub and sank into the hot water.

Long she lay, soaking in the lemon-lime fragrance of the hotel bath salts, then she scrubbed herself hard with oatmeal soap. Finally she showered in clean water. She sniffed herself: no trace of that odour now.

She lay on the bed, warm, clean, lotion moist, hair damp. Outside the window it was quite dark, the snowflakes now illuminated by the streetlight visible over the hotel wall.

Three hours later she awoke to the sound of the door opening. Ananda entered.

He was in a foul mood. Where the hell had she been last night? He kept trying the hotel, but they said no one was in the room.

Nina embarked nervously into a flurry of explanations, fellow students, late night, bar, dinner, but Ananda was not interested.

'I'm here now, it doesn't matter.'

'Didn't you want to come?'

Again he grew irritated. 'It's too late to discuss this. Of course I *wanted* to come, otherwise would I have made all these arrangements? Or booked us into the Ambassador, which is costing me, I can tell you.'

They could move out tomorrow if he so wished.

'No, let it be. Now I'm here.'

He opened the mini bar and looked for something to drink.

'There is also tea if you like. They have a kettle and some tea bags.'

'A drink is what I need.'

'Well, why were you trying to get in touch with me?'

'Thought I could come tomorrow instead of today. Not feeling well.'

Indeed, he did look rather dreadful. She was sorry she had not been there to look after him.

He also had a cold, did she realise how terrible it was to be a dentist with a cold?

No, but she could imagine.

Was there any problem when she checked in?

262

'Not at all. Everything was fine.'

Finally he saw her. 'You look pretty. Ottawa suits you.'

She smiled deceitfully back at him. 'I have been waiting for you,' she said.

And so their time together started. After dinner, by candlelight at the hotel restaurant, they returned to the room. Touched by good food, novelty, wine and adventure, Ananda's bad mood dissipated. Nina changed into a white silk and polyester lace slip: slinky, low cut, certainly sexy. She wanted to give, she owed him one. Ananda, meanwhile, was looking at the crouched, racing figures in a hockey game, praising Wayne Gretzky. It was a while before he could be persuaded to turn his attention to Nina. After they made love, Nina marvelled that adultery could be so imperceptible to the partner.

It was fortunate the couple's first experience of the nation's capital was during winter. There was little temptation to wander around outside, and every incentive to absorb the culture so essential to an aspiring immigrant.

As they walked through the halls of the National Gallery, Nina kept telling herself, here she was, actually looking at *originals*, at Picasso, Pissarro, Monet, Cezanne, Degas, Chagall, Braque, Matisse, Dali, Klee, *themselves*. United, she and Ananda assured each other that such viewing would never ever have been possible at home.

The lesser known names inspired the same awe; they had gone beyond the universals. Now they could talk knowledgeably of Maurice de Vlaminck, Andre Derain, Fernand Léger, Jackson Pollock and Francis Bacon.

In the Canadian section, Ananda led Nina firmly to the Group of Seven—early twentieth century artists, they really are very famous. Nina looked on indifferently at landscapes that were surprisingly small, but she had to admit, very vivid. But then if you lived in Canada, landscape assumed an excitement that might be lacking in more populated countries.

Inuit art, simple, clear lines, strong and interesting, not much colour. Their ivory and whalebone carvings were beautiful, again something she would never see at home.

You are wrong, Anton. You made fun of the Archives—I laughed too—but you forgot that great art can only be seen by people like us as part of a collection. You really are a philistine. But then what can one expect from a descendant of Russian peasants?

She turned to her husband and smiled. 'Aren't you glad now that you came?'

He smiled back. It was thanks to her that he had at last seen Ottawa, he acknowledged that.

A little shopping and they returned to the hotel, savouring its fine French cuisine and generally enjoying a sense of luxury. Ananda, by now completely restored to his former self, apologised to his wife for his temper the day before. Travel, ill health and stress had taken their toll.

It was all right, she replied, they had been working hard, the best thing for them would be to enjoy the weekend.

That night was a restless one for both.

'Can't you sleep?'

'No.'

'Why?'

'Not sure. Too tired, I guess.'

'Let's make love.'

'Yes, let's.'

It did help some.

They woke late and had to take a taxi to Parliament Hill, instead of going on the city tour which left their hotel at eight am.

Nina had passed the Ottawa River, had seen the Parliament buildings in the distance, but it was only when she drove up the hill with Ananda that their full magnificence hit her. As they alighted from the taxi and walked towards the Centennial Flame, both felt some pride at being associated with this country;

they had nothing quite like this in India. The guidebook said the old building was burnt down in 1916, but it had been built again, with a grand gothic tower rising from the centre, symbol of Canadian democracy.

Strolling about, holding hands, they surveyed the Ottawa River below and the city buildings that stood against the cloud-streaked sky. In order to create their own private record, Ananda took Nina's picture in front of statues of former prime ministers, in front of the Centennial Flame, in front of the Peace Tower. Eventually, chilled but with enlarged minds, they caught a taxi to the Ontario Museum of Culture, highly recommended by their guidebook.

It didn't quite generate the awe they had felt on Parliament Hill. As they examined the exhibits, Nina wondered whether it was compulsory to be interested in different types of bird houses, quilts, weather vanes, puppets, chests, Easter eggs, violins and rattles. Anton's comment came to mind, and involuntarily she smiled.

'What's the joke?'

'This country is obsessed with itself—up to a point it's ok, but fancy keeping Easter eggs.'

'You are a librarian—you should understand that. It's an example of folk art.'

'Still, one can see the funny side.'

He looked wary; funny sides were not for him. She linked her arm in his and said she was tired, she was glad that time did not allow them to visit the Bank of Currency Museum, the Royal Canadian Mint and the Canadian War Museum.

Later that evening they caught the plane back to Halifax, saturated with the history of their adopted country.

We must do this again, they mused to each other, yes, we must.

v

Monday. Library School. Nina enters the Killam uneasily. She will see Anton, what will it be like?

He is as he always is. Talks to her as usual in the coffee break.

For the first time this unsettles her.

What are the rules that govern affairs? In Ottawa she had thought she would take her cue from him, now she wants more contact. Above all she wants to talk, it is the way she will come to grips with what has happened. But Anton, it seems, is going to deny her the pleasure. For days he maintains his distance. Nina suffers from his indifference, though she tells herself she has no right to expect anything.

The sense of autonomy she had had in Ottawa turns out to be illusory. It stemmed from a man finding her desirable and her own sense of adventure as she responded. In her group they teased out meanings from such incidents to raise their consciousnesses. Her consciousness is obviously on the floor, and to see it writhing does not augment her self-esteem. She has the wherewithal to acquire a lover, but not the ability to sustain a life in which her emotions were independent of men.

She walks home slowly in the falling dusk. She can see a few stars in the sky, she can see her breath vaporising as it leaves her body. Ananda will be home, he will be cooking. She will enter the building, take the lift, walk down the drab neon lit corridor to number 602, put her key in the lock, turn it and the first thing she will see is Ananda's back bending over the stove. She will smell warm, fragrant smells, she will ask what he is cooking and he will tell her in great detail. The Western smells of his meat will mingle with the Indian smells of the tomatoes and onions he is frying in butter with cumin and coriander.

Today he is braising a trout with a lemon parsley sauce. He covers the pan and looks at her. 'Doesn't that smell good?'

Yes, she murmurs, it does.

Lemon parsley butter sauce—how often had she smelled this? Cooking trout was one of Ananda's favourite food activities, combining simplicity, health, taste and freshness. By now she was even used to the way the dead eye glared at her from the pan.

When she first came to Halifax, not eating meat had been a way of remaining true to her upbringing. In Halifax her vegetarianism was treated respectfully, as part of her beliefs, but she felt false every time she concurred with a picture of herself as a traditional, devout Hindu. Really, what did she care about a religion she never practised? After she had had sex with Anton, it seemed especially hypocritical to hang on to vegetables.

Down with all taboos.

She looked at the pyrex lid, steamed over, heard the fragrant sauce bubbling around the lone trout. 'Looks good too.'

He raised his eyebrows. 'Want some? I can thaw another.'

'I don't want a whole one. I will have a little of yours.'

He understood the gravity of what she was doing. 'You won't regret this. It will make your life easier.'

The first forkful was for her. 'Bite?'

She opens her mouth, he puts the piece in. She holds her breath and cautiously chews. Underneath the lemon, the butter and the parsley is a faint fishy tang. She washes it down with some water.

'Not so difficult after all. Another bite?'

'That's all for now.'

That weekend was spareribs, the real test. Red meat. Flesh. Mammals. Cow. Cows that looked into your eyes—cows that her mother worshipped on fixed days of the Hindu calendar. She could have graduated to chicken from fish, but Nina did not want the dishonesty involved in these slow, cautious steps.

She chewed the leathery mass lurking beneath the rich tomato sauce.

'Do you like it?'

'Um.'

'Eventually if one lives here one has to eat meat. I started when I moved out of Uncle's house. Here I cook for you so it is not so complicated.'

'In Rome, do as the Romans do.'

Ananda beamed and helped her to another small piece of spare rib. He watched as she cut it into still smaller pieces, watched as she carefully covered each morsel with sauce, chewed and gulped. It was hard at first, but in a few months he would have her eating sirloin steak and loving it. From now on, there wouldn't be the trouble of always cooking dal for her, of making sure there was enough salad and veggies when they went anywhere. Also, he would have the pleasure of sharing responses to food.

'What are you looking at?'

'You. You'll find life easier from now on.'

This grated on her nerves. Her meat eating was the result of fragmentation and distress, not a desire for convenience.

'Just think how much more pleasant it will make dining out,' he continued.

'We don't go out that much.'

'Well, now we can.'

'My poor mother. She would not like seeing this.'

'We can always turn veg when she comes to visit.'

She kept quiet. He was so determined to see the bright side of things, that at times she shrunk beneath the glare of those spotlights as they searched harshly for her shadows, those shadows that made her what she was.

That Monday Nina walked to the library, fish and beef indelibly part of her being. Feeling less Indian had its advantages. There were more possibilities in the world she could be open to. Her body was her own—and that included her digestive system and her vagina.

March and still the snow, still the biting wind. From time to time she felt a deceptive thawing in the air; but the snow softened only to freeze into ice again. At home the sun would be beginning to burn, in a few weeks there would be no stopping its onslaught on the north Indian plains, whereas here the snow still had to melt, buds still had to appear, spring was still far away.

In the midst of this everlasting cold, one sunlit day, Anton approached her after class at twelve thirty.

'Want to come to my place for a bite?'

'I was going to go to Fader's.'

'I'll make you a sandwich. We have three hours.'

As before his message was clear. But why had he said nothing all this time?

'Let's walk outside while you decide.'

She picked up her books. She already knew she was going to go. Tension and excitement gathered in her, but shyness and fear too; she didn't dare catch anybody's eye as they waited for the elevator.

It was so pretty outside. Blue sky, stinging air, everything crisp and sunny.

'Nice day, isn't it?'

'Yes. So different from home. There when the sun shines, it means warm in winters and bloody hot in summers. Here, alas, it means no such thing. '

'You must miss your home.'

'I do. My husband says I must think of this as our home, otherwise I'll never get used to it.'

By this time they had reached the corner of the football field. They skirted the stands and cut across the snow-filled ground.

'How far is it?' she asked after another five minutes.

'Oh, not far. Murray Place. Soon they are going to tear the house down, so the room's pretty cheap.'

'I live close to Dal too.'

'Really? You must show me.'

'I'd love to,' rose automatically to her lips, even while she resolved to never let him near her home.

Two hours later, Nina walked down the same sidewalk with a spring in her step. She felt buoyant, one with the day, the cold sun, the buildings, the city, the Killam Library, one with

Information Sources, one with its teacher Dr Mannheim, one with all her fellow students.

She had forgotten how liberating sex could be. It was the force of life, she thought, remembering her Lawrence. Anton and she were not into having a relationship; it was purely a meeting of bodies, a healthy give and take. He had explained everything. He hadn't wanted this to develop into anything serious, that is why he had not approached her. Their Ottawa encounter had made a deeper impression on him than he had expected, and he needed to be careful. She may not have known, but he had even made an extra trip to New York in the interim to strengthen his resolve. After two months of self-control, he had thought what was the harm? Why not just one more time?

The words one more time are a fatal drug and, despite the long ago experience with Rahul, Nina was not wary of them. I am not taking anything away from my husband, I am not, she rationalized, as it became clear that her trysts with Anton were not going to stop. All around her she heard of open marriages, of no bonds but the voluntary, of no living according to the rules of others. Her life was her own; she didn't owe anybody any explanations. If Anton gave her pleasure, if his easy acceptance of her gilded her studies, didn't she owe it to herself to sleep with him? Besides they had all of Library Science to discuss, their colleagues, their assignments, their deadlines, shared concerns, which increased the satisfaction that lay in shared bodies.

It was just as well she had no children, how would she have managed then?

Ananda was still seeing Mandy—this kept him tolerant and loving at home. Because Nina was so busy he didn't realise how demanding his lover was getting. After his Ottawa visit, she had forced him to make it up to her with time, money and attention. Sometimes he thought his liaison was getting out of hand, but each time he came away from Mandy he left a piece of himself behind—retrieving it with difficulty. It was amazing how she got under his skin. Sometimes, in the day, overcome with longing, he would write her a little note, showing it to her when they met, then carefully taking it back to tear it up.

'You think I'm going to blackmail you, huh?'

He was indeed protecting himself, but it was better not to admit to such things.

'I wish I didn't love you so much,' was all he said, a little miserably.

'Hey, it's ok.'

'I'm being unfair to my wife.'

'And I thought I was the one you were being unfair to.'

He turned to her, a blind look in his eyes. 'I could never be that, it's not in me.'

Nina didn't really notice what Ananda was being to her. Instead she was relieved that he expected so little.

'I know what a graduate student's life is like,' reassured Ananda. 'Why, for days I got by on four hours sleep.'

'But you were not married.'

'It's just till you finish.'

'Still, not every husband would put up with being neglected so much. I don't know how I would have done this course without you. In India I certainly couldn't have spent so much time in studies.'

'Baby, things are really different here,' he replied. 'Besides you forget, I have looked after myself for years.'

Indeed, Ananda cooked, shopped and vacuumed the house. She only had to do the washing. After dinner she attended to the dishes in a dreamy manner, her hands encased in rubber gloves, enjoying the easy way in which the soapy water got the dirt off, enjoying wiping around the tiny stove and counter. As for the clothes, she took them to the basement laundromat every Sunday, often sitting there with a book till they were done, breathing the warm steamy air that smelt of many different detergents.

Nina's balancing of the different spheres of her life broke down when it came to her group. Its whole raison d'être was honesty. Secrets were considered debilitating. There was no way in hell she could hold Gayatri's hands, look into her eyes and lie, even by omission.

On the other hand, telling was inconceivable. She had to protect her marriage, the bedrock of her life in Canada. It felt safer to abandon the group even though it was strictly non-judgemental and confidentiality was absolute, even though she herself had heard many stories of affairs, joyous flings and sorrowful betrayals. Now when it was her turn to reveal one such story, she chose the easy way out and prevaricated.

'I'm so busy, I'll have to leave the group for a while.'

Gayatri was the most upset. 'I'll miss you—why can't you manage? I manage with my PhD.'

A PhD was different. If she didn't master the technical details of Library Science, she would not be able to maintain her A average, and she would lose her funding. She had already been given a warning, she added in a lie so inspirational she impressed herself.

Who could argue with this? All right Nina, go into the world with what we have taught you. Remember your lessons, and come back if you need to.

Bye, bye, bye.

Spring came and with it daylight saving time. She could now see purple and yellow crocuses, peeping out besides clumps of melting snow and green shoots of grass. There were snowdrops, nestling near the steps of some of the houses, on the roads she walked along. Tiny nodules began to appear on the bare branches of trees. The moist, cold air ceased to have so much bite. The loo would be blowing at home, hot dusty winds, while here, the air was fresh and damp. The season made her glad she was here, glad. Anton's bed had the same effect.

'I think we are totally compatible,' she said one afternoon.

'It is good, which is why it has continued.'

272

'What is it like with your wife?' Nina asked, beginning to transgress.

'What's it like with your husband?' responded the lover, dealing with her transgression without a moment's pause.

'Oh, ok.'

'Same here.'

There was a gym attached to her building. She joined it, devoting even more time to her body. There she worked up a sweat that was innocent, there in the ladies shower she strutted her stuff, and the fact that no one cared gave her confidence.

Her attitude to Western clothes changed. All that walking had made her leaner. Clothes were no longer something to be invisible in. At home she had made her best shopping decisions by herself, undisturbed by another's opinion. Now with the image of an elegant, well-dressed Nina, she headed on her own towards Mills Brothers on Spring Garden Road.

The salesgirl understood her requirements. Effortlessly, clothes were selected. Black pants, grey pants, a white cotton blouse, a black sweater. The bill was for three hundred dollars, and cheap at the price, said the sales girl. Normally those cashmere sweaters go for a hundred and ninety nine dollars. Nina stroked the soft wool, admiring the deep, dark inky black. She would cherish it forever. That sweater is a beauty, said the cashier, as she wrapped it in tissue paper before sliding it reverently into a bag. It was Mills Brothers' policy to make their customers feel special.

The special feeling lasted when Ananda complimented her on how she looked, lasted when she put on her new clothes and looked in the mirror, lasted till the American Express bill came.

'Three hundred dollars! You spent three hundred dollars on your clothes? Why, my most expensive suit is a hundred and fifty.'

'The cashmere sweater will last a lifetime. And it was on sale,' defended Nina.

'You could have bought an ordinary sweater. Why do you have to dress in cashmere?'

Wasn't the beauty of cashmere enough justification? And the way the wool responded to her stroking hand?

'I should have come with you. You go alone, you lose your head.'

'I haven't spent much on clothes in the two years I've been here. You keep saying you want me to dress like the natives.'

'That was two years ago. Even you saw the sense.' Ananda continued to stare at the bill, evidence of wilful, selfish, thoughtless extravagance.

'Well, you tell me how much can I spend,' demanded Nina resentfully.

'A reasonable amount like any normal woman.'

'I am a normal woman,' she retorted. 'It is you who are not normal. Who knows what you earn, you never tell me, never share, how am I supposed to know?'

'I'm self-employed,' he shouted. 'I don't earn one fixed amount, is that so difficult for you to understand?'

'You never even give me a basic idea.'

'Ok, you want to know what I earn, then know my debts as well. Know what I have to pay each and every month along with these bills.' He slapped his hand on the American Express total of Nina's sins.

She had heard the list of his debts so often, she blanked it out. The whole thing took five minutes, starting with the first one to his Uncle and ending with the annual insurance rates. By the time he had finished, the pleasure in the black sweater had gone.

'From now on, I will only buy clothes when I have money of my own.'

'It's not as though I don't buy you things,' responded Ananda bitterly. 'I don't think you can accuse me of stinginess. But at this moment I'm not in a position to spend so much.'

That night Ananda lay with his back to his wife, clutching the offending bill in his troubled thoughts. He didn't like denying Nina clothes, but he was still paying for his therapy in California.

He thought of his mistress and her needs. Mandy was tied to the uncertainties of temping; whenever he urged a permanent job, she said she refused to be stuck in one place, with one set of people. She wanted to be free.

Free. Did that mean she was sick of him?

No, silly, she had replied, why are you so insecure?

I am not insecure, he said with some annoyance.

Then what's the problem? she had laughed.

All he meant was that if she had a decent paying job—one that didn't involve temping—she would be financially better off.

And not in a position to meet so many men. She had made the initial moves—what was to say he was the only one in her life? Yet, when he asked once, she laughed and said, 'You're a fine one to talk, you with your wife, suppose I phone and tell her, then?'

'You do that, baby, and it's all over with us.'

He was never harsh and now his tone made her retreat.

In general, however, he could insist on nothing with her, though often baffled and frustrated. No matter how many times he thought he would break up, he couldn't do it. She represented too many things. Indeed she was his Newfoundland—something he had stopped saying because she got irritated.

Meanwhile, an overwrought Nina's conscience began to talk. She spent a lot of time avoiding its company, but it came persistently, an unwanted guest, its rhinoceros hide impervious to rejection. Is it right or fair to be upset with your husband about a bill, when what you do is so much worse?

What he doesn't know won't hurt him. Anton will soon finish and return to New York. It's not as though I am taking anything away from Ananda.

275

Don't quibble. You are guilty, guilty. Look how scared you are lest he hear something, suspect something.

I will never spend any of his money, never. I will earn on my own, buy ten cashmere sweaters on my own.

The dialogue continued all night as Nina tossed and turned. Morning came. Dreary eyed, unrested, she got out of bed and pulled on her clothes. Outside, she walked and walked in the weak early morning light. Street after street was silent; she was the only person in the world. Within the neat, tranquil houses she passed, rested the happy families of Halifax. The bushes bordering their walls glowed whitely with dew. Here and there, she could see a spider's web, specially encrusted.

The stillness around her added to her desolation. Her warm bed now seemed cosiness itself, as did her kitchen, her routine and meals cooked with Ananda. It was not a bad life. Ananda was always saying keep it simple. She would go home, and make up with him. For her world to be in order, there had to be love between her husband and herself.

vi

Nina and Anton found it convenient to have sex on Wednesday afternoons. The three hour gap between The History of the Book and Introduction to Systems Analysis did nicely.

By now Nina had grown to love the room in which Anton lived. The walls were painted black, so was the furniture. In the middle hung a light enclosed by a red paper Chinese lampshade with hanging golden tassels. The room was in perpetual shadow, blurring the distance between night and day, between sex and fulfilment.

The previous guy was a ghoul, said Anton, but made no move to change any of it. The rent was sixty five dollars a month, he was trying to live as cheaply as possible. A woman called Sue Lin lived in the next room, he and she cooked on a stove in the landing. Next to the stove was a small, rickety fridge—one shelf for Sue Lin, one for Anton.

Sue Lin was a graduate student in English. Her long black hair hung limply to her shoulders, her round face had little pouches under black eyes. Her mouth was small and red, her teeth white and uneven. Nina asked Anton a lot of questions about Sue Lin; she was jealous of any young woman with an undetermined future.

On this particular day Nina was lying in bed, her post-coital shawl wrapped around her. She found Anton's room cold. The intense black added to the chill. The summer holidays were approaching; Anton would leave for New York, and the thought of no contact for three months gave Nina a hollow feeling. She pulled his arm around her chest, and idly gazed at the contrast of their skins. With Ananda her skin was so much lighter, with Anton so much darker.

He raised himself on one shoulder. The bed sighed, a muted sound compared to the groans it had emitted earlier.

'I've got a summer job.'

'You have? Where?'

'The New York Public Library.'

'Oh.'

Invariably he curbed her curiosity with facts: bare, dry and reluctant.

'Is it nice, the New York Public Library?' she asked.

'Is it nice! It's beautiful. Like being in a cathedral.'

'Really?'

'Why, it's one of the tourist spots of New York.'

'Really?'

'Uh-huh. Why don't you come and see it one day?'

'Perhaps I will.'

'What are you doing this summer?'

'I don't know—maybe going to India.'

'Wow! Lakshmi and I would really love to visit India.'

'Well, why don't you? Lakshmi should discover her roots.'

'I know. But we can't afford it yet. For now we are going to explore the Maritimes. She's coming up in the first week of June.'

277

This was too much for Nina. His relationship with his wife was obviously flourishing, while she was an unimportant pastime. To be sure he had never offered any reason to think differently.

He proved his noble non-attachment to the woman he so casually fucked by telling Nina how little leave Lakshmi got, and how much easier it was for him to go down one weekend in the month.

What he was really doing was reminding her of the limits within which they operated. They were rigorous, these limits, and they demanded severe compartmentalisation of body, mind and heart, of word and thought, of the apartment at Hollin Court and of the little black room at Murray Place.

She got up and started dressing.

'Hey, you ok?'

The feelings which had driven her to this situation were now being told to die. Yes, she said, yes, she was ok.

The last day of term. Among the students, general jubilation, exchanging of summer plans and job information. Between Anton and Nina, nothing. Anton seemed to consider their goodbyes said. Nina had to run to catch up with him on his brisk way home.

'Anton, wait up.'

'Oh, hi, Nina.'

'I wanted to say bye to you.'

'Oh, baby, didn't we say bye to each other that afternoon?'

How could one man's voice sound so sexy?

'Yes, but you know I am going to India.'

Silently they walked along, parting at the corner with goodbyes that touched no depths. The summer stretched long and lonely in front of Nina, with only Ananda and her thoughts for company. All the holidays held was a part-time job at the HRL, a lie about a trip to India and the slowly forming resolution to put Anton behind her. No marriage could take such strain.

*

278

'I wish we lived in India,' she said to Ananda that night. 'Can't we at least visit?'

It was after dinner and there was silence between them. This was very dreadful for Nina. A couple who have nothing to talk about are in a bad state, and she often babbled simply so this would not happen. Today she was tired and depressed, babble did not come easily.

How had they spent all those evenings together, when now one of them seemed so unending? Her heart was heavy, in other circumstances she might have considered it to be breaking. She contemplated the months that would pass without the particular comfort of seeing Anton and found she couldn't bear it. Her state alarmed her; it was so inimical to marriage.

'Please, can't we go to India?' she repeated.

'What for?' asked Ananda.

'I think it's easier on marriages. You have a family, you have friends, they all back you up. I loved being with your sister, Ila, Ishan... '

'Why do you need backing up?'

'Oh, I don't know. There is just you and me here. Not even children.'

'We have our work, recognition, status, a better standard of living. Look at the way your mother lives.'

'You judge by superficials,' she replied crossly.

He felt she was denigrating all he had given her.

Although he tried to never compare the women in his life, Ananda ended up doing this constantly. Now he thought one nice thing about Mandy was that he never had to have conversations about India with her. She wasn't even curious; she had never said, like so many people did, that India was a place she had always wanted to visit. Occasionally he realised she thought people lived in trees among tigers roaming the jungle; these impressions he never bothered to correct. In her company he was just a man, a man who happened to have a dark skin—really anybody from almost anywhere.

Meanwhile Nina was hurrying on—she knew her husband was fixated on this country, and she didn't think she could stand another conversation on how grateful she should be.

'Everything is clearer at home.'

'Clearer? What do you mean?'

'Nothing, nothing. Still it's unnatural to not even visit. It's been almost two years.'

'If you ask me it's unnatural to live in one place and be always thinking about another.' And, he continued, people's teeth did not know vacations. His first visit had been after seven years.

Seven years. Did he want her to do likewise?

She kept to herself how much she longed to see her mother. That love had a purity it would be a relief to experience after all the complications she had suffered in its name.

A few days later, Ananda announced he had a surprise. He had bought her a ticket home; she could spend two months there.

A gift from heaven. Thank you, Ananda, thank you.

Privately she was suspicious. A man who objected to a Mills Brothers purchase, who constantly told her of his debts—why was he spending four hundred and fifty dollars on a ticket to India?

Ananda congratulated himself. He had dealt with the whole thing nicely. Nina's trip to India would give him space to sort things out with Mandy. He was going to be circumspect next time, confine himself to flings. The strain and secrecy of his affair were getting too complicated for him to handle. He liked to keep things simple, and the longer his affair lasted, the less simple it was.

'Two months is a long time,' said his wife uncertainly.

'I thought you would be pleased.'

'Yes, of course I am.'

She was going home. Suspicion could wait.

So Nina's summer lie turned true.

'Why don't you join me?' she asked Ananda, guilty in her relief.

He had equal cause to be relieved, but those causes lay in Halifax. For two months he would enjoy a close approximation to bachelor status. One woman was a prison, many contained the variety of the world.

Idly he thought he should have been born in an earlier age, when Hindu men could marry as often as they pleased.

'I have to catch up with things here. Besides, two tickets to India is more than I can afford.'

As usual the spectre of money silenced her.

Ananda, driving to Clayton Park, thought of all that Mandy had done for him and regretted that its novelty was wearing off. Her charm had lain in her generous, white, uninhibited body. His gratitude that at last he had entrance to an unexplored country had been strong. But Mandy was also fixated on receiving, and therein lay the rub. No country should levy such high taxes.

At the very least he must loosen her stranglehold on his spare time. He went over the story he was going to tell her and admired its cleverness. It ran thus: his wife had found out about his affair and was going home to his sister, giving him two months in which to chose. Family honour did not allow him to abandon the woman they had selected for him. This might be hard for Mandy to accept, but she must know that immigrants came with old world values.

Mandy was not moved by this tale. He was a doctor, a huge step up the social ladder for her, and she had hoped for permanence with him.

'I think you're a coward,' she said, 'using your wife as an excuse. Maybe she came to Canada because of you, but she's studying for a library degree, she's going to work here. How does it matter what some family in India thinks? If you cared so much, you would have gone with her.'

He looked hunted, the weak point in his narrative only now apparent.

'Are you trying to get rid of me?'

'No, no.'

'Good. Because you and me are an item, aren't we, Andy?' She stood behind him, her arms folded around his chest, her fingers inside his waistband, unbuttoning, searching, touching. These methods had often been very successful.

'Maybe I should meet your wife,' she murmured. 'After all we have a lot in common.'

He stiffened. 'Don't even think of it.'

'Why? Are you ashamed of me?'

'Of course not—besides, I told you, she's not here.'

'I know how to wait,' said Mandy.

Meanwhile the wife was preoccupied with thoughts of home. Every hour on the flight brought her five hundred miles closer. Her mother and Alka would be at the airport to greet her. During her visit, she would make sure her mother did not worry about money for a single second. Now that she was the mistress of convertible currency they could even go to a hill station for a holiday.

As she walked down the plane steps, she encountered a heat so severe she could hardly breathe. How would she manage months of this, was her first thought, her second amazement that in two years she could become so delicate. She had been careful not to change, careful that her accent remain the same, that she not get used to convenience, comfort or cold air, but unbeknownst to her she had.

Her mother greets her with tears in her eyes. Her daughter is looking lovely—taller, thinner, clear skinned.

'Beta, beta,' she murmurs. She chokes with happiness while Alka looks indulgently at the sentient drama in front of her, repeated in groups all over the airport.

They drive home. As the hot air blows against her face and dries the sweat on it, Nina looks eagerly out of the car window. She experiences some disappointment: the landscape is inextricably poor and third world, low squat hovels line many of the roads, their decrepit nature obvious even in the moonlit night.

The nostalgia she has anticipated comes as the car nears Jangpura. There is the bend into the colony, the bus stop, the shut iron gate of the house, the hooded car in front.

The driver deposits her suitcases inside, and after many goodbyes and thank yous, Alka drives off. Mother and daughter are alone in their two rooms, which memory had made less mean and cramped. When Nina opens her suitcases to quickly put the cheese and chocolate in the fridge, the lids occupy all the free floor space.

Conversation takes up the rest of the night. The living arrangements of the widowed woman that were buried under wedding minutiae two and a half years ago, are now scrutinised.

The annual visit that Mr Batra made to Lucknow was gone over in great detail. Theoretically, in-laws might suggest company and security, but in fact age had not sweetened them, nor had custom lent them consideration. They had offered the lonely woman a home, but in return it was expected she serve, slave, look after and endure. This was too heavy a price, even for the meek. She preferred to manage on her pension, in fact the money Nina sends is unnecessary.

'God, Ma, don't embarrass me. Fifty dollars, a hundred dollars, what's that? One patient, two patients. When I get a job as a librarian, you see what I do for you.'

'Till then, don't send, beta. Ananda must pay his debts first.'

'Everybody there has debts, they mean nothing. Why, I spent a hundred dollars on a single sweater.'

The mother looked appalled.

Nina glanced around the poky room and the tiny screened-in veranda. 'Ma, aren't you lonely here?'

'Beta, since your father died, it has never been the same. You can be lonely in a room full of people, but thank God you are too young to know that. You are settled and I am happy.' And she steered the conversation back to her daughter.

Over the next few days Nina detailed all her activities, the group, Gayatri Gulati, Library Science, part-time job, field trips, Ottawa, the friends, the *very good* friends—'But beta, what about your husband?' interrupted the mother finally.

'What about him? He goes early to work, but I go even earlier.'

'Then who sees to his breakfast?'

'Ma, don't be so old-fashioned. He gets his own breakfast like every person in the West.'

'He eats alone?'

'Only during the week. I also eat alone, by the way.'

'He married for companionship.'

'We have companionship,' declared the wife, 'we cook dinner together every night.'

Mr Batra examined her daughter. 'Is that enough?'

'Of course. Don't I look happy?'

The mother was silent. Indeed, Nina looked different. Her skin glowed, her flab had gone; the result of regular gym visits and energetic sex. Two years of cold damp air, walking everywhere and studying hard made her seem younger.

'Why haven't you conceived?' went on the mother, nosing around. That topic mentioned on the phone, its urgency lost in transatlantic distance, could now be resurrected in all its might.

'We have been trying, Ma, what to do?'

'Doesn't Ananda mind?'

'I don't know,' said Nina irritably.

The mother stroked the daughter's hair with her thin hand.

A week later Ramesh sent the driver to pick up his sister-in-law for a ten day visit. Nina drove over armed with presents:

whisky, chocolate, jeans for Ishan and Ila, makeup for Alka.

She was welcomed with open arms. In being hospitable to her, they were showering Ananda with affection. It was this seamless identification that Nina had to get used to.

After she had married, she had gloried in being part of a larger whole, loving the novelty of being two in one. Now she felt oppressed by the blind acceptance accorded to a visiting daughter-in-law. She could be just anybody she told herself, then blushed at the way she sounded—so un-Indian, so tainted with Western individualism.

Did she, in this brief period, want that Alka should start getting to know the essential her? Who was this murky creature, had she herself any idea?

Marriage was a social institution, she reminded herself. A certain amount of pretence was necessary for its successful functioning.

Her in-laws were meanwhile uninterested in her heart, mind and soul. They were civil servants, intent on enjoying the good life. Nina went regularly with them to the Gymkhana Club, entered enthusiastically into the little party thrown for her and every evening responded indulgently to Ila's attentions. In Ananda's family, she acquired the weight of aunts, uncles and cousins, all with a flattering interest in her Library Science degree and her daily life abroad.

Politics was in every conversation. After two years Morarji Desai was finally ousted. Charan Singh was now PM, the result of deal making between the erstwhile foe, Indira Gandhi, and himself. The public had become fed up with the power mongering and self-serving incompetence of the Janata party. Inflation was on the rise, the price of onions much talked about.

'Are things never to get better?' Nina asked. Her in-laws laughed gently and told her she was lucky to be out of it all.

Nina left Ananda's family with sadness; her interaction with them had been easy and uncomplicated. If only she could live in the same city, within the sense of community that their presence created so effortlessly. 'Please come and visit me,' she pleaded. 'We are so alone.'

'It is hard,' agreed Alka, 'to be without family. I know Uncle is busy, and Aunty does not understand our ways.'

'At least send the children for higher studies. Dalhousie is a very good university. Small, but good. And the fees are more reasonable than the USA.'

Ramesh was thinking of putting both his children into dentistry. Ila of course would have to stay in India—there was the question of her marriage—but Ishan, yes, for him Dalhousie could be an option. Which led Alka to reflect that if Ananda did not have children he would be even more interested in hers.

Once back in Jangpura, Nina got heat stroke. As she lay in the darkened room with high fever and cooling liquids she thought of the country she had left with longing. Why did her heart have to be so divided? She vented on her mother.

'Ma, living here is hell. I am going to send you money for an air conditioner.'

'The cooler is enough, beti.'

'It's something, but not enough.'

'Who will pay the electricity bills? I am all right the way I am.'

'Come and live with me.'

'When the children come.'

'Why are you obsessed with children?'

'You live in the West. Have you tried everything?'

'Not everything. It's expensive.'

'He's a doctor.'

Nina was silent. The situation was difficult to explain.

'How expensive can it be?'

'Very.'

'Both of you come here. AIIMS is very good, Ramesh can help you get a bed. He is still an important man.'

'Let me finish my degree.'

'Only a year left.'

286

'Then I have to look for a job.'

'Job can wait, children can't.'

'Ma, I feel too sick to talk about all this now. You just come, you will love it in Halifax, it's not as cosmopolitan as Brussels, but still the West. You need a holiday.'

The mother let her daughter talk on. Seeing her so beautiful, lively and graceful was like manna to her heart. Now her responsibilities were truly over. She felt tired, she didn't want to travel all that distance. Which husband likes shouldering the burden of his wife's mother, even a husband as nice as Ananda?

Nina became better and dragged her mother off to Mussoorie. Come on, you know you love the mountains. For one week they stayed at the Roselyn, down the Mall from the fancy Savoy, and breathed fresh, pure air. After a week in such an atmosphere Mr Batra looked positively healthy. Really, if she came to Halifax she could be in such an environment all the time, thought Nina. It did not seem right that a life of privation should never end.

'Aren't you going to meet your friend?' asked the mother once they returned to Delhi.

'Of course,' but Nina did nothing. When she lay down at night, the thought of Zenobia pressed on her like an unfulfilled obligation. Her experiences in Canada made her feel flawed, as though she lacked integrity. When she did eventually phone it was to spin stories about jet lag, heat stroke, fever, recovery and weakness.

This was such a wonderful surprise, said Zenobia, she must come over as fast as possible. She couldn't wait to see her.

Nina had flouted the expectations of friendship—she had postponed meeting Zenobia, she had lied, not only now, but for two years.

By her second term of Library Science, Nina Sharma, née Batra had taken for a lover a married man, a man who did not even pretend to love her, with whom she continued to have a sexual relationship. She had to somehow say all this; if she didn't, what was the point of meeting? But would Zenobia condemn, judge, look down on her, betray the friendship that Nina had betrayed? Whatever she did, Nina would have to deal with it.

Two days later Nina took a scooter to Zenobia's barsati in Defence Colony. The forty degree air whipped against her and coated her freshly made up face with dust. As the grime of the city settled into her pores, she thought of Ananda's remarks about Canadian air and wondered whether she was becoming like him. If this was what it took.

She hoped that the chocolate she had taken from the freezer would not liquefy.

Defence Colony. Hurriedly she paid the scooter wallah the fare he demanded, not bothering to check his metre card for accuracy. It all came to a few piddly cents anyway. The surprised scooter wallah roared off and Nina stood at the entrance to Zenobia's house. The gate was heavy, and as she pushed it open, she observed the contrast her arms and bangles made against it, the metal, the flesh, the translucent red glass, the peeling black paint on the iron. She walked towards the back of the house, towards the narrow staircase that led to the barsati. Round and round, in slow motion, the steps carried her into the past, towards a Nina less experienced, more naive and straightforward than this one.

She reached the top and banged the bolt loudly against the rickety door. Zenobia had no bell. Footsteps, the sound of a latch being opened. Zenobia. After two years, Zenobia. She threw her arms around her neck and said with an intensity that embarrassed them both: I missed you, I missed you, I was here earlier, I didn't call you, I didn't know what to say, Zen, I'm having an affair. He's a married man. Nobody knows. That's why I didn't call.

There. Problem of what to say to Zenobia solved.

'My goodness. But come in, come in—tell me everything. How lovely you are looking, Nina! Whoever he is, obviously suits.'

Nina looked around the terrace, marking each change: the champa tree in an enormous clay tub, the madhumati creeper that trailed across the bedroom window, the bougainvilleas that bloomed in rows against the balcony wall. In the last two years her friend had become a gardener.

Inside she avidly studied the books that marked Zenobia as an English teacher, the ikat spreads on the takht in the corner, the cane two-seater and single chair next to a low marble coffee table, its sameness so familiar it hurt her chest. Meanwhile Zenobia made lemonade in the tiny kitchen, not forgetting Nina's preference for a pinch of black salt.

Holding their glasses they settled on the bed where the AC made life bearable, and there half reclining against the soft cushions, head propped by further pillows, Nina began the story of her life in the last two years.

It took till evening.

It must be because she didn't have any real friends in Halifax that her sense of friendship had atrophied, thought Nina on her way back. Why hadn't she run to Zenobia the minute she landed? Really, marriage made you do strange things.

Why had she wasted ten precious days in Alka's house, actually rejoicing in a new-found family before whom she had to lie all the time? Though she had felt she belonged, essentially she was Ananda's wife. The minute that ceased, all doors closed.

'You look happy,' commented her mother as she walked in.

'What's for dinner? I smell good things,' said Nina, sniffing the air violently.

'Lauki kofta.'

'Oh, Ma, you shouldn't have. I would have helped you.'

'It's all right. You can't stand for so long in a hot kitchen.'

As Nina mashed the delicious, melting lauki kofta into the fragrant basmati rice along with some cold dahi, she thought life had no greater bliss. She was unburdened of a secret she had carried for a year, and she was eating one of her favourite foods. There were so many little things to enjoy that if one was able to live in the moment, one could actually survive without too much grief.

That night Nina sat in bed, rubbing immense amounts of cream into her dry feet, going over every detail of her conversation with Zenobia. If she could memorise it she could carry its sympathy with her when she returned to Halifax.

Nina's marriage, for the rest of the trip, was their favourite topic of conversation. Sometimes Nina felt she wasn't paying enough attention to her friend—what had she been doing these past two years, how was college, her love life—but in essence all Zenobia said was 'Same old shit', and in the pause that followed, Ananda, Nina, Anton, Ottawa, Halifax, Library School, were the topics that surfaced.

Nina's situation was such that Zenobia's sympathy eventually came to be marked with a certain amount of criticism. 'It sounds totally schizophrenic—the life you are leading. You will have to do something about it, leave Ananda or confront Anton. That man is getting the best of both worlds. He sounds a bit like Rahul.'

Nina gazed out at Lodhi Gardens from the upstairs windows of the IIC dining room. She could see the white flowers of the champa, sitting squatly against broad, long leaves, the remaining red blossoms of a coral tree, the pale purple clusters of the jacaranda. Down below was the club pond with its scummy green water, bordered by the overhanging bottle brush. Why did she have to think about her life, when the summer looked so pretty from air conditioned rooms?

'I can't do anything till I have finished my degree,' she said petulantly. A friend so close had its drawbacks. She saw the nasty things in your life and did not hesitate to point them out, all out of love.

'You were wise enough not to get pregnant, that is one saving grace.'

Nina couldn't bring herself to say this act of wisdom was involuntary.

The monsoon came, the academic year began, Nina visited Miranda House. She timed her visit for the twenty minute coffee break. Her ex-colleagues clustered around her, gave her tea, asked about her life in Canada. They wanted to hear all about it, she must tell them everything, everything. Library Science? What was that?

She describes it—her courses, her fieldwork, her trip to Ottawa, the lab work, the Friday get-togethers. She can hear the glamour she is giving a course that really has none and she feels sorry for her erstwhile colleagues. Sorry that they believe her, sorry that they think she has gone to a better life. She will never tell them how she misses the world of ideas. Despite the discomfort of poor teaching facilities and the pain of stupid students, she had known the excitement of breaking into minds. That is entirely missing in her new life.

When she finally finishes with her account of life in the West, she is introduced to unfamiliar faces. The new recruits look pleasant, blank and uninterested. They do not care that it is her absence that has given one of them a job.

The bell rang, the coffee break was over. The teachers disappeared with their registers under their arms, that badge of belonging. And Nina had to accept the fact that she was now an outsider.

It wasn't the institution she missed, it was the community. What had she been searching for ever since she left but community? At the La Leche League, the HRL, the consciousness raising group, the Killam. She strove to find a place into which she fit easily but every way she turned, she scraped against jagged edges.

As the day approached for Nina's departure, Mrs Singh vociferously assured Nina that her mother was very lonely. 'How she waits for your phone calls, talking of you all the time, all the time. You must take her back with you. What is there for her here?'

Nina, tightlipped, said yes, Mrs Singh, instead of yes, aunty. She knew her formality would offend.

'Stupid bitch,' stormed Nina later. 'She can't resist interfering.'

'I hope you weren't rude to her. She has a good heart. Who else do I have to ask about me?'

'Why don't you come and live with me, Ma? I am your only child,' said Nina thinking if only her mother would agree to immigrate to Canada, her life would assume the simple sweetness she yearned for.

'We'll see, beta. You have just married. You need to be alone with your husband.'

This silenced Nina. God knew what her mother would think if she came, how many dark corners her piercing maternal gaze would uncover. Let her own life get sorted out, then she would call her, then insist, then finally give her the comfort she deserved. After her life got sorted out.

July end. Sitting on the plane, back to Canada.

This was the trip that was supposed to give her peace, clarity and wisdom, but two months later peace, clarity and wisdom are still playing hide and seek. The corners in which they hide have multiplied, and Nina is angry and upset about this.

To fly angry and upset is to prolong an already long journey. Nina as usual does herself no favours. Her head feels dull, and when the air hostess arrives with the drink trolley, she takes a beer. At the sight of the golden froth in the plastic glass and the little packet of roasted almonds, she decides once again that one should only live for the moment, as advised by the Bhagavad Gita. It is clearly useless trying to do anything else.

viii

Back in Canada. Back to Ananda, back to jet lag, back to silence and isolation. Two months, that's all it had taken, two months to forget the solitude that ran through her days when

292

she was not working or studying. If Zenobia could only see her as she roamed, distressed, from room to room, no one to talk to, alone and lonely, she might understand a little better.

Back to cleaning, shopping, borrowing books from the library. Back to walking the streets, gazing at the maple trees and admiring their beauty. Back to eating chips, Cheetos, brownies, and drinking root beer. Back to waiting. Waiting for Ananda to come home. Waiting for term to start.

In the evenings Nina asked Ananda about his day, his patients, Gary and Sue. Ananda was full of conversation—he must have missed talking when I wasn't here, poor man, mused Nina. Everybody needs someone, and fate has joined us together.

'It's strange being so alone here, after India,' she remarked.

'At least you don't have a thousand people poking their noses in your business.'

'It's a small price to pay.'

He grunted. She looked at him. Who was he? At times so distant, at times so attentive. Their marriage was in the bright flat colours of a child's painting.

His obvious pleasure upon her return contributed to her guilt. She had transgressed, her discontent was her fault. From now on she would devote herself to him, but in this endeavour she experienced a barrier impossible to cross.

Laughing to show she was not serious she asked, 'Well, did you have an affair while I was away?'

His lips pursed, his eyebrows drew together. What made her say that?

Nothing. She just wondered. He seemed different. To herself, she thought, how could a man look blank and tense at the same time?

'Don't talk rubbish.'

Ananda should have known how to forestall his wife's suspicions, especially since he had missed her. His emptiness during her absence brought home to him how comfortable he had grown with his Indian counterpart by his side. Maybe he could only have sex with white women once his older self was housed, safe and secure. Did his uncle ever feel totally at ease with Nancy? For seven years Ananda had yearned for a Canadian wife, but his body had made its preferences clear and he had followed its dictates.

Fortunately that body was now comfortable with a larger playing field. He had experimented while Nina was away; it would have been foolish not to make use of the time he had paid so dearly for. In jeans and an open shirt, an old silk scarf tied around his neck, he had made his way to the bars near the quay. The first girl was blonde, he liked the look of her slender white legs as she sat perched on a high stool. They reminded him of the long ago Kim. He looked at her, she smiled and suggested he buy her a drink. It was easy, so easy. He was a traveller passing by, he said, on his way to India. India was always exotic enough to create interest and make sure that there was no future.

After this fling he had told himself, enough. He had proved himself beyond a doubt. True, he had lasted only ten minutes, but he had compensated by doing it twice in the night. The girl had seemed satisfied. She had moaned and arched, he had done some of the things Mandy had taught him. Then a few weeks later, again the yearning for this kind of adventure.

In bars, he was anonymous, he could experience the thrill of being anybody. Why stick to the familiar? The second time he claimed he was Egyptian, Omar Sharif.

'Isn't that the name of an actor?' the girl had asked.

'My parents named me after him.'

'My name is simple. Patricia.'

'A lovely name. So Patricia, what are you doing tonight?'

Patricia looked at him. He looked different, sexy and intense at the same time. She knew what he was after, and she knew it wouldn't be repeated. He was leaving for Cairo the next day. But, might be fun with an Egyptian man.

It was.

*

294

Ananda did want to bring excitement into his marriage, but too many potential sources of conflict bogged him down. For one thing Nina had reverted to her earlier obsession about children. Going to India had influenced her in this direction, he accused.

'I can be pregnant and still study. There is someone in my class who has just had a baby. She said being a student meant her time was more flexible.'

'Well, I think we should wait till you finish. That is what we had decided. It's not a game, you know.'

But still she talked of motherhood, continuity, infertility treatments and her biological clock. His wife was conservative after all, in different ways he kept coming to that conclusion. He was the true Westerner, she the true Indian.

Did she know how much these things cost, he asked irritably, trying to shut her up.

Yes, she did. They cost but not that much. If he wanted, she would pay him back when she started earning.

At this he got really angry. Their fight lasted three days, the coldness another week.

The many faces of Ananda did not amount to a man Nina comprehended. It was obvious from the joy with which he greeted her at the airport that he had missed her. And then he had insisted on making love as soon as she put her foot inside the apartment, never mind her fatigue, the day and night journey, the jet lag. Just a quick one, he pleaded, just a quick one, I missed you so much.

She found this passion reassuring. I'm going to try really hard from now on; this marriage is the main thing in my life, she vowed as the quick one got over.

'Let's start again,' she murmured.

'Yes, let's.'

'Two months was a long time.' Now she felt it, who hadn't felt it before.

'Too long.'

'Well, you were the one who bought the ticket.'
'I didn't know how much I would miss you.'
'You didn't, huh?'
'I love you, baby.'
'Thank you, dearest.'
'Welcome home.'

Come September she was definitely going to ignore Anton. In the arms of his wife at night, and behind the desk at the New York Public Library in the day—between these two poles there was no room for anybody else. He had never said there was, but she didn't have to agree to such terms. She wanted permanence and after her degree, she would do all it took to conceive. Her mother was right, this was the West, anything was possible.

In her mid thirties she felt insecure about a future with no children. Her profession was being taken care of, but on the home front she needed more than Ananda. In India husbands were not expected to meet one's entire needs. Here it was all man—woman—relationship—love—fulfilment, screaming at her till she wanted to give up the ghost. The anchor she was forging out of the iron mined from the virgin soil of Canada needed a broader base on which to rest.

The passion Ananda had exhibited on her arrival soon waned, leaving her empty and dissatisfied. His crimes loomed large. He wouldn't address himself properly to the issue of their children, he kept calling her baby, which she hated, he had taken to wearing a ridiculous silk scarf around his neck when they went out. Did he think he was a gay lothario rather than a middle class immigrant from small town India?

Above all her feeling of isolation was creeping back. It was borne on her that she was living with a man who never understood a word she was saying. He exhibited concern for practical things. Cooking, housework, car rides, tickets home, all taken care of, but who was the wife he worried about? Nina didn't think she had ever known the woman, though she would have given her right arm to be her.

The first day at the Killam. Nina spent some hours imagining the ways in which she was going to ignore Anton.

But she was destined to be thwarted. No greying head turned out to be his, no matter how piercingly she gazed at it from a distance. Seven days passed in this manner, with the desire to ignore him now raised to fevered proportions. Perhaps he had decided to drop out—how would she ever know? She grew tense thinking of this possibility.

When he finally returned, Nina heard, eavesdropping on the explanation he gave the teacher, that his wife had sprained her ankle; there was no way he could have come earlier.

His wife again. Was there no end to his concern? Nina left the classroom, turning left to avoid him at the elevators.

Anton's priorities were clear. Staying away or seeking him, both were fraught with emotional intensity. She would be natural, friendly, only interacting with him as a colleague.

The beginning of October, Nina's third autumn in Canada. It is the afternoon break on Wednesday—the day associated in Nina's mind with extramarital sex, and a day on which she had to struggle even more with the sadness in her nature.

'Hey Neen.' It was Anton. He was running to catch up.

She stopped.

'Long time since we talked.'

'I thought this was the way you wanted it.' Moodily she kicked the few leaves her feet could find on the pavement.

He was too intelligent not to know what she was saying. His wife had been sick and he had been distracted—nothing to do with her. And now, he went on, would she like to come to his room? He had missed her.

Her traitor heart stood still at the prospect of simple, joyful sex with a man who understood what she said the minute she said it.

All of her longed to say yes, to forget, to go.

But he had been too silent. She was not to him what he was to her.

'I think it better we don't see each other in that way.'

He might argue, try and convince her; she would have to be firm. She steeled herself to resist.

She was not tested. 'See you then,' he said and loped off.

The following months she hurt more than she had bargained for. She sat alone in the deep purple armchairs ranged against the big glass windows overlooking the courtyard, pretending to study while thinking about her life. Even though she could see that Anton had been using her, she grieved over him. Humiliated by her own longing, she wondered why she was such a sucker.

No satisfactory answer was forthcoming. She only knew she missed the black room, the intense well-being she felt after love making. But he didn't care for her, so it was impossible to continue.

Her pain warned her never to try an affair again. To bargain away her peace of mind for an ephemeral satisfaction made no sense. And when the man was married, it meant he always had an excuse for not committing. Her own marriage did not protect her, while his protected him—one way street from start to finish. Initially it had seemed an adventurous thing to enter into, but once the exhilaration wore off, all the tawdriness lay revealed, along with the heartbreak.

Once or twice, from the corner of her eye, she saw Anton's footsteps slow down as he approached the purple armchair but she forced herself to ignore them.

So Nina went through her assignments, the Friday evening meetings, her job in the department library, through the shortening days.

The winter was long, cold and hard. Snow fell and fell and fell. The wind blew. By four it was dark, and the whole of

December the sun didn't appear. Nina's DNA, programmed by years in India to love cloudy skies and drizzling rainy days, began to wilt under this onslaught. When people around her groaned about the weather she did too.

'What a winter,' said Ananda admiringly. 'They say it's the worst snowfall since 1928.'

'Why won't the sun ever shine?' demanded Nina. 'Day after day, nothing but grey. It is so depressing.'

'It's called seasonal affective disorder.'

'What?'

'Feeling depressed by lack of sunshine. SAD for short.'

'Do you feel this way?'

He laughed while she looked drearily out of the window.

ix

A field trip to New York was planned for March. They would leave on a Sunday, spend Monday to Wednesday touring the library and cataloguing systems of the city, Thursday would be devoted to individual areas of special interest, then the weekend was theirs to do as they liked. Just like Ottawa.

'I thought you were learning to be a librarian in Canada,' remarked Ananda, patriot and critic.

'The school follows the system recognised by the American Library Association. It makes it easier to get jobs. Why don't you join me later for a holiday like you did last year? If you come out on Friday we could have the weekend together.'

Ananda grunted. He was bent over a cookbook, there was a glass of beer at his side. His lips were faintly pursed, his Mandy encouraged moustache stuck out a little.

'I don't want to go to New York,' he now said.

'Why? Please.'

Too much money, too unsafe, too many rumours about mugging, the prices too high and not quite the Canadian notion of an ideal destination.

She was disappointed. He was ignoring the opportunity to be together, away from daily preoccupations. The class was buzzing with the excitement of going to New York, many spouses were coming. Again she longed for somebody to share her life with, to be interested in her. How could she build a bridge between Ananda and herself if she had to provide all the materials? The construction would collapse at the first footfall.

In school they were given detailed briefs of what they were to see. They were going to visit the New York Public Library, the UN Library, of interest particularly to international students, they were going to tour HW Wilson, the leading indexing company in the Bronx, they were going to the JP Morgan Library, specialising in rare books and early publications. Here they would witness the care that went into the preservation of old books, the humidity control, the temperature control, the specially built display cases.

Nina spent Saturday packing. Something momentous had happened to her on the trip to Ottawa, maybe something would happen again, though she couldn't imagine what.

She had heard there would be some parties. Opening her cupboard she stared at her beautiful, unworn saris, for which conditions were never right. The ground was mostly wet, the wind mostly high, the sari too liable to embarrass her by flying up to reveal petticoat and legs. No, leave the sari. She would take Western clothes, all the black stuff that had served over the year for both formal and informal.

Ananda drove her to the airport. The trees undulating on either side of the road appeared almost black in the dull winter light. The sky was a blotchy grey. Patches of dark earth showed amongst the piles of snow in the fields beyond. It was all as dismal as her heart. Flurries began to drift against the windshield. They clung for a moment and then slid down against the onslaught of the wiper. They were just flurries, damp, soggy and ill formed, without the staying power of snowflakes. She felt like one herself.

As Ananda drove into the airport portico Nina could see the massed vehicles to her left in the car park sea. The flurries were getting larger, coating the roofs with a faint film of white. Ananda jumped out, opened the trunk, took out her small suitcase. He didn't say anything about parking and joining her, neither did she. The wind was tossing the flakes about, clearly the weather was going to get worse. It was important Ananda hurry back.

'Ok, bye,' said Ananda, getting into the car and strapping on his seat belt.

'Ananda?'

'What?'

'I'll miss you.'

'Me too.'

A wave and he was gone. She dragged herself and her suitcase into the building, and stood in the line snaking between ropes. There were her classmates, chatting, looking at ease.

'Hey Nina,' from Andrea.

'Hi Nina,' from Tim.

'Hi, hi,' and then to Anton, 'Oh hi,' for wasn't he like one of the others?

'How're you doing?'

'Fine, fine, and you?'

'Me too.'

They found themselves next to each other in the plane. Her skin prickled slightly at this proximity, but otherwise everything was under control.

'Are you pleased to be going home?'

'Yeah.'

'I've never seen New York.'

'I hope you like it, some people don't.'

'Does your wife?'

'Loves it. She tells me all Indians do.'

'Will she be at the airport?'

'Nah. She is on night shift at the hospital. That's why I'll be staying with everybody else at the Y, instead of at home.'

It was time to mention her husband. 'Ananda doesn't like the idea of New York. Maybe he is more Canadian than Indian.'

'Let's see what you think.'

Nina loved New York from the moment she arrived. Everything was to her taste: its variety, size, parks, multi ethnic people, first and second hand book shops, little eating places, its assurance that it was the only place in the world.

They were booked at the International Student House, an old red brick building, somewhat rundown. The fourth floor had been reserved for all of them. Nina put away her things, inhaled the slight odour of the room and gazed meditatively at the wall that formed her view. It was a bit depressing inside, obviously the place to be was the streets. Their cheap flight meant they had arrived late at night, their education would start on the morrow.

At breakfast the next morning there were loud complaints about cockroaches. They hadn't had to put up with this in Ottawa. Andrea said she had never seen a cockroach before, just read about them; she had almost taken the next flight home. Anton said in New York cockroaches were part of the wallpaper, especially in an old building like the ISH. Nina said in India cockroaches were everywhere, one waged a constant and losing battle with them; there were mating and birthing seasons, plus seasons of baby cockroaches. Andrea shuddered and said she would never go to India.

The dining room was on a lower level than the lobby. From where she sat Nina could see people's feet going up and down on the sidewalk outside, a purposeful New Yorker walk. They too were going to join the march of purpose as they got into the bus organised for them. Their first stop: the New York Public Library on 5th Avenue and 42nd Street.

As Nina climbed the steps of the library she marvelled at its magnificence. Was this the entrance to a hall of books or some exquisite palace? Mammoth, magnificent, colonnaded, its entrance flanked by majestic stone lions, the respect given to print by this building reflected all the glory of the city. Inside, its pillars, halls, arches, imposing staircases, beautiful chandeliers, high ceilings, marble floors and walls, rotunda, main reading room with its painted ceiling, vaulted roof, long windows, wooden tables with brass lamps, the balcony running around the mezzanine—all this made the building a temple to the written word.

Unlike other libraries the NYPL was run by funds from both the city and patrons of culture. An early exemplar of money made and well spent was John Jacob Astor, immigrant, fur trader, America's first millionaire and founder of this institution.

Only four other libraries in the US could compete with the NYPL: the public library in Boston, the Library of Congress, the university libraries of Yale and Harvard. The NYPL was among the largest research as well as circulating libraries in the US; its magnificence drew ten million visitors a year, while its telephone reference section attracted up to a thousand questions a day from all over the world. Detail after detail their guide piled on as they toured the great building and glimpsed the stacks that were not open to the public, as they saw the rows of card catalogues, examined the system of reference code and number that the readers used.

Plans had been sanctioned to extend the library westwards under Bryant Park. When it was finished, one hundred and twenty five thousand square feet and miles more shelf space would be added.

Surely to work in this building was to know the high point of being a librarian. As they emerged, past the lions that they now knew had been nicknamed Patience and Fortitude by New York mayor Fiorello LaGuardia during the Depression, Nina turned to Anton and said, 'Wow, your city is so extraordinary.'

'I didn't know some of these facts myself.'

'Even though you worked here?'

'Just one of hundreds. You saw the reading room and stacks? I was among those scurrying around to fill requests.'

'Must have been so interesting.'

'Not particularly. Didn't require special skill.'

'Are you going to come back here and work?'

'In a way it would be ideal, but I want to see other parts of North America. Its Lakie who refuses to move—she needs to be near her family. I love Halifax, but she couldn't wait to get back the one time she came.'

So, his wife was difficult in some ways. She was glad. Other people should be unhappy, it added to her pleasure.

'I told her other immigrants are not so set in their ways, but how many do you know, she asked. I had initially told her about an Indian girl in my class, but later I stopped mentioning you.'

Treacherously her heart read significance into this statement. She turned away, confused.

They were going to eat at a McDonald's. Everyone groaned, is this what they had come to New York for, but, can't help it, folks, the place has a parking lot. You are on your own for dinner, do what you like then.

'Do you like Japanese food?' asked Anton.

'Never had it.'

'Would you like to try? We could have dinner together, I know of a nice restaurant within walking distance of the ISH.'

There was a familiarity about Anton that made the suggestion a gesture of friendship rather than romance. In the city of his marital happiness, any thought that indicated otherwise was indecent. They knew how they stood with each other. She would be neither prudish nor expectant.

That evening at seven thirty they walked the six streets down to Meri-can. The evening was cold but not freezing. They walked down 7th Avenue, past 14th, 15th, 16th, 17th, 18th, 19th streets, talking of Nova Scotian versus New York winters, the Canadian dollar versus the American, dreary office jobs, the value of a Library Science degree. The easiness she felt with him had both to do with the distance she had established during the year and the fact that once they had been lovers. There was no need to create an interest; it had been there and now it was dead.

On the corner between 19th and 20th streets was the small restaurant. Red lanterns hung over the tables, large stick fans curved archly against the walls, huge curly bamboos guarded the cash. In the centre was a raised dais with tables. Nina and Anton sat there, next to the large windows, looking out.

The menus came, and Anton gazed at his with the eyes of a lover. Nina imitated Anton's order: sushi, salad.

'Sushi is the one thing I really miss in Halifax,' said Anton dreamily. 'The cuisine there is so boring.'

Next to New York the whole world was bound to be boring. Perhaps it was not fair to compare a Canadian small town with this megalopolis.

The conversation broke, then Anton amused himself by asking whether Nina knew sushi was raw fish.

No, she didn't.

Dread filled her.

A carafe of house wine would help with the coming ordeal. Life was all about pushing yourself and doing new things.

The sushi arrived. The rolls looked pretty—black, white, with a dot of colour in the middle. She slathered one in soy sauce and red chilli paste. Gingerly she ate, quickly she gulped the wine. It was not so bad. Now let's talk about the wife.

'Where does Lakshmi work?' she asked.

'At the Union Memorial Hospital. Not far from here.'

'It's a pity she had to work nights this week of all weeks.'

'Don't worry about her.'

She lapsed into silence. They finished their sushi. 'Another glass of wine? It's quite good.'

They drank slowly, talking of the day. Outside Nina could see the yellow-orange street light fall on the many passersby and the changing traffic light. Next to the restaurant entrance was an old man, sunk against the lamppost. At his feet was a dog and an open guitar case.

'Why is he sitting like that?' she asked.

'One of the homeless,' said Anton briefly.

'Homeless? You mean no home?'

That was what he meant. Yes, in the world's richest country, in its richest city, there were people on the streets. Such was the heart of the administration.

Nina thought of the Indian government's heart. So far as its millions of poor were concerned, it too was weak and feeble. Ananda claimed Canada had heart, thus it was the best country in the world.

Anton paid and they walked out into the cold night. It was nine, and a light rain was falling. The homeless man did not move.

'Should we give him something?'

'Nah, he's probably on drugs.'

She could see the brown spots on the man's balding scalp. His clothes were a greasy, dark colour. The dog also looked as though it were on drugs, as immobile as its master. In India Nina knew what to do when confronted with misery. Here she was less certain.

'Are you sure he's on drugs?'

'Of course. Can't you see? Let's go now.'

'Well, thanks for dinner. Let me treat you to a taxi.'

Anton stepped out onto the road with an outstretched arm. Within seconds a taxi drew up.

'Thank you for a wonderful evening,' she repeated as they reached the ISH.

'Thank you for agreeing to come.'

They opened the heavy old doors and walked towards the ancient elevator. Nina waited till they were inside before she said, 'Why shouldn't I agree to come? We are friends after all.'

'You haven't behaved in a very friendly manner to me all this term.'

'Good heavens! How can you say that? You made no attempt to communicate all summer, I can't be on again, off again... '

'You were the one who was so afraid of your husband knowing anything.'

'What about honest to goodness friendship?'

'We are both married. How much friendship is possible?'

'One wants to be thought of as more than a sex machine.'

'You didn't seem to mind.'

He was insulting her. Anton, the patient, good-tempered, uninvolved, where was he? Her head felt heavy. She needed to go to her room and think.

The elevator arrived at the fourth floor, clanking and shuddering. She got out, he followed her down the dingy corridor. She pushed the key into her room lock and struggled fruitlessly. He took the key, unlocked the door, followed her inside and before she could put on the light, took her in his arms.

'Baby, let's make it a romantic evening.'

Nina stiffened. Too late it was obvious that the dinner's hidden agenda had been sex. The fact that a bigger fool than herself did not breathe in the universe presented itself forcefully.

'I am very tired,' she now said.

'This won't take long.' He edged her towards the bed.

'Anton, please, too much time has passed. I don't feel close to you anymore.'

'We must rectify that, mustn't we?'

'I don't feel like it, Anton, please.'

'But why—when you used to feel like it all the time? I've missed you, baby, I'm lonely without you. I thought in New York, we could recreate our Ottawa night.'

'Yes, with your wife in the same city.'

'That's why I chose to stay here with you, rather than at home.'

What on earth was he getting at? He didn't care beyond a point—he couldn't—he had made that very clear. She tried to

307

disentangle herself from him, his grip tightened, her suffocation increased.

'Come on, Neen, it was wonderful what we had going between us… ' His hoarse voice made her long ago desire seem sluttish and despicable.

'Well, for me it's over.' She tried to get up, but his weight pinned her down, while his hands simultaneously worked his zipper and her waistband.

Was he trying to have sex forcibly? The idea of it was so startling and then so revolting, it collected her wits. With all her might she shoved at him, trying to get her leg under his so she could use her body as a lever.

'Come on now, baby,' grunted Anton, more and more beast-like.

'Anton, get off me, get off me this second, you bastard,' she screamed in a low voice, mindful of the place, as he put his mouth on hers, bruising her lips.

Her legs were wide apart now, his pants off, he was pushing himself into her. Her tightness and reluctance increased her pain, but could not keep him out. His arms were heavy weights against hers, her breath was caught inside her chest, she was panting and gasping.

What was once so pleasurable was now agonising.

'Come on, baby, don't say you're not enjoying it,' the beast grunted some more.

At last he shuddered and groaned, grew limp, slipped outside and sank to the side of her bed. She got up and held the door open, 'Get out, get out, or I'll tell Dr Hartley. Just get out,' she hissed, violent, but controlled.

'Alright, alright, don't lose your shirt.'

His pants were up and he was ready to face the world, having raped a woman he had slept with for six months.

She shut the door behind him. The lights were still off, but she didn't want to see anything. She collapsed onto the bed, one of many defenceless creatures in an uncaring city.

*

The next morning she did not go down for breakfast. Andrea came knocking at the door. Dr Hartley wanted to know if she was all right. The bus had arrived; they were going to leave in another minute.

So, morning had come without her noticing the lifting dark. But she could go nowhere, she was not feeling well.

Andrea had to agree with this assessment. Nina looked terrible, should she call a doctor?

No, no, she would be fine, she only needed some rest, but thanks, Andrea.

The door shut, the footsteps receded, the clank of the elevator also receded. She fell back into bed, and covered her head with the musty smelling blanket.

Hours passed. Her helpless feeling spread to every pore, reducing her to a baby. If she exposed him, that would mean exposing herself as well. He would use their liaison to defend himself. The whole affair would be out, and her integrity questioned. She shrank from any gaze, so inevitable once she opened her mouth.

Around noon she got up. The smell on her body, the grey dreary room, made her feel sicker. At the end of the corridor were the bathrooms. Numbly she stood under the shower. As the hot water ran over her, her mind grew quieter.

She got dressed and went outside. It was cloudy, a billboard announced it was forty degrees Fahrenheit. Slowly, slowly she walked. The streets of New York must be the most fascinating streets in the world, the most commercial, the most busy. How much she had enjoyed them yesterday.

A few steps lead into a park. Benches, trees, the slanting sun and a sign that said Union Square. She entered and sat, as still, as resigned as the old man across from her, as the young girl with a homeless card near the steps, sat like them as the sun stepped slowly across the sky.

When she got up, her limbs were stiff. She was cold, thirsty and hungry. At a little magazine shop she bought a packet of tortilla chips and a coconut filled chocolate bar. Her mouth closed over the excessive salt and sweet and she crunched mindlessly. At Broadway and 21st, she noticed a bookshop with rows of bookcases outside. The sign above said 'The Strand, eight miles of books'. Their pull was strong. She entered. She would be among friends.

Only to feel that if this was yesterday, she would have been able to revel in paradise. Books, books, every one of them half the cover price, many of them less. She wandered past the display tables, between the racks, examined the many review copies, picking, flipping, picking, flipping. Eventually everything was put down, nothing was desirable enough to buy.

By now it was dark outside. From an early age fear had been fostered in her, the empty road, the increasing night, all to be avoided. She had been grossly misled. It hadn't happened like that, not like that at all.

The streets were still crowded. Through big windows she could look into small eating places like the Meri-can, feeding the multitudes. No one cooked in New York. She turned into one shop on 7th Avenue, Murray's Bagels it said. Bagel, another thing she had just heard of—like rape.

She stood in a long line and ordered something that turned out to be massive, doughy and unpleasant, the thick bland cream cheese adding nothing to the flavour. At three dollars fifty cents, this was an experience dearly bought.

The heavy food did this much, it pulled her towards considering strategies. Tomorrow she would get up and go on the tour. She would eat breakfast with the others. She was not going to let Anton ruin her life. If this was not much of a strategy, she was not much of a confrontationist.

It was late when she crept back into the ISH. There was a note from Andrea under her door: how was she, she had come to visit, hoped to see her tomorrow. Yes, Andrea, you will see me tomorrow. No message from the rapist, no apology, no concern.

She could not sleep. Her stomach responded with anger to the bagel, capturing it as hostage, refusing to release it.

310

Shifting uncomfortably in bed, Nina for a moment did not register the significance of the door knob moving. He was on the other side.

Mesmerised she gazed at that rotating movement. Her room was on the corner, she could hear cars from the street, a pallid light filtered through the net curtains.

Then a soft knock. Once, twice. A long wait, and once again. Finally footsteps getting fainter, down the corridor and out of her life. She knew Anton would not try again.

Next morning he approached her. He smiled, his eyes crinkled; he didn't know what had gotten into him that night, he had heard she was ill, he hoped it wasn't on his account, that would be too stupid for words, after all they had been lovers, hadn't they?

Nina turned, incapable of addressing such effrontery, and after some hesitation Anton moved away. The rest of the day in the library of *The New York Times* passed in a daze.

That evening Professor Hartley told them, beaming at the pleasure they were about to receive, that they had been invited to a party. It was at a penthouse on 99th and Broadway owned by John Berry, publisher of the *Library Journal*. How many of them remembered what he had said about the *Library Journal*?

In Nina's mind flashed that it had started in 1876, and such had been her school training, that despite all that had happened, she vouchsafed the answer.

Professor Hartley looked pleased. Nina could always be counted on to produce dates.

They took the subway to 99th. As they emerged into the open, Professor Hartley said, 'John has the most wonderful swing in his loft. It's bolted into the ceiling, and you can swing right to the windows and see all of New York.'

'In India, Gujarati homes have swings too,' said Nina pedantically.

'Yes?' said the professor absently.

The apartment was big, beautiful, minimalist, modern, with glass walls on two sides. It bespoke of fine and expensive cosmopolitan living. They would probably never in their lives find themselves in such a place again, face to face with an aerial view of this overwhelming city.

Nina sat in the swing, flew over the lights of New York, infinitely more alluring than the stars which could barely be seen. The earth, instead, was covered with moving stars, thick and bright. Something to tell her mother in her next letter.

Trip over. Journey home. Nina sat at the back of the plane, next to Andrea and Sam. Anton had stayed behind, presumably to repeat his sexual acts on unsuspecting women friends in New York. He would be back in time for class on Monday.

She would take the airport bus to the Lord Nelson Hotel. From there a taxi to her hearth and husband. Three more months to the end of term, the end of Anton, the end of being a student. She would be a qualified librarian, one who had the promise of a job anywhere in North America. She would believe in that promise, believe in new opportunities. Certainly those seemed more within her reach than her companionate marriage plus children dream.

And she made another vow. She would be happy. How was less clear than it had ever been. But to not be meant she had fallen victim to circumstances, and that was even more terrible.

Her father, fond of eternal verities, used to quote lines from Lin Yutang, one of his favourite authors, 'The art of being happy, though poor, consists in one phrase, to think, "it could be worse… "' Simple truths sometimes console the heart.

Back in Library School, assaulted by Anton's tentative smile, Anton's efforts at apology. She ignored him, but it was hard to put the incident behind her when she saw him all the time.

Had she invited this on herself in any way? The aggressor in him connecting to the weakness in her? She, who had been trained to be careful around men from the moment she could walk, she would not have let down her guard unless she were with someone she trusted. And she had felt safe with a man who was once her lover.

How could she have been so deceived in another's character? Been foolish enough to be unaware of the links between former desires and present danger?

This was her female conclusion, and she knew it had flaws.

She contemplated going to her group, discussing the incident, putting it in a larger context, drawing sustenance. They would be supportive, more than supportive. They would discuss options—go to the police, expose him, tell Dr Cunningham, get him expelled, lodge a complaint. Violence required counterattack. Now was the time to break that mindset that made women victims. Now, now, now.

Her thoughts made her very tired. They kept needling her to do something when she didn't want to. She had been through enough. Perhaps one day, in the distant future, with another set of women, she might be able to discuss the rape and its aftermath, the self-flagellation, the helplessness, the confusion, the lack of action. Perhaps one day, but not now.

Sex with her husband became difficult. After a few days she gave him a bowdlerized version of what had happened during the trip. It hadn't been so late, around ten, she had decided to take a walk to clear two glasses of wine from her head, when a man attacked her from behind. He had snatched her gold chain, then dragged her into an alley leading off from the street. She had screamed, but he put a knife against her neck. From somewhere a shape appeared, the attacker's hand momentarily slackened, she had run like the wind. Though she had escaped, she was still in a state of shock.

As a story it was full of holes, but he didn't notice them.

'Why didn't you let me know at once?'

'For what reason? To upset you?'

'We are husband and wife.'

'It hurt to talk about it.'

She started crying, tears coming down her face, followed by great ghastly gulps. He patted her, long awkward strokes, up and down her back, rumpling her clothes. She did not like the feel of his heavy hand, everything furthered her irritation.

'Did you tell them? Your Library Science people? They were responsible for you.'

'I was afraid, I didn't know what would happen. Suppose they had insisted on an inquiry, a police report, a medical examination—maybe having to stay longer, lots of talk, the whole trip ruined for everybody—I didn't think I could do it.'

Yes, she couldn't ruin the trip for everybody. As Indians, they were together on this. 'Remember I told you New York was a dangerous place.'

'What choice did I have? It could have happened to anyone, anywhere.'

'But not so easily.'

'Please—do you mind—I don't want to talk about it.'

He looked injured. How could he console her if she refused to talk?

'But it must have been quite traumatic,' he encouraged.

'It was.'

She seemed so remote. He had instinctively felt—and how right he had been—that this trip was bad news. Every day the papers told of violent crime in the States. Nina couldn't take care of herself the way these Western women could. He doubted Mandy would ever find herself in such a situation.

'Even a child knows better than to go out alone in New York at night,' he said, his annoyance increasing by the minute.

The face she turned towards him was blank. He wanted to comfort her, but she had to protect herself against him. What would he say if he knew what had really happened?

The days dragged on. This was her third winter, harsh, never-ending cold, snow and icy wind. As she walked home, her shawl wrapped tightly around her head, her hands in their gloves, her feet in fur lined boots, her long down jacket keeping her warm till her knees, she wished she could escape into the purity of the landscape and be separated from her thoughts forever.

Snow fell, her feet marked out boot prints in the fresh soft whiteness, the sky was pale and grey, damp flakes speckled her dark hair, her coat, shoulders, shawl, everything quiet and pristine, except for the polluting storms inside her. She passed the Citadel, where she had gone with Ananda to celebrate Canada Day. This is our country, he had said, a new country, a clean country. That was also true.

x

The weather turned warmer, the piles of snow began to dwindle, a few daring green shoots appeared next to protective houses. Storm windows were removed, on sunny days glass shutters slid slightly open. Come May she would be qualified to look for a job anywhere. Any change would be welcome. She was tired of the life she was living.

The phone rang one evening after dinner, dishes, channel surfing and conversation. Nina could tell from Ananda's tone that he was talking to his sister. A minute into the conversation she felt something was wrong. Her mouth became dry, her heart beat heavily.

'What is it?' she asked as he put the receiver down and said nothing.

'Nothing.'

'Why was she calling? What is it? Is it Ma?'

'No—I mean, not really.'

And then she knew, of course she knew. 'Is she dead?'

'Why do you say things like that?'

It was the link that bound mother and daughter together as well as her own expectations from life. 'Just tell me.'

He tried to hold her, but she wouldn't let him. So he had to tell her, with no softening touch, that her mother had died that morning in what appeared to be a heart attack. The landlady had discovered her in bed, she had phoned Alka and now Alka wanted to know whether they should keep the body or not. He was going to phone her back as soon as he talked to Nina.

Nothing he said made any sense to her. Her face was wet with tears, her mouth was open, she sounded like an animal.

'Well, she was old, and you always said she was ill,' he tried to reason with her. 'This was to be expected.'

The animal sounds increased. Ananda made her lie down on the bed, then got on the phone to consult with Alka. Should Nina decide to go it would take her at least thirty six hours in flight and transit, let alone the time difference. No, they decided, that was too long. The body had to be burned.

He set about phoning his uncle, Gary, the travel agent, and then Gayatri. Gayatri, whom he had never met, but with whom Nina had spent so much time. The number was there in the phone book. As he dialled he considered calling Sue as well, but no, maybe an Indian would be better at such a moment.

Meanwhile Nina sobbed and sobbed, while her husband circled uneasily around her.

Half an hour later the bell rang. Uncle is here, said Ananda, but Nina pushed her head into the pillow and refused to see anyone. After what seemed hours, Ananda came to say that when somebody was making an effort, the least she could do was make one too, people were concerned, uncle had offered every kind of help, maybe if she had met him she might have felt better.

She heard his voice from so far away, he could have been in another country. Her knees were scrunched up, she was lying on the bed with the pillow against her face, her whole body trembling. He stared at her for a moment, then rubbed her shoulder, but she did not respond.

Still later in the night Gayatri arrived and moved fearlessly into Nina's anguish. Arms around her, she murmured, 'Oh poor poor Neen, poor Neen, never mind, she has attained moksha, she will not be born again in this world full of pain and sorrow, she is free. She left no debts unsettled, no duty undone. Don't be sad, Neen, she died in her sleep, only great souls do that. Everybody has to become an orphan one day, what can we do?'

The stream of familiar sounding words continued, words that accompanied any death Nina had ever known. Grief for her father added to the loss. She sobbed and sobbed, pulled tissue after flowered tissue from the box thrust under her hand.

Finally Gayatri asked, 'When is the funeral?'

'Over by now.'

'When are you leaving?'

'Day after. Tomorrow was all booked.'

'We live so far away,' murmured Gayatri.

At such times the price they paid was heavy.

The next day Gayatri put some things together in a suitcase, not helped at all by Nina. Her mother was dead, why should she think of clothes, toiletries and footwear? Her Delhi stuff would do.

As Gayatri left she hugged Nina—if you suffer, she will not be able to rest. It was a way of thinking that had its uses. Nina struggled to control herself. Ananda was returning soon, he had gone to pick up her ticket, she would be leaving early next morning.

And so began the long, stiff journey home. Four hours of waiting in Toronto, six in London. At the Heathrow duty free she bought Scotch and chocolate for her in-laws; the funeral arrangements had fallen on them, it was the least she could do. She bought her stuff and sat in the departure lounge, staring mindlessly outside the window at the big silver jets slowly wheeling around on the runway. She could not bring herself to open the book between her hands.

Eventually, the last leg of the journey. They were flying over the Middle East; she was just a few hours away from home. Her chest grew tight with pain. She should have somehow insisted that her mother immediately come and live with them.

317

But there had been reluctance on all sides, and no apparent need for hurry.

She was sure her mother's last thoughts had been of her. Had she felt alone, frightened? She had been found dead by her old friend, the landlady. How right her mother had been to value her.

Delhi. A wave of April heat struck as soon as they emerged from the hole of the plane. She looked up at the windows of the terminal and an hour and a half later emerged to Alka and Ramesh.

As soon as she saw them she began to cry. They in turn clutched her sympathetically. She cried while they took over her trolley, cried on the way to the car and all the way home.

'Bas, bas,' they murmured. 'You must be brave. She finished her earthly duties and left.'

In the car Nina was forced to hear how the landlady had called them, how they had immediately gone over. They found her lying in bed, legs dangling from the side. Shards of broken glass glittered on the floor, a stainless steel jug lay on its side, the mattress was dark with water.

Around and around her heart these images circled, that hand reaching for a glass of water, those feet groping for their slippers, the glass slipping and breaking, the arm brushing against the jug as the body sank back on the bed.

Nina spent the night dozing intermittently. Dawn awoke the birds, then her. Alka and Ramesh were drinking tea in the still cool garden; she joined them, they discussed the chauth. A small notice in the newspapers would do, as small as her mother's life.

Now it was time for Nina to get ready for Jangpura. She wanted to go alone.

There it was, that narrow rutted bend in the road, down which she had travelled for ten years. She unlocked the padlock on the front door with the keys Alka had given her. There the little verandah, there the one room.

Everywhere was dust and emptiness. She sat on the bed where the body had last rested. How pathetic and futile it seemed. How could these miserable one and a half rooms contain a life? When she herself had been living there it hadn't seemed so wretched, maybe because she was young and was always going to leave. Her mother had made sure she did leave, even if it meant sending her ten thousand miles away and her own certain loneliness.

The bed strings moaned as she shifted. She had come prepared to touch, to connect, to go into the past, yet all she could sense was the sadness of her mother's life. Except for bank and medical papers, there was hardly anything to go through. Slowly, over the years, her possessions had eroded, with no replacements.

She pulled the suitcase wrapped in plastic from under the bed, then opened the cupboard to reveal the pitiful little store of clothes. Not a single new item purchased since the daughter left. Had her pension really been enough?

Nina's hands moved among the covered, carefully wrapped things. In a corner were two framed photographs. One of her father, the other of her and Ananda. Next to them the daughter's letters arranged date wise in a cloth bag with a drawstring, a notebook with lists of wedding presents and estimated values, lists of the things they had given to Ananda's family and the price of each one. Now these lists were hers forever. She emptied the cupboard, filled the single suitcase and tied a bedcover around everything else.

These were the personal effects, but what about the bed, desk, dishes, bedding, bits of linen? Give them all to Mr Singh—the true inheritor. Mr Singh, here, you deserve them more than me. I have this suitcase, which contains my mother's life, the rest is yours.

This done, she closed the front door and left the place that had been so resistant to her mother's impress.

Nina wondered how many people would come for the chauth, to be held the next day, four days after the funeral. Her mother's life had been thinly populated. The daughter was its centre and when she left, the centre could not hold. Hollowed out, she died.

A small shamiana was spread in the lawn for the evening hour-long function and fans put up in four corners. A table nearby held glasses of water. A portrait of Nina's mother stood on a small covered stool, garlanded with jasmine and roses. Ila, who was learning classical singing, sang two bhajans along with her music teacher. This took twenty minutes. Then the pundit gave a small talk about death. The tropes were familiar, people nodded. And finally those who wanted to say a few words about Mr Batra were invited to do so. Mr Singh, Zenobia, and Alka shared some polite praise.

Then the few mourners lined up to condole. There were some who had known Nina's father. They introduced themselves. Shanti, lovely lady, so brave after your father's death. Where had these friends been all this time, thought Nina but said nothing. They had come. They didn't have to. Everybody had their own lives to live.

Her mother had been bitter about them. Once he died, your father's friends vanished, while he, poor man, imagined that those who ate at his table would be true to him. People save money and build houses, but not your father, oh no. He wanted the good life, he wanted to entertain, time enough to settle down when we are old, he said so often, so often, but the only one old is me.

And the only one left is me, thought Nina.

The next day Nina was to go to Rishikesh to immerse the ashes in the Ganga. Her mother's last remains would flow in their final journey across India into the sea. Another two days and she would leave for Canada. Her round the world trip, as Ananda put it.

In the morning she got up early to catch the train to Haridwar. As she followed Ramesh's office peon through the crowds at New Delhi station, Nina clutched the matka which contained what was left of her mother. It was bound with red and gold cloth. People, recognising its contents, edged away.

Though she was wearing a sari with her head covered, many taxi drivers in Haridwar accosted her in English. Madam, I will take you best place for immersing, madam, madam, whole day taxi five hundred rupees only, madam, guest house nearby? She chose an older taxi driver. Whole day four hundred, she said in Hindi, to indicate that he couldn't take advantage of her; four hundred, she repeated, and jumped in.

The road towards Rishikesh was slightly winding. In the distance Nina could see the hazy outline of hills. The green fields were dotted with small white temples flying saffron flags. Barefoot sadhus trod the road, sadhus in orange, ash-smeared sadhus of all ages. The river glittered in the distance.

In Rishikesh, the taxi driver took her to all the sacred spots of the city, the banks of the bigger temples, places replete with holy men, devotees, piety. Nina hated every place she saw. No, not here, not here, she kept repeating to the taxi driver. At Laxman Jhoola the driver swore that, if she were to walk down the winding lane to the banks of the river, she would find a very good spot. Head covered against the beating sun, she picked her way around dirt and debris, past places smelling of piss and shit, and nothing of that changed as she reached the water's edge. Back she climbed, take me out of this town, take me into the mountains.

'Madam, how will you reach the river from the mountains? The road is too high.'

'You just take me.'

'Hundred rupees more.'

'All right. Now go.'

She slumped in the back of the taxi, her arms around the urn. She had to find a place before it was time for the evening train. How many thousand million ashes and bones had the Ganga swept away? Did it matter where exactly you immersed them? This was no burial; they would end up in the sea as they were meant to.

321

Higher they climbed, the river winding beneath them, then down again, then up. It was four o'clock, she couldn't search much longer, she would miss her train. Her anxious gaze swept the dense trees, looking for a path. Finally she saw a woman emerge from the wilderness, a pot of water on her head. There, stop there, she said.

It took almost twenty minutes to follow the faint path among the trees. As she walked, she slipped occasionally on pebbles, her sari caught on thorny branches, the matka grew heavier, but the river was getting nearer.

At last the trees gave way to sand and stones. There it flowed, the Ganga, emerald clean and swift between two green mountains. She tucked her sari high into her petticoat and waded in as far as she could, the cold water swirling around her legs. Carefully she undid the red cloth around the mouth of the matka. It was almost full with powdery ash, her mother's charred teeth and bones embedded within. Slowly she tipped them into the river. The grey ashes swirled in the eddies forming around her legs, the blackened bones sank into the dark water. Once it emptied she threw the cloth in, and then the matka. She watched the red earthen pot bob along the waters before it filled and sank.

That was the last of her mother's body. She splashed her face and wondered if those water drops contained ashes that had been floated further upstream. Like this the whole world was connected. She lingered, balancing on stones, feeling the strong current against her legs as the sun gradually withdrew till the line of trees on top of the opposite mountain. Missing the train now seemed insignificant. She had done what she came to do. Wading to the bank, she arranged her clothes and climbed back up, some of her burden left behind in the green water.

In the taxi she rested her head on the seat and closed her eyes, impervious to the jolts and complaints of the driver—he would have to drive very fast in the growing darkness to make it to Haridwar on time. Only when they arrived at the station did she sit up, pay attention to her surroundings and find that the train was two hours late.

Two hours on the platform, in the first class waiting room, in the restaurant drinking boiled tea, with wavering faith as to whether the train would ever come. The coolie, waiting embedded in the luggage he carried, could gaze vacantly around him for a lifetime, of which only two hours had passed before the whistle announced the train's arrival, and the platform gathered itself for its assault.

All night Nina was wakeful, lying on the upper berth, absorbing her loss, temporarily soothed by the motion of the train. Soon she would be back in Delhi, in a few days back in Canada. What was there to bring her to India again?

Maybe her parents were together now. Their union had been a success, and the strength of its tie would no doubt continue to operate in their next lives.

Her own existence seemed poor in comparison. With no mother to disappoint, nobody's expectations to meet, the bonds of her marriage assumed a different feel. Her life was now completely her own responsibility, she could blame no one, turn to no one. She felt adult and bereft at the same time.

xi

Ananda was there to receive her at the airport.

'How was it?'

The concern brought tears to her eyes. Blinking, she reached for a tissue as he took her trolley.

'Well, how was it?' he repeated in the car, pulling out of the car park.

'Now Ma will never be able to visit.'

'Who was to know this would happen?'

'She was still so young.' Though God knew her mother had stopped being young the day her father died.

Ananda did not reply. His parents could have been called young too.

They drove on in silence.

'Well, what did you do while I was away,' she thought to ask eventually.

'Nothing much. Clearing up some stuff that needed to be cleared.'

'Oh, well now I am back I can help you.'

He held her hand for a moment, then let it go.

'I missed you,' he said.

She sighed, 'Now there is only you.'

These thoughts remained with her till next morning, when, upon making up the bed she found a wavy blond hair next to her pillow. She would have missed it had she not switched on the bedside light to stare more closely at the picture of her mother placed on the table.

She took it to the window and turned it around. Light glinted on the surface. Its root was darker, the glint must be the effect of dye.

With it still in her hand she sat on the bed. The hair explained much—the distance, the silence, the ticket for two months in India, his strange indifference interspersed with tenderness, the shifty look that skittered about her. She didn't blame him. His body spoke, when his tongue could not.

Absentmindedly she twisted the hair around her finger. Going to the bathroom she fetched some tissue paper and carefully folded it around the evidence. Then she opened her accounts notebook and taped it to the cover. This way she would always see it, always wonder what to do with it.

So the marriage was based on more than one person's lies. Discovering this made it worse. Her transgressions had been against a faithful husband, her constant understanding that any exposure would cause ruin and grief.

The yellow hair put paid to all that.

How long? Long enough to explain the absence of the clock? It couldn't have been before, when he could barely sustain sex with her. She knew he had done it to prove himself, knew as clearly as though he had written a thesis on the subject and dedicated it to her, thus ensuring a reading of every word. This discovery was definitely mistimed. She had just come home the day before. Her mother had died and she was entertaining thoughts of Ananda being her solitary anchor in the world.

Anchors. You had to be your own anchor. By now there was no escaping this knowledge. Still she had been trained to look for them and despite all that had happened, she had not got over the habit. Marry me, love me, above all, *look after me.* Somebody had to be responsible for her, besides herself. That was what women had been led to expect and hardly any price was too high. Loneliness, heartache, denial, all grist to the mill.

Which spirit could grow in these circumstances?

The red account book lay closed on her knee. She was wearing her old faded nightgown. Today was the day she was going to rush off to school, she had missed so much already. Her personal life, the mess that it was, kept intruding into the routine of a Library Science student.

She got up and carefully placed the notebook in a drawer. She would not do anything for now—she couldn't. The present was calling her attention with too much urgency. Its demands could not be delayed because Ananda had been venturing into the realm of golden hair and white bodies.

During her time away, spring had arrived. Warmer air, bumps on bare branches, clumps of crocuses and snow drops blooming against the walls of houses. Walking to the university, Nina thought of the work she had to do, the colleagues she was going to meet. The Killam was a place to be happy in, despite contamination by Russian peasants.

In ten days, Nina had missed much. There was sympathy in the department, offers to help make up. Anton made a point of coming when he saw her alone and asking if he could assist in any way.

'After what you did to me, Anton, I don't believe so.'

'I'm sorry, really sorry,' he said eagerly. 'I don't know what came over me.'

'Surely you can think of something better? That's the oldest excuse in the book.'

'That doesn't take away its meaning. I'm ashamed of what took place that night. Let's put it behind us.'

'Words are cheap.'

'Come on, Nina, please. After what there was between us, you can't say I raped you.'

'I can. You did. In any other situation I would have reported you to the police.'

'I got carried away—that can happen to anybody. And it was not as though we were—you know—strangers to each other.'

So, he wanted absolution from her, something she would never give. He would have to live with his crime. Coldly she said that he was beneath contempt. Mate or rape was his motto, especially where Indians were concerned. The hurt that crossed his face gave her pleasure. At least she hadn't fallen victim to his words; instead she had used her own to wound as much as possible.

It was a small victory, but one to savour.

At home she could not respond to Ananda's pretence that everything was all right. Each time she considered confronting him with his infidelity, she felt the futility. For that to have any real purpose, she would have to confess her own, they would have to examine why they had betrayed each other, they would have to be a woman's group, knowing that the only way forward was to function with honesty, trust, all judgement withheld.

Was the love between them strong enough to persuade her to venture into this quagmire?

She looked at the cards of her life as she wondered which hand to deal. In any game she would have flung them down and said 'I pack.'

Pack, pack.

*

326

Ananda persisted in his efforts to cheer his wife up. She was taking the New York incident hard. That, followed so closely by the death of her mother, had made her a bit unstable. Repeatedly he told her he understood how bad she felt, he too had gone through similar trauma. Success at work would make her feel better, but she had to give it time.

Nina mumbled an agreement, but did not enter the discussion. Helplessness overtook Ananda. Stubbornly the woman sat there, morose, lugubrious and moody, obstinately refusing to be a different person. The atmosphere in the house was so oppressive he dreaded coming home. He had done so much for her, and all she could do was sit there with a long face and behave like a deprived immigrant.

Life was what you made of it. You could look at a glass and call it half full or half empty. You could look out of the window and see the sky or stare at the mud. How often had he heard his parents make these distinctions between types of people. Well, he knew what manner of person he was. And Nina was definitely his opposite.

He voiced these comparisons. If she had to chose between half full or half empty what would she chose?

She stared at him. What he was insinuating was so clear. Who wouldn't want to be the half full variety? To warm oneself and others, to become a ray of sunshine? But what did one have to do? Did one have to live with yellow hair under the pillow?

'I don't know,' she replied.

'You are a drifter. One needs some purpose in life. One needs to give back. You are always taking.'

'To whom should I give back? You? Canada?'

He replied with dignity, 'I am not talking about myself. But, yes, this country has offered you a lot. Did you get a full scholarship or not? Do you think such a thing is possible in India, or even in the US?'

'I am sorry, Ananda, I can't be as grateful as you want me to be. Consider it a character defect.'

He frowned. He hated levity, the kind of cleverness that allowed people to take refuge from serious issues. 'Many people would kill to be in your position. You have everything, and still you sulk and behave like one of those heroines in the novels you are always reading.'

'What novel are you referring to? They are not all the same—or maybe you wouldn't know.'

'No, I wouldn't. I live in the real world.'

'And I in the unreal?'

'You said it, not I.'

'You think anything not material is worthless. What kind of value system is that?'

Ananda looked angry, then bewildered. He hadn't married for these kinds of scenes. He was a simple guy. He said as much. If Nina wished to do drama she should go somewhere else.

Nina said nothing. For him all feelings except the most obvious were drama. She could not be happy living on the surface where he floated. For her that was not living at all. But how to explain these things? Either you understood them or you didn't. Still she couldn't free herself from her husband. Her sense of security in Canada lay with him.

Ananda kept his own stress close to his heart. He had chosen according to his family's wishes, but in doing so had experienced a fresh set of difficulties. And how would he not? He was not the boy they had planned for, he was as much someone else as he could possibly be. There was not a single other immigrant like himself that he knew. They all clung to some notion of home, gathered at the India Club, trying to recreate the motherland. That was so bloody stupid. There was more to the West than just a comfortable lifestyle. You had to have the courage of an explorer to step out of the mindset most immigrants mouldered in.

Marriage had been the most significant step in the remaking of his old self. There was no one to appreciate the irony of this. After he married everything changed, his mind, his heart, his penis. In this change his wife had been left far behind. It was not her fault. It was the situation. Given his social position, he hoped it was a temporary situation.

Buds blossomed, leaves emerged, the grass turned green. Nina enjoyed every breath of air, despite her heavy heart. Alas that her own regeneration was not as inevitable as the revolving earth and the tilt of its axis.

She graduated and applied for jobs everywhere but in Halifax.

'I need to go away and think,' she told Ananda.

'Why can't you think here,' he demanded. 'As usual you are making excuses.'

And as usual his way of putting things pissed her off. She stared at him, he looked back at her. These two that fate had brought together through death and marriage. Who did they have besides each other? Yet to a certain extent this country freed emotional needs from the yoke of matrimony and social sanction.

The things that might have made separation in India difficult for Nina were hers to command in Canada. Financial self-sufficiency, rental ease, social acceptability. She hoped independence would facilitate her thought processes. She looked down the path on which there would be no husband and saw the difficulties, the pain, the solitude. Nevertheless treading it was not unimaginable.

'I need to be by myself,' she clarified.

'Away from me. Why don't you say it?'

'Yes, away from you.'

He had anticipated the answer, but not the pain.

Her letters of recommendation were glowing, her academic record excellent, the responses she got were encouraging. The University of New Brunswick called her for an interview.

She packed her bags and left for Fredericton on a Greyhound bus. In her bones she knew she would get the job. Interviews had always been easy for her.

The empty prettiness of the landscape drew her attention. The last time she had gazed at moving scenery her mother's ashes had lain on her lap. Now there was nothing tying her down anywhere. She was travelling away from Halifax, deliberately pulling at the bonds that held her.

She thought of those who had been nice to her, wayfarers on the path, nothing permanent, but interacting with them had made that stretch easier. Colleagues at HRL, the women's group that encouraged her to be angry and assertive, Beth, Gayatri, Library School; the sense of community was there, warming but temporary—everything temporary.

Perhaps that was the ultimate immigrant experience. Not that any one thing was steady enough to attach yourself to for the rest of your life, but that you found different ways to belong, ways not necessarily lasting, but ones that made your journey less lonely for a while. When something failed it was a signal to move on. For an immigrant there was no going back.

The continent was full of people escaping unhappy pasts. She too was heading towards fresh territories, a different set of circumstances, a floating resident of the Western world.

When one was reinventing oneself, anywhere could be home. Pull up your shallow roots and move. Find a new place, new friends, a new family. It had been possible once, it would be possible again.

Acknowledgements

In Halifax for their information about libraries and Library Science, I thank Susan James, Vivian Howard, Judy Dunn and Professor Norman Horrocks.

Dr Paul Downing and Dr Rupa Raghavan gave me crucial information about dentistry in Canada and India. In New York Penelope Anderson was generous with her home and her knowledge of the city.

My husband Gun Nidhi Dalmia has been a source of encouragement, support and reassurance. His memory has been infallible, his patience inexhaustible.

I thank Katharine Bowlby for all the gaps she plugged in my knowledge of Halifax, for her photographs, observations and clarifying instincts, for her house and her unstinting hospitality. To her generous husband, Craig Laurence, to her daughters, Marion and Anna, thanks again.

Ira Singh has as usual read my work in progress more times than anybody has a right to expect. From beginning to end she has been with Nina and Ananda—at last she can say goodbye to them.

Anuradha Marwah criticised the manuscript as ruthlessly as only friends can.

I thank my editor, Julian Loose, at Faber, my publisher Chiki Sarkar and Rajni George, my editor, at Random House India, and Ayesha Karim, my agent, for their insightful comments and enthusiasm.

A writing fellowship from the Civitella Ranieri Foundation—a bequest made by the late Ursula Corning—in New York enabled me to spend six productive weeks in the Civitella Ranieri Castle in Umbertide, Umbria, Italy, where thoughts were stimulated by fine food, the fellowship of artists and the Umbrian countryside.

At the Delhi Gymkhana Club, the library staff, Hans Raj Parihar, Praveen Kukreja, Harish S Negi, Joginder Goswami, Ram Sewak, Mahadev and Santosh went out of their way to make sure I had a comfortable, undisturbed writing environment.